T0329223

"It Can't Be True!"

She threw back her head and screamed, her cry caught by the wind like the murder-scream of a hawk. How could that tender knight be the calculating bastard who had hated her father, who had only married her to capture a castle?

She let out a dismayed little snort of laughter at her own folly. Even now she wanted him there, wanted to feel his arms around her and hear him murmur softly that all would be well, that he was her true heart's love. One night in a pretty devil's bed, and she was ready to betray a lifetime's love and duty.

She looked up at the lowering gray clouds the wind was sweeping across the sky, and her thoughts flew to the white falcon that had fallen to her death in a savage act of will. Her heart cried out in perfect sympathy. She must escape; there must be a way to escape!

She seemed to hear her mother's voice in the wind, a hundred voices that were both strange and familiar as her own secret thoughts . . . now she felt light and whole, not happy, but serene, accepting of the wind that combed her thoughts into meaningless shreds like the clouds that now seemed close enough to touch. . . .

For orders other than by individual consumers, Pocket Books grants a discount on the purchase of **10 or more** copies of single titles for special markets or premium use. For further details, please write to the Vice President of Special Markets, Pocket Books, 1230 Avenue of the Americas, 9th Floor, New York, NY 10020-1586.

For information on how individual consumers can place orders, please write to Mail Order Department, Simon & Schuster, Inc., 100 Front Street, Riverside, NJ 08075.

JAYEL WYLIE

A FALCON'S HEART

SONNET BOOKS
New York London Toronto Sydney Singapore

This book is a work of fiction. Names, characters, places and incidents are products of the author's imagination or are used fictitiously. Any resemblance to actual events or locales or persons, living or dead, is entirely coincidental.

An *Original* Publication of POCKET BOOKS

A Sonnet Book published by
POCKET BOOKS, a division of Simon & Schuster, Inc.
1230 Avenue of the Americas, New York, NY 10020

ISBN: 978-1-5011-0996-6

First Sonnet Books printing July 2001

10 9 8 7 6 5 4 3 2 1

SONNET BOOKS and colophon are trademarks of Simon & Schuster, Inc.

Front cover illustration by Ben Perini

Printed in the U.S.A.

for my parents, still my first, best loves

Acknowledgments

Heartfelt thanks and much deserved credit to the following: My agent, Timothy Seldes, for being as supportive as he is brilliant; my editor, Lauren McKenna, for her enthusiasm and great ideas; Marcia Addison, M.L.I.S., for every kind of research assistance and truly astonishing technical support; my reading coven (Mama, Grandmama Wylie, Alice, Isabel, Petey, Sarah, Rachel, and Laura), for their feedback; my office mates for their support; and my unimaginably fabulous family for everything, now and then and always.

Historical Note:

King Henry II; Queen Eleanor; Henry's mother, Maud (aka Matilda); Thomas à Becket; and the late and mostly unlamented King Stephen were all real people, and many books have been written about them. The other characters herein are entirely fictional.

Balladry Note:

The falcon ballad is a version of a traditional song of medieval England; the other was written by the author, for better or worse.

A letter from Fra Paolo Bosacci to his sister, Serena, translated from the Italian

Near Falconskeep Castle on the coast at the English-Welsh border 1139

My dearest friend—

I have only the force of my own poor hopes to comfort me that these words will ever reach you. Florence seems as far from me this night as the stars above my head, farther than the throne of Heaven itself. But the events of this day have been so sad and in their way so beautiful to me, I must share them with you.

The Lady Bianca—Blanche, as she is called by her lord—died this day after many weeks of wasting illness. As soon as her servants knew that all hope for her was lost, a terrible fear spread through the castle and even into the peasant village that in these days of war has grown up within the outer walls. The mercenaries of the Angevin duchess were seen marching this way two days ago, with no sign, no word of rescue from the King's men or our own

Lord Mark. So long as the Lady lived, the people here seemed to believe her castle invincible to the coming siege, but as soon as she began to fail beyond hope, all confidence was lost. By midmorning, the people had begun to flee west into Wales, and by noon, Falconskeep was all but empty. All that remained was the tiny garrison of soldiers charged with the protection of the castle proper, myself, the dying Lady Blanche, and her daughter, Alista, a tiny child barely four years old.

When I went up to the Lady's chamber to give her the final absolution, I found the child Alista there already, a little ruby in her bright silk gown with her dark hair plaited down her back. Some nursemaid had dressed her to meet disaster as if it were a festival night. "Good morning, cara mia," I said. I held my hands out to her, and tears came into my eyes at her trusting smile and the way she ran into my arms.

"Good morning, Brother Paolo," she answered, holding on tightly around my neck. "Are you quite well this morning?"

The woman already lying still as death on the bed made a shuddering sigh that might have been a laugh. "Si, cara mia, quite well." I held the child at arm's length, studying her, but I saw no tears, no sign of distress. "But your mama is sleeping," I said, determined to spare her what pain I might. "You must go downstairs and play."

"No, Brother," she said, quite serious, laying a tiny hand on either side of my face. "Mama says I must stay with her. But you may go if you like."

"Alista is right," Lady Blanche spoke up, her voice weak but certain. "Though I don't think Brother Paolo will leave us, not without performing his duty." She held out a

hand thin and pale as a willow branch, and the child moved to her side without hesitation, without the slightest fear, as if she could not smell or see death, only her precious mother. "You must stay out of his way, little bird," Lady Blanche told her, caressing her plump, pink cheek. "Be very still and quiet."

"Yes, Mama." She raised up on tiptoe to reach her mother's face for a kiss, then went over to the window ledge and climbed up. The heavy shutter had been opened, and outside the window I could see falcons circling, as numerous and quarrelsome as the gulls that swooped over the beach far below.

"The servants must have opened the mews," I said absently, hypnotized by the falcons' orbiting flight.

"Fra Paolo," Lady Blanche said, breaking my foolish reverie. She held out her hand to me as she had to the child, and I took it, suppressing an unmanly shiver—she was already so cold, and yet so lovely still, her pale blond hair spread on the pillow like a halo behind a face worn translucent with pain and fever. Her eyes were bright, as if all her spirit were now contained in their gaze, and they captured me, burned into my heart. "I entrust my child to you, Fra Paolo," she said, looking past me for a moment to the figure perched on the window ledge. "And something else as well."

She laid her free hand over her throat, plucking at a chain with powerless fingers. "Let me help you, my lady," I said, lifting the chain with my fingertips, barely touching her flesh before unfastening the clasp.

The chain itself was as fine as any I have seen, its tiny links so cleverly wrought of some pure white metal it seemed a single, fluid piece. But the pendant that had hung between Bianca's breasts seemed worthless, a dull pink stone worn smooth as if by time and water into the vague shape of a heart. A deep crack flawed the center of the heart, revealing a deeper, but still dull, red color inside. "You must hide this heart away," Bianca whispered, her voice all but lost, but her eyes still bright. "This heart and my prayer book, there on the chest beside the window." She reached for my hand again, and this time her grip was like talons. "No English queen must ever have them for her own."

I looked down at the stone I still held with new interest and, I must confess, a little fear. Since I had come to this strange place a year ago, I had heard many times that Lady Blanche was a sorceress. She was said to be descended from the Picts, the wild race of blood drinkers who had lived here even before the Welsh. But her husband, Lord Mark, was of fine Norman lineage, and the Lady had shown herself to be a good Christian, keeping the commandments of Holy Mother Church and rearing her daughter to do the same. Still, I had seen enough (as I have written you oftentimes before!) to know that what she called a prayer book was not of Our Lord, and if the stone I held were connected to it . . .

"You must take them now and hide them," she repeated urgently. "There is not a moment to lose."

"I must hear your confession, my lady," I protested, taking refuge in my office. "Give you the final rite—"

"And so you will." She smiled, and her beauty still lived in her face and in my heart, a pain I could not refuse. "For my daughter's sake, Paolo, I beseech you."

I looked again at the child in the window, and at last I understood. Lady Blanche had herself been tainted against her will by whatever evil clung to these relics. But even in death, she meant to keep her Alista in God's grace. "I will hide them well, my lady," I promised, silently swearing to Our Lord that the little one would never know of them again. "I will be back very soon."

Her eyes fell shut, but her smile never wavered as she released my hand. "Thank you, my friend," she whispered.

The Lady's bedchamber was at the top of the castle's tallest tower, and I ran down the circular stairs, faster and faster, barely seeing the sputtering torches as I passed them, barely thinking where I meant to go. When the last of the arrow slits was behind me, I still kept running, into an underground room of which I had heard the servants speak but which I had never seen. In it was a spring, a natural well that could be used in time of siege. Squinting in the flickering light, I could see it, sealed with a great, moss-covered stone that looked as if it had not been touched in a thousand years. Surely this would be a hiding place that could never be found.

Using all my strength, I rocked the stone in its jagged cradle until I could roll it completely away. The smell of fresh water and distant decay filled the room in a choking rush, making me back away. When I could breathe again without gagging, I lifted my torch and peered down into the well. I could see a reflection of the torch's flame wavering far below, at least a hundred feet down, and I was satisfied. I had dropped the book and necklace at my feet; now I picked them up again, my eyes straying to the book's cracked leather cover. Symbols were tooled into the leather, like words in a language I had never seen, and for a moment, I was fascinated, reached to turn the cover back, see what mysteries must surely be written inside. Then I stopped, my heart pounding in my chest—was damnation such a casual slip? I dropped the book into the yawning mouth of stone and flung the necklace after it, waiting until I heard the distant splash. Then, muscles aching, I rolled the boulder back into place, then turned and ran back up the winding stair.

Alista still perched in the window ledge, her knees drawn up beneath her chin, but now tears glistened on her cheeks. The woman on the bed no longer stirred. I went to the bed, lifted her wrist, held my hand in front of her nose and mouth. "She has gone," I said, speaking aloud but to myself, my failure.

"I know," Alista replied, her cherub's chirp roughened with weeping. "She flew away."

I looked at the child, uncertain I had heard her right, even less certain how I should answer her if I had. "Alista—" I stopped. A sound was coming through the window, a low rumble. Looking out, I saw a long line of men and horses coming around the near curve in the road as the child's arms crept around my neck. "Come," I said, scooping her up as the garrison sounded the alarm.

I took my charge into the tiny chapel off the castle's main hall, setting her down and falling to my knees before the altar. "We must pray," I explained, and she knelt obediently beside me. As she folded her hands and began to lisp the Our Father, I heard the distant creak of the drawbridge being lowered, the portcullis being raised. Traitors! The garrison meant to surrender without a fight. Laying a hand on the child's shoulder, I joined her in prayer, praying for the strength to preserve this innocent's life.

"Alista!" The door to the chapel was thrown open with this shout, and a man, who from my present vantage looked

like a mountain clad in mud-spattered armor, came thundering up the aisle, throwing back the visor on his helmet to reveal a dark, matted beard and bright blue eyes.

"Papa!" The little girl beside me broke free of my grasp and ran to him without a trace of fear, flinging herself, sobbing, into his arms. "She flew away, Papa. She flew away."

I couldn't hear what he said to her, but his answer seemed to calm her, make her quiet against his shoulder. I was relieved, but surprised—I had heard from the child's own lips that she had no memory of her father, that he had been away fighting this most uncivil civil war for most of her short life. Yet she had known him at once, and he her. Never had I seen a man hold a child with more tenderness, answer her cries with more patience, even though it was plain in his face that his own grief was overwhelming.

"My deepest condolence, signor," I said, rising from my knees. "I fear you come too late to say good-bye—"

"I would not have said it even if I were not," he snarled, sparing no tenderness for me but looking me up and down as if somehow I were responsible for his trouble. "Blanche's priest," he muttered, turning his full attention back to the child. "There is no time to waste—Maud's brother and his army are biting my soldiers' heels." He set Alista back on her feet. "Let this friar help you gather your things," he told her. "We must fly in our fashion as well."

And so we did. From where we are encamped with Lord Mark's army, we can see the glow of flames in the distance—Falconskeep put to the torch. I do not know what this man means to do, whether we are to return to London or if this army will turn and fight. But watching him now as he watches his little daughter, I cannot but think well of him. I know he will do all in his power to keep her safe. And I will do all in mine to help him, not for his sake or even for the child herself, but for the promise I made to Bianca.

One

Alista grew up, and her father did keep her safe, with Brother Paolo always nearby to watch over her as well. When King Stephen finally managed to drive his cousin Maud back to Anjou and her husband, he drove many of her supporters among England's noble class as well, and the home and holding of one of these, Brinlaw, was given to Mark as compensation for the loss of Falconskeep. By the time she was eighteen years old, Alista barely remembered any home but Brinlaw.

The bloody civil war was finally ended. Maud's son, Henry, had won many battles, while Stephen's son had died, so the beleaguered king made the peace by making Henry his heir. As one of Stephen's strongest and best-liked retainers, Mark first became the target of a certain amount of espionage, which he neatly avoided, and a great deal of charming diplomacy, which he returned in kind, doing much to reconcile the rest of the nobles to the prospect of a king born in Anjou. Now Stephen was finally dead; Henry was to be crowned; and Mark was leaving Brinlaw once again for the coronation in London.

"Tell me honestly, Papa, why must you go?" Alista asked, standing knee deep in snow beside her father in the courtyard as the final packing was finished. "I know how little you care for ceremony, and Henry has already heard your pledge. Geoffrey said he said as much himself before he sent the invitation. It's the middle of winter—"

"So he's Geoffrey now, is he?" Mark teased, trying to change the subject. "Not 'Sir Knight' or even 'the King's cousin' any longer?"

"As if I should remind him," she retorted. Geoffrey of Anjou held no title of his own, but he missed no opportunity to mention his blood kinship to England's new king. "And you didn't answer my question."

"Didn't I?" he answered with a sigh. "Your friend Geoffrey also said that Old Brinlaw's son was back in London, renewing his friendship with Henry."

"What of it?" A groom led her father's horse into the courtyard, and she went and took the reins herself. "Why is that reason enough to leave us without you for Christmas?"

"Because in future I would prefer to keep my Christmases here," Mark answered, swinging into the saddle with an ease that belied his years. "Now that Stephen is gone and Maud's pup is to be on the throne, the boy means to reclaim his father's forfeit title, and I would think this castle with it." He patted the destrier's neck to calm his prancing. " 'Tis what I would do in his place."

"But he can't!" Alista protested. "Henry couldn't—"

"Of course he could; he is King." He swung the horse about, trusting Alista to get herself out of the way. "Particularly if I'm not there to remind him how dearly I do love him myself."

"And so you will be there." She stroked the horse's

mane, trying to push her disappointment away. In all her eighteen years, she could remember only two or three times she'd had Christmas with her father, and now there would be one less, but she wouldn't whine and raging wouldn't help, not this time. "You don't really think we could lose Brinlaw, do you?"

"Not for a moment." He smiled down at her, this strong, young creature he loved before all else in the living world. "Go inside and tell your Geoffrey to make himself seen, or I'm leaving for London without him."

"Will you not go back inside to say good-bye to Druscilla?" she asked. Dru was her father's mistress, a beauty barely older than Alista herself, and she had been weeping piteously in fits and starts since Henry's messenger had arrived.

Mark suppressed a weary sigh. "I think best not," he answered. "Hurry, girl, before it starts to snow again."

Inside the Great Hall, all seemed to be chaos, but she knew it for a well-practiced ritual. Men-at-arms were being sorted into who would go to London and who would stay to guard the castle; cooks were packing enough hampers of food to supply a manna-less flight from Egypt; maidservants were running up and down the stairs with compresses and sweets to comfort the miserable Druscilla. All the regular business of a December midmorning continued on apace. Yesterday's rushes were being raked up and discarded by a team of boys while another team of women spread the new. The dog boy was frantically trying to keep Mark's hunting hounds from devouring Druscilla's ill-tempered spaniel bitch, perched on a cushion on the hearth bench and taunting them shamelessly with high-pitched yelps. Last night's guards, long delayed by preparations for their commander's journey, were finally breaking their fast with cold meat and bread, some near to nodding off in their cups of ale, others still fresh enough to pester the women with voices rubbed rough in the winter wind on the battlements. Alista looked around the teeming human hive with a sudden sentimental pang. What if her father was wrong and Henry did mean to give this holding to the traitor's heir? She knew all these people by name, had been cared for by them as a child and as a woman cared for them in turn. It was unthinkable that she should leave them, unimaginable that she could ever feel anything but misery anywhere else. But hadn't she felt the same at Falconskeep? She had known those people, too, as well as she knew herself, yet now she couldn't remember a single name or more than a single face from the life she'd led there. Even her mother's image had become little more than a dim shadow in her mind that only came clear in dreams. She remembered the horrible days she'd spent at Stephen's court before they came to Brinlaw, she the motherless mite pitied and ignored by the ladies charged with her care while her father rode away to war. If Brother Paolo had not been with her, she would almost certainly have grieved herself to death.

"Alista?" Brother Paolo was so near in her thoughts, his voice couldn't capture her attention. "My lady?" he persisted, shaking her arm.

Her eyes snapped back into focus, her mind coming back to the present. "Forgive me, Brother," she smiled. "I was thinking again."

"Of something very sad from what I saw," he answered, studying her. For a moment, every trace of childishness had flown from her face, and it made him feel old to see her so, a woman deep in contemplation. "What troubles you?"

"Nothing," she insisted. "Have you seen the Angevin knight?"

His heart sank even further. "Why?" he asked suspiciously. "What use do you have for him?"

"Little if any at all, but Papa sent me to find him." The hounds broke free of their attendant for another barking pass around the hall, scrambling over Alista's feet and tangling themselves in her skirts as they went by. "Peter, why don't you drive them outside?" she complained to the boy flying after them.

"Pardon, my lady," Peter begged, red-faced. "But if they should see his lordship on his horse, 'twould break their hearts when he left them behind."

"Aye, so it would," she relented, refastening her mantle. "Come, we'll take them out back." Druscilla's maid passed on her way to the stairs. "Jane!" Alista called, stopping the girl in mid-trot. "Tell Dru that if she wants to bid my father farewell, she must pull herself together and come down at once. And send someone to find Sir Geoffrey." She turned back to the Franciscan with a smile. "You need have no fear for me, Brother," she promised. "I have no real call to be sad."

Together she and Peter were able to herd the pack through the narrow pantry and out into the deserted back garden where they broke free, baying joyfully as they plowed through the night's fresh fall of snow. She had first come to Brinlaw in an early summer, and this garden had been magnificent, thick with colorful blossoms, many of which even Brother Paolo couldn't name. But Mark's servants were not the careful gardeners that whoever had planted the garden had been, and many of the plants had died before the next spring. For years only soft, green turf had grown beneath the ancient oaks, and now all was bare, black bark and blue-white snow under a leaden sky.

"Is that not the Frenchman you were looking for, my lady?" Peter asked, pointing out a figure in a pale blue mantle coming into the open from a thicker copse of trees.

"So it is," she sighed, resigned. She didn't dislike Geoffrey; on the contrary, she found him charming company in large groups, quite the most witty and cultured creature she had ever known. He was the usual intermediary between Mark and Prince Henry, and she had come to look forward to his visits to the castle. But whenever she found herself alone with him, she seemed to lose her mind, become utterly tongue-tied. She couldn't even keep a proper silence—everything he said to her made her laugh, even when he obviously hadn't intended to amuse her. He was a courtier, a gentleman, and she couldn't help but find him a wee bit ridiculous. Try as she might, she couldn't quite think of him as a man. He was perfectly handsome, a paragon of current masculine fashion, with bright blond hair that curled slightly over his shoulders and a neatly shaped blond beard. He was said to have distinguished himself quite well on the battlefield, and he was preternaturally well-spoken. But even standing close to him, Alista couldn't help thinking of some cleverly whittled mannequin, all beauty with no spark. Tall for a woman, she was nevertheless accustomed to being towered over by her father and his men. Geoffrey's eyes were level with her own.

"My father sent me to find you," she explained without preamble when he reached her. "He says he's ready to go."

"So in an hour or so we may depart," he teased. He held

out his hand, and she gave him her own to kiss in the French fashion. "The cold suits you, Lady Alista. You are quite aglow."

In truth, she was blushing, but she nodded her thanks for the compliment. "Papa says it will likely snow again before nightfall," she offered. She tried to retrieve her hand, but he had tucked it through his arm so that when she walked away, he walked beside her. Seeing this, Peter discreetly took his leave to busy himself with the hounds.

"I have no fear of snow," Geoffrey said. "I only wish your father would allow you to go with us."

She laughed; as ever, unable to help herself. "He didn't forbid me, Geoffrey," she explained. "I didn't want to go—I've always hated being at court."

"That was when you were a child," he pointed out, undeterred. "I think you would find it very different now." He stopped and seemed to study her, stepping back to the length of his arm to peruse her face. "I can see you in a velvet gown the color of burgundy wine," he mused. "You would be magnificent."

"You have a vivid imagination," she teased. She tried to look away, but he touched her cheek, turning her face back to him, and she started, her eyes wide.

"Forgive me, my lady," he said, serious. "I didn't mean to frighten you."

"You didn't frighten me," she said, offended. "I was just surprised—"

"Now that my cousin is finally to be crowned, I don't know when we shall see each other again," he went on, looking deep into her eyes but seeing nothing of her dismay. "I had hoped that if you would come to London for the coronation, I could convince you to stay."

"That seems unlikely," she said, laughing again. "Brinlaw is my home. I love it here."

"But what of when you marry?" he persisted. "Won't you leave then?"

Her laughter snuffed out. "I have no thought of that," she said, freeing her hand from his grasp and backing away. "My father has never mentioned—"

"He cherishes you, Alista—of course he would wish to keep you with him." He reached for her again, then let his hands fall before he touched her. "I have no castle, no lands of my own," he went on more gently. "But my name is good, and I have the King's favor. I could care for you, and for Brinlaw—I would never ask you to leave here, to leave your father."

This sudden turn of the conversation was so unexpected that for a moment she could only gape at him, speechless. Geoffrey here at Brinlaw forever? Geoffrey as her husband? The very idea seemed absurd, like shutting up a peacock to lay eggs with the chickens. "I don't . . ." she finally stammered. "I had no idea—"

"That I loved you?" He took her hands then, smiling.

"Love . . . me?" Her heart was pounding just as Druscilla said it must when confronted with one's beloved, but she couldn't get over the feeling that the whole thing made no sense, like a silly dream where only she knew she was dreaming.

"How could I not?" he insisted. "You're like an angel, all innocence and light—"

"Hardly—"

"Tell me, then, that you feel nothing for me." He unlaced the leather binding of her glove and pressed his lips to her bare wrist. A shiver ran over her, made her face turn hot again. "You don't even know what love is," he said, his voice soft but vaguely frightening, husky in a way she had never heard. "You don't even know what you feel."

She stared down at her wrist, trying to get hold of the sensation radiating through her to give it a proper name. "Geoffrey . . . my father is waiting," she finally said, avoiding his eyes.

He let her go, watched with secret amusement as she snatched her hands back, clasping them behind her like a child struggling with the urge to steal a sweet. "Promise me, Alista," he said. "Promise me you will think on what I've said."

Her wide black eyes turned on his. "Of course I will," she said. "How could I possibly not?"

The church bells of London were still ringing as the sun began to set on December 19, 1154, ringing in triumph for peace, for the crowning of handsome, young Henry II and Eleanor, his beautiful queen. Watching as the shadows grew long across the floor of the audience chamber, Mark of Brinlaw suddenly realized his head ached as if it had been split. "Shouldn't they be tired by now?" he mused softly to himself, meaning the bell ringers.

"They say King Henry has the stamina of a bull," a nearby baron answered in friendly incomprehension. "One assumes his queen can match him, but the rest of us may starve."

The King had indeed been busy that day, hearing his nobles' petitions almost from the moment the crown was placed on his head and for many hours since, long after Queen Eleanor had retired. But night was finally coming on; soon all would adjourn for the banquet, and the day's more serious business would be done. Perhaps Mark had worried for nothing; perhaps he had wasted a trip. Then he recognized the figure now approaching the dais.

"William of Brinlaw, Majesty," the young knight was saying, shouting it out as if he meant to address the throne of Heaven as well as England. "Will you hear my suit?"

Mark had seen Old Brinlaw's son from across a battlefield enough times to know him even without his armor. How old would he be by now? Twenty? Thirty? The face half-obscured by a dark, close-cropped beard suggested even older, but that hardly seemed possible. He'd been no more than a child when his father had turned tail for France. He was as tall as Mark or taller, broad-shouldered—a warrior, no question. His clothes were plain, as befitted a newly returned Crusader, but not ostentatiously drab or poor. He was a noble, not a monk, an adversary worthy of caution. He had turned to look at Mark as he spoke the title "Brinlaw," daring the castle's true lord to dispute him, and hate burned unmistakably in his eyes. Mark had spoken to his new sovereign in private the night before and knew his claim was secure, barring any sudden change of royal heart. But it was clear this William would not give up without a fight.

"England holds you dear as my own heart, Will," King Henry answered with obvious affection, cutting short Mark's thoughts. "You know I am glad to hear you."

Will stopped and frowned. Something in this answer was wrong, for all the words were so pleasant. Ever since he was a boy of eleven, he had lived for two things alone: to see his friend crowned King of England as was his right and to reclaim his own father's lands. Now that one dream had at last come true after years of pain and bloodshed, the other seemed assured, this public request no more than a formality. But now that the moment was at hand, something in Henry's smile was wrong, a flicker of pity in his eyes. He turned and looked again at Mark, the old villain who had held Brinlaw for the dead usurper these many years. He looked like a statue of Zeus even without his armor, as imposing in a gown as he was astride his war-horse. He knew what Will would ask; he must, but he didn't seem the least bit concerned.

"I want Brinlaw," Will said aloud, suddenly too furious to feint and flatter through the forms of court. "My father was your mother's faithful servant, wrongly stripped of his title and lands. As his son, I ask my king for justice."

Many whose thoughts had begun to drift from the proceedings to the anticipation of supper suddenly snapped back to attention, and a ripple of whispers crawled around the room. Henry's smile dimmed but didn't vanish, and his tone when he answered was fond. "Your king believes you deserve far more than justice," he said. "You know the love I hold for you and for your father's memory." He turned and looked on Mark with apparently equal affection. "But Lord Mark has been a faithful servant of the Crown as well. Is it just for me to now repay him—?"

"A faithful servant of the Crown?" Will cut him off, sending a gasp of horror through the crowd. "In what way, Majesty? Was he serving the Crown when we faced his armies in battle not so long ago?"

"The rightful Crown of England, yea, sirrah, and well," Mark cried before the King could answer, other nobles making way for his approach. "I was protecting the sovereignty of England when you were a suckling babe." The phrase "sovereignty of England" was no more popular with the nobles looking on than Will's rudeness had been. No one had forgotten the new King was technically from Anjou. But Mark pressed on undaunted. "And I never left England or my children to save my own hide."

Will turned in a flash of rage like lightning, the King and England both forgotten. "My father did not break faith. He followed the queen to whom he was sworn—"

"Your father was a traitor to his country and his king!" Mark shouted, his craggy face gone red with fury.

"Enough!" Henry's roar was as impressive as any feat he had accomplished so far, at least in the minds of the assembly. After more than twenty years of civil war, everyone's nerves were still rather tender, and the peace seemed as rare as rubies and fragile as glass. The last thing anyone wanted was to see it shattered by a pair of ingrates with no more sense or courtesy than to dredge up old quarrels over a backwater castle no one had ever heard tell of anyway. "I will have peace in this Hall!" Henry continued, fixing each combatant in turn with a baleful glare that belied his tender years.

Will needed every ounce of self-control he could muster and then some to obey, every muscle in his body drawn so taut it trembled. No man would call his father a traitor and live, Henry and his bloody peace be damned. But he would not force his sovereign's hand, not on the very day of his crowning. He glared at Mark's face, purple with rage, for another long moment, then dropped his gaze to the floor.

Henry relaxed a bit, though he kept his expression stern. He had known Will would balk at his decision, and he'd hoped to settle a better manor on him before he made a public fuss. But somehow he'd never found the time. At least the single-minded fool hadn't lost his head entirely—no blood had been shed, and the situation could still be fixed. He even had a brilliant idea how. But now, when they were ready to slit one another's throats in the presence of every English nobleman and half those of France, was not the time to suggest it. "Lord Mark will keep his castle," the King said aloud. "I will not punish him for his loyalty and friendship with the loss of his lands."

"You prefer to punish me for mine," Will couldn't help but answer through clenched teeth, making the nobles murmur again in shock. Treason, they clucked like hens on their nests, their own futures secured, their own accounts well paid. He had no doubt that Henry meant to give him some manner of compensation for his loss, but nothing he had, not even his crown, would be enough. The wound he carried had burned and bled for fifteen years; nothing but to be master of Brinlaw would heal it. And Henry ought to know as much. If he didn't, Will would have to show him. "You are my king, and I will die in your service," he said aloud, speaking to his friend more than to his sovereign. "You know my love for you as friend as well as lord." He looked up, his expression cold. "But I will not accept this. I cannot."

Mark's head was pounding harder than ever, hard enough to make him feel faint, and he was still angry enough to spit in the eye of Satan. But something in these words touched him, made him feel a grudging respect for the stone-headed boy even as he despised him. "You needn't risk hanging for treason on my account," he said not unkindly. "If you would take my manor, lay siege to it. Attack me, not the King. I assure you, you will not succeed." He almost smiled. "To have Brinlaw, you will have to kill me."

Will looked at him, his face unchanged. "I can think of no better way."

As the sun was setting on coronation day, Alista finally worked up the courage to tell Druscilla about Geoffrey's odd proposal. "I thought for a moment he meant to kiss me on the lips," she finished, sprawling onto a chair in the solar, exhausted with relief from finally having it out.

Dru kept her eyes turned conscientiously on her needle. "You mean he didn't?" she asked.

"No, thank heavens. I told him Papa was waiting."

"Oh, Alista, really." Dru was a widow, born in Paris, so she considered herself wise far beyond her twenty-two years.

"He surprised me, I suppose." She pulled her dagger from its sheath at her waist and traced the swirling pattern of knots worked into the silver hilt. "You don't really think he was serious?"

"Of course he was," Dru laughed, an edge of bitterness in her usually dulcet tone. "You are a most marriageable maid."

Alista silently cursed herself for a blundering fool. Her friend's lack of a husband was the great ill of her life. The knight who'd widowed her had been no great prize to hear Dru speak of him, and he'd been a fool as well, refusing to give up plotting mischief after Henry's peace was made and losing his wooden head for his trouble. Mark had first seen Druscilla when he arrived at her London house to supervise the confiscation of all her worldly goods. Moved to pity by her plight, he had offered to escort her to a convent and pay for her entrance there, but on the way she had convinced him he'd really rather keep her for himself. But he would not marry her, nor would he ever. He had told his daughter as much. "Marriageable, eh?" she sighed, twirling her dagger with its point poised on the arm of her chair. "You'd never know it to look at me."

"No, in faith, you would not," Dru admitted, laughing in spite of herself.

Mark had feared for his daughter's safety to the level of obsession since he'd lost her mother. Consequently, he had insisted she learn not only to defend herself but also to take the offensive if necessary. Practice with her sword was as much a part of her daily routine as needlework and infinitely more to her liking. When her father was away, as he was now, she rarely even bothered with skirts at all, dressing like a squire with her long, dark brown hair tightly braided down her back. "The next time Geoffrey comes, I shall greet him dressed exactly like this," she grinned, sheathing her dagger again. "That should rattle some life into his brain."

"Milady, help!" Sophie, one of the serving maids, came in with an arm around the shoulders of Tom, the boy who kept the castle mews. He seemed to be covered in blood, and more streamed from beneath the rag he held against one eye.

"Tom, what happened?" Dru leapt to her feet, her sewing tumbling unnoticed to the floor.

" 'Tis the Greenland falcon, the white," he explained as Dru lifted the rag and Alista and Sophie gasped as one. Deep gashes were scratched into either side of his face. "She broke her jesses, milady, I know not how."

" 'Tis not so bad," Dru said, dabbing blood away with her white linen veil. "The eye is whole."

"I fear the bird will take more hurt than me," Tom said,

allowing himself to be seated on a footstool by the hearth. "She is mad to be free, flying against the walls. I tried to calm her, and she gave me this." He winced as Dru probed his wounds. "Something has frighted her, but I cannot say what."

"I'll go see," Alista said, getting up.

"Alista, no," Dru protested.

"If she isn't quieted or freed, she will kill the other birds," Alista pointed out. "I'll take care, I promise."

A small crowd had gathered in the courtyard just outside the mews. Clarence the castellan was consulting with one of his bowmen, and the screams of the birds could be heard even through the heavy oaken door. "You can't mean to shoot her," Alista cried, running to join them, her feet sliding on the icy ground.

"I only wish we could," Clarence grumbled. "It's dark as Satan's pit in there, and she flies at any show of light."

"A white falcon is a creature of the devil," one of the cooks said sagely. " 'Tis a priest we're needing, not a crossbow."

"Don't be ridiculous," Alista snapped. "Everyone step back."

"Oh, no, you don't," Clarence said, blocking her way. "I can't let you go in there. Did you not see young Tom?"

"You fear for my beauty, Clarence?" she grinned. "I have Brinlaw for my dowry; why should I need a pretty face?" A keening cry was suddenly cut short inside the mews. "She's killing the others, and she knows me well—I must at least try to set her free." He didn't budge, and the expression on his face told her he was not convinced. "In my father's name, I order you to stand aside!"

Clarence obviously wanted to argue, but he nodded.

"You heard her," he ordered, his jaw clenched. "Step away and douse the light."

As she slowly swung the heavy door open the smallest crack through which she could squeeze, Alista knew she should be afraid, but she wasn't. The Greenland falcon was her father's prize possession, fierce and beautiful with feathers so pale they seemed white. "Like my mother's hair," Alista had said when her father had first shown her the bird, stroking the soft breast as broad as his spread hand. Now, standing so still in the darkness she felt every breath, she cared only for saving the magnificent creature from harm.

The other falcons that still lived and Brother Paolo's owl had all fallen silent, sensing her presence. As her vision adjusted to the darkness, she could see the staring owl blink at her, hear the faint tinkle of a bell tied to a restless talon. Then suddenly over all, drowning every other sense, was the savage scream of the white. A fierce breath of air passed by Alista's face with a whir of beating wings. "All will be well, my lady," she called softly, holding out her arm, bare but for the thin sleeve of her tunic. "Come to me so I may set you free."

The scream faded to a sound like a woman's sigh. Alista could see the pale glow of feathers in the rafters just over her head. "Will you tell me your sorrow, my lady?" she crooned, sure somehow that the falcon understood. "My father would serve you himself, I know, but he is gone away."

At this, the cry sounded again, more furious than before and growing louder, deafening, as the bird swooped down to her arm. But the lethal talons were delicate, barely holding on as if loath to break her skin. "Thank you, lady," Alista whispered, moving toward the door.

Once outside, she motioned the others back, and Clarence made them obey, his face drawn with tension. "Only a moment more," Alista promised, her voice barely more than a whisper, as she untied the falcon's hood. One golden eye fixed on her face for a moment, then the bird took flight in a leap so powerful its force knocked Alista backward into the snow. The moon was full in a cloudless, starry sky, and she could see the white falcon climbing higher in a circle that seemed to shrink smaller and smaller until the bird was another, paler, star. Then a sound filled her ears, piercing, like the sound of an arrow leaving its bow, only louder, so loud she covered her ears with her hands as the shape in the sky grew larger again, coming toward her. The falcon plummeted toward the courtyard as if intent on a kill, and one of the women screamed, and Clarence ran to Alista, grabbed her arm to drag her to safety. But instead of extending her talons, pulling up her downward flight to attack, the falcon came on headfirst, crashing to the ground mere inches from Alista's feet.

"No!" Alista screamed, scrambling for the creature on her knees. The bird was stone dead, her feathers soaked with blood. Pressing her fingers to the carcass, Alista could feel no flutter of heartbeat, no sign of life at all. "No," the girl kneeling in the snow repeated, weeping with horror and a grief all out of proportion for the death of a falcon. She felt something warm falling over her and looked up to see Brother Paolo wrapping a mantle around her shoulders. "What is happening?" she demanded, as if she truly believed he knew. "Tell me what this means."

"Nothing, cara mia," he promised, lifting her to her feet. "It's only a bird, sweet love."

* * *

The church bells had finally stopped ringing by midnight, but the general air of celebration continued all through London. Even in this miserable Cheapside tavern, the air was thick with joy, every drunkard beaming with reflected glory. Every drunkard, that is, but one.

"Will, for the sweet blood of Christ," this melancholy creature's sole companion swore, thumping down his tankard with enough force to make their other empties dance. "You act dead and sour as old Stephen rotting in his tomb."

"Shut up, Raynard," his friend muttered, taking another long swallow. William of Brinlaw hadn't realized how completely he had counted on Henry until the new king, his boyhood friend, chose to break his hopes to bits.

"You oughtn't to be so surprised," Raynard said, signaling for more drink. "Henry has always been one to think first of his own want and hide—'tis why he's tupping the lovely Eleanor this night with the crown on a bedside table." The soldier meant no treason or even malice; indeed, it was this very self-preserving instinct that had drawn him to give up the mercenary life to follow Henry a decade or more past. But Will Brinlaw was his friend, the only real friend he could boast, and seeing him grieve so for a single plot of mud made Raynard want to crack open his skull to let some sense inside.

"My father died for him," Will answered, his blue eyes clear with a fury too powerful for any liquid spirit to quench.

"As did a thousand others, with his mother's count taken in," Raynard said, meeting his gaze. " 'Tis naught but politics, nothing to do with you or your father, either." The barmaid set down two more brimming vessels and hurried away, chilled by the look in the big, pretty one's eyes. "The war is over, and old Mark is of more use."

Will knew Raynard was right; 'twas why he felt such pain. Henry saw him as no more or less than a weapon for battle, a well-wrought, lethal sword, invaluable in wartime, but in peace good for little more than gathering dust. Could the man with whom he'd shared so much truly know him so little? "You can't understand," he said aloud. "You've never known what it is to have a home and lose it, to lose a family." In his mind, he could see his mother cover her face with her hands to weep as King Stephen's troops escorted them from their home, could still feel the blood pouring over his own hands from his father's chest as both of them sprawled in the mud of a battlefield. "It all means nothing to you," he finished, speaking not to Raynard but to Henry, the boy to whom he'd sworn allegiance with his dead father's blood still wet on his hands.

"Aye, you must be right," Raynard muttered, drowning his own anger in another swallow. The boy was drunk and miserable; his words couldn't be held against him. "But what can this fine fellow want?" he said, glad to see a distraction heading their way.

The royal page had obviously taken great pains to disguise his office, his usual livery exchanged for a plain tunic, but the expression of horrified distaste he wore with it was a dead giveaway. He started to speak to Will, then, seeing his face, decided Raynard was the more receptive audience. "His Majesty the King sent me to find William of Brinlaw," he explained. "He said he must come to him at once, but all quiet."

"Well, lad, we'll be pleased to come," Raynard answered, lumbering to his feet with such force that his chair fell over with a crash. "But I can't promise we'll be quiet."

Paolo had been certain the falcon's death meant nothing, that the bird had simply been captive too long. "Its nature broke free of its wits," he had told Alista, hustling her off to bed. But his own dreams were troubled with falcons in flight and the memory of Bianca. . . . *She flew away*, the child Alista cried from the misty cliffside of the dream as the sea roared far below. *My child is yours, Fra Paolo,* her mother spoke, urgent and fond, as if she stood just at his shoulder. *You must not let her fall*. . . .

He woke to familiar darkness, his own warm room, but the chill of the dream seemed to hang on his sweat-slick flesh. He lit the candle and climbed out of bed to huddle at the hearth, building the fire back up into a blaze. The Lord in His mercy had given him little bodily hurt with the passing of the years, but suddenly he felt ancient, a lonely old man in the dark.

He and Lord Mark had quarreled in this room, the same old struggle grown more heated with time instead of burning out. Burning. Bianca's husband had said she must be burned, her daughter taught the heathen tongue. Blasphemy! Paolo had cried, but the knight wouldn't listen, would never hear.

"It is her nature, Brother," Mark had said again before he left for London, here, in this room before this fire as the daughter they didn't quite share slept in her room down the hall, a woman grown but innocent. "You cannot protect her from herself, even if there were need—"

"There is every need!" Paolo had shouted, the old fear freezing his blood. Mark was blind, still, after all these years; blind with love, yes, but the horror was no less for that. "Alista's very soul is in danger—"

"Her soul is pure, and it is her own!" Mark had shouted back. "Not yours, good Brother, not mine. We cannot even understand—"

"Then what are we to tell her?" They had spoken these words to one another so many times, repeating them again seemed like a joke or a catechism, the meaning already soaked into their hearts. "What will you say—you say you must tell her the truth? What is this truth that you would tell?"

"I will tell her who she is," Mark had answered, his tone suddenly calm. "What she might become. When I return from London, my daughter will be told."

All argument had ceased. Paolo loved Alista more dearly than life, but her father was Mark of Brinlaw. Now alone in the darkness, the monk gathered his robes more tightly around his shoulders. "Protect my child, dear Father," he prayed, his head bent toward the flames. "I commit to You her soul."

Down the hall in her own little room, Alista hadn't slept yet. She sat on a chest by the window that was no more than a narrow slit, the stars and moonlight just enough to let her see what she wanted. On her lap she had spread a paper, a piece of vellum creased and thinned from years of folding and touch.

"Alista" was written across the top, first in beautiful letters, then again more raggedly—her own childish script. "Little bird," Lady Blanche had written beneath the names, spelling each letter as it was drawn while her daughter watched, enthralled.

Under the writing were two pictures. The first was a falcon in flight, its wings beautifully rendered, feather by delicate feather. "Lovely," Alista had whispered, making her mother smile. Then Mama had drawn a lady clothed only in her own long hair, looking back over her shoulder as little curlicues of sea-surf played around her slender ankles. "Who is she?" Alista had asked, studying the picture so closely its lines seemed to waver into life.

Her mother had kissed her forehead, gathering her against her side. "You are she."

Now the woman the child had become touched the drawing-woman's face, remembering the feel of her mother's kiss, the sweet smell of her gown, the softness of her cheek. Sometimes when she tried to remember these things, she felt like she was remembering the memory instead of the reality, as if her mother had been no more than a story told to her as a child. But tonight the past seemed very close, and this picture she had kept secret for so long, secret even from Brother Paolo and her father, seemed vitally important, a message from the past. Something was happening to her; she could feel it.

She folded the page again and tucked it back into its hiding place, a tiny crevice between the stones of the wall where she had kept it from the first night she had spent in this room. But the image of the woman and her falcon still burned in her mind like the shape of her own name.

Will and Raynard were taken to the King's private bedchamber. The heavy draperies were drawn around the bed, but Henry had obviously emerged from it only minutes before their entrance, and was still dressed in nothing but his hose with a fur-lined mantle flung over his shoulders.

"That was quick," he said, grinning, as they came in. "So how drunk are you?"

"Not near drunk enough," Will answered sullenly, refusing to be charmed. "What is this, Henry?"

"That's Your Majesty the Bloody King to you, Brinlaw," Henry shot back pleasantly, filling three cups with his own hand as a squire struggled to coax a warmer blaze from the fire. "Here, have another drink."

Raynard took a swallow. "The vintage and company are much improved," he admitted, settling into a chair with his legs stretched long before him. "But the hour still makes a man uneasy—a midnight summons from the King?"

Will was still standing, his expression as grim as before as he looked down on the friend who was now his king. "Will, for pity," Henry grumbled, kicking a chair toward him as he sat down himself. Will sat and grudgingly reached for the last cup. "That's a fine way to behave when I'm about to grant your heart's desire."

The wine cup froze halfway to Will's lips. "How so?" he asked, still wary, and even Raynard's lazy pose tensed up a bit.

"Brinlaw," Henry replied, taking a satisfied swig. "I'm going to give you Brinlaw."

For a moment, Will thought he must be the butt of some cruel joke, and he waited, still scowling, for the cream of the jest. "What of Mark?" he heard Raynard ask.

"Dead," Henry answered, leaning forward to look Will in the eye. "Dropped dead as a stone not two hours past, and none do know it but his own squires and we three." He smiled again, as if Mark's death were a gift he had himself produced for his friend's pleasure. "May God assoil him."

"So you mean to claim his holding." Will's own voice

sounded distant to him, the voice of a stranger in another room. An hour before, he had been plotting treason, a war that would be like suicide but inescapable nonetheless. Now the cause was to be won without a fight? "What of his heirs, his son—"

"No son, just a daughter." Henry flung a roll of parchment across the table. "I witnessed his will myself and am charged with her protection."

"And this is how you mean to fulfill your office?" Even Raynard was shocked, and he thought he knew how little conscience their friend possessed. "By depriving this woman of her inheritance?"

"I mean to deprive her of nothing," Henry protested. "I will give her the greatest gift any woman can receive."

"Oh, no," Raynard laughed, understanding.

"A husband," Henry finished.

Will's momentary confusion at the King's sudden burst of generosity cleared up in an instant. His kind but faithless king had a stake in his success after all. Not that it mattered, so long as he had Brinlaw, but still . . . "You think I will marry Mark's daughter and hold his district loyal," he said aloud.

"I think you can if you hurry and keep it quiet," Henry answered, the good-humored boy giving way to the man with a design. "Mark's daughter is now one of the richest heiresses in England, and once the word gets out, the road to Brinlaw will be churned to mud with would-be husbands. As King, it is my duty to see her appropriately wed, and I intend to do it by keeping my faith with you. I will endow you with your father's title, then you and your men will escort Mark's body back to Brinlaw. You'll leave before first light."

"So Will is to wed and bed the wench before any other contender can reach her." Raynard raised his cup in salute. "Sometimes, my liege, your wit can astound even me."

"I thank you both for your good wishes," Will answered sarcastically. "But what if Mark's daughter won't have me?"

"Then you must convince her." The softly accented voice came from the bed. Emerging from the draperies was Queen Eleanor, as exquisite as her legend proclaimed her, even—especially—in her nightshift with her long, black curls in disarray. "Her name, by the way, is Alista," she went on, taking a sip from her husband's cup. "I dare say Henri has forgotten."

"She'll have who I send her, whatever her name may be," Henry grumbled.

Eleanor gave him a fond smile. "Of course she will, my love," she agreed. "But if William truly wants what he has always claimed, he will do far better to win her heart." She turned to Will, her eyes serious. "You say, my lord, that you wish to reclaim your home, to rebuild your family. You will need an ally, not a slave."

Will flushed red, not with embarrassment but with new rage. How dare Henry discuss his private hopes with this woman? Henry couldn't know Will's reasons for thinking so little of his queen, but just knowing she knew his desires made the betrayal seem even more ill meant. Were his life's hopes no more to his friend than pillow talk? "I thank you, Majesty, for your good counsel," he said with perfect courtesy.

"But you don't believe it," Eleanor answered with a world-weary sigh. "I wish you good fortune, Lord of Brinlaw."

* * *

At Brinlaw, the snow had turned to a hard, cold rain that drove every human creature indoors. Druscilla had set up her loom in the relative light and warmth before the fire in the castle's Great Hall, giving her an excellent vantage point from which to watch Alista's training. "Clarence, no!" she shrieked as the castellan swung his broadsword in a whistling arc, missing the other girl's head by inches as she ducked into a crouch and rolled to safety.

"Hush, Dru, or he shall kill me indeed," Alista scolded with a laugh, leaping to her feet in an instant.

"I will if you don't have a care," Clarence agreed, already behind her to give her a solid slap to the behind with the flat of his sword just to get her attention.

"Bloody varlet!" Alista swore, happily furious as she turned on him again.

"Alista!" Dru cried.

" 'Tis true, you know," Clarence said as their swords clashed again. "Such language is hardly ladylike." She was advancing on him steadily, but not fast enough, and mischief danced in her eyes. He feinted with an upward stroke and lunged, meaning to push her off her feet, but she neatly avoided the blow, stepping back and up on a bench, then up again on the table, momentarily out of reach. "And now you're walking on the furniture," he continued.

"Shocking, isn't it?" Alista agreed, pleased to see her acrobatics work so well. Clarence had been her teacher since she was a child, but he had only recently begun to spar with her himself. A full foot taller than she was and outweighing her two to one, the great Viking had probably worried he'd accidentally break her to bits. But if her usual bruises and currently stinging dignity were any indication, he had finally decided she could manage, and she was quite pleased with herself. " 'Tis a good thing I have no fear of heights," she laughed, leaping back from another swing of his broadsword with nimble grace.

"Maybe you should." Before she could lift her sword, Clarence suddenly reached up and grabbed the front of her tunic, dumping her unceremoniously face first on the floor.

"Mon Dieu!" Dru scolded, running to her fallen friend. "Clarence, you should be ashamed!"

"Yea, Clarence," Alista agreed, rolling onto her back, her wind still knocked out from the blow. "I hope your conscience pricks you."

"Dancing works better for jesters than it does for fighters, my lady," Clarence said, unmoved. "A battle is never a game."

Shouts from the battlements interrupted her reply—men beneath the Brinlaw banner were riding over the drawbridge. "Papa!" Alista cried, scrambling to her feet and racing for the door.

"Alista, wait, you'll freeze!" Dru called after her. "Think how you're dressed!"

Alista barely heard her, so intent was she in reaching her father. Ever since the death of the white falcon three nights before, her fears had run colder than the rain, fears only the sight of her father would dispel. She ran out into the courtyard just as he was climbing off his horse.

Riding into the outer bailey of Brinlaw, Will had been surprised at how little he felt, how dim his memory of this place had grown in the fifteen years since he'd been forced to leave it. In the drenching downpour, the gray walls looming over them could have belonged to any castle in England. But when they entered the courtyard and he saw the Brinlaw dragon hanging over the arching door, such a sense of belonging and vengeance washed over him he felt sick. "Not much of a day for a triumphal entry, is it?" Raynard teased, then he turned his horse about to give the order to dismount. Will swung down from his own horse and was pushing back the hood of his chain mail when a young boy ran down the steps from the front door and threw himself into his arms.

As soon as Will touched her, he knew this boy was no boy, and she obviously knew he was not whomever she'd expected. He felt a fleeting press of feminine curves against his chest and arms around his waist before she recoiled so quickly she fell backward on the mud-slick stones. "Who are you?" she demanded, the rain plastering loose strands of dark hair to an elfin face and thin muslin to pale pink skin. "Where is my father?"

Father? he thought, incredulous. This was his intended bride, this sodden, unseemly creature in boots and hose? If he hadn't been so lost in his own chaotic thoughts, he would probably have been less blunt, more quick to realize that Mark's death would be a matter of far greater personal import to this girl that it was to him. As it was . . .

"He's dead," he answered. Another girl, this one blond, pretty, and wearing a proper dress, was coming out the door and let out a blood-chilling scream, but the baggage on the ground just stared at him, deathly pale in the weak and watery light. He had seen that look many times before on the battle-field, the stunned shock of a corpse who in the first moments after the blow can't believe he's really dead. He bent down and offered his hand, beginning to regret his lack of tact.

"Sweet saints, Will," Raynard muttered, echoing his thoughts.

"Will," Alista said, her reeling mind catching hold of the word like a drowning woman grasping at reeds. "Who are you, Will?"

"William of Brinlaw, Lady Alista." He gave up waiting for her and grasped her hand, a tiny, trembling thing. "King Henry has sent me to you."

Two

"Alista, please," Druscilla pleaded, watching her friend prowl the solar like an anxious cat. "At least change your clothes—"

"For what, my wedding?" Alista demanded, turning on her. "Or for my father's funeral? Who is it I should impress?" Brother Paolo gave her a painful look, and she flushed, but she didn't back down. "No, Dru, I think my clothes will serve right well for hacking that bastard's head—"

"Alista, don't be ridiculous," Brother Paolo cut her off.

"Why is it ridiculous?" She flung off the heavy mantle she'd thrown over her wet tunic, its weight more oppressive than the chill. "Why have I trained so long if not to defend my home—?"

"From the King?" the monk asked mildly.

"Why should we believe this man truly comes from the King?" she persisted. "That letter could be forged—"

"But the King's seal could not," he finished.

"It's no good trying to reason with her, Brother," Dru

said in an uncharacteristically petulant tone. "She is in love with Geoffrey of Anjou."

"I am not!" Alista shouted, feeling ready to explode with fury.

"Fine, you are not, but please, keep your voice down," Dru hissed urgently, glancing at the door.

"Of course you are not," Paolo soothed, casting Dru a baleful glance. "Cara mia, listen to me." He laid a hand on her shoulder, and she flinched, but to his relief she didn't pull away entirely. "Do you think I wish to see you married to a stranger?" He wanted to put his arms around her, hold her close and let her cry out her misery as she had so often as a child, but he didn't dare. As wild and inappropriate and foolhardy as her raging might be, just now it was her greatest strength, and she needed it more than comfort. "Do you think I would ever urge you to do such a thing if there were any alternative? You are strong, my love, but this William is a seasoned soldier—did you not read the King's letter? He has just returned from Crusade—"

"So he is too holy to oppose?" she asked bitterly.

"You would never have the chance to oppose him," he answered, his tone just as sharp. "He would strike your sword from your hand before you could raise it and likely beat you for your impertinence." Alista had never been struck in her life, and he knew this would make an impression. "And with the King's seal and an army at his back, I would not dare speak a word to defend you."

"Not a word?" she scoffed, not fooled for a moment. Woe betide the King's man if he raised a hand to her, Crusader or not.

"Even so," he conceded without backing down. "Would you wish to cause me such pain?"

"I don't care," Alista insisted, but her sudden pallor and a quaver in her voice said otherwise. "I can't marry him." *And my father can't be dead,* she silently added.

"Then all of us are dead," Dru said simply, sinking into a chair.

Alista snapped her head around, her loosening braid flying, to look at the other girl, ready to blast her with the full force of her wrath, but Dru was crying, almost silent, her pretty face hidden in her hands. She believed what she had said, that if Alista refused to obey the King's command . . . She had never seen Dru look so scared, even during her first tense days at Brinlaw when she'd jumped out of her skin every time Alista's father spoke to her, no matter how kindly. King Henry had written that Alista's marriage to Old Brinlaw's son had been arranged before Mark's death, an ideal solution to their mutual problems. William had no lands; Mark had no sons. Now that their political differences were eliminated, an alliance was all but inevitable. Alista had no doubt that most men would reason so—hadn't Geoffrey said nearly the same thing, the practical pith of his airy declaration of love? But try as she might, she couldn't imagine her father using her heart so callously just to win an ally or please his sovereign. All she remembered of her mother was entwined in Blanche's love for her husband and his for her. She had told Alista again and again how they had chosen one another, how their souls were one, and after she was gone, Mark had mourned her as if his soul were truly lost, had never stopped grieving for her. He had known Alista had expected to one day find the same sort of love, had spoken of it with her more than once—'twas the reason he had allowed her to remain a maid when any other woman her age would have long been a wife and mother.

"You will know him," he had laughed when she had asked. "No one else may see any good in him, but you will know." He had touched her cheek, the black eyes so like her own turning soft with love. "And when he finds you, I will have to let you go." Was this what he had meant? Was this Will the man he believed she would choose?

Dru was still crying, and Brother Paolo was still reproaching her with his sad, dark eyes. That was always his way. When her father was angry with her, he railed and raged, but in a day or so, his wrath was forgotten by both of them. Brother Paolo never raised his voice or even really told her what she must do, but when she displeased him, he looked so disappointed, his look would haunt her for months. "Brother, before he left, did my father speak to you about finding me a husband in London?" she asked.

"No," Paolo answered, a sharp hook of regret digging deep into his heart as he watched her give in to the inevitable. Even if she could bear it, how could he? "Perhaps he didn't think of it until he met this man," he said, grasping at some semblance of comfort for them both. "He is well-spoken, well-made—King Henry has much praise for him. Perhaps your papa believed he would please you—the King says he meant to wait until you knew one another before he mentioned it. Perhaps he thought this man would be your choice."

You will know him, her father had said. She didn't, couldn't even imagine—her father was dead; how could she think about a husband? Her father, the one soul save Brother Paolo who truly knew her, had known this William of Brinlaw. The King said he had chosen him to be her love. The same father who had come for her when her mother was gone and disaster was on its way had wanted her to accept this Will as her own, had told his king as much. If this were true, it could not be ignored. She could defy a stranger; she could even defy her king. But she could not defy her father.

She went to Dru and pulled her close for a moment, stroking her hair as she cried. "I'm sorry, Dru; don't cry," she murmured softly. "I swear I will make us all safe."

Will had been trying to examine Brinlaw's Great Hall with a critical eye ever since they had come inside. He wanted to find more reason to hate dead Mark, to be appalled at the changes he had wrought on Will's family manor. If he could despise Mark with all his bitter heart, maybe it would harden against his daughter, look on her as the inconvenient addendum to his castle he had left London knowing she would be. For three days of a grim, forced march across a wintry England, he had ridden with the smell of Mark's corpse in his nose and an image of his daughter just as offensive taking shape in his mind. She would be cold and disdainful and plain—if not, why hadn't her father brought her to court? To have his rightful inheritance, he would have to bed an icy, overaged virgin with nothing but contempt for his family and himself. Steeling himself as if for the most wretched battle, he had promised himself he would hear no protests, force her to do the King's will, then allow her to flee to the sanctuary of the nearest convent just as fast as he could drive her away.

Then he had seen Alista. Nothing in his plan—indeed, nothing he had ever known—had prepared him for her. He was not without experience with what he had imagined to be every possible variety of woman. He remembered his mother, all quiet dignity, and his sister, May, a bundle of vanity and giggles until disaster struck—much of the revenge he craved was for the sake of May. He had learned about whores alongside Henry, God's Anointed, the two of them Raynard's willing apprentices in the stews from London to Jerusalem. He had flirted with the ladies of Aquitaine after Henry's marriage and found them little different, only better dressed and more given to deception.

But now, staring at the bolted door of the solar, he turned these over and over in his mind, and none of them seemed to have anything in common with the wild little witch from the courtyard. Even in the boyish clothes, he had found her fair to look on, and he could still feel the shape of her against his chest and thighs an hour after her hasty, mistaken embrace. But where the other beauties he had known had possessed charm and serenity and guile, Alista seemed all bitter innocence and passion. Compared to the spark he had seen in her, every other woman seemed lifeless, no more real than a painted statue in a church nave or mounted before a bawdy house.

"What is this?" she had shouted, waving Henry's letter barely read and making no ladylike attempt to hide her pain and fury. "To the devil with all this—just tell me what happened! How did my father die?"

"My lady, calm yourself," the monk had urged as the other girl looked frankly terrified. Even the brawny castellan had seemed a little nervous. But this Alista was fearless in her grief, facing Will squarely and demanding an answer with her eyes.

"I cannot tell you," he had told her, as much truth as he was willing to give her. "I only know he died."

"Then why are you here?" she persisted. There were

tears in her eyes, a softness at odds with her anger that was shockingly feminine. "To marry me, the King writes, but why?"

"To keep you safe," Will answered easily, unoffended. Why should she want to marry him? She would, of course, but he wouldn't think ill of her if the prospect didn't make her swoon with joy. "To keep Brinlaw safe."

She shook her head before he finished. "No, this is wrong," she insisted, turning away from him. "Everything about this is wrong."

"Come, my lady," the monk had said, putting an arm around her shoulders. "You must excuse us, Lord Brinlaw. Lady Alista is distraught." She had allowed Brother Paolo to lead her to the solar with the other girl, Druscilla, close behind, and there they had been ever since.

The front door was pushed open, admitting a blast of icy wind and Raynard. "Still sitting here by yourself?" he asked, flinging his soaking mantle on a bench by the fire. "What does your lady say?"

"Nothing more yet." Will pushed his own cup to his friend. "Any problems outside?"

"None to speak of." They had decided to relieve the usual guard of Mark's men and replace them with soldiers of their own. "The castellan is suspicious, but he recognized Henry's seal." He glanced around the crowded Hall. Everyone was subdued, quiet, but he sensed no malice in the air. "The others are just thankful to be in out of the rain." He tore a lump of bread from the loaf Will hadn't touched. "They're all loyal to the girl, that much is certain," he went on in softer tones. "As she goes, so will go the garrison."

"Loyalty is no bad thing," Will answered. "Old Mark made sure she was protected. I would have done the same in his place if I were able."

"I doubt you'd have given her a sword and let her dress herself in breeches," Raynard said. "They say she's a deft little warrior in her way. In truth, I think they love the lady for her own sake. Mark was away much, if you'll recall."

Will grimaced. "As if I could forget." Some of the most miserable battles of his life had been fought against Mark's troops before the peace was made.

"He was as spry at home as he was in the field, by the way," Raynard grinned. "The other girl, Druscilla? She's no lady-in-waiting for your mistress; she was Mark's doxy."

Suddenly the solar door opened, and Druscilla came into the hall. Will noted with wry amusement that though her eyes were red with weeping, she had taken the time to change her rain-sodden gown and put her crowning glory back to rights. This, at least, was a woman he could read.

" 'Swounds, but 'tis a goddess," Raynard teased loudly, getting up to sketch a deep, courtly bow.

Druscilla barely spared him a glance. "My lady will do as the King has asked her," she said to Will. "She will even marry you this night and bury her good father on the morrow, though 'tis against all that's natural to her heart."

"Yea, lady, but 'tis infinitely safer," Raynard laughed, unperturbed by her scorn.

"Tell your lady that I thank her for her sacrifice," Will answered, ignoring him.

Dru made a tiny curtsey. "You may expect her in the chapel within the hour." She looked at Raynard, her wide blue eyes suddenly blazing with hatred. "And you, sir, may go to the devil."

* * *

By the time her wedding ceremony began, Alista felt awful, not just sick at heart but physically unwell. When she'd first come in from the rain, she had barely noticed she was wet and cold. She couldn't feel anything but horror, as if her body only existed to contain the screams of her soul. But now she could barely think straight, barely keep clear in her mind what had happened, what was happening still. Her father had died in London; she was about to be married to a stranger—the words had no meaning. Brother Paolo was standing right before her, speaking the words of the rite, but he sounded far away, as if he were calling to her from the bottom of a watery chasm. Her head was swimming; her face was burning hot; her mother's red silk gown, the only garment she owned that seemed remotely suitable to the occasion, clung to her flesh like seaweed, the skirts dragging at her legs, dragging her down to the floor of the chapel. She longed to give up the struggle and sink, to press her burning cheek to the smooth, cold stone and close her eyes. Her knees started to buckle, and she reached instinctively to catch herself, grabbing the elbow of the massive knight at her side. My God, he's huge, she thought, gazing up at him in wonder.

Will felt his bride grab hold of him and turned to her in alarm, but she seemed calm enough. In fact, she was gazing up at him in perfect serenity, almost smiling, her huge, black eyes alive with avid interest. Her cheeks were flushed with blood, but the effect was charming, another colorful contrast to the creamy white of the rest of her skin and the stark ebony of her eyes and fine-drawn eyebrows and the glossy hair that now fell to her shoulders in waves. Her blush matched her lips and her gown, made her seem even more vividly alive, and for a moment, looking into her eyes, he felt dizzy with the knowledge she was his. He made himself smile at her in what he hoped was an encouraging manner, and she smiled back, apparently satisfied, before returning her attention to the monk.

Such a nice giant, Alista thought, her teeth beginning to chatter. A moment ago she'd felt ready to burst into flame; now she was freezing. I hope he won't be too distraught in a moment when I drop stone dead at his feet, she thought with fatalistic humor. But everything was so mixed up. . . . When this Will person had shown up and told her . . . this horrible thing he had said that she didn't want to remember, she had barely seen him, paid him no mind once she knew he wasn't . . . her father; she had wanted her father so much, and this person wasn't him. But suddenly now all she wanted was to look at him, this Will, and looking made her feel strangely happy, almost dizzy with a joy that made no sense. He was handsome, she discovered, had a good, strong chin under his little beard and a full, sensuous mouth and blue eyes, darker than her father's, more midnight sky than crystal, but lovely, taken in all. And when he'd smiled that tiny bit a moment ago, she had noticed he had all his teeth in front, a rare blessing for a Crusader. Her father had done a fine job of finding her a husband whether she wanted one or not, and she may as well want one. Brother Paolo was right; she could never hope to bring down this mountain by the sword.

Brother Paolo was drifting away again . . . no, he had stopped speaking altogether to look at her groom-giant. "I will," Will answered, and his voice was so close, she jumped—whatever bubble in the air had swallowed her had apparently swallowed him, too, made him the only seeming-solid object she could find.

I have a fever, she realized, remembering similar bubbles from her childhood. The first had been at Falconskeep with her mother—her mother had held her hand, held her fast to the real world until her fever broke and let her drift back down to earth. She reached for Will's hand now, felt it close warm and strong around her own. "Thank you," she whispered, barely even a whisper, a fleeting wisp of breath.

Will turned to look at her again, her unexpected touch racing through his blood. Her head was bent as if in concentration or prayer as the cleric asked her the vows, no indication she had spoken beyond the gentle grip of her hand. Either she truly was a guileless innocent, or her play-acting was more sophisticated than any he'd ever seen, even more accomplished than the masque Eleanor kept whirling for Henry. If he hadn't known better, he could have believed she was happy to be his.

Except that she wouldn't speak the vow. Brother Paolo had reached the end of his questions, but Alista was still staring at the floor. Will gave her arm a shake, and she looked up, but she seemed to have no idea what was expected of her. She looked at him, at Brother Paolo, then back at him. . . .

"I will," Alista blurted out, realizing what they wanted. Good, it was almost over—at least she might survive to see the end. *Married,* she scolded herself. *Pay attention, idiot. You're being married.*

Brother Paolo had been concentrating his entire attention on his English prayer book, trying not to think too deeply about what he was doing or to see the fear and helpless rage he knew must be in Alista's eyes or the smug triumph of her captor. But looking at them now, he saw to his shock that he'd been wrong. Alista looked quite calm; it was William of Brinlaw who looked utterly at a loss. "Then as God's earthly servant, I say you are man and wife," he said, finishing the rite.

Raynard, standing at Will's side, fully expected his comrade-at-arms to beat as hasty a retreat as courtesy would allow. Taking a wife in a public ceremony was all very well, but Raynard couldn't imagine him making any manner of show over it—even with camp-following whores, Will was the fastidious soul of discretion. So he was most surprised to see his friend kiss his bride on the lips, nearly as surprised as the maiden herself.

When Will moved to take her into his arms, Alista's first response was purely gratitude—he felt so warm, and she was freezing. But when he touched his lips to hers, she was seized with an entirely new sensation, so powerful she nearly forgot she was ill. She shivered in his embrace, feeling fragile and protected, and his mouth felt so strange, soft and hard at once—alive. He was alive and separate but so close to her his breath could have come from her lungs, and this should have been appalling, but it wasn't; it seemed to be perfectly right, the only possible way for her heart to go on beating. She opened her mouth to breathe him in more deeply, and she felt him shudder, pull her closer, and she slid her arms around his neck and raised herself on tiptoe to reach him. The fever shook her from deep inside her bones as his tongue tasted hers, a flame flickering into her mouth to give her new life, and she fainted dead away in his arms.

For a moment, Will couldn't think what had happened, couldn't think at all, only feel this burning, yielding, living creature, this Alista, cling to him and conquer him completely. No woman had ever given herself so completely to his kiss, even in the deepest throes of love play. He felt as if he had been bewitched, lured by some fairy to an enchantment that only looked like Brinlaw, his longed-for dream of home. Then she went limp in his arms, her head falling back, breaking the kiss. He opened his eyes to find hers closed, ebony lashes staining cheeks as pale as moonlight.

Brother Paolo dropped his prayer book as Will scooped the unconscious woman off her feet. "Holy Mother, she is burning up," the monk swore, pressing a palm to her brow. "Come, bring her upstairs."

By the time Will had carried her up the treacherous stairs and laid her on her bed, Alista had begun to stir in his arms, but it was obvious from her incoherent fretting that she had no idea where she was or who held her. "Papa," she moaned as he let her go, ". . . away . . . must fly away . . ."

"Hush, cara mia," Brother Paolo urged, brushing Will aside. He loosened the laces on the tight-fitting gown and took the basin of herb-strewn water from the maid who had brought it up. " 'Tis no great wonder she caught a chill," he told Will, bathing Alista's brow. "She was soaked to the skin when you arrived, running to meet . . . running outside."

"Will she live?"

The monk looked up, surprised, but there was no mistaking the man was in earnest. His face was as taut and grim as his voice, as if he expected no more or less than utter disaster. Even so, the hunger in his eyes was unmistakable, a desperate hope that made him seem as young and vulnerable as the girl lying helpless on the bed. "Of course she will live," Paolo scolded, suppressing a smile. The poor knight was undone, and in less than a single day, just as he himself had been by Bianca. "She is a healthy woman in the prime of life. A winter chill won't harm her overmuch."

"Stop it," Alista muttered, pushing the wet cloth away without opening her eyes. "I can hear you."

"Good," Paolo retorted, pushing her hands out of the way. "Now hush and go to sleep."

"No," she fretted peevishly, but she stopped struggling. In another minute, she was breathing evenly, lost to all cares of the world.

Will watched the rise and fall of her breasts under the taut fabric of the gown. "Is she often ill?" he asked, trying to sound disinterested, a man thinking of buying a horse.

"Very rarely." Paolo stepped back to let the maid and a companion undress his patient. Discreetly turning his back, he noticed Will made no move to do the same. "But when she has a fever, she is likely to say things that make no sense. Lady Alista dreams very near to the angels, I believe."

Will tore his eyes away from his bride to look at him, appalled. "You mean she is mad?" he demanded. And wouldn't that be the perfect coup de grace to his miserable quest, to be tied for life to a lunatic?

"Not at all." One of the maids laid the red gown aside while the other pulled the blankets up to Alista's chin. Then both dropped a clumsy curtsey to Will before scurrying out, chattering to one another in awestruck tones before the door quite closed behind them. Paolo laid a fresh compress on Alista's forehead, but she barely stirred. "She will sleep 'til morning, my lord," he said. "You may as well go to your own rest."

"I'm not leaving," Will said stubbornly, feeling both like a villain and furious with himself for feeling so. If anyone in Brinlaw Castle had a right to take offense at this whole day's turn of events, it was he, not Alista, and certainly not this spider-skinny nursemaid of a monk. "She is my wife," he went on, sounding brutal even to himself. "She belongs to me now."

The monk's eyes widened, but he didn't flinch. "None in this house can doubt it, my lord," he answered mildly. "Just as you are hers."

Will's eyes narrowed, but the Franciscan seemed ready to stand his ground 'til Judgment Day. For a brief, heady moment, Will considered flinging him bodily from the room, hopefully with enough force to send him tumbling down the stairs. Unfortunately, he could think of no way to do it without seeming both a heartless cad and a hopeless idiot. "I'll be back," he muttered, heading for the door.

Paolo smiled. "My lord, we will be here."

Will found Raynard in the cozy solar, taking his solitary ease before the roaring fire. "So is she dead, or was she faking?" he asked pleasantly as Will came in.

"Neither." He collapsed into a chair, leaned his head back, and closed his eyes, becoming gradually aware of a persistent ache pounding just beneath his skull.

"That woman in Damascus swore you had hidden fires, but I never thought to see you fell a sturdy English lass with a single kiss." In truth, Raynard was a little worried. He had known the man sitting before him since he was a boy and in all manner of passion—rage, fear, grief, even joy.

When he had first met Will, Raynard was a mercenary, fighting in the hire of the Duke of Anjou, Henry's father. Twenty years old and already officially damned—all professional soldiers-for-hire being automatically excommunicate from the Church—he had cared nothing at all about the justice of Maude's claim to England, no more than he did her husband's petty squabbles in France. But something about the skinny boy sitting by a watch fire after the day's battle, seemingly bathed in blood but making not a whimper, piqued his curiosity. "Are you hurt?" he asked, sitting down beside him.

"It isn't mine," the boy Will answered, still staring into the flames. Tears carved twin rivers in the grime on his face, but his voice was steady as any man's. "The blood was my father's." He looked up at this stranger who fought for money alone. "I have sworn myself to serve Henry and to make him King of England. His father has made me a knight."

Raynard's first thought was that their situation must be more perilous than he'd realized if Duke Geoffrey had begun knighting infants. His second was that this poor kid wouldn't last a week. "Change your shirt and get some sleep," he advised, tossing a less-gory garment from his own pack at the boy. "Then tomorrow, you stay close to me."

He had taught the orphaned nobleman to fight to survive as well as to impress his fellow lordlings, to make snap judgments in the heat of battle without pausing to pray for guidance or consider the rules of chivalry or any such fatal nonsense. As Will and Henry had become friends, Raynard had grown to like the other boy as well, eventually even giving up the mercenary life to serve him, though the baseborn soldier could never be a knight. But it was to Will Brinlaw his loyalty was sworn, not the future king. Even when Will decided to leave the comfortable diversions of Aquitaine to go on Crusade to atone for a sin that wasn't his and shouldn't have been a sin in the first place, Raynard never considered letting him go alone. Never one for self-study, he had never considered the reasons for this, nor would he begin now.

But he knew Will Brinlaw, knew him better than he knew himself. And he knew he had never seen him like this. Carrying that girl out of the chapel, Will had looked haunted, as if he no longer trusted his own eyes. Now he just looked stunned, as if something had sucked the life right out of him.

"Alista is sick." The pounding was sending colorful splashes of light through the dark behind his eyelids, or maybe it was the fire. He was also dimly aware of a different sort of throb lower down, the lingering effect of the very kiss for which Raynard now chose to taunt him. "She caught a chill in the rain, and now she has a fever."

"So that explains it." Raynard leaned forward to give the fire a bit of encouragement with the poker. "How disappointing." Will snorted a bitter laugh as his only answer. "So your marriage isn't consummated."

Will's eyes snapped open. "The woman is unconscious."

"An unconscious virgin with your future between her legs." Raynard had never been a poet, but he felt the present situation required even plainer speech than usual. "We can't have more than half a day's start on any other contenders for her sacred treasure, and she looked willing enough to me."

"She was out of her senses." Will looked at his friend with undisguised disgust. "Even you couldn't take her in such a state."

"Your youthful worship of my virtue never fails to warm my heart," Raynard shot back. "Tell me, gentle knight, have you read Henry's suit on your behalf?" He tossed a scroll into Will's lap. "I found it in here after you and your lady retired."

Frowning slightly, Will unrolled the scroll and read.

"Holy Christ . . . he told her Mark chose me for her husband?"

"Appalling, isn't it?" Raynard grinned. "But if you know Henry, it sounds just like him. By now, he believes it himself, assuming he's given it another moment's thought."

I know you to have been the one true joy of your father's life, dear Alista, Will read, hardly able to believe his eyes. *I know you will not defy him now in death.* "Bloody bastard . . ."

"So it's often been said, though his mother the empress doth most heartily deny it," Raynard agreed.

So that was the explanation, the reason why she had come to marry him so willingly. The ache in his head was suddenly sharp enough to make him sick. He balled Henry's letter into a clot without thinking, crushing it in his fist. "I suppose I should tell her the truth."

"Wait another day, and I'd wager someone else will do it for you," his friend said, relentless for the boy's own good. "Most of the lords of the realm heard your quarrel with Mark on the very day he died, and most of the ones who aren't looking for a rich wife for themselves have sons to think about. If one of them turns up to tell tales before you wed the Brinlaw heiress, what's to stop her and her monk from annulling your claim and letting another suitor turn the lot of us out?" Will didn't answer, only tossed Henry's letter into the dancing flames. "Will, listen to me. Lady Alista is a darling, I grant you, and no doubt she deserves to be better treated."

"I don't know what she deserves," Will muttered grimly.

"But you've already made up your mind to have Brinlaw, and the wench is the way to the castle," Raynard went on.

"Thank you, Raynard; I had forgotten," Will sarcastically shot back. "I've just never been much of a rapist."

"Nor will you be one now," Raynard answered in kind, dismissing this as the foolishness it was. "The woman is your wife; she isn't a child; and she doesn't seem to be an idiot. She should know what's expected."

"I'm sure she does," Will agreed, the thought making him no happier. His own sister, May, had been a wife, and she had known what was expected, too, had meant to do her duty. But she found over time that she couldn't; eventually being a wife had become more than she could bear. The word had found Will in Aquitaine as he was wasting his days pretending to be smitten with this or that of Eleanor's ladies. Lady May had hanged herself, her sweet soul banished forever from God's grace just to escape her lawful husband. Will had taken the cross at once, praying to lose his own life to absolve her for taking hers, half-mad with rage at the world that had driven her to it. A stupid twit, Eleanor had called her, not realizing Will could hear; a fool who could think of no better way to dodge an unwanted husband.

"You will tell her the truth," Raynard said, cutting into his thoughts. "Just wait until it's too late to matter. She'll be furious, no doubt, but she'll get over it. She'll have no better choice."

"And what does that make me?" Will mused, though he knew Raynard was right. Brinlaw was his; nothing would change that. Better he should marry Alista than turn her out of her home.

"A man sure enough in his course to keep it, no matter what the cost," Raynard answered evenly. " 'Tis a little thing, Will, taken in all."

"Compared to Brinlaw, yes," Will agreed, standing up. "A little thing indeed."

* * *

Alista was slowly rising from a dream, passing through murky layers of meaning that had seemed joyously important a moment before but that now made no sense as she lost the thread of context to connect them. In the distance, shrinking ever closer, she could hear the voice of Brother Paolo in a heated argument with another man—in the dream, her mother was with her, and the sound of this other man's voice made the fading Lady Bianca smile, or maybe she smiled for Paolo. "Get out!" the stranger ordered, and Mama continued to smile, fading back away from the dream-Alista who tried and failed to hold her fast, the hand her daughter held melting to mist. She'd said something before that Alista had sworn to remember, but now she was silent, and her words were lost. . . . The heavy wooden door slammed shut, and the last heavy tendrils of the dream world disappeared.

"Alista?" The bed creaked as the stranger sat down beside her, barely touching her cheek. She opened her eyes to find Will looming over her, not a stranger at all. "Are you all right?"

She frowned, her scant memory of him hopelessly mixed in with the scattered fragments of her dream. He had kissed her. . . . "I think so," she answered carefully, not really trusting her voice until she heard it, clear and plain as ever. "I think I'm sick."

Will smiled in spite of himself. "I think so, too."

She squeezed her eyes shut tight, testing . . . the pounding in her head was gone, but her brow and skull still felt tender, bruised from the inside out. "I'm getting better," she decided, opening her eyes again. "But I need to stay still a while longer." A sudden thought occurred. "We finished the wedding, didn't we?"

Ah, there, dearie, lies the rub, Will thought wryly in the privacy of his own aching skull. "Pretty much," he agreed aloud.

Alista's mind was clearing fast enough to catch the hint in his tone. "Oh, damnation," she muttered, shocking a laugh from her brand new husband. She had spent enough nights as a child on a pallet in her father's room to know exactly which part of their joining had yet to be celebrated, but even if the entire prospect of lovemaking didn't already put her into a proper maiden's panic, she still couldn't have accomplished it in her present queasy state. "I'm sorry, my lord, but I just can't, not tonight."

Will, who like most men of his class had been brought up to believe sex would be a surprise he must spring on an innocent, all-unknowing bride once he'd lured her to the altar, didn't know whether to laugh again or be furious. "Can't what?"

"Oh, please," Alista grumbled, pushing herself up on her elbows. "Like you don't know right well." Even sitting up, she had to tilt her head back to look into his eyes, and she found she rather liked it. "I did like it when you kissed me," she confessed with a smile.

Will smiled back, a bit more warily—was she flirting with him, or just daft? "Did you truly?" he teased. "'Twas hard to be certain, what with your fainting."

"If it makes you feel any better, you may believe I did swoon from passion," she answered. Sitting here with him on the bed with only one candle and the fire for light, she found him easy to like, as if they were old, fond friends. She made bold to touch the fine-drawn line that had appeared between his eyebrows. "Are you angry with me, Will?"

The easy way she spoke his name was as damnably

provocative as the sight of her breasts and belly shadowed by candlelight through the thin cloth of her shift. But then, she thought she knew him, believed her father had come to know him on her behalf. "No, lady," he promised, kissing her hand. She smiled, utterly trusting, as she sank back against the pillows. "Alista," he began, leaning closer.

She had let her eyes fall shut again. "Yes?"

He pressed his lips to the dark smudge of lashes on either tender cheek. "Nothing," he promised. "Go to sleep."

Raynard knew he'd been right to speak with Will as he had, right to advise him to choose hard reason and convenience over a fool's tenderness and honor. But for once being right didn't make him feel any better. Dashing the dregs of his cup into the dying fire with a blasphemous oath for good measure, he left the solar for the Hall in search of a diversion.

Unfortunately, in Brinlaw Castle all was apparently well. The midnight watch was set and ready, the home garrison taking to the new additions as naturally as hens to chicks—indeed, many of them were none-too-distant kin, Mark's men being as largely native to the region as Will's. The scouts he'd sent back to keep an eye on the roads had all settled in and sent back their first reports—no sign of trouble in any direction. Those not on duty were bedded down in the Hall, snoring as peacefully as the old man's dogs before the fire. "Something wrong, Captain?" asked the bleary-eyed sentry, meeting Raynard beneath the arch.

"Aye, Duncan," Raynard muttered. "The world is a terrible place." Duncan opened his mouth to answer, but the captain was already gone.

He was headed for the stairs to have a look out over the battlements when he heard a woman weeping, an eerie sound that crawled and echoed along the narrow passage from the direction of a glowing, distant light. Dropping his hand to his sword hilt, he crept down the passage to the chapel.

The light came from tall racks of candles set at the head and foot of Mark's corpse. And the weeping came from Druscilla, kneeling at its side. Her head was bent to the armored chest; her hands were clenched tight around the arm that held the sword.

"I'm so sorry," she cried on, oblivious to Raynard's entrance. "I never thought . . . 'twas me and only me who did the wrong. . . ." The rest was lost in a wracking sob.

Ordinarily, Raynard would have been unmoved except to steal back the way he'd come. Women's tears were a ploy to him, another weapon in a lethal lady's arsenal. But something in this girl's posture, the rawness of her sobs, the utter lack of grace in the picture she presented made him pause. "Lady, what pains you so?" he asked, his own voice echoing in the shadows.

Dru sprang back from Mark's body, struggling to her feet, tripping on her tangled skirts. "How dare you?" she demanded, her hauteur coming out as a shriek.

"I heard you crying and thought you might need help," the captain answered easily, obviously amused by her struggles.

"From you?"

"From someone wiser than you." His tone was teasing, but his eyes were serious, even sympathetic. "Trust me, poppet, nothing you can have done could be worth so much remorse."

For a moment, he thought she would tell him. Her expression softened, considering, her tear-reddened eyes full of hope. Then something else seemed to dawn there, to shut him away from her completely. "You only think you are wise," she answered, turning back to her dead lover. "I'faith, you know nothing at all."

Three

Will woke up from his first night as lord of Brinlaw feeling like he'd slept a hundred years in a cave. Every muscle in his body was stiff and aching from the awkward night's rest after three days and nights on the road, and he was chilled and smothered at the same time, his legs bent under him on the cold, stone floor while the rest of him sprawled across the bed. He had sat on the floor by the bed for hours, watching Alista sleep, trying to decide if he should join her on the bed or leave her alone. Apparently he had fallen asleep before he made up his mind. He pushed off the heavy fur someone had flung over him and slowly sat up. At least his headache was gone.

Alas, so was his bride. "Alista?" He climbed to his feet, ignoring the pains that shot down either leg. The red gown she'd worn for their wedding was still neatly laid across a trunk where the maids had left it, but Alista's shoes were gone, too. A plate of bread and cheese had been put on the table along with a flagon and cup. His breakfast . . . but how long had he been sleeping? And where had Alista gone?

He half-staggered to the window and threw open the shutter to let in a blast of cold, wet air. The chill cleared his head, but the view wasn't much help. The sky was so thick with clouds, it could have been any hour from dawn to twilight. He leaned out and breathed in a deep lungful of damp, surveying the empty courtyard below. Maybe Raynard was right, and he was crazy to come back here to reclaim Brinlaw at any cost. Henry, faithless liar that he was, would still have happily given him charge over any of a dozen manors in England or Anjou, some of them probably more profitable than this one. *And most in better repair,* he thought with an inward groan as he caught sight of a crumbling gap in the outer bailey wall he hadn't seen riding in the day before—this window faced the back of the castle and the frozen lake beyond. But Brinlaw was his. By all rights it should always have been, and he would put it back to what it had been or die in the attempt.

He pulled the shutter closed again and looked back at the rumpled bed. Now Alista was his as well—a thought to chill the bone and fire the blood all at the same time. He knew nothing about keeping a wife, even a placid one—how was he to manage this wild faery of Mark's? But remembering the way she had clung to him and the fire of her kiss, he knew he had to do it. Alista was as much his as Brinlaw, and he would not give her up.

She wasn't in the Great Hall, either, though most of the household seemed to be, the business of his new holding carrying on without him. Even Raynard seemed perfectly at home, sitting near the hearth trading tales of glory with some of Mark's guardsmen. But as soon as Will was spotted, everyone fell silent to stare at him. Not sure what else was required, Will stood in the archway and stared back.

"Good morrow, my lord," Raynard grinned, coming to meet him as activity slowly resumed. He dropped his voice to a conspirator's rumble. "I'm glad to see you looking so well. You slept so long, I had begun to fear your bride had slain you."

Will gave this the scowl it deserved. "Where is she?"

"Who?" his friend asked merrily.

"Alista," Will answered, scowling even harder. "Where is she?"

Raynard's grin faded a bit. "I thought she was with you."

Will made a comic show of looking over his shoulder. "Seemingly not," he said dryly. "Where is she?"

The grin disappeared entirely. "Will, God's truth, I haven't seen her, and for all I know, neither has anyone else," Raynard swore. "They've all been waiting to see if you both survived the night." Their eyes met in miserable understanding. "Bloody hell . . ."

Will noticed the castellan watching them from the group at the fire, his red-blond beard hiding none of his suspicion. "Somebody knows something," he muttered. "Somebody left me breakfast."

"You didn't eat it," Raynard said, alarmed.

Will shook his head, knowing immediately what he meant. "I wanted to find Alista first."

"Thank God." He had a sudden flash of Druscilla, sobbing her remorse, and he suddenly felt as sick as if he had eaten poisoned porridge himself.

"Forgive me, my lord." The monk had come upon them so quietly, neither of them had noticed until he stood at their side.

"What is it?" Will asked, his tone neutral, his face a mask.

"What about Lord Mark?" Brother Paolo asked. The two knights obviously had little experience of domestic life, or they would have chosen a better spot for their private conversation. Alista's nonappearance at breakfast had inspired great unrest in the castle, igniting the general suspicion that had naturally been laid by the strange events of the day before. Half the garrison was on the brink of slitting their new lord's throat for murdering his lady, so ready were they to assume the worst of him. Luckily, Paolo knew better. "Something must be done with his body," he patiently explained. "He is beginning to decay."

Both Will and Raynard gave the air an experimental sniff. After the battlefields of the Holy Land, Mark's stench was but a trifle, but it was unmistakable, nonetheless. "Of course," Will answered. He met the monk's brown eyes steadily, studying him. If Alista had fled, Brother Paolo would know where, had likely been her accomplice. But the brown eyes never flinched. Raynard suspected the girl of poisoning. Will thought of her own eyes, dark and serious as these of the monk, her kiss, her sudden laughter, and he tried to imagine these as part of some grand design to keep him at bay until she could escape him. . . . No, Will was no fool to be duped by a maiden's wiles. Alista hadn't run away. He briefly considered asking the monk where his wife could be found, but he didn't want to admit he didn't know—a foolish point of pride, not like him in the least, but inescapable, nonetheless. "Do what you think best, Brother," he said aloud. "I'll be back soon."

Raynard shook his head. Predictability had always been one of Will's finer virtues, so far as he was concerned, but apparently it was gone for good. "As will I," he muttered, following his friend into the rain.

* * *

Alista tilted her head back, turning her face full into the icy wind, but she could still smell the stench that had driven her out before the sun was fully free of the horizon. She had awakened at first light to find the fever gone, her body warm and comfortable in the cozy depths of her father's bed. Stretching like a cat, she yawned, something nagging at her waking mind, dragging at her early morning sense of well-being like a sodden shroud. . . . The smell washed over her, filling her nose and mouth with something too thick and vile to breathe. "Sweet Christ," she prayed and swore, sitting up with both hands clapped over her face like a veil, but even her own living flesh smelled putrid. She stumbled from the bed and grabbed the chamber pot, gagging and retching so violently she lost her footing and fell forward on her knees. But even when her stomach was empty, the stench remained, worse as she realized what it was. Papa . . . Papa was dead. Her stomach rolled again, but she fought the nausea back down. Wiping her mouth with the back of her hand, she made herself stand up.

Will, her husband, was sleeping, oblivious to her suffering, sprawled half-on and half-off the bed. Creeping closer, the stone floor like ice under her feet, she peered down at him, this prize sent from the King to console her for her loss. When he was still and sleeping, he seemed younger than he had the night before, his mouth and the skin of his face as fresh and smooth as her own in spite of the short-cropped beard and moustache, dark brown flecked with gold in the dim light of the dying fire. His head was pillowed on one arm, powerful muscle bunched across his shoulders, dark-shadowed under the thin white fabric of his shirt. She had touched him, clung to him, and he had kissed her, put his tongue inside her mouth, carried her in those arms. . . . She longed to touch him again, to trace the curves and hollows of him, to feel the softness of his face and the hard planes of his body beneath her fingertips. But she was drowning in death; the smell of it clung to her flesh and would cling to his as well. Suddenly the memory of his kiss made her tremble with revulsion—how could she even think of such a thing when her father lay dead and unmourned? Dragging the heavy bed rug over him to ward off the chill, she turned from all thought of Will and fled the castle. Saddling her father's war horse, she had clattered over the drawbridge and away, seen only by the guardsmen at the gate and Brother Paolo, returning from an early morning ramble of his own. He had called out to her, but she had ignored him, standing in the stirrups to urge her great mount into a gallop. She had ridden miles in the misting rain and freezing wind, stopping only when the destrier's red-brown coat was lathered black with sweat.

Now she stood on the bank of the river, the snow covering her boots, letting the horse drink from the thin rivulets of current still too swift to freeze. The future seemed to be spread at her feet like the river, gleaming and treacherous, daring her to venture forward to shatter the crust and be swept away under the ice. A shadow skimmed the surface, and she looked up to see a falcon slowly circling overhead.

The huge horse had been easy enough to track through the melting snow, but even now, looking down the steep embankment to where Alista stood beside him with the reins still in her hand, Will could hardly believe she had ridden such a mount so far. He had been forced to ride the beast himself from London because it would not be led, and he knew how hard it was to control. Enswathed in a long, black mantle that pooled in folds behind her like a train, she looked like a child, an orphan turned out into the snow. "What is she doing?" Raynard mused, pulling up beside him. "You don't think she means to jump?"

As if she'd heard, Alista turned and looked up at them, her eyes deep wells of sadness, and Will's heart leapt to his throat. "She wouldn't dare," he swore, spurring his horse forward down the treacherous slope. "Alista!"

The madman was bearing down on her like she might be a jousting target. Alista grabbed the reins in both hands and dug her heels into the mud as her father's horse pranced and tossed his massive head in alarm. "It's all right," she insisted, yanking back with all her strength and struggling to keep her balance. "He means us no harm."

Will jerked his own mount to a rearing halt in front of his runaway bride. "Madam, are you mad?" he began angrily, then stopped. In her struggles with the horse, the mantle she wore had fallen open. All she wore underneath was the shift in which she'd slept, now muddied to the knees. "What are you doing here?" he asked, getting down slowly, afraid to move too quickly lest he frighten her into the river. In her present state, she seemed too fragile to live.

The horror in her bridegroom's face made Alista look down and see just what a sorry spectacle she made. "I . . ." she began, then stopped. What possible explanation could she offer that would make the slightest sense? "I don't know," she admitted, grief writhing in her belly like a viper. "I woke up, and I could smell it, all through the castle." She looked up into his eyes, aching to make him understand, see that she wasn't a half-witted, hysterical girl. "I can still smell it, even out here," she pleaded, tears threatening to undo her completely. "My father is dead."

Since she'd first flung herself into his arms by mistake, Will had been trying to make some sense of this creature who was to be his for life, but she had eluded him. Nothing she had said or done since that first moment had seemed logical or even conceivable to him. But looking down at her now, her beautiful face drawn and distorted with grief, was like looking back through time at himself, the boy he had been, the boy who had been lost on the day his father died. Suddenly she seemed anything but mad. "I know," he promised, reaching out for her as Raynard finally reached them. She stiffened, her hands hard fists against his chest, but he could feel her shudder with swallowed tears, and she didn't fight against his embrace. "I know," he repeated, a whisper as he kissed her hair.

"You gave us a fright, milady," Raynard said, looking quizzically at his friend.

Alista wanted so much to let go, to hold on to this knight who meant to save her and cry out her heart on his breast, to close her eyes and pretend 'twas her father who held her so. He seemed so like Papa just now, so strong and kind. But what would he think if she did? What must he think of her already?

She flattened her hands against him and pushed him away. "I can't think why you were frightened, sir," she answered Raynard, her brisk tone only slightly shaky. "I only went for a ride."

The prideful thrust of her chin made Will want to kiss her again and better. "You have to tell me when you want to leave the castle," he scolded instead as he let her go. "It isn't safe for you to ride out alone."

"I've come here alone my whole life," she retorted.

"Even so, we should go back now," Raynard suggested,

confused. A minute ago, she had seemed hysterical, a damsel in most dire distress. Now she looked and sounded like nothing so much as a peevish, willful brat. She was even looking up at him as if he were the one who had dragged them out into such miserable weather in the first place.

"Who are you, anyway?" she asked.

"This is Raynard, my lady, my most trusted friend," Will explained, suppressing a smile. "Henry wanted him to help him in London, but I beseeched him to come here with me."

"At your service, Lady Alista," Raynard said, making the best courtly bow he could manage on horseback. "Now may we all go back to the castle?"

The very idea made Alista cringe inside, but she knew what she must do when she got there—had known before she left. She just hoped she could convince Brother Paolo. "Yes, I think we must," she answering, picking up her reins again.

"Here, lady, you must be tired," Will protested.

His wife looked at him like he was crazy. "Not a bit," she assured him before swinging into the saddle as nimbly as a monkey, her mantle billowing around her.

"At least she wore her boots," Raynard remarked as the object of their search rode away from them again.

"Her father is dead, Raynard," Will shot back, wheeling his horse around to gallop after her.

"Aye, I know it," Raynard muttered to himself. "I'm just surprised to see you noticed."

By the time they made it back to Brinlaw, the drizzle had become a stinging sleet, and Druscilla was waiting on the doorstep, wringing her delicate hands. "Alista, look at you," she cried, coming out to meet the girl and ignoring her escort entirely. "What were you thinking?"

"I have to see Brother Paolo," Alista answered, allowing herself to be bundled toward the door without a backward glance.

"You have to come upstairs and change your clothes," Druscilla retorted. "Do you want to die of fever? There are easier ways, you know."

"Hush, Dru," Alista ordered. "I am perfectly all right."

"Damn Henry's eyes," Raynard muttered as they watched the women disappear into the castle. "He might have warned us there were two of them."

"I doubt very much that he knew," Will agreed, handing his reins to a groom.

One of their most trusted foot soldiers, dressed for the moment like a peasant farmer, came out of the shadows of the arch. "You were right, Captain," he began without preamble. "We were followed from London. But ye'll never guess who it is."

"Dru, for pity's sake, leave me alone," Alista snapped, trying to sidestep the other girl's efforts to adjust her fresh gown. "I can manage—"

"Oh, yes, and I see how well," Dru scolded back, tugging her down to a stool set before the mirror. "And your coiffure would put all of Paris to shame." Alista opened her mouth to reply, then closed it again at the sight of her reflection. She did indeed look like Queen Guinevere's ghost. "What would your father say if he knew?"

"I don't know," Alista admitted, flinching as Dru took a comb to her hair. "Nothing good, I suppose—Ouch!"

"So sorry, milady," Dru simpered sarcastically. "As

beautiful as you are, you could have this man turning somersaults for you, but no . . . honestly, darling, you can be such a child."

The black gown she had put on made her skin look blue-white, and her dark brown eyes were ringed with purple shadows. "I know," she admitted, watching Dru's clever fingers work tangles into sleek braids. "I don't know how to be anything else."

Dru's eyes met hers in the mirror. "Oh, dear," she sighed, leaning down to hug her close. "I didn't think . . . was it truly as bad as all that?"

Alista stiffened. "What?"

"I know, dearest, I know." Dru let her go to finish braiding. "But I swear to you it does get easier in time. And if you can pretend to be a bit interested, it's done with so much faster, as silly as that sounds."

Alista frowned. "Druscilla, what are you talking about?" Her expression cleared, and she blushed. "Oh . . . that."

Dru couldn't help smiling, but she did manage not to laugh out loud. "Yes, that." She tied a temporary lace around the end of the first braid and started on the second. "The morning after my wedding night, I considered drowning myself in the moat, but I got used to the wretch after a while. At least Brinlaw is handsome."

She was already calling Will by her father's title—Dru, who had cried like a baby every time Mark left her sight. "He's beautiful," Alista agreed, pushing the thought from her mind. "But we didn't do anything. I was too sick."

Dru raised a golden brow. "Indeed?" She fastened both braids with a single clasp of beaten copper. "I'm surprised that made a difference."

Alista was spared answering by the timely appearance of

Brother Paolo. "Feeling better, I see," he said, laying a palm against her forehead. "Or do you mean to court the plague?"

"Dru has lectured me quite enough already, thank you," Alista grumbled, getting up. "Now we have to talk about Papa." She picked up the dagger lying on the chest and slipped it into its sheath now strapped to the silver girdle at her hip.

"I've already made the arrangements," Brother Paolo answered. "The reeve has been told of his death, and word has been sent to the village. His burial—"

"No." Alista turned to look first at him, then at Dru. "You know my father cannot be buried."

"I know no such thing," the monk replied, "nor do you."

"What are you talking about?" Dru asked, confused. "Of course he must be buried—"

"He must be burned," Alista explained. "It was what he wished, to be burned on a pyre like the ancients. My mother's family—"

"Ancient barbarians," Paolo cut her off, visibly upset.

"When I was a little girl, Papa made me promise him this," Alista went on. In her mind, she could still see the flames of her mother's pyre, see her father's face as he made her swear he would have the same. Brother Paolo had been outside with her father's soldiers; he had known, had wanted to stop them, but Mark would not be stopped, even when he knew the enemy was almost upon them. That night after everyone but the sentries was sleeping, he had taught her the words to be sung in the ancient tongue, promising her that it didn't matter that she didn't know what they meant or why she must say them. She still didn't know, and over the years she had forgotten them, pushed them from her mind along with the memories she hated. But now she remembered, and even if she wanted to forget, she couldn't. "I don't ask or expect you to approve," she said to the priest she loved as dearly as any parent. "I want my father to have a Christian funeral, and I beg you to give it to him. But I must give him this."

"As if it matters now," Dru said bitterly. "What difference does it make now?" Alista looked at her, uncomprehending, as Dru turned and ran from the room, the sound of her sobs trailing behind her.

"She is right, you know," Paolo said gently. "Your father is gone, my love. He does not need—"

"He does," Alista cut him off. "I have to believe he does."

The fear and fury in her eyes made his heart ache. "And I have to believe he does not," he said. "What is it you hope to accomplish for him with this pagan ritual?"

Alista suddenly thought of the white falcon climbing higher in the cold, dark sky, the despairing triumph in her cry as she plummeted to the earth. *He will never fly,* a voice spoke sadly in her mind. *A man may never be a falcon.* The voice was like a thought, like something she had conceived on her own, but she didn't understand it—it made no sense. "I don't know," she admitted to Brother Paolo as other words seemed to echo in her ears, words in a tongue she couldn't quite understand, a memory of sounds. "I only know I promised. Please, Brother." She put a hand on the monk's arm. "When I said good-bye, I didn't say enough, didn't know what I should say." She had cried so much, her eyelids were raw, making the fresh tears sting. "Please let me do this much."

As if he could deny her. "You cannot believe me that this

is a meaningless gesture?" he sighed. "Not to mention the fright it will probably give your new husband." She didn't answer, only looked at him, and he shook his head. "Never mind then," he gave in, hugging her close. "I will not say you nay."

Will stood on the lowered drawbridge and gazed down at the weedy ice that was the moat. Frozen over, it was ugly, but otherwise not much good. "How soon do you think we can expect them?" he grimly asked Raynard.

They had taken Henry's warning most deeply to heart, had fully expected to defend Will's claim to Brinlaw before the week was out. But never in their wildest imaginings had they thought to hear a challenge from Harold FitzCammon.

Dubbed "Harried" by Thomas à Becket, FitzCammon, at the distinguished age of twenty-three, was already a notorious coward. His father, also called Harold, had switched sides no less than half a dozen times during the war between Henry's mother and her cousin, Stephen, before finally giving up the ghost to blood poisoning from an untreated canker on his majestic, yellow arse—or so 'twas said. Since his death, poor Harold the Younger had upheld the family legacy with vigor if not with pride, swearing fealty and friendship to whichever sword seemed most likely to find itself at his throat at any given moment. He had been in London when they left, paying his respects to Henry too little and far too late and asking for royal assistance in ejecting the Welsh cousin who had put him out of his own manor the month before. All in all, hardly the sort of fellow one might expect to trudge across England on Christmas Eve to challenge a seasoned Crusader for the hand of an orphaned damsel, no matter how rich she might be.

"Before nightfall, I should think," Raynard glumly replied. "Moreau said he and his men were no more than a day and night behind us."

"His men?" Will echoed, incredulous. "Where in God's name would FitzCammon acquire men?"

"From Henry, I imagine," Raynard opined. "It has to be . . . a joke to punish you for not being properly grateful. He knows FitzCammon can't possibly best you, but he's back in London right now laughing his bloody crown off imagining how he'll try."

Loud banging from the courtyard behind them interrupted Will's swearing the blasphemous oath their sovereign so richly deserved. "Now what?" he finished instead.

Several men of Brinlaw's home garrison were piling heavy logs around a makeshift, man-sized platform in the center of the courtyard. "What's this?" Will asked, hoping it wasn't what it looked like.

"His lordship's funeral pyre," one of them cheerfully explained, confirming his lord's worst fears. Since Alista's return to the castle, seemingly uninjured, the household's attitude toward Will had warmed considerably.

"For Lord Mark, my lord," another hastened to add, lest they be misunderstood.

"Well, that's a relief, anyway," Raynard muttered. "At least it's not for you."

Will knew from experience that Mark's men were lethal in battle, but apparently they weren't particularly bright without the guidance of their lord. "Passing over for the moment the question of why Lord Mark needs a pyre," he began, "you can't build a fire that size inside the bailey without burning down the castle."

"That's what we thought, too," the first helpful soldier

agreed. "But when you gave the order for all to stay in and prepare to make a defense, we knew we couldn't build it by the lakeside like we'd planned. We told Lady Alista, and she said she cared not where we built it, so long as 'twas built before sunset."

Will looked back at Raynard. "We need this," he assured him. "Testing is good for the soul." He turned back to the soldiers. "Where is Lady Alista now?"

"Inside," the second soldier said. "She's telling those that came in from the village about the pyre. She said not to disturb you and the captain, but that if you was to find a moment, you might come in and meet them—the reeve and such like."

"That sounds like an excellent idea," Will said. "In the meantime, go on and build your pyre beside the lake, then come back inside and raise the drawbridge. If it's safe at sunset, fine. If not, the funeral can wait."

The two exchanged a look, then turned to their comrades, all of whom looked just as doubtful. "Just as you say, my lord," the first man said with a sigh.

"Here," Raynard offered, shooting his glance at Will, "let me lend you a hand."

If Will hadn't expected to find his wife in the Great Hall surrounded by retainers, he might not have recognized her, she was so changed from the pitiable waif of an hour or so before. Her hair was neatly arranged beneath a linen veil, and her gown, though somber, was becoming and perfectly suitable for a lady of their class. And her demeanor when she greeted him was perfect as well, warm and slightly deferential as befitted a new wife in the presence of inferiors. She made the introductions all around, remembering each man's name, and the look of adoring sympathy on each man's face spoke volumes of her history as mistress of the manor. But as she stood quietly at his side while he talked with the men and received their oaths, he couldn't help thinking she was playing a part, doing her duty while her mind and heart drifted far away. "Are you all right?" he asked her point blank as soon as the delegation had gone.

"No," she admitted with a wry smile, sinking down on a bench. A spaniel that had been pacing the Hall came and nuzzled her hand, and she stroked its silky head. "I'm not really ready for any of this." She looked up and half-smiled again as if the two of them had a secret. "Surprise!" she said softly, an ironic joke.

He smiled back, unable to help himself. Yesterday at this time, they had never clapped eyes on each other, had never exchanged a single word, barely knew the other existed and wouldn't have cared if they had. Today he could speak to her and listen to her in ways he had never imagined conversing with any woman, certainly not the beautiful daughter of his sworn enemy. Yet it seemed perfectly natural to talk to her, to want to protect her, to be interested in her thoughts.

"How could you be?" he said aloud, joining her on the bench. He scratched the dog under the chin, and it preened and whined with pleasure. "Your father seemed able to live until Judgment and beyond." How strange to speak of Mark as a man with a daughter who loved him, a man he might have known as a friend. "You obviously thought well of him."

"I love him with all my heart." She left off petting the dog to fidget with the sheath of a dagger she wore at her hip, a strange ornament for a maid. "He was away so much when I was a child, all my life, really, but I never once believed he wouldn't come home. Even when he was fighting and so many others were killed, I knew he would live. I knew someday the war would be over, and he and I would be here at Brinlaw together forever. But now . . ." She shook her head, biting her lip.

"I know." He reached out and took her hand, marveling again to feel how small it was, how fragile. "When my father was killed, I felt exactly the same, as if I had been cheated."

She nodded, holding tight. "Now I don't know what to do . . . I know he meant for me to marry you and be happy, but I don't—" She shook her head again, her nails digging into the flesh of his hand, she was holding him so tightly. "You have to help me, Will."

"I will, Alista." He pressed a fervent kiss to her fist so entwined in his own. "I swear it."

"No more time for wooing, lad," Raynard said tersely, coming in from outside. "Our guests have arrived."

"Guests?" Alista could see from their faces he didn't mean a few friends who'd come for Mark's funeral.

Will kissed her hand again quickly as he stood up. "Is the drawbridge up?"

"Just," Raynard answered. "The last of those pyre men had themselves a merry trot to make it."

"The moat is frozen over in any case," Alista pointed out, raising her voice to be heard. "Why have you raised the drawbridge—and why is my father's pyre outside if you have? My father's funeral—"

"The funeral may have to wait," Will said. Outside, Harried FitzCammon could be heard shouting his name.

"No!" She leapt up and cut Will off before he could

reach the stairs. "We've waited too long already. I demand you explain what's happening! Who is that outside?"

"Not that anyone cares, but the bastard brought a catapult," Raynard casually remarked.

"Alista, listen to me." Will put his hands on the girl's shoulders, trying to make her understand the urgency of the situation without giving her an insult she didn't deserve. "I am your husband, charged by all that's holy with your protection. Is that not so?"

"Yes, but I've never required so much protection before," she persisted. "Who is it that threatens me now?"

"You must trust me." She was still frowning, her dark brown eyes searching his with the sharpness only a blameless innocent could manage, and he felt a perfect villain. "It's nothing serious," he promised—that was true, at least.

Alista could see he was hiding something, and that made her afraid. "Are we at war again?" she asked.

"Everyone or just us personally?" Raynard asked, mock-polite.

"Alista, please," Will said, shooting him a murderous glance. "Stay inside and wait." She opened her mouth to protest further, and he kissed it, then left before she could recover.

"A neat trick, that," Raynard grinned, following him up the stairs to the battlements. "Not to worry, by the way—the idiot didn't even bother to ride around and find that gaping hole in the outer bailey wall."

"Does he really have a catapult?" Will asked.

"Aye, and near sixty men to arm it," Raynard answered. "Mercenaries from the look of them. Harried himself is no great threat, but those could be a problem."

Will stepped out into the freezing wind, now armed

again with sleet. "Let's hope you're right, and Henry let them in on the joke."

"Brinlaw! Show yourself!" FitzCammon's voice was obviously unaccustomed to so much shouting in the open air; he was already hoarse as a toad.

Will moved to the edge. "Look up, Harold," he called down.

The man obeyed so quickly, the visor on his heavy helm snapped shut. "God's blood," Raynard snickered, and the guardsmen on the battlements around them exchanged grins of relief.

"I demand you release this castle at once!" Harold shouted back with admirable pluck if little logic.

"Harold, why must I release my own castle?" Will answered.

"Your own castle, my arse!" This would have been more impressive if it hadn't ended in a squeak. As it was, the poor knight's own soldiers were beginning to snicker. "Where is Mark's daughter?" Harold continued undaunted. "Let us ask her whose castle this is." The mercenaries were even less impressed with this—what did it matter what a dead man's daughter thought? Discontented grumbles rolled through the gang clustered on the opposite bank of the moat loudly enough to be heard clearly from above.

"Idiot milksop," muttered Clarence, Brinlaw's castellan. "If that rabble should turn on him, they'll be more hot for plunder than they are now."

Will had commanded enough mercenary troops fighting with Henry to know how right he was. "FitzCammon, I have no wish to kill you," he called. "But if you insist—"

"I do say Brinlaw is his!" Alista shouted, appearing at his

elbow. Every man on the battlements turned to gape at her, none so aghast as her husband.

"Alista, go back inside," Will ordered in a tone as icy as the weather as he yanked her back from the edge.

"Lady Alista?" Harold's hoarse shout was now positively timid.

"Aye, of course," she called back, wrenching free of Will's grip with a reproachful glare. "Am I not who you seek?"

"Yes, but . . ." He took off his helm to get a better look. "Are you in distress?"

"You mean besides mourning my father?" She looked back at Will and Clarence without the slightest hint of remorse. In fact, she looked ready to shove them both over the side. Raynard had to turn his back to hide his smile—this was Old Mark's daughter, indeed. "No, Sir Knight, I am content, though I thank you for your concern. 'Twas most chivalrous."

"Lancelot reborn, in truth," Will agreed with a scowl.

"But . . . you have given him your castle?" Harold plaintively responded.

"I had no choice, Sir Knight. He is my husband." Now she did smile at Will as the wind whipped tendrils of black hair free of their braids to dance around her face in a demon's halo. "And I like him well enough."

"I am moved, mistress, truly," Will muttered sarcastically for her ears alone before he moved forward to address himself to Harold. "Are you satisfied, FitzCammon, or must my wife catch her death while you think it over?"

Their besieger was obviously at a loss. "I . . . that is, we are on our way north. To reclaim my manor."

"Invite him to spend the night here," Alista said urgently. "Anything—it's nearly sunset."

Something in her voice made Will turn to look at her, a desperate fear undetectable in her banter with FitzCammon. "The funeral?" he guessed, putting a hand on her shoulder.

She nodded. "It can't wait another night, Will. It may already be too late."

She looked so certain and afraid, he didn't have the heart to tell her she made no sense. "Then join us in honoring our dead lord tonight," he called down to Harold, ignoring Raynard's dropped jaw. "You and your men are welcome."

He watched her as the others left the battlements, her forehead drawn in obvious anxiety. "Alista, what is it?" he asked, catching her as she started to follow.

She turned back, a flash of irritation on her face that quickly dissolved into a weary smile. "What is what?" she asked mildly, though he could see from her eyes that she already knew what he meant.

"This fear you have, this insistence that your father must be burned on a pyre today, this instant, before the sun goes down." Saying the words aloud gave him a flesh-crawling chill he'd been too busy worrying about FitzCammon to feel before. "Why not give him a Christian burial in the morning?"

"Because I can't," she said, jerking free of him. "I know it makes no sense to you, Will, but you must believe me when I tell you it's important."

This was the first time since he'd met her that she had hesitated to tell him every thought in her mind, that she had hidden any piece of her heart from him, and he found he didn't like it in the least. "Obviously I do believe you," he said more coolly. "I just don't understand."

You don't have to understand! she wanted to scream, her eyes turning helplessly to the orange-turning sun. But he was trying; any idiot could see that, and he did deserve some sort of reason, she supposed. "The pyre is a family tradition," she said slowly, trying to think of words to make the pagan sound perfectly normal. "My father—"

"Your father was a Norman, just like mine," Will stubbornly insisted.

"My mother was not," she retorted, more sharply than she'd planned. "She was . . . sort of Welsh, I guess," she continued more gently. "To be honest, I don't really know; I don't remember very much about her or the place where I was born. I was only four years old when she died."

This surprised him, though it shouldn't have—surely he had known once that Mark's wife was dead, that his daughter had been half an orphan most of her life. But of course, he hadn't. He had never thought of Mark as having a family at all, daughter or wife, dead or alive. A family was what Mark's usurper king had ruined, what Mark's need for a castle had driven from Brinlaw, his family, the ones who must be avenged. "So your mother believed in pyres," he said aloud.

"Yes, very much," Alista answered, relieved. He didn't sound particularly appalled, just a little curious. "And because of her, my father did as well. He made me promise long ago that even though we had left our home in Falconskeep, when he should die, I would keep the old ways, see him burn, and . . ." She trailed off, unable to think of a way to tell him what else she must do. She was only becoming certain now herself, only now remembering, and it made her shudder. How could she explain it to Will? But the ritual was coming clearer in her mind as the sky began to darken, and with it came a terrible urgency more powerful than a promise, an almost physical need to see it done.

"Then you will," her husband decided. "Come on, let's see it done."

They made a strange gathering at the edge of the frozen lake: Mark's entire household; Will, Raynard, and most of their sworn men; all the men and most of the women from the village of Brinlaw; and bewildered Harold Fitz-Cammon, standing just within Raynard's reach, looking as if he expected to be tossed on the bier with the corpse at any moment. Mark's body was laid out bare-faced on the hastily constructed platform, and Will found he couldn't look directly at it; the sight of his old enemy's bluish face made him sick with guilt and fury. The last time he had seen this man alive, his face had burned red with fury, with life. To see this face cold in death was like feeling a part of himself turn to ice, but what he felt wasn't grief. He felt cheated. What was he to do with his hatred now? What would thaw his heart? He glanced over at the woman at his side, Mark's daughter. His wife.

Brother Paolo began speaking the Latin blessing for the dead as the sun began to slip into the lake, and Alista reached for his hand. He looked at her, saw her make the sign of the cross with her free hand, her eyes red-rimmed with unshed tears but her features as placid and cold as the darkening ice. On the other side of her stood Clarence, holding a flaming torch. Feeling Will's gaze, he turned to him and nodded, tears streaming over his wind-reddened cheeks and into his gray-frosted, red beard.

"Let me go," Alista whispered as the monk finished his last prayer. Giving her hand a final squeeze, Will let her slip away, with Clarence following close behind. Seeing them, Druscilla let out a sob, falling into the embrace of her maid, her face buried in the other woman's neck as if she couldn't bear to watch.

Alista drew her silver dagger, the dying rays of winter sunlight dancing on the blade, all glitter with no heat. She had never felt so cold, frozen to the innermost kernel of her heart, and this was no fever that would break before the dawn. She looked at Clarence, and the sight of his tears was almost too much, but she couldn't cry, not yet. "Light it," she ordered softly.

The wood was damp and slow to catch, but finally flickering tongues of flame licked all around the bottom of the pyre, painting writhing shadows on the faces of the mourners. She turned to look at her husband, to gauge his reaction, but his handsome face was a mask. Turning back to the fire, she raised the dagger, the first phrases of the ancient chant rising to her lips before she could form them in her mind, as if some other woman's spirit had taken control of her voice.

When she started to sing, Will felt the hair on the back of his neck stand on end, so eerie was the sound. She was holding a dagger aloft, and he took a step toward her, alarmed, but she only cut her hand, slicing the blade across her palm with a shudder as she sang on, her eyes full of dancing fire. He started toward her in earnest, and a powerful hand clamped down hard on his wrist. "Leave her alone,"

Brother Paolo said softly, his own displeasure apparent in his expression. "It is almost finished."

Her hand throbbed like she cradled her own heart in the palm, blood welling thick in the cut. She turned it over and let the blood drop onto her father's face, the drops sizzling in the flames as his cold flesh began to melt. When the chant was done, she stepped back and lowered her hand, but she couldn't look away, paralyzed with horror.

"Now," Brother Paolo urged. "Go to her now."

She heard people behind her beginning to murmur amongst themselves, but she couldn't move. The fire was burning her face, but her heart was still so cold, sunk back into the frozen depths of her breast. *Gone,* her mind whispered, a witch's crazy whine. *Papa is truly gone, and I shall be alone.*

She was as beautiful and sad as some ancient queen of legend, and for a moment, Will was almost afraid to touch her for fear she would melt away to mist. "Alista?" He touched her cheek, the wind entwining wisps of raven hair around his wrist. She looked at him, her lower lip beginning to tremble. "Come home with me now," he ordered. "It's finished."

She smiled a little, her mouth twisted up at one corner. "I know." She touched the back of his hand at her cheek, staining his skin with blood before she walked away.

Mark's funeral feast may have been subdued, but at least it was crowded. The Hall was full to overflowing with more soldiers encamped in the meadow outside the outer wall. Will was hospitable, but he wasn't a fool. FitzCammon claimed he was leaving at first light; Will just wanted to be certain that he did. He had spent the past hour patrolling the battlements with the guard, making certain no tricks were afoot. But now he figured he had no choice but to go in and play the host. He scanned the crowd for Alista, but he wasn't surprised not to find her. He found Druscilla sitting near Clarence, who was keeping his sword near to hand by pretending to sharpen the blade. "Where is your lady?" he asked her, skipping courtesy when he could think of nothing appropriate to say.

Druscilla looked up at him but didn't speak, just stared. "She's upstairs with the friar," Clarence answered for her. "FitzCammon has gone to bed as well, frightened out of his wits." He smiled. "Our lady gave him a bit of a turn at the pyre."

He's not the only one, Will thought but didn't say. "Harried scares easily," he answered instead. "Is all well otherwise?"

"As well as might be hoped," Clarence said as Druscilla turned away in disgust. "Alista . . . " His voice trailed off, and he shook his head.

"Clarence, what is it?" Will prodded, curious.

"She's not so brave as she pretends, my lord," Clarence went on, the title obviously coming hard to him. "Though she is a brave one, no mistaking. But . . . she's still a maid, whether she will own it or not, and a young one at that. You must—" He broke off again, unable to find the words.

"I know," Will answered. He clasped the older man's arm in a warrior's salute. "I'll make certain she's all right."

He found Alista alone, curled on the sill of the open window of the main bedchamber, wrapped head to toe in the heavy fur from the bed. She turned her face toward him as he came in, and he saw her tears at last, glistening in the light of the fire. "I'm sorry," she said softly as he closed the door.

"For what?" He moved to her slowly, uncertain just how to approach.

She shrugged, and the bed rug slipped down from one bare, alabaster shoulder. "For whatever I ought to be."

He framed her face with his hands and looked into her eyes. "You've nothing to be sorry for." He pressed a kiss to her brow, and she cried out a broken sob. Her face was a child's mask of tears, a grimace that was beautiful to him in a way that artful charms could never be, and his heart ached for her as he kissed her twisted mouth. "I know," he soothed as her arms slid around his neck, gathering him close.

Alista laid her cheek against his shoulder, clinging as hard as she could as she finally gave in, every muscle soaked with the sweet ache of release. He was a stranger, but he was hers, and the way he held her and the low rumble of his voice seemed to say he knew her grief. She nuzzled his bearded jaw, and his mouth found hers again, kissing tears from the corner of her lips before covering them completely with his own. She shivered as his tongue slid inside, but tonight she wasn't cold or faint, only his, needing to keep him this close and closer still. His hands slid under the robe and around the bare skin stretched taut over her ribs as she reached up for him, and flames seemed to lick her flesh in spite of the chill from the window. "Yes," she murmured, the word a moan as she pushed her own tongue against his.

Will felt dizzy, drunk with a want that seemed a completely new sensation, nothing like the animal urge so easily satisfied a thousand times before. He broke the kiss to look into her eyes, luminous black in the moonlight pale of her face, her lips swollen and dark pink from his kiss, slightly parted for sweet breath. Cradling her in one arm, he reached past her to close the shutter, and he closed his eyes, struggling to think, regain his reason, but she wouldn't be shut out, the hot silk of her skin as potent as the fire of her gaze. He bent and kissed her shoulder as his hand slid upward, cradling a soft, round breast. She gasped as he brushed a callused thumb across the nipple, the same deep rose as her lips.

She let her head fall back against the window frame, gasping for breath, her heart still broken but her body tingling with life. Her hands slid deep in his thick brown hair, cradling him to her as his mouth closed over her breast, hardly believing this could be her, burning for a lover, the girl who had ever feared a kiss. His hand caressed her hip, strong fingers kneading her flesh, and she wrapped a leg around him, pressing him closer. Tears slid hot down her cheeks as his mouth sought hers again, as natural a part of this as of her lonely grief.

He could tell she had never been touched so before—her kisses were endearingly clumsy, and her touch was tentative, delicate as the flutter of wings. But there was nothing tentative in her response to him, no coyness or feigned alarm. He kissed her cheek, aching for her but loath to spoil this innocent surrender with even a moment's pain. Her arms circled his neck again, and he lifted her from the windowsill and carried her to the bed as the heavy robe slid to the floor. "It's all right," he whispered, a tender wisp of breath against her ear as he pulled away to pull his shirt over his head. She reached up to touch the bare flesh of his chest as he leaned back down to her again, and for the first time he noticed the bandage wrapped tightly around her hand. "Does it hurt very much?" he asked her, lifting the wounded palm to his lips.

"No," she promised, smiling through her tears. "Not very much." He was staring at her nakedness with no pretense of shame, and she blushed, though it seemed silly to be embarrassed now.

"Good." He held her arms over her head and kissed her softly, then moved down, suckling each breast in turn. She let out a long, soft sigh, and his mouth slipped lower still, a flickering caress in the shallow hollow of her navel. He ran his hands down over her hips, and she arched up to meet his caress, the sweet musk of her making his senses reel.

She turned her face into the pillow and drew a long, shuddering breath as he pressed brief, wet kisses along the curving crease at the top of her thigh. As a child, she had blushed and giggled for the women Mark had taken to bed and the silly sighs and moans they made, certain nothing on earth or in heaven could make her do the same. But now as his mouth covered the deeper, pinker crease of her sex, she cried out loud, as powerless against the cry as she was against her tears. "Stop it," she ordered, but she didn't fight him when he lifted her legs over his shoulders. She was his; he would not hurt her. *Only drive me mad,* she thought with another gasping cry as his tongue flickered hot inside her.

Will had expected her to be shocked, to have to overcome her maiden's modesty with his passion, but beyond the single weak protest, she didn't resist him at all, even when he tasted her sweetest inner core. *Who are you?* he thought, feeding gently on her flesh, his own sex so hard it hurt him. Could an angel surrender so completely? Could a demon give him anything but pain? He scraped his teeth lightly across the throbbing bud between his lips, making her cry out again.

Alista thought she must be dying, burning up from the

inside out, and he must know it, must be doing it on purpose. Suddenly she felt bereft, tortured, and she cried out to him, wordlessly begging him for comfort, and somehow he understood, moved back up to kiss her mouth, strange sweetness on his tongue another tender torment, but now he was holding her close, and she could bear it. She wrapped her arms around him, rising with him when he would pull back again, kissing his face and jaw and throat, feeling the hard muscle of his back and shoulders under her hands and harder, hotter flesh insistent against her thigh. He caught her lower lip between his teeth, a gentle nip as he broke free of her kiss, and she saw his eyes, the blue so dark it was like gazing into midnight. "I'm scared," she whispered, touching her fingertips to his mouth, tracing his full lower lip.

As simple as that, he marveled, a phantom fist closing tight around his heart as he met her gaze. "No," he whispered back, nuzzling her ear. "No need." He kissed her cheek as he struggled free of his hose, and she laughed softly against his jaw, reaching down to help him. He smiled at her as he bent to press another kiss to her lips, soft as a silent prayer. "It's all right," he said again as he guided himself inside.

Alista's eyes opened wide, and for a moment she couldn't breathe. The first sharp pain was nothing, a spark that quickly faded. But the strangeness, the intimacy of it—another life throbbed inside her flesh, but it wasn't her—filled a hollow she'd never felt before. Her arms fell slack to the bed, and her eyes fell shut, every fiber and thought focused on the invader opening the way for another living soul.

Will felt the change even through the blessed torture of

being engulfed, the two of them intricately molded into one, two parts of a single, perfect whole. He kissed her eyelids, struggling to stay still and wait for her to look at him. "Do I hurt you?"

"Yes," she answered truthfully, looking into his eyes, and suddenly he wasn't a stranger at all, and she framed his beautiful face in her hands . . . this was the mystery, her mother's great secret, this lover she held here now. "Kiss me," she whispered through her tears. "Don't stop."

He did as she asked, and her mouth opened to him, her arms and legs enfolding him in blood-warm silk. He rocked deeper inside her, helpless to resist another moment, and she rose to meet him fearlessly, awkward at first, then matching her rhythm to his. Drawing a deep, strong breath, Alista thought it was like swordplay, a thing of instinct, felt in the blood and sinew and bone, impossible to reason out or plan. He moved faster, and she pressed her hands to his chest, pushing him away even while she longed to pull him closer, the sudden ripples of pleasure radiating through her too powerful to bear, trembling down her thighs and upward to her heart. *Wait*, she thought and tried to say, but her voice was lost in a helpless sigh. He caught her hands and held them to the mattress, overpowering her resistance, and she was lost in dizzy waves, like plunging over a cliff. He kissed her, and she breathed him in with all her strength as if her life's breath came only from him. Just as the waves began to subside, she felt him shudder over her, falling full into her embrace, and the world spun away again. "Yes," she heard herself murmur as she stroked his hair, and his hands slid under her, encircling her in his arms as he rolled onto his side. He kissed her face and throat, as desperate as she felt herself, and her fear melted into an intense desire to protect him as he had sworn he would protect her. She brushed back a fallen lock of dark brown hair to press a kiss to his brow, feeling the blue-white crease of a long-healed wound against her lips. "Go to sleep," she murmured, the warm wet inside her leg as he shifted only making the glow inside her burn brighter. This was meant; all was what it should be; she had never felt so certain.

Will had never felt so sleepy in his life. Every muscle seemed melted to water—if she raised her dagger to slay him, he would die, helpless to resist. Her head was cradled in the hollow of his shoulder, and he pulled the blankets up around them, a possessive hand laid on her breast. "Will?" she said so softly he barely heard. "Happy Christmas."

He opened his eyes to find her smiling up at him, a perfect faery imp. "Happy Christmas," he mumbled, squeezing her close.

That night she dreamed of Falconskeep, but she was not a child. She stood at the edge of the sea, breakers foaming around her ankles, cool sand between her toes, warm sunlight on her skin. She was naked, but she felt no shame or fear. Looking down, her body seemed impossibly beautiful to her, a newborn thing, gleaming pink and gold. Falcons circled high above her, their cries like the sound of her name, and she lifted her arms to them, but she was an earthbound creature; she couldn't fly. For a moment, she was sad . . . a shadow fell over her shoulder, the shadow of her lover on the sand, and sadness was forgotten. She turned with a laugh, her arms outstretched—

And then she was awake. Brother Paolo was ringing matins on the chapel bell—Christmas morning. Will was snoring, the rumble under her ear pressed to his chest making her smile and shiver at the same time at the sweet comfort and terrible intimacy of it. She raised up to look at him, her eyes adjusting easily to the dark. Her handsome husband . . . *You will know him,* Papa had said, and she did; finally she felt as if she did. "Thank you, Papa," she whispered, sinking down again to nestle back into sleep. "You chose for me right well."

Four

A letter from Fra Paolo Bosacci to his sister, Serena, translated from the Italian

Brinlaw Castle
Christmas Morning, 1154

My dearest one—

I do not pretend this will reach you before Easter, but I still wish you and your beloveds all the joy of this blessed day. My thoughts and prayers are with you as ever, and I live in anticipation of the day we shall meet once again.

The two things you have long believed would bring me home to Florence have come to pass, one hard upon the other. Lord Mark, my ancient friend and adversary, has died, and his daughter, my darling Alista, has married his successor. In telling you these facts I come near to exhausting my knowledge of both events. No one can tell us how it is Mark came to die. I examined his corpse in secret and could find no sign of violence, but when he left us to travel to London for the King's coronation less than a week past, he seemed as hale and full of life as any man I have ever known of any age whatever. So I am quite troubled and pray we will somehow learn more.

The only one who might have given us the answers we seek is the man who has taken his place, William, the son of the man who held this manor before our coming. But he says he knows nothing of Mark's death, only that his king sent him to take possession of Alista and with her Brinlaw Castle. His father built Brinlaw in the reign of Henry I, then lost it when he supported the old king's daughter, Maud's, claim to the English throne against the man who won it, Stephen. (You see? English politics are every bit as complicated as Florentine, just less subtle in practice.) King Stephen gave the forfeited manor to Lord Mark in compensation for the loss of Falconskeep, and the man who lost it took his family to France, as near as I can tell. But now Maud's son, Henry II, sits on the throne of England and much of France, and he and this young William are said to be great friends. This was why Lord Mark felt he must attend the coronation, to defend his claim to Brinlaw Castle against that of William, or Will, as he is called.

But now Mark is dead, and Will has the castle and Alista, all based on a letter from King Henry attesting him as Mark's choice as heir through marriage. I can see your frown as you read this, little sister, and I confess I must agree—it all seems quite suspicious. Alista herself was quite adamant at first that she would not do the King's will without further explanation, but being the practical coward that I am, I persuaded her that she must. Indeed, what choice did she have? This man she has married, this Will . . . he is kind to her, and the King spoke very highly of him. Only the vagaries of politics made his father

Mark's enemy, and those matters are settled now. But I must confess I am not entirely easy in my mind about this marriage. Will Brinlaw is said to have just returned from Crusade, but I have yet to see any evidence of his piety . . . indeed, Serena, he indulged Alista yesterday in an act no pious knight could ever have allowed.

I have never told you about this, my love, though it happened long ago. I couldn't find the words, couldn't bear to remember. For fifteen years, I have told myself it doesn't matter and put it out of my mind. But now I am most fearful that it does matter very much and always has, that my sin of omission will cost an innocent dear.

On the day Lady Blanche died and her husband returned, rebel troops were marching on Falconskeep in pursuit of him—were expected at any moment. I was sent to gather my belongings and Alista's as quickly as I could while Mark and his garrison made ready to dispose of his wife's mortal body. But when I returned to the chapel, I found it empty. I heard voices in the garden, and it was there that I found Mark and the body of Lady Blanche burning on a pyre. Alista was beside me, but when she saw this, she ran to her father, toward the flames. I tried to stop her, but a soldier, Clarence, the man who now serves as castellan of Brinlaw, caught hold of me and held me back. "Don't be afraid, Brother," he said, his gruff voice rather shaky. "She isn't."

And it was true; Alista was not frightened by the horror before her. Her eyes were bright with interest as she watched her mother burn. "Go ahead, little bird, if you can," her father said softly.

"I can do it," she answered him in a voice and manner far beyond her years. She looked up to the sky where falcons

still circled and cried, and she seemed to call out to them, words that had no meaning in a voice too big for her tiny body, words that became a song.

"Alista, come to me!" I ordered, struggling in the soldier's grip, but she paid me no mind at all. Mark looked back over his shoulder at me, something like hatred in his eyes, and Clarence and another soldier dragged me away, Alista's singing still echoing in my ears.

Later, as we camped some few miles from the castle, I tried to question the child, but she didn't seem to remember anything strange at all beyond her mother's death. "Our house is burning," she told me sadly in her usual baby's voice as her father set guards for the night. "It is going to be all gone."

And so I believed it would be, all gone, a part of Falconskeep's past that was lost just I had lost Blanche's book and her strange pendant in the well. But beloved, I know now it is not. Alista does remember much more than my most horrible fears could have imagined. Yesterday she insisted Mark's body must be burned just as he burned Bianca's. She shed her own blood on his corpse to feed the flames, sang the same pagan song. She would not be dissuaded, not be me, not by anyone, and her new husband allowed it, made peace with an enemy to give Alista her way. He doesn't understand it; he can't know what he has done, but I believe it has become a bond between them, stronger than the empty marriage vow ordered by the King. It frightens me, Serena.

So you see you were wrong, my friend. Mark is dead; Alista is married; but I must stay to protect her even so. I fear she will need me even more.

* * *

Will was as comfortable this Christmas morning as he had ever been in his life, but his eyelids still snapped open at dawn's first light—a habit learned the hard way as a squire, now impossible to break. Alista was still sleeping, curled on her side, one hand laid on his arm on the pillow by her head. Her color was better, more pink than pale, and the shadows beneath her lashes had faded a bit. But as the room lightened, he saw a ruddy scrape on her chin.

Moving slowly, careful not to wake her, he raised up on his elbow and lifted the blankets away. Similar scrapes stained her shoulder and the side of her breast. Exploring further, he found another on the delicate skin of her inner thigh, this one more painfully red than the rest. He moved to gently touch it, and Alista stirred, rolling away from him with a shiver. He pulled the blankets back up and kissed her cheek, and she smiled, still dreaming, nuzzling up against his mouth. When he drew back, he saw a pale, pink mark on her skin.

"Bloody hell," he grumbled, wishing he still had a proper squire.

Paolo left the castle through the quiet throngs of Harold FitzCammon's departure, Captain Raynard giving him a soldierly nod as he passed. He reached the lakeside just as weak, yellow beams of sunlight broke free of the trees at his back. Mark's pyre was very near to burning itself out. All that remained were a few glowing embers scattered over the bare-scraped circle of earth and a few wisps of gray smoke that rose from the chain and plate mail armor now scorched black into the empty shell of a man. He poked at the ashes with his staff, and the late lord of Brinlaw's sword slid free of the pile, clattering at Paolo's feet as the embers popped and rolled. But every morsel of flesh and bone had been consumed by the flame's embrace.

He unlaced a waterskin from his belt, muttering every blessing he could think of in Latin and Italian, feeling both fearful and foolish. He shook the holy water over Mark's ashes and armor, his heart beating faster as steam rose and hissed around his face. But the steam was gone in a moment, leaving the ashes clumped and dampened but otherwise unchanged. "Idiot," he muttered, putting the waterskin away. What had he expected, a legion of demons to rise and tear him to bits?

Again he remembered the day of Bianca's death, the talismans of evil she had trusted him to destroy just as she had given her daughter over to his protection. Alista had never mentioned them, had never shown the slightest sign of being infected with sorcery. As strange and unsettled as her childhood had been, she had always shown herself to be a pious and dutiful Christian maid, and he had convinced himself that she had forgotten everything else. But now he knew better, knew the ancient rites that had plagued Bianca had their hold on her daughter as well, and that knowledge was like a cancer in his heart. Surely now that her promise to her father was fulfilled, Alista would abandon such things, but he could never be certain again. The book and the heartstone were lost, but their spirit still haunted Bianca's blood, the blood that lived in Alista, the blood that had burned in Mark's pyre.

He stepped back and made the sign of the cross. *"In nomine Patris, et Filii, et Spiritus Sancti,"* he said, a defiant reclamation, a humble plea for strength. "Amen." A cry drifted out over the icy air from the direction of the castle, an alarm or a greeting, impossible to tell which. *What now,*

Heavenly Father? he thought as he gathered his talismans and turned toward home.

Alista awoke to the unfamiliar sound of masculine voices in her bedroom. "You did well enough," Will was saying to one of his men, looking at his own face in Druscilla's silver mirror.

"Thanks, my lord," the soldier said, wiping his own brow in exaggerated relief. "I wouldn't want to spoil you just now as you're finally married." Catching sight of Alista watching him, he sketched a clumsy semblance of a bow. "Good morning, my lady."

"Good morning," she answered warily, pulling the blankets up to her chin. Will jerked a nod in the direction of the door, and the man made his escape. "Who was that, please?" she asked.

"Rolf," Will answered, coming to sit on the bed. "The world's oldest and least graceful squire."

"Oh, he shaved you," she said, sitting up. She kept a firm grip on the blanket as she touched a tiny cut on his chin.

"Do you like it?" She was frowning so, Will was beginning to feel rather foolish.

"You're beautiful," she said. "But you were beautiful with the beard."

"Alista, men are not beautiful," he scolded, embarrassed, pleased, and vexed all at once. He had truly married the strangest woman in Christendom.

"Oh," she said, suppressing a smile at his scowl. "Forgive me; I didn't know." He seemed to be content to stay sitting there. She supposed he would; this was his bedroom now. "Are you going to watch me get up?" she asked pointedly.

He couldn't help but laugh. "I had thought I might," he admitted, her look of shock making him laugh harder. "I am your husband, you know."

"Aye, my lord, I remember," she muttered, shock darkening to a frown. "And a beastly rude one you are." Ignoring her embarrassment and flinging the blankets aside, she stood up and stalked past him to the chest, entirely naked and utterly shameless—if he didn't care, why should she?

He just sat there, stunned, for a full long minute as she took out a gown and dropped it on the bed. "Alista?" he said as she turned to the mirror to comb her hair.

"What?" she grumbled, yanking at a particularly stubborn tangle.

"You are . . ." His voice actually failed him; he had to start again. "You are beautiful."

She smiled at her reflection. "Thank you." In truth, she was freezing, and the very idea of being naked in front of this stranger made the Alista she had always been shudder to the bone with horror. But since Will had come, a strange new Alista seemed to want possession of her body, a willful sprite made entirely of feeling with no thought, as changeable as the air. The woman she knew herself to be was frightened of Will, angry at King Henry, heartbroken at the loss of her father—this woman had demanded that Will explain himself, had run away from Brinlaw to escape the stench of death, and had surrendered to the inevitability of this marriage. But the faery inside her had wanted Will from the moment she saw him—she grieved, but she hungered more. *Am I going mad?* she thought, half-despairing, half-amused, as she fastened her braid.

Will watched, still hypnotized, as she dressed herself quickly in a few efficient movements. "Are you ready?" he asked as she laced her shoes.

She sniffed her sleeve. "No," she answered. "This stinks of smoke." He could see the memory of the pyre pass through her mind, a shadow of pain on her face. "I have to put on something else." She looked around the room. "All my clothes are still in my old room."

He stood up. "We'll have them moved later." He pressed a kiss to her forehead, his hands closing over her shoulders. "I'll meet you downstairs."

Will came out into the courtyard just as Harold FitzCammon was mounting his horse. "Godspeed to you, Harried," he called, ignoring the gape-mouthed stares of all his men, Raynard included. "I hope you kill your cousin."

FitzCammon was as astonished as the guardsmen. Who was this good-humored, clean-shaven stranger, and where had he stashed the surly monster's corpse? "Yes, well," he stammered. "Yes, I shall certainly try . . ."

"Sweet Christ," Raynard muttered. "You look as if you've been skinned."

In truth, Rolf had drawn a bit more blood than Will would have liked, but this seemed an exaggeration. "Safe journey," he said, giving Harried's horse an encouraging swat to the rump.

"What I want to know," Raynard said as their guest and his troops rode out of sight, "is how she convinced you to do it."

"She didn't," Will answered. Villagers were hurrying over the drawbridge in scattered groups, crossing the courtyard, and disappearing into a narrow side entrance to the castle. "What's all this?"

"Holy Mass," Raynard explained, still giving his friend's face a doubtful eye. "It's Christmas, or have you forgotten?" Something about this gave Will an expression of addlepated bliss so nauseating, Raynard dared not wait for an answer. "The priest, alas, is out wandering in the wilderness—I saw him go myself. But no doubt he'll be back."

Will caught his tone and sobered back to something more near his customary scowl. "Did you talk to FitzCammon's men last night?"

"Aye," Raynard nodded. "His captain fought with me in Harry's father's last Normandy campaign. He was properly cautious, but he did admit they were hired by one of the royals, though he swore it wasn't Harry." He grinned. "Perhaps you offended the Queen when you all but ignored her advice."

"Then I shall have to beg her pardon," Will answered.

"Was she right?" Raynard persisted with the start of a monstrous leer. "Has the lady been won at last?"

"I'll make you a drawing someday," Will retorted. "Now come to Mass."

"I think not," Raynard demurred with a sour look. "You may have all my share of salvation."

Will's smile faded a bit. "Would that I could," he answered. "But we both may be saved yet."

Alista was in such a hurry to change she was out of her gown and tearing through the trunk at the foot of her narrow maiden's bed before she saw Druscilla. "Dru, good Lord," she swore, yanking a fresh gown over her head. "What are you doing in here?"

"Forgive me for invading your room, cherie," Dru said lightly. "I wasn't sure where else to go."

Alista suddenly understood. As Mark's mistress, the young Frenchwoman had been accustomed to share his room, to sleep in his bed. But with the arrival of a new Lord Brinlaw, she was rather at loose ends. "I'm sorry, Dru, truly," Alista said, closing the trunk. "Of course you must stay here—when we move my things out, we'll move yours in. I just didn't think."

"Don't be ridiculous; you have nothing to be sorry for," Dru answered, waving off the apology. "It's not your place to see to me. Besides, from what I've seen, you've been busy enough as it is, don't you think?"

"I suppose," Alista admitted. She sat down, hurrying to Mass forgotten for the moment as she found herself remembering the night before, how she had felt in Will's arms. Pretend to be interested, Druscilla had advised; have it over quickly. At the time, this had seemed wise, had made Druscilla herself seem wise if rather indelicate, but now it seemed laughably foolish. Had Dru ever been possessed by the kind of desire that had Alista's mind reeling even now? Had she ever looked at Mark and ached to touch him, to taste his mouth as Alista found herself longing for Will even though she had just left him, even though she barely knew him? She found it impossible to imagine, and that made her feel strangely sad. She wished she could tell Dru how she felt, share this madness and get her help sorting it out, but she couldn't. Dru, she decided, for all the blows dealt to her virtue by the fates, was at heart a proper lady. Alista, alas, was apparently not. "We have to hurry," she said aloud without making any effort to get up even so. "We'll be late for Mass."

"As if Brother Paolo would ever start without you," Dru smiled, sitting down on the other side of the bed. "Besides, there's something I must tell you."

Ordinarily when Dru was upset, it was painfully easy to tell, but now though her wide, blue eyes were stormy, her expression and manner were calm. "What is it?" Alista asked, reaching for her hand.

The other girl hesitated, chewing her pretty lip, then suddenly the words came out in a rush. "I . . . I cannot stay here, Alista; I have to go away—home, to Paris, or somewhere else, anywhere else but here—"

"Why?" Alista asked, cutting her off as she gave her hand a shake. "What are you talking about?"

"I don't belong here—"

"Of course you do," she insisted before Dru could finish. "I'm all topsy-turvy, too, but we can neither of us just run away. We'll manage—"

"No, cherie, not this," Dru said, shaking her head before Alista's words were out. "We will not manage this." She stopped, seeming to gather her forces. "I am going to have a child, your father's child," she said softly, looking down at the bed. Alista couldn't answer, only gaped at her in shock. "You see?" she said, looking up with a sad smile. "How will we manage that?"

Alista closed her mouth with a snap. "The usual way, I should think," she began slowly. Her father's child . . . another daughter? A son? The idea was too bizarre for contemplation, but Dru certainly didn't seem to be joking. "You will have a baby, and both of you will live here."

"What makes you think so?" Dru asked with a bitter laugh. "You are your father's heir and have brought

Brinlaw to your husband. How do you think he will feel about another child turning up—"

"Dru, he shouldn't care," Alista said, wishing to be kind but knowing they must be practical. "Your child will be beautiful, and we will all adore it, but even a son would have no claim to Brinlaw—"

"Because he will be Mark's bastard," Dru finished for her, apparently taking no offense. "But that doesn't mean the new Lord Brinlaw will want him in his house."

"It's my house, too, is it not?" Alista answered indignantly, incensed at the very idea of her kin being so disregarded, even kin not yet born—the only blood kin she would have, for that matter. She had thought herself alone in the world now that her father was gone; now she would have a brother or sister, legitimate or not. "No one, not even my husband, had better dare suggest my father's child should not be in my home, not while I live."

"Brave words, cherie," Dru smiled. "Are you sure you can make them true?"

"They are true," Alista insisted, getting up. "Don't even think of leaving—I will explain this to Will, and he will understand. And if he doesn't, I will make him understand." She grinned. "But just to be certain, we'd better go to church."

Will was getting a small taste of Harry's life as king. The castle's chapel was filled to overflowing, and every pair of eyes was focused squarely on him. He shifted a bit in his spot, and a whisper swept through the room. "I'm sure she'll be along," the reeve's wife made bold to murmur from across the aisle with an encouraging nod and smile.

As if on cue, Alista came running in, followed at a more

ladylike pace by Druscilla. His bride stopped short at the top of the aisle with a grimace as if remembering her dignity too late, and Will couldn't help but smile. "Promise me you won't faint this time," he said softly as she took her place beside him.

"If you kiss me, I might," she retorted, just loudly enough to make the reeve's wife gasp as Brother Paolo began the Mass.

Must everyone stare at us so? Alista thought, singing the first responses. It wasn't as if they hadn't been looking at her every day for most of her life. At her wedding, no one had been present but the castle household; at her father's funeral, she had been too miserable to notice who was there at all. But now she could all but hear the speculation swirling around them, all these good Christian souls wondering how she liked her new husband and how he liked her back. A slow, hot blush rose in her cheeks.

Brother Paolo was calling for Communion, and she waited for Will to move forward; as lord of the manor, it was his place to be first to take the Host. But he didn't budge. She jogged his elbow, thinking his mind had wandered, and he jerked his chin toward the altar as if to tell her to go ahead. She looked up at him, questioning, and he smiled, giving her a slow, rather lecherous wink that startled her into a laugh. Blushing harder, she hurried to the front.

Brother Paolo raised an eyebrow as she knelt before him, and she shrugged. Will was supposed to be a Crusader; why shouldn't he take Communion? She tried to concentrate her attention more on the Body of Christ and less on the oddness of her husband as the wafer was placed on her tongue, but she was troubled nonetheless.

Later, after the service, she watched him in the courtyard with the villagers. Yesterday at the funeral, he had been an object of furtive curiosity. Today, he was known, and many were bold and curious enough to come forward and pay their respects. And to Alista's surprise, no one was disappointed. Each man who spoke to him received Will's individual attention, a smile, a serious nod; he cared to hear these people, she realized as she listened. They were important to him. "So how are the harvests?" he asked a man with the bent back of a lifelong farmer.

"Last year not so bad," the man replied, leaning on his stick, as much at ease as if he and his new lord were old friends. "Once the fighting stopped, and the fields weren't being trampled by soldiers and horses every time a man could turn around, things perked up right smart."

Will smiled. "May it long remain so," he answered.

"As God wills, my lord, but aye," the farmer agreed, smiling back.

"Your lord seems to be settling in," Brother Paolo said softly, appearing at Alista's side.

"Yes," she nodded, still watching Will. Her father had always held the awe of the village and the love of his men—he was a soldier, first and foremost, and the pursuits of peace rather bored him. Because he was a soldier himself, she had assumed Will would be the same. "He's so different, Brother," she mused aloud. "I don't know what to make of him."

"New wives often feel that way, I'm told," Brother Paolo answered, relieved. The haunted, near-demonic light of the night before had left her eyes, replaced by a new interest altogether of God's world. "New husbands as well, I should think."

She looked at him and smiled. "I suppose," she said, blushing a bit. A village wife was bringing her newborn twins for her lady's approval, and Alista turned away to exclaim over them with delight. "They're beautiful," she pronounced, taking one of the babies. *Will I have one of these next Christmas?* she thought, the first time she could ever remember considering such a thing. She looked down into the infant's face, so serious he seemed to be contemplating the eternity of time, and she smiled.

"You look sweet and natural so, my lady," the child's mother pronounced.

Alista laughed. "You're kind to say so," she answered, bending to kiss the baby's wrinkled brow. Looking up, she saw Will watching her and smiled again at him.

Will felt a little dizzy from the chaos of emotions he felt as Alista handed the peasant babe back to its mother. Seeing her so was like looking on his dreams come to life, too perfect to bear. Mark's daughter, he thought, but the words had no meaning, no power to quiet his heart. She was his now, would be the mother of his children, and an almost angry love came over him, caught him by surprise, made it hard to breathe. He turned away, was watching the last of the villagers disappear over the drawbridge when his wife came to him and took hold of his arm. "You said I should tell you when I mean to leave the castle," she said. "There's something I must do. Would you care to come along?"

The pyre was no more than cold ash and dusty metal that gleamed dully in the morning sun. The outline of Mark's armor and shield remained where they'd been laid, but his sword had slid from its half-consumed scabbard to the ground. Alista crouched beside it, her fingertips barely touching its hilt, tears sliding down her face. "It's heavy," she said, grasping it and slowly standing again. "I don't think I've ever picked it up before." She held it out to him. "Will you take it?"

A superstitious chill crept along Will's spine. "If you want." He reached out and grasped the hilt, still warm to the touch. A falcon with its wings outspread was worked where the hilt met the blade, its eyes a pair of sparkling blue jewels.

"It's yours," Alista said, her living eyes black and wet with tears still waiting to be shed.

He hesitated, a shadow of doubt passing over his heart, but he couldn't refuse her. "Thank you," he said, still holding the sword as he took her into his arms. He held her close as he had beside the river, but this time she clung to him, her arms wrapped tight around his waist as she sobbed against his chest. "Alista, what does all this mean?" he heard himself ask before the words formed in his mind. He had promised himself the night before that he wouldn't ask, that it didn't matter. Brinlaw was his; she was his willing wife; they would build a family together, and the pagan nonsense he had seen would be forgotten. Watching her at Mass had only confirmed this conviction—a family tradition she had called this pyre, and that was explanation enough. But something about the way she touched the sword and the way she trembled now in his embrace—this was more than a daughter's natural grief. "Those words you sang last night," he pressed on, his lips at her brow, every word a kiss. "What do they mean?"

"I don't know," she wept, nestling her face against his shoulder as if to hide from the world. "I don't even know how I know them, or why I had to bleed . . . he made me promise, but he never told me anything." *She flew away,* she cried inside her head, the voice of a little child, but she didn't know why, didn't understand this any more than she did the rest. "Brother Paolo didn't want me to do it; he thinks it's evil, but I swear that isn't so. My mother . . ." She drew back to look into his eyes. "My mother wasn't evil."

"Of course she was not," he answered quickly, rushing to comfort her, desperate to drive the terrible fear from her eyes.

"Tell me it doesn't matter, Will," she said softly, her voice intensely tender. "It's over now—it's never meant anything before. Tell me you don't care."

He bent and softly kissed her mouth. "It doesn't matter," he promised in a whisper, promising himself it was true. "I don't care."

Raynard watched the household drift back into the Great Hall from the chapel and the women begin to set out what would pass for the Christmas feast in this grief-stricken castle, but neither Will nor his lady appeared. Brother Paolo didn't seem alarmed; he gave the captain a nod as he passed through on his way to the stairs. But Raynard wasn't entirely comforted. Will seemed happy enough, but he had reasons for contentment that had nothing to do with his head, and his judgment couldn't necessarily be trusted. The fool had already shaved his beard, for pity's sake—to Raynard this seemed a symbolically perilous gesture of the highest order. The mystery of Harried FitzCammon's appearance still worried him, too. Someone had spent a great many silver pennies for a siege campaign that lasted less than half an hour. At first he'd believed it must be a joke of Henry's, but Henry wouldn't have paid enough to let Harried take his troops home with him. Those men wouldn't have followed a man they obviously considered an ass if they hadn't been paid well in advance. But by whom? Not by Harried, that was certain. A royal, his old acquaintance had admitted. Raynard had joked about it being Eleanor, but in truth this wasn't entirely impossible to imagine. Will didn't care for the Queen, which was silly, and made no secret of it, which was stupid. But would Eleanor have wasted so much money just to irritate a man who was pretty well out of her hair already, safely put away in his castle miles away from London? Not to mention risk alienating her husband—Henry had already proven time and again that while he found his wife endlessly fascinating, he considered his loyal nobles the rock on which his hard-won throne was fixed. Perhaps that was reason enough for Eleanor to take offense. . . .

"Are you truly such a heathen, then?" Druscilla teased, breaking into his thoughts. In truth, she had been watching him for some minutes now, ever since she had come in. He made a great show of laughing at everything and everyone, this Flemish captain, but he wasn't laughing now. Something had put him in quite a study, and she found herself curious to know what it was. "You cannot be bothered to come to Mass even on Christmas Day?" she continued, putting on a rueful face as if she quite despaired of him.

Raynard knew well enough when a woman was flirting with him, and he smiled, letting his worries go hang for the moment. "Someone had to guard the castle, poppet," he answered easily. "Yesterday, 'twas the ferocious FitzCammon; who knows who might turn up today?"

"So that's what you've been doing?" she asked, eyeing his empty mug. "Guarding the castle?"

"Of course." She shook her head, and he laughed. "All right, then. I will confess I am a heathen."

"I knew it," she said, almost smiling in spite of herself.

"But it isn't all my fault," he protested. "The good Christ made the quarrel with me, not I with Him."

"A blasphemer as well!" she cried, more genuinely shocked than she let on.

"Nay, 'tis true," he insisted, refilling his mug. "Can I help it if war is my vocation? Some men were born to pray; I was born to fight. Why should I not be paid for it and fight for whomever can pay?"

"Because 'tis a sin to do harm for no good but money," she said, watching his eyes for some sign he was making fun of her or at least regretted what he spoke of. Her own morals were hardly the whitest in England, but even she balked at this. But he seemed perfectly in earnest and showed not the slightest sign of shame.

"Exactly." He took a long swallow. "So because I can be nothing but a soldier, Jesus and I are at an impasse."

"You might repent," she pointed out, flirtation all but forgotten. "You serve Brinlaw now—"

"I do not serve him," he cut her off, his hazel eyes turned deadly serious in a single moment. "He is my friend, and I will defend him to Satan's own dooryard, but I do not serve him."

"A delicate distinction, cherie," Dru teased, intrigued and vaguely disturbed by the look in his eyes. Alista had come in while they talked, and though her eyes were red from crying, she seemed well enough. "In any case, who knows? You may turn saint before it's over."

Raynard's grin returned, but a shadow remained of the change. "Do you mean to reform me, then?"

"Not me," she demurred, but a spark that was something more than flirtation flared for a moment in her own blue eyes. "You are far too much for me." Before he could answer, she went to join Alista.

Will was up late that night, consulting with Raynard and keeping watch on the battlements with his guardsmen. Like his friend and captain, he knew the matter of FitzCammon had been resolved much too easily. Their scouts reported that Harried and his mercenaries had continued on their slushy, snowy way toward the purloined FitzCammon manor as promised, and the only activity of note on the London road was Will's own baggage train, sent from Henry as promised to bring all the possessions Will had left behind in his rush to reach Brinlaw. Still, neither he nor Raynard would rest as easily tonight as they would have hoped.

On his way to the master bedroom, he passed a straggling parade of men, each struggling under the weight of a massive leather bucket full of water. So he wasn't surprised to find Alista drying her hair in front of the fire. "You were struck down with a fever less than three days ago," he pointed out, bolting the door behind him. "Do you think that's wise?"

"I couldn't bear it any longer," she explained, ruthlessly tugging her comb through the tangled, wet curls. "My hair reeked of smoke." She yanked at a stubborn knot so hard the comb slipped from her grasp. "Damnation," she grumbled, trying again.

"Here, let me help," he said, more to keep her from snatching herself bald than anything else. But when he sat down behind her, the spicy scent of her hair washed over him in a wave, making him feel drunk. "You smell fine now," he said, his voice catching in his throat.

"Good," she answered softly. He was being so gentle, it was almost ridiculous, working each lock smooth with his fingers before pulling it through the comb. At this rate, they'd be all night about it. *Not such a terrible notion,* she thought, her hands twisting in her lap. "Will? Could I ask you a question?" she said softly.

He picked up the rough cloth she'd been using and ran it over the wet-silk mass. "If you want."

"Today at Mass . . ." He was rubbing her down like a horse, she thought with an inward giggle. "Why didn't you take Communion?"

Will frowned. "Oh, that." He went back to work with the comb, the knots now smoothed to waves that sprang back into shape as they dried. He had seen the finished product of pretty well every feminine coiffure fashion had yet to devise, but he realized he had never been privy to the process before, and he found himself strangely fascinated.

"Yes, that," she answered. "One of the cooks said it proves you must be quite wicked." Before he could respond, she laughed. "Though she didn't seem to think this was a bad thing, mind you."

He smiled, marveling again at her familiar tone, teasing, even affectionate, but honestly so; his wife was no coquette, flirting to turn his head. She seemed to either take his admiration as a given, inescapable fact or not think of it at all. "That cook is very wise," he said aloud.

"Hardly," she retorted. This was the same stupid woman who had declared the white falcon a creature of the devil. "So will you not tell me, then?" she persisted.

"I haven't made confession," he said flatly.

She turned to look at him. "Since when?" she asked, one eyebrow raised. "And what have you done to cause you to need absolution? What is it you haven't confessed?"

Just like that, he thought, incredulous. *Tell me all your secrets, Will; I truly want to know.* "Not since I came home from Jerusalem," he answered, handing back her comb.

"But that's just it," she protested. "You've just come back from Crusade; surely your soul is clean—"

He started laughing before she could finish, but it wasn't a happy sound. "You've obviously never been on Crusade," he said as he got up.

"No, of course not," she ventured, a little hurt. "But I thought—"

"That it was a holy war; yes, I know," he cut her off again. Watching his face, she thought he didn't mean to be cruel or even rude to her, but something was torturing him, twisting like a knife, something he couldn't tell her. "And so it was, maybe, once. But Jerusalem is won." He sat on the chest at the foot of the bed and started unlacing his boots. "Now the problem is keeping it and trying to expand . . . it's a different sort of war, and not everyone fighting is a soldier."

"I see," she lied. She got up and went to help him, kneeling at his feet. "Is it true Queen Eleanor went on Crusade when she was married to the King of France?"

"Oh, yes," he answered, the tension melting from him. "I understand it was quite a picnic for everyone concerned." She was such a sweet and pretty thing, and she was his. He was home, and nothing that had gone before could touch them.

"Is she as beautiful as they say?" she asked, getting up.

"She certainly thinks so," he said as she banked the fire

for the night. “Yes, Eleanor is beautiful,” he admitted. *But not so beautiful as you,* he thought but didn’t say.

“My father said the same,” Alista said. “But he didn’t think . . . he told me she was a great deal more intelligent than she let on and that King Henry might live to regret it.”

“Your father was an excellent judge of character,” Will said as he stood, the words dry as dust in his throat.

She looked at him and smiled. “I should hope so,” she said as she stepped into his arms. She kissed him, fearless, rising on tiptoe to reach him, and he felt pain again in his heart, as if she’d reached into his chest and taken it in her fist. “What’s wrong?” she said softly as she drew back. “You look so sad.”

“No,” he answered, shaking his head for emphasis. “Not sad.” His hands went to her waist as he kissed her again, lifting her off her feet.

Everything changes in an instant, Alista thought as her arms went around his neck. One minute they were talking; the next . . . but it wasn’t really so different, either. Kissing him, feeling his hands on her, warm in sweet contrast to the room’s winter chill—these things were extensions of the talk, no more awkward, no more strange. He was carrying her, leaning her against the tapestried wall, cold, rough stone at her back she could feel even through the heavy fabric, and she clung to him more tightly. He was so close to her, hers to hold. Last night he had moved slowly, every touch at first a question, but now his hands seemed to know her as they sculpted her shape, and his kiss was fierce, familiar, possessive, capturing her mouth. She slipped down the wall as her hold on him weakened, and his hands slid under her behind to lift her up again, shift her closer.

She sighed into his mouth, powerful little legs entwined

around his waist, and he was dying for her, desperate. He ripped the thin shift from her shoulder, tasting her flesh, tracing the hollow of her collarbone with his tongue, her still-damp curls a silken curtain against her cheek. Her grip on his shoulders loosened, became a caress as his mouth moved lower, tasting her cream-soft flesh, the hard bud of a nipple against his lower lip then drawn gently between his teeth.

She slipped her fingers into his hair, caressed his neck, his shoulders, the long, smooth muscles of his arms, seeing him with her hands, her eyes blind with want that pulsed red as blood. He kissed her mouth again, and she felt a sudden pressure against the in-turned curve of her hip. She slipped a hand down between them to trace the shape of this as well, hot and pulsing in the tender cup of her palm. Will moaned against her cheek, a vulnerable, animal sound that made her shiver to the marrow of her bones. He was a giant, a mountain, yet she could make him make this sound. His hand closed over hers, and together they guided him inside her.

Last night she had gone so still, he had been afraid he had hurt her; tonight she wrapped herself around him, drawing him closer as he pressed deeper. He thrust upward, and she gasped, a sound between a laugh and a scream. She rocked with him, easily finding his rhythm, and he wrapped her in his arms, a precious thing to be adored.

Safe, she thought as sweet waves of release broke over her, setting her consciousness adrift. *I am safe.* She lay her head against his shoulder and let sensation have her, felt his sweet explosion as a rebirth of her own.

"Alista," he murmured as he held her, a whisper through a kiss. Their clothes were tangled and twisted around and between them, bonds that had been forgotten a moment ago now unbearable. He pulled at the shift she wore, heard a tearing sound as the garment gave way, and he expected her to protest, but she laughed, helped him to fling it away before wrapping her arms around him again. She kissed his mouth, broke the kiss to drag his shirt over his head, then he pulled her into his arms again, and picked her up to fall with her on the bed. As he tore out of his hose, she watched him, the serious black eyes he had already learned to love warm with desire. He turned back to her, and she reached out for him, drew him down into her kiss, the soft silk of her embrace. He fell asleep with his head pillowed on her breast, her fingers caressing his hair.

He dreamed of the desert. The sun was setting, turning the hills of sand to blood, but the hills were already soaked, the desert people hacked and strewn over them in pieces. The bodies lay all around him, the ground so thick with blood the sand clung to his boots and flies clung to the sand, crawling black on red on dusty brown, and their buzzing was driving him mad. "It isn't just me!" he screamed, sick and terrified. "I am not alone!" But no one else was standing; everyone else was dead—men, women, children, infants even, split open like suckling pigs and dropped beside their mothers—all tangled in the black wrappings and robes of the Muslim tribes. A flock of vultures settled into a valley in the sand below the hillside where he stood, and he cried out again, raised his arms to drive them away, and a shooting pain raced up his right arm, a shriek of swollen muscles worked past all endurance. He turned his head, a sob rising in his throat . . . he held a sword, coated with flies and blood.

* * *

He opened his eyes on darkness, but the stench of the dream dissolved in the scent of his new wife's hair. "Wake up," she was saying, bending over him. "It's only a bad dream."

He reached up and caught her to him, rolled over her in the blessed warmth and comfort of the bed, his bed, his home. "I'm home," he said aloud as he caught his breath. "I'm at Brinlaw." Alive with relief, he kissed her face, her eyelids, her cheeks, her mouth again and again, tasting her breath, assuring himself that she was what was real. He would not lose her, would not give her up.

"Yes," Alista soothed, mystified but tender. "You're home with me now." She kissed his cheek, tasted tears, and her heart ached for him, for the pain that haunted him so. He entered her quickly and hard, making her gasp at the force of it, but there was tenderness even in this brutality, a strange sort of reverence in his touch. She held him to her and opened herself to his thrust, the initial shock quickly melting into pleasure as he moved faster, still kissing her, framing her face in his hands. Even in the dark she could see his eyes, see him looking down on her as if he hungered for the sight, and this was sweeter still. "You're home," she repeated, touching his cheek as he climaxed inside her.

He felt her shudder with him, a tiny wrinkle of concentration in her brow as her eyes closed, and fresh tears spilled on his cheeks. He lowered his head to her breast again, and she caressed his hair, seemingly content. *Please, God, I will make her happy,* he prayed as he drifted back to sleep. *Please don't take her away.*

Five

The room was still pitch dark when Will felt Alista climbing out of bed. "Boxing Day," she said in answer to his questioning grunt. "I have to help get ready." None of this made any sense to his still-groggy brain, but it didn't sound bad, so he went back to sleep. He felt her kiss him briefly on the lips some time later, but before he could force his eyes to open and reach for her, she was gone.

He found her later in the Great Hall with most of the women of the castle. Leftover food was spread on all the trestle tables, along with stacks of clothing. The women were packing it all into bundles and stacking the bundles in baskets. "There you are, finally," Alista scolded as he came in.

"Yes, there he is," Raynard teased with a grin from his chair near the hearth.

"Sophie, bring Lord Brinlaw his breakfast, please," Alista went on, giving the captain a sharp smack to the back of the head as she passed behind him, startling him into a laugh. "Turn around, please," she ordered Will.

"Don't do it," Raynard warned, making a show of rubbing his offended skull.

Will ignored him and obeyed. "What are we doing exactly?" he asked his wife, who was holding up something behind him.

"I want to see if my father's shirts will fit you before I give them all away," she explained, testing the width of the shoulders.

"They won't," Will said quickly, mildly horrified at the very idea.

"No, you're right," Alista agreed, suddenly a bit shaken by the notion herself in spite of its practicality. "Here, Dru, put these in with the others."

"Fine clothes for a farmer," Dru remarked, taking the stack of shirts. "And rather large as well."

"The peasants can cut them down for nightgowns," Raynard suggested, helping himself to cold mutton from one of the trays.

Will suddenly realized what was happening—Boxing Day, Alista had said. On the day after Christmas, the nobles of the manor would package the surplus food from the castle celebration and distribute it throughout the local peasantry, along with any other items of charity they saw fit. Thinking back, he could remember his mother doing the same, packing bundles in this very room while May tried to help and he mostly got in the way. "As long as they don't ask me to do it," Alista was saying now, holding up a tiny tunic with one sleeve noticeably longer than the other. "You may as well know, Will; your wife can't sew to save her." She packed the tunic into a bundle. "Luckily Dru can, or we'd all be in a pitiful state."

"Don't listen to her, my lord," Sophie advised as she set

his breakfast trencher before him. "She does right well when she can be bothered to pay attention."

"Thank you, Sophie," Alista said, mock-sweetly. "Is that finally everything?"

"Everything we can spare and then some," Druscilla agreed.

"Then I suppose we are ready to go," Alista answered. "Has my horse been saddled?"

"I'm coming with you," Will announced, standing and swallowing a huge bite at the same time.

His wife looked surprised for barely a moment before she smiled. "Of course you are," she said. "So hurry."

As the final preparations were done, Raynard found his attention drawn to Druscilla. She helped Alista fasten her mantle with a predictable admonition to be careful, and she smiled and kissed the other woman's cheek. But when Alista and Will left the hall, Druscilla followed to the archway to watch them go, and her pretty face lost all animation. "They seem to get on well, don't you think?" Raynard said.

"Alista is an angel," Dru answered without looking at him, standing in the doorway looking out. Alista was allowing Will to hold her horse for her as she mounted, elegant for once in a proper gown and lady's fur-lined mantle for her official visits. "She loves everyone because she has always been loved."

"A pleasant way to live," Raynard pressed, keeping his tone casual.

She turned to him, her blue eyes cold and calculating in the doll-like mask. "Only until one learns the truth, Captain," she answered. "Then it is very hard indeed."

"What truth is that, cherie?" he asked, perfectly aping her Parisian accent.

"That love is an illusion, bien sûr," she said with the barest hint of a smile. "Would you not say the same?" Before he could answer, she was gone, following the other women into the kitchen.

The people of Brinlaw Village were no less startled to see their lord making visits than his wife had been to hear he intended to do it, but they were infinitely less skilled at hiding their surprise. Lord Mark had been a generous master, a fair-minded landlord, but he had never once crossed the threshold of a peasant cottage—any noble visitations had been carried out by his daughter alone. " 'Tis sad to think," Alista sighed in pretended regret as they finished their last stop. "For all anyone cared to see me, I might as well have stayed in bed."

Will looked around at her, concerned for half a moment before he realized she was teasing. "I shall ease your feelings by taking you with me to war," he suggested, helping her back onto her horse. "Everyone there will certainly like you better."

She smiled, but her black eyes suddenly looked troubled. "I should hope neither of us will be thinking of war any time soon," she said as he mounted Goliath. Her father's war-horse still didn't care to have this stranger on his back, showing his displeasure by prancing sideways every time Will stepped into the stirrup, but when Will refused to be discouraged, Goliath no longer tried to buck him off.

"Not before spring, I shouldn't think," Will answered, wrapping the reins more tightly around his fist.

He said it as if it were a matter of course, as if some kind of fighting were the natural state of man, and Alista supposed it might be, but she hated it just the same. Her whole life had been spent waiting for her father to return from war, all the time thinking he might never return at all. Must she now do the same for her husband? "So is it the same as you remember?" she asked aloud, changing the subject. "The village, I mean? Or do you remember it?"

"I remember." This was the first time either of them had mentioned his life here as a child—indeed, they had avoided the subject of his father's loss of Brinlaw like a cat avoids water. He had begun to wonder if she even knew who he was exactly, but apparently she did. "Some things have changed." Their horses were standing at the cross in the center of the village, so Will could look up and down the entire length of the single, muddy street. All of the inhabited cottages were well-kept, their thatched roofs intact with no signs of rot, their walls smoothly plastered. But many homes at either end of the street were obviously empty and had been left to decay as they would. "I'll fix it," Will said aloud, his familiar resolve as powerful as ever at the sight. Brinlaw was his; he would restore it to what it had been, and his father's shame would be forgotten. Mark would be forgotten.

Alista watched her husband's face change, feeling a chill that had nothing to do with the icy wind. What he'd said was benign enough—some things about the village probably did need fixing. But the way he'd said it, the look in his dark blue eyes, said more than words. She saw triumph there, even vengeance, determination over all. Her father had looked that way when he spoke of battles to be won. Who was the enemy Will Brinlaw meant to vanquish now? She thought about Dru's unborn child, her friend's fears, and suddenly they didn't seem quite so silly. She had begun to relax with him, to believe she was coming to know him.

The man who had cried out to her in the dark the night before had seemed as familiar and vital to her life as the throb of her own pulse. But this man was a stranger. It was as if they were each two people, two Wills and two Alistas. In the dark, no one and nothing could touch them; they were tied—no, forged into a circle of two. But in the daylight the world rushed in—Brinlaw, King Henry, her father, his father, both dead but neither forgotten.

"My lord!" One of Will's soldiers was riding out to meet them from the castle. Pulling to a stop before them, he gave Alista a friendly nod, but he addressed himself to her husband. "Your baggage train is here, and some friends of the old lord have come with it."

When Will had returned from the Holy Land, his estate, if it could be called that, had fit on a single packhorse without taxing the animal's strength. But now the castle courtyard was full of wagons and packhorses, all seemingly laden to capacity. "Henry sent you some wedding presents," Raynard grinned as he met them just inside the gates.

A pair of knights in armor stood in front of the castle doorway, talking to Druscilla. "Michael!" Alista cried, flinging her horse's reins at a groom to run to one of them, flinging herself into his arms.

"Sir Michael Pettengill," Raynard explained to Will in an undertone as the unpacking went on around them. "He was Old Mark's squire for years, knew Lady Alista as a child. The other one is Henry's cousin, Geoffrey."

"Lady Alista, I am so sorry," Michael was saying as he hugged her. "Your father's death was not known until . . . until after his body was gone."

"You mustn't trouble yourself, Michael," Alista promised, stepping back to take his hands. "Wherever he has gone, my father knows your friendship."

Suddenly she saw Geoffrey d'Anjou, hanging back with Druscilla. "You are kind as ever, my lady," he said, the corner of his mouth twitching in half a smile.

"Not at all," she demurred, letting her old friend go to take another step back, bumping into her husband in the process. "Will," she said, turning to take his arm. "This is Michael Pettengill, a dear friend." *Fool,* she silently scolded herself. After Will Brinlaw, Geoffrey looked even smaller and less real to her than he had before; why should the sight of him upset her? "And I expect you know Sir Geoffrey d'Anjou."

"No, I don't," Will said in a coolly neutral tone.

"Lord William had already left on Crusade when I joined my royal cousin in Aquitaine," Geoffrey explained easily with his charming diplomat's smile. "But I did see him at the coronation."

"As did I," Michael added. Geoffrey looked perfectly at ease, but Michael was looking at Will with barely concealed suspicion, giving Alista more cause for concern. If Pettengill didn't like her husband, he had good reason—her father had often joked that Michael was far too good-natured to ever make a knight.

Suddenly an ear-splitting cry tore through the air from the courtyard behind her. "Holy Christ," one of the grooms swore, springing back from a cage in the wagon he was unloading. "The thing's run mad!"

The thing in question was a magnificent peregrine falcon, tricked out in a ridiculous purple hood with a headdress of nodding white plumes. "He isn't mad; he's embarrassed," Alista joked, pushing the groom aside gently. "Poor prince . . . what have they done to you?"

"Alista, be careful!" Will ordered, alarmed, as she opened the cage, paying the bird's screams and flashing talons no more mind than the snowflakes that had begun to fall around them.

"I shouldn't worry if I were you," Clarence said, coming out of the castle.

"That's quite enough," Alista scolded softly, stripping off one of her gloves to put a bare hand into the cage. "You've every right to be angry, but this smacks of common rudeness." The falcon gave another halfhearted shrug of his wings as he settled back onto his perch. "Much better," she smiled, stroking the downy feathers on the magnificent chest. The falcon cried out again, more softly, almost plaintive as its head flashed back and forth, the plumes on its headdress dancing madly. "I know," Alista soothed. "I shouldn't care to ride blind from London either." She untied the hood's lacings. "Shall we have a better look at one another?"

Will could have sworn the bird really did look at her when she removed the hood, the yellow eyes fixed on her face. "You have a talent for falconry, I take it?" he said softly as he joined her.

"Not really." The falcon stepped onto her half-bared wrist with great care, and she drew it from the cage. "I don't like forcing them to hunt. It isn't dignified."

"His name is Hector, my lady," said the servant who had come with the falcon, charged with its care. "He was tamed for Queen Eleanor herself. Her Majesty sent him to you."

"To me specifically?" Alista looked up from caressing the creature. "He is truly mine?"

The man glanced at Will, who nodded. "Aye, my lady."

Hector wore jesses on his ankles nearly as elaborate as his hood, purple-dyed leather with golden spurs. She untied these quickly, handing them to Will. "There, you see?" she almost whispered. "So much fuss for nothing." Taking a few steps away from the others for safety, she raised her arm, launching the falcon into flight.

"My lady, are you mad?" the servant cried, aghast. "The place is strange, and Hector is already in a pique. He will never come back!"

Alista looked at him as if he were the one without wits. "Of course he will not. I never expected he would."

"Not the most gracious way to accept a present, sweet," Will scolded mildly, secretly amused.

Raynard heard very little of this; he was too occupied watching Pettengill and Geoffrey. When they'd first arrived, it had been Pettengill who had worried him. An obvious partisan of Mark's, he couldn't be at Brinlaw by chance. Geoffrey d'Anjou he assumed had been sent by Henry to smooth things over, something at which he was reputed to excel.

But as soon as Alista appeared on the scene, Raynard's concerns reversed. Pettengill was frankly affectionate with her but not overly so, and she with him, and that knight, while courteous, showed his feelings plainly in his face. He didn't like or trust Will Brinlaw, but at least he wasn't trying to hide it. Geoffrey, on the other hand, was slick as goose flop, smiling and saying all the right words while his eyes never left Will's wife. What was worse was that Alista obviously knew she was being watched. She'd turned red as a strawberry as soon as Geoffrey spoke to her, and while she'd embraced Pettengill like a long-lost brother, she'd been careful not to lay so much as a finger on his companion. Will and Henry and even Raynard himself had believed Mark's daughter to be an innocent virgin, and perhaps she was. But something was going on between her and this Geoffrey d'Anjou.

"How fares your cousin, Sir Geoffrey?" Raynard asked as Eleanor's gift flew free. "Is he still king?"

"Yes, indeed," Geoffrey answered with another friendly smile. "More than ever."

"Come," Alista said, coming back to them with Will beside her. "Why don't we all go inside?"

The men were all still in the Great Hall, but Alista had managed to escape to the solar on the pretense of sorting through some of the King's gifts. "So now what will you do?" Dru said, coming in with another hamper.

"Open the rest of the bedchambers, I suppose," Alista answered. "There are enough linens and draperies here for this whole castle and three others like it."

"You know perfectly well what I mean," Dru retorted, not fooled for an instant. "What are you going to do about Geoffrey?"

"Sir Geoffrey d'Anjou is no concern of mine, nor has he ever been," Alista said. She took out a stack of linen sheets, worn soft and darkened ivory with age. A dragon was embroidered in green and gold at the center of the sheet on top, the threads beginning to ravel at the edges—Will's dragon, the same as on his banner and shield. The Brinlaw dragon. "I am married to William Brinlaw, or hadn't you noticed?"

"You needn't be such a cat with me, cherie," Dru answered. "You aren't hiding anything."

"What exactly am I supposed to be hiding?" Alista asked coolly, more angry than she was willing to show. She loved Druscilla, but the woman had a perverse gift for choosing when and with what to torment her most sorely.

"Geoffrey proposed to you," Dru pointed out with exaggerated patience. "You were considering—"

"I never!" Alista protested, realizing as she said it that this was absolutely true. She might have told Geoffrey she would think about being his wife, but she could never in a thousand years have done it. Now that she had found or been found by Will, the idea was even more absurd.

Dru was staring at her, mouth agape, a most unbecoming expression. "In faith, you did not?"

"No, goose-brain, I did not," Alista grumbled, going back to sorting. "I told you as much before."

"I suppose I wasn't listening." Dru sat down on a bench, still looking vaguely addled. "Don't you think he's handsome?"

"I suppose, but what difference does it make?" Alista answered impatiently. "Handsome or not, he isn't an idiot—he can bloody well see that I'm married. Besides, I don't care for him and never have."

"All right, I understand," Dru said, surrender in her tone. "But Alista, do you care for Will Brinlaw?"

She said this as if it were the most unimaginable notion she'd ever heard, annoying her friend all over again. Alista wanted to talk to someone about her mixed-up, crazy feelings about Will and Brinlaw and her father, but Druscilla would apparently never be that person. "Dru, he is my husband," she repeated, gathering an armload of linens. "Don't you think I had better at least get used to him?"

"Of course," Dru agreed, getting up to help her. "I just think you have no sense of romance."

Alista almost laughed. "Perhaps I take after my father," she said, heading for the door.

Dru did laugh. "C'est vrai, cherie, et touché," she said, following. "That is very true."

Brother Paolo came into the hall just as Mark's falcon banner was being taken down from over the fireplace to be replaced by the Brinlaw dragon. "A sad sight," Michael Pettengill said for the friar's ears alone.

"The castle's new lord would likely disagree," Paolo answered mildly, generally unmoved. The loss of Mark the man was a grievous hurt to him, but the loss of his pagan symbol was not. "I suspect the dragon hung in that spot long before Lord Mark came to Brinlaw."

"And one like it hung in a mud hut on this site long before that," Raynard agreed, joining their conversation as casually as if he'd been invited. "Will traces his line to a Saxon chieftain as well as a Norman lord."

"Indeed," Pettengill mumbled with a token effort at a smile that never reached his eyes. Paolo had known this young man since he had first come to foster with Mark as a twelve-year-old squire. He was a good-hearted man, little given to fits of temper or melancholy. If he were troubled, something was truly wrong.

"Sir Michael was very dear to Lord Mark and his family," the friar explained.

"Yes," Raynard agreed, his own smile tinged with malice. "I can see that."

Will was looking at his father's banner, oblivious to

everything else. When Stephen's soldiers had torn it down, he had attacked them with all the fury of a ten-year-old betrayed, managing to knock one of them to the floor before the other dealt him a blow with a sword hilt that had knocked him out and made his ears ring for days afterward. "That was very foolish," his mother had said as she tended the cut over his eye. "Pride is a sin, William, not a virtue." He must have shown on his face what he thought of this, for she had laughed, a bitter sound that hurt his heart. "Never mind, my champion," she had sighed, kissing his battered brow. "Someday you will put it back again."

And so he had.

"My lord, what about this?"

Turning, he saw Clarence holding Mark's banner, his bearded face carefully neutral. "Where shall I put it?"

For some reason he could not or would not pause to define, Will found himself remembering Alista's face in the pouring rain, her wet-black hair plastered to her shock-whitened brow as he told her Mark was dead. "Give it to me," he said, holding out his hand to take it the same way he had reached out to her. For a moment, he thought the castellan would refuse; he made no move to obey. "Please, Clarence," he pressed. "I would give it to Lady Alista."

The big man's expression softened at once. "That's good," he said, handing over the banner. "She will like that."

Paolo was pleased as well, but if anything, Sir Michael looked more miserable. "Brother Paolo, may I come to your room later?" he asked, glancing quickly at Raynard. "I fear I need spiritual guidance."

"Of course, my son," Paolo said, mystified but ever discreet. "I will be glad to help if I can."

* * *

Will found his wife in the midst of redecorating their bedroom. "No one told me my new husband was so rich," she said as he came in. Looking up, he found her at the top of a ladder hanging a tapestry while Sophie the maid fretted with worry below.

"He isn't," Will admitted, trying not to sound surprised. No other woman he had ever known would have dared to climb a ladder, but Alista didn't seem bothered in the least. "Nearly all of this is new to me."

"Nearly, but not all." She climbed down without so much as a shiver. "Are those not your mother's sheets?"

He looked down at the stack of linens still folded at the foot of the bed. "Yes," he admitted, barely touching the embroidery, his vision clouding for a moment. "I had forgotten I still had them."

"They're lovely," she said, moving the stack to the chest. "I'll never work any so fine, I can almost promise." Sophie moved quickly to help her strip the bed. "What do you have there?" Alista went on as she worked.

"Your father's banner," he answered. "I thought you might want it."

"Yes, certainly, but—" She stopped in mid-turn and mid-sentence. He had taken it down, of course, and put his own up instead. "Thank you," she began again, taking the banner and smoothing its folds. Her mother had woven it all in one piece, and her father had carried it into a hundred battles, the simple silhouette of a white falcon in flight on a field of blue. The edges were tattered; a long, jagged tear had been mended by Mark himself—Alista could see these details in her mind without unfolding the cloth. When King Stephen and Prince Henry had made their peace at last,

Mark had brought his banner home in triumph and hung it over the mantel, never to be taken down again. “Forgive me,” she said softly, blinking back tears. “It’s just strange to think of, I guess.”

“It’s all right,” Will said quickly, hardening his heart against her tears. He would be kind to her, and she would feel better soon enough.

“My lady, what about this?” Sophie said, holding up the mangy fur coverlet from the bed.

“Burn it?” Will suggested.

“Don’t you dare!” Alista cried, running to take it herself, but she was smiling again.

“Why not? It’s heavy as iron and stinks to high heaven,” Will said, scowling but relieved.

“That well may be, but I’m keeping it,” Alista said, spreading the fur across the foot of the bed with exaggerated reverence. “It’s my trophy; I killed this wolf myself.”

“Bollocks,” Will retorted.

“No, my lord, ’tis true,” the maid assured him. “When she was barely more than a snip.”

“Fourteen, I think I was,” Alista agreed.

Will eyed the wolfskin doubtfully—it was longer than his wife was tall. “And just how did you manage it?”

“I didn’t have any choice.” She sat down on the chest and buried a hand in the coarse fur. “Papa had come home for the Christmas peace, and we had gone riding together. It was very cold, early December, and the first deep snow had just fallen. We had stopped to fly the white—my father’s white falcon—when suddenly the horses began to shy back from the woods and make that sort of chortling sound that means they smell danger. The falcon swooped down screaming over our heads, and at first I thought that was what had frightened the horses, but then Papa saw the wolf."

"Me, I would have died on the spot," Sophie shuddered, going on with making the bed as if she'd heard this tale before.

"I wouldn't blame you," Will agreed, watching Alista.

"I don't really remember being scared, not then, at least," she insisted. "Papa didn't seem dreadfully concerned, so I wasn't either. He got down off his horse and handed me the reins—he told me to be still, to hold them still." Her brow was wrinkled slightly in concentration, remembering. "The wolf came out of the trees, circling around him, trying to get between him and the horses. He had his sword out, was crouched down, waiting for the beast to spring. My only worry was that I would be sick when I saw the blood. But then Papa slipped on the ice. It was a hillside, rocky under the snow, and he slipped and fell, and the wolf leapt on top of him, too quickly for him to stab it with his sword. It was snarling, and I could see its eyes, see blood in the snow, and I wasn't scared; I was angry. I grabbed Papa's crossbow from his saddle and tried to fire it, but I wasn't strong enough to pull the string back to load it." She laughed softly. "It's probably a good thing—my aim would have been so bad I probably would have killed Papa and saved the wolf some trouble."

"So how did you kill it?" Will asked, astonished and vaguely appalled.

"I used this," Alista said, drawing her dagger from her belt. "I just jumped out of the saddle onto the wolf's back and started stabbing at anything with fur just as hard as I could—my arms were sore for days." She lifted the top corner of the fur as if to demonstrate, and Will could almost see the missing head with its deadly fangs. "He whipped his head around to snap at me, like this, and I stabbed him in the throat." She stopped, catching sight of her husband's face. "He meant to kill my father," she finished with a slightly embarrassed shrug. "I couldn't just sit there and do nothing."

"Like as not the beast would have killed you as well if you had," Sophie added. "Wouldn't you say so, my lord?"

"Yes," Will agreed, still staring at Alista. "So your father kept the pelt as a reminder."

"And as a kind of magic, as silly as it sounds," she answered with a smile that could have meant she was teasing. "He said that he would always sleep under this wolfskin because every time he saw it, he would know I could take care of myself and would never have to worry." She stood up, still holding the fur. "So you see, we can't burn it."

"No," Will agreed, taking it from her. He held it up, skin side out, and he could see all the little sewn-up slashes, all the little stab wounds. A living wolf's hide was as thick and tough as tanned leather; how could a fourteen-year-old girl have found the strength to pierce it so many times? Still, it didn't seem like her to concoct such a tale, and Sophie obviously believed it. "We'll hang it in the solar," he decided. "Then we can tell our children how their mother killed a wolf with a dagger."

"That should make them behave," she laughed, coming to kiss his cheek. "I think it's an excellent plan."

He put an arm around her waist and drew her close, letting the wolfskin fall to kiss her mouth. "You shall have to tell the King's cousin your story," he said, smiling. "He'll think he's come to the pagan wilderness indeed."

Something about this made her smile fade, her face turn

pale, and Sophie beat a hasty retreat, barely pausing to bob a curtsey before disappearing through the door. "I'm sure he already does," Alista said, moving out of his embrace.

"Alista." He caught her gently by the arm. "What's wrong?"

"Nothing," she insisted, trying to pull away, but he wouldn't let go. "Will, don't."

"Don't what?" he pressed, his scowl returning. "Why are you—"

"It's about Geoffrey—the King's cousin," she suddenly began in a rush. "He said . . ." She tried to pull free again, and this time he allowed it. "King Henry used to send him here to see my father all the time," she went on. "He's the one who came and told us Stephen was dead and Henry was to be crowned, and before my father left with him to go to the coronation, he asked me to marry him, or rather asked me to consider whether I wanted to or not. I suppose he meant to speak to Papa in London, and maybe he did, I don't know." She paused, giving him time to say something, but he just stood there looking at her with no emotion showing on his handsome face. "Not that it matters now," she finished weakly.

"You're right," Will said. "It doesn't matter." He kissed her on the forehead, but his lips were as cold as his tone. "You are my wife, not Geoffrey's."

Didn't he even care what she had felt, what she might have said to Geoffrey's proposal? "Well, obviously, but—"

"We don't have to talk about this," he cut her off. "I won't talk about it. It's over, Alista." His blue eyes were like ice. "It's over."

She just stared back at him, nonplussed. If he would just listen to her, she would gladly explain that she'd never had any intention of marrying Geoffrey, could imagine it even less now that she knew him. But no, he preferred to treat her like a naughty child and shush her up before she could tell him anything. "It's more than over, Will," she shot back. "It has never even begun." Before he could answer, she turned and stormed out.

Will sat down on the bed as soon as she was gone, his hands shaking, cold sweat breaking out on his brow. Before he knew her, Alista had had a lover . . . no, she had been a virgin; he could at least be certain of that. But she had had a sweetheart, an intended—Geoffrey d'Anjou, the King's cousin, a pretty courtier. Will couldn't even begin to imagine it, but she had said it herself. He was near Alista's age, this Geoffrey, nearer than Will was himself. Did Will seem old to her? "Sweet Christ, who cares?" he swore aloud, his fists clenched tight as he stood up again. She was his; Brinlaw was his; nothing else was important.

He thought again of his dream of the desert. In reality, he had not been alone there; a hundred men had fought beside him, if the slaughter of nomad tribes with barely any weapons could be considered fighting. But he had felt alone, cut off from any hope of peace, of anything but pain and blood. Returning to England, he had sworn he would make his own peace, a haven, an absolution. At Brinlaw, he would forget the butcher of the desert; he would be the man of peace he was born to be, the man his father would have been, given the chance. Looking into Alista's eyes, holding her in his arms, tasting her innocent kiss, this had all seemed possible, and his heart had gone out to her. But Alista was not what he had thought. Alista was the faery who sang of death over a pagan pyre. Alista was the warrior who killed a ravaging wolf knife-to-fang to save her father, Will's own sworn enemy. Alista had talked of marriage with Geoffrey d'Anjou.

"I don't care," he repeated, pushing these thoughts from his mind. "It doesn't matter."

Alista was still fuming when she found Dru in the downstairs corridor. "Thank God," the other girl breathed, catching her by the arm. "Come quickly; we're going to church."

"What? What are you talking about?" Alista protested as she was hustled into the chapel. "Dru, for pity—" She stopped. Brother Paolo was standing near the altar, along with Michael Pettengill and Geoffrey d'Anjou, and all three of them were staring at her. "What is going on?" she asked Brother Paolo.

"Michael wants to tell you something, sweet love," the monk said, looking grave. "I'm afraid you must listen to him."

"Afraid?" she echoed, her anger at Will turning to alarm. Geoffrey was just standing there, staring with those cat's green eyes. "Michael, what's wrong?"

"Forgive me, my lady," the knight began. "The good friar told me that King Henry wrote you a letter saying your father chose Will Brinlaw to be your husband. May we see it?"

"I don't have it," Alista answered, glancing back at Dru. The other girl looked almost as scared as she felt, but there was another queer light in her eyes as well, almost anticipation. "I haven't seen it since that night. But what Brother Paolo has told you is quite true—why can't you just believe him?"

"I do believe him, of course," Michael said quickly,

obviously horrified at the mere suggestion that he might doubt the cleric's word. "I just thought if I could see it, I might be easier in my mind. Alista, I just don't see how the King could write such a thing or how it could be true. Lord Mark hated Will Brinlaw—he would have married you to the Pharaoh of Egypt first."

A cold chill crawled over her skin, and her vision seemed to frost over as well. "Papa didn't hate him, Michael," she heard herself insisting. "He just didn't want to lose Brinlaw. He said he would have done just what he expected Will to do in Will's place. But he didn't have any feeling toward him personally."

"That was before they met, mon âme," Geoffrey said sardonically.

"At Henry's coronation, Will Brinlaw claimed this manor, just as your father expected he would," Michael explained, frowning slightly at the other knight. "The King refused him, saying he would not deprive Lord Mark of his holding but that he would give Will some other castle instead. But Will wouldn't hear it—he openly defied his sworn sovereign and said he could not accept his ruling."

Alista looked at Brother Paolo, aghast. Will had defied the King in his own court? This was tantamount to blasphemy—no knight of honor would even think of such a thing. The King was ordained by the Almighty, and an oath sworn to him was sworn to Heaven as well. To defy the King was nearly the same as to defy God Himself. "If that's true, why would King Henry have written to me recommending Will so highly?" she protested.

"I don't know, my lady," Michael replied. "That is why I wanted to examine the letter—perhaps it was a forgery."

"Oh, I doubt that," Geoffrey protested. "Alista, Will

Brinlaw is one of my cousin's most dear friends. He could and would forgive him nearly anything." He came closer to her, his tone obviously meant to be soothing. "Besides, this open defiance that so appalled Sir Michael didn't seem nearly so dramatic to me. Brinlaw also said in the same breath that he would gladly die for his king. He just wanted his castle back."

"At any cost," Michael said grimly.

Geoffrey looked surprised. "You mean to tell her that, too?" he asked. "What purpose—?"

"The truth," Michael cut him off. "Whatever King Henry may or may not have written or forgiven or believed, Lady Alista deserves to know what manner of man she has married."

Geoffrey opened his mouth as if he meant to protest further, then he closed it again, shaking his head. "Tell her then," he muttered, turning away.

"Yes, by all means," Alista insisted, her stomach rolling in dread. She'd heard enough already to make her sick; what could be worse?

"When your husband said he would have this castle regardless of his king's command, your father bade him come and take it," Michael said slowly, as if it hurt him to even speak the words. "You know—you knew your father; he feared no man living. He invited Will to lay siege to Brinlaw if he wished, to do his worst, for he would never take Mark's castle so long as Mark lived; he would have to murder him to have it." His eyes met hers. "Will said he would like nothing better. I thought he was bluffing, saving face before the other nobles. If I had for one moment believed your father was in danger—"

"Michael, slow down and tell me," Alista said, blood

roaring in her ears. She thought she must be dreaming, or that she must be the butt of some perverse joke they had all concocted together to drive her mad. She hadn't wanted to marry Will; she hadn't wanted to marry anyone, but she had because her father wished it. She knew this because the King himself had written the words. If none of these things were true . . . "Did Will Brinlaw murder my father?"

"All I can say is that the next thing I knew, your father was dead, the body was gone, and Will Brinlaw had his castle," Michael answered.

"Which in and of itself means nothing," Geoffrey insisted, catching Alista's arm. "There is no proof—"

"How did my father die?" Alista demanded, pulling free, though she did feel faint—the floor seemed to pitch and roll like the deck of a ship in a storm. "Why won't anyone just tell me—?"

"Because no one can tell," Geoffrey interrupted. "By the time anyone but Will Brinlaw and the King knew Mark was dead, Will Brinlaw had left London with his body."

"To hide his crime," Dru suddenly insisted. "Of course he killed him—"

"We can't know that for certain," Geoffrey cut her off.

"No," Michael doubtfully agreed. "We cannot."

"But you believe it," Alista said, looking back and forth between the two knights. The nausea was beginning to pass, replaced by something more powerful, a kind of frozen rage. "You believe Will murdered my father."

"If I were certain, I would have come here with troops," Michael said. "But I think so, yes. Alista, what did Will tell you? Did he say anything of what was said before the King?"

"No," she admitted. "He only said he didn't know how Papa died."

"A lie," Dru said bitterly.

"My lady, please," Brother Paolo scolded gently. "I examined Lord Mark's body myself and saw no sign he was murdered by anyone."

"He was dead, n'est-ce pas?" Dru retorted. "What other sign could you need? Have you never heard of poison?"

"Dru, stop it," Alista ordered. Her mind was racing, sifting through every detail of what she knew of Will Brinlaw, trying to imagine him as a murderer. It didn't seem possible. But why hadn't he told her the truth? He had said he couldn't take Communion, that he carried an unconfessed sin on his soul—could it be her father's murder? But he had kissed her, made love to her, held her close while she grieved for her father. What sort of villain would he have to be to behave so if he were her father's killer? If he had hated Mark enough to kill him in cold blood, how could he treat her, Mark's daughter, with such tenderness? "I can't believe it; I won't," she said aloud, shaking her head for emphasis. "I have to talk to Will—"

"My lady, you can't be serious," Michael said, alarmed.

"Of course I am," she answered. "Mark was my father; Will is my husband. I will know the truth." Before they could protest further, she turned and ran from the chapel.

"Alista, wait!" Geoffrey caught her at the foot of the stairs. "What about me?" he said, as if he were highly offended. "Will you dismiss me so easily, too?" He took her by the arms. "I love you; let me help you—"

"Geoffrey, for pity's sake," she protested, struggling free. "You don't love me; you don't even know me—"

"I do, far better than Will Brinlaw," he insisted. "I know

you loved your father more than life, that you would die before you would live as his murderer's wife. I can't let that happen; I have to save you—"

"Are you mad?" she demanded, a desperate whisper. They were standing in the shadows of the corridor, but the Great Hall was only a few steps away.

"Yes," he retorted in kind. "And I will do something desperate if you won't listen to me."

"I have listened to you already," she insisted. "Now leave me alone."

"Meet me later where we can talk without the others," he pressed. "In the back garden where I first proposed—"

"No," she was saying before he could finish. "That's stupid; I won't do it."

"You will," he said, his eyes brilliant green in the dark. "Or I will openly accuse your husband. I will tell him that you love me—"

"You wouldn't dare," she breathed, horrified. "He would kill you!"

"Very likely," he agreed. "Would you have my death on your conscience?"

"If you are such a fool—"

"Will you meet me?" he interrupted.

Alista just glared at him, thinking how happily she could kill him herself just then. "Yes," she said at last. "At midnight in the back garden." Before he could say another word, she turned and ran up the stairs.

From his own hiding place around the corner, Raynard watched with clenched fists and a heavy heart. Alista ran away, and the Angevin bastard slipped back into the chapel. "Bloody hell," he muttered, going to find Will.

He finally found him on the battlements of the castle

proper, looking up at a tall, thin tower pointing into the sunset like a sorcerer's bony finger. "That shouldn't be here," Will said by way of greeting. "I've been trying to remember it, but I'm sure now. It wasn't here before."

" 'Tis not so strange," Raynard answered. "Old Mark wanted to see us coming."

Will's smile was as bleak as the tower. "And yet he did not."

Raynard nodded, collecting his thoughts. "Will, it's happened," he began at last. "That Michael Pettengill, he's told Alista about your quarrel with Mark."

"How do you know?" Will asked, his attention snapping into focus in an instant. "Did you hear—?"

"No," Raynard said quickly. "But he went to see the monk in his cell; the monk sent Druscilla for Alista; and they all met up with Sir Geoffrey in the chapel behind closed doors for quite some time. Alista came out crying with Geoffrey hot on her heels." He paused, picking his words with care. Whether he was admitting it or not, Will had begun to be fond of this strange girl he had married, and he would not hear the rest of this sad tale well. "Will, you've made it clear that it's none of my business, but I have to ask—has your marriage been consummated?"

His friend's eyes flared blue fire for a moment before he answered. "Yes," he muttered at last.

"Can you prove—?"

"Yes!" He looked away. "The sheets were kept."

"Good," Raynard nodded, relieved but not happy. "Will, it pains me to tell you this, but Geoffrey d'Anjou—"

"Wanted to marry Alista; yes, I know," Will finished for him. "She told me."

"She told you herself?" Raynard echoed, surprised. This

was good; perhaps the girl was salvageable after all. Raynard was beginning to rather like her himself. "What did she say?"

"She said he asked her to marry him and that she had not yet given him an answer," Will said, turning to gaze out at the gathering night. "I told her it doesn't matter, that she's my wife now."

"Well, perhaps we had better remind her and tell Sir Geoffrey while we're at it," Raynard replied. "I heard him swear his love to her, and she has agreed to meet him, alone, at midnight." Will's head snapped around to look at him, and his face looked as if he'd been struck. "In the back garden," the captain finished.

Will just stared at his friend, speechless. *It doesn't matter,* the stern voice in his head repeated. *I have Brinlaw; nothing else matters but that.* "Guard!" he called out, summoning one of Mark's soldiers standing some hundred or so feet along the wall.

"Yes, my lord?" the man replied, half-running to obey.

"Tell Lady Alista to go to bed without me," Will ordered. "I'll keep watch out here tonight."

"My lord?" the soldier asked, confused. "We are plenty to keep watch—"

"Just do it," Will snapped, scowling.

"His lordship and I have business this night," Raynard explained with a grin, pulling a set of dicing bones from his pocket. "His lady will have to manage without him."

"Aye, Captain," the main grinned back. "I will tell my lady."

Raynard watched the soldier go, then turned back to Will, staring into the setting sun, his expression like stone. "What do you mean to do?"

Will glanced back at him for a moment. "Only what I must," he said, his voice gruff with bitter resolution.

Alista paced the floor of Brother Paolo's room, unable to sit still. "I still believe this meeting is ill-advised," the monk was saying as he watched her.

"Geoffrey is the very least of my worries," she answered. She was dressed in her boy's clothes, ready to meet the Angevin knight in a few hours. If he insisted on being a lovestruck ass, she intended to show him that he didn't know her nearly so well as he believed, and if he still dared to lay a hand on her he'd get a dagger in his gullet for his trouble. "With five minutes away from anyone who might slit his throat, I can make him see reason and be done with him forever. It's Will who is driving me mad." She picked up a paper from his desk and set it down again, barely seeing it. "I don't care if he and Raynard have decided to spend the night dicing—they can go whoring for all I care," she insisted. "But I have to talk to him—and what's more, he knows it. Otherwise he wouldn't be hiding."

"I think hiding may be an overstatement," Paolo said mildly.

"What would you call it?" she demanded. "You know what vexes me most? All these idiots seem to believe I'm some piece of furniture, incapable of reason, to be passed from one to another without a word to say. Geoffrey doesn't want to tell me anything except that he loves me, which is either a damnable lie or the most ludicrous truth I ever heard in my life. Michael wants to tell me all he knows, but he doesn't want me to do anything about it. And Will—" She broke off for a moment, her voice catching in her throat. "Will wants to stay on the battlements, standing guard and dicing with his captain. Standing guard against what, I want to know? Dicing for what—is Raynard to have his chance to win Brinlaw now?"

"You could go and ask him," Paolo suggested.

"Yes, if I wanted to ask him if he murdered my father in front of all his troops," she retorted more sharply than she'd intended. "I'm sorry . . ." She sank into a chair. "Brother Paolo, what could have happened to that letter?"

"I couldn't say," the friar admitted, thinking this was rather a small point compared with everything else. But nothing she was saying was making any sense. One moment she seemed to believe her husband was a murderer; the next she was furious with him for not rushing to her side. "Do you honestly believe it could have been forged?"

"Of course not." She took out her dagger and balanced it on the arm of the chair, a nervous habit that made him nervous as well. "If King Henry didn't truly want Will at Brinlaw, why would he have sent that baggage train? No, if my father was murdered, Henry either didn't know it or knew and didn't care. That's why I want to read his letter again. I was in such a state when I read it the first time, I'm afraid I might not be remembering clearly. He did write that my father had specifically chosen Will to marry me, did he not?"

"Yes," the friar agreed.

"But Will himself has never said it," she went on, leaning forward in her chair. "Not once. I've been wracking my brain, and I am sure of it. So if it was a lie, it was Henry's."

"Unless Will told the King—"

"But that's just it," she insisted. "The King said my father told him he meant for Will to marry me, not Will. My father." She got up and sheathed her dagger. "I have to talk to Will."

Six

Alista found her husband on the battlements, as expected, with Raynard and a small crowd of guardsmen, none of whom, she noticed, had ever served her father. "I got your message," she said, almost shouting to be heard over the wind and the general babble of conversation.

Will looked up, startled. He had seen the boyish figure coming toward them from the arch, but it had never occurred to him that this could be his wife. Since his arrival, she had worn a proper gown. "Why are you dressed that way?" he quite reasonably asked.

"Why not?" she shot back. "I have to talk to you."

"Because it's unseemly and obscene, and I forbid it," Will answered. "Go inside and change your clothes."

She wanted to believe in him, to believe he couldn't possibly be the monster Michael said he was, but he wasn't helping his cause. "Why don't you come inside and make me?"

Will could not believe his ears, but he must have heard right—why else would his men be laughing? "Alista, I said go inside," he repeated, slowly standing up.

"I heard you the first time," she answered, forcing her voice not to quaver. Even her father, the most patient man in Christendom where she had been concerned, would likely have beaten her for such insolence as this. "But I can't go inside unless you come with me because I have to talk to you."

"Will," Raynard began. "Maybe you should—"

"Take pity on her, my lord," another guardsman, a little drunk, interrupted. "She misses you."

Will wanted to smash his fist into this idiot's face, but he wouldn't give his bride the satisfaction. Taking her ungently by the arm, he escorted her back toward the arch, far enough away to be out of earshot of his men, if not entirely out of sight. "What exactly is so damned important?" he asked her instead.

Shouting in a high wind before a crowd of drunkards, even from a distance, was not how she'd planned this conversation, but he was apparently giving her no better choice. "I can't find King Henry's letter," she began, as good a place as any.

Will thought back to when he arrived. "I burned it," he admitted, remembering. He hadn't even realized what he was doing at the time, and besides, what difference could it make? "Was there anything else?"

"You burned it?" she echoed, aghast. "That was mine!"

"And you are mine," he finished, closing the subject. "Go to bed, Alista."

What evil purpose could have been served by burning Henry's letter? Alista thought, turning red more with rage than embarrassment. *Could it have been forged after all?* "You villain!" she began.

"Alista, your father may have allowed you to torment his every step when he was here, but I am not your father," he cut her off, determined to put an end to this once and for all. He was furious with her, and if she did as he expected she intended at midnight, he might well wring her neck. He had determined to stay away from her for the very purpose of avoiding just such a conversation, or any conversation with her until he knew for certain just what her intentions with this damned Geoffrey were. But apparently he wasn't to have that luxury, would not be allowed to keep his distance even for a few short hours. Still, he would not have her mocked by his men, nor would he allow her to bait him into a brawl before them. He briefly considered scooping her up and carrying her inside, but he didn't trust himself to touch her so much, even for a moment. "Now for Christ's sake, leave me alone!" he finished, forcing a heat he didn't really feel into his tone in the hope of frightening her enough to send her scurrying away, out of his sight, out of his heart, to give him peace to think.

But Alista didn't scare so easily, and she wasn't one to scurry. "No, my lord, you are not my father," she agreed, now deeply hurt as well as angry, but not afraid. "And I will most happily leave you alone." She turned to do as he asked, fighting tears she would not let him see if she could help it.

Her tears were genuine, Will realized; she wouldn't have fought them so hard if they were not. "Alista," he said, following her to the arch.

"Don't you dare!" she hissed, turning back and flinging off his hand as he touched her shoulder, making him glad they were no longer within sight of the guard.

His own anger flared again, but he didn't make another move to touch her. "So now my touch offends you?" he said coldly.

"Yea, my lord, I am most sorely offended, but you needn't fear for me," she shot back. "When I was a child at court, there was a little boy there who I thought was my friend. We played together every day for weeks, and he was very kind to me. But then one day his older brothers came to London with his father." She looked pointedly over his shoulder in the direction of his men. "They teased him about being friends with a girl—his little true love, I believe they called me," she continued. "To prove it wasn't so, he hit me and pushed me down."

"A sin against the angels, in faith," Will said sarcastically.

"Brother Paolo told me that when I grew up, things would be different," she went on, her black eyes narrowed. "I told him yes, that when I grew up, if anyone tried to push me, it wouldn't be me that ended up with skinned knees and a muddy face."

In his time, Will had been both coddled and cursed by women, lied to, flattered, scolded, kissed, deceived. But this was the first time he'd ever been threatened by one. "You were how old when this tragedy occurred? Four? Five? While you were playing hobby horse at Stephen's court with rude little boys who hurt your feelings, would you like to know what was happening here?" He was moving closer, daring her to run. "I was having my skull cracked open trying to defend my father's castle from Stephen's troops. While you and your father were settling into our home, my sister May and I were wandering the streets of Calais with no money and nothing to eat while our mother begged the holy sisters to take us in until my father could be found." He was now so close his breath stirred the strands of ebony hair on her brow, but she still hadn't backed down an inch. "When you were being so clever and killing a wolf to save your father from his own stupidity, May was killing herself," he went on, the words tearing at his guts as he spoke them, and Alista's face went pale. "She hanged herself in a ruined village church because she could not stand to be beaten and raped any more by a husband who told her she deserved it because her father was a traitor to the crown." Tears had come back to her eyes, but this time he didn't care. "So push me if you must, Alista," he finished. "Just be very certain you're prepared when I push back."

Alista couldn't speak, could barely breathe. The pain in his eyes was so terrible, it made her heart ache for him, but it frightened her as well. Pain so deep as that could surely drive a Christian soul to murder, could turn the dearest love to hate. And he had hated her father. She reached out without thinking to touch his cheek, and he jerked his face away as if he couldn't bear to even look at her, much less feel her touch. "He didn't know," she said softly, her mouth so dry she could barely form the words. "My father—"

"Of course he knew!" he shouted, turning back to cut her off, his blue eyes wild with rage, but something in her face made him stop. "Stupid child," he muttered, turning away again instead.

She flushed hot, far more humiliated by this than by the guardsman's jokes. "I am not stupid," she said coldly. "And I don't deserve to be hated."

Something about the way she said this touched him where her tears could not, made the thought that she could love Geoffrey d'Anjou too hurtful to be borne. She wasn't some mindless lady-in-waiting playing at romantic intrigues. If she loved, she would love with her soul. "I don't hate you," he answered, allowing himself to touch her cheek. She flinched, but he didn't let go, caught her with his other hand and drew her into a kiss.

His face as he moved back was impossible to read, a beautiful mask with dark blue eyes cold as midnight. *Tell me,* she wanted to beg him. *Tell me who you are.*

But she would not. Wiping his kiss from her mouth with the back of her hand, she turned and walked away.

Raynard thought Will would go after his wife, or at least leave the battlements, but he seemed determined to stay there until midnight. "I'll be back," the captain said softly, taking his cup and heading for the archway. Someone knew something more than he did about what was going on, and he suspected he knew just who.

Druscilla was in the chapel again, weeping her prayers alone. "Go away," she ordered as soon as he drew near. "I don't want you here."

"Who says I came here for you?" Raynard shot back, sitting down on the other end of her bench. "Is self-love not a sin? Such as you have ought to be."

Her eyes narrowed. "Why can't you just leave me alone?"

"You're irresistible, remember?" he laughed. "My very soul is aching."

To his surprise, she smiled. "You know, I believe it is," she said. "Poor, ugly fool."

"Ugly?" He pretended to be shocked. "Fool I may be, poppet, but I am no one's idea of ugly."

"You are mine," she said, her pretty face serene. "Old and scarred—your face looks like a map to Damascus."

"And so it is," he agreed, unfazed. "I suppose you would prefer some pretty boy like Sir Geoffrey."

"Or your friend, Will," she agreed, barely missing a beat. "Except that he's a heartless, murdering liar."

Raynard leaned back on the bench. "Why would you say that?" he asked in a conversational tone.

"Because he is," she answered. She had been crying before; he could still see the stain of her tears on her creamy cheek, but nothing in her voice or manner betrayed anything but calm contempt. "And what's more, Alista knows it."

"What does she know?" he pressed, maintaining his own casual pose.

"Mark did not choose Will Brinlaw for her husband, and the King did not rule in his favor," she answered. "Brinlaw defied the King's ruling and killed Mark to steal his manor."

"Did he indeed?" Raynard laughed with genuine amusement. "And how precisely did he kill him?"

"You would know better than I," she replied with a deadly smile.

"And Sir Geoffrey knows best of all, no doubt," he said. "Or is it Michael Pettengill?"

Her blue eyes narrowed. "Pettengill is gone," she said.

"But not Sir Geoffrey," Raynard answered quickly, pretending this was not new information, that he already knew quite well that Pettengill had fled. "Sir Geoffrey is in love with Alista."

An intriguing light flared in her eyes. "Was," she corrected. "Not anymore."

"Oh poppet, I fear you are mistaken," he pressed. "I heard him tell her so this very afternoon. Perhaps you shouldn't speak so easily on matters you know nothing about."

Her pretty face was unreadable as she gazed unconcerned at the candles on the altar. "I know enough," she said without changing her expression. "You, for example. You pretend to think me an empty-headed fool, much too low to notice." She turned and lay a hand on his chest, her eyes half-veiled beneath her golden lashes. "But I could make you lick my shoes if I hinted you could have me for it."

Raynard suddenly thought he knew what had killed Old Mark. "Silly poppet," he said, keeping his voice even with an effort. "I think you might truly believe it."

"Don't you?" She touched his mouth, traced the shape of his lower lip. "Don't you want to kiss me?"

His hand closed around her wrist, and she gasped, then smiled, delighted. "Sorry, Dru," he said, leaning close enough to taste the sweetness of her breath. "I would sooner kiss a snake." Letting her go, he left her to her prayers.

He went out into the corridor and whistled to the guard near the doorway to the hall. "Where is Sir Michael Pettengill?" he asked.

"Gone to bed, Captain, more than an hour ago," the soldier replied. "Shall I go roust him for you?"

"Don't bother." He turned away, shaking his head in disgust. Less than a week of domestic tranquillity, and they'd all gone thick as mud. "Watch Druscilla," he ordered, pointing at the chapel door. "Don't let her out of your sight—and for God's sake, keep her from Lady Alista."

At midnight, the back garden was still and cold as death. Alista stood in the shadow of the tower and listened as the chapel bell counted off the hour. The snow had stopped, and the sky was clear with stars like chips of ice. "Papa, please," she whispered, closing her eyes. "I don't know what to do." In truth, she had never felt so alone or so confused. When Michael had first suggested that her father had not only been murdered but murdered by Will Brinlaw, the idea had seemed ludicrous, a sick joke. Now she couldn't be so sure.

She had always known Brinlaw Castle had once belonged to someone else and that this someone had not given up his manor by choice. But she had never considered what had happened to this knight and his family after they had gone. She had been a child; she was just happy to have a home again, to be away from London. Later when her father told her about facing Old Brinlaw's son in battle, she'd been only mildly curious—he was just another enemy from France. But now he was here, her husband, the man who shared her bed, and she felt she knew him even less. He had hated her father, of that much she had no more doubt. But had he hated him enough to kill him in cold blood? Before she couldn't imagine it because she couldn't imagine him believing he was justified in doing so. Now that she'd heard him tell what had happened to his family, his sister, had seen his face as he told it, she knew better. He may not have done it, but in his mind he had reason enough.

From far above she heard the cries of a falcon—Hector, perhaps, celebrating his new freedom—and for a moment, she envied him. *I can fly, and I am free!* he seemed to cry. *I am fierce, and I am free! I can kill, and I am free!* Her attachment to the birds of prey, while eccentric, was not sentimental; she didn't find them adorable; she knew them for the killers they were. What must it be like to kill without remorse, to be the most deadly creature in the forest? And having known such freedom, what must it be like to be captured?

Will watched from the trees nearby, his crossbow drawn and loaded, his finger on the trigger. He didn't actually intend to kill anyone, not even Geoffrey—he had promised Raynard as much. "Why bother to let them meet at all?" his captain had quite reasonably asked. "Tell your wife what you know, put her sweetheart out of your house, and be done with the whole situation." To the Fleming's mind, the fled Pettengill was a more immediate concern, and the soldier in Will knew he was right. If Pettengill had gone to gather troops, he had bigger problems than Alista's fidelity or lack thereof. But try as he might, he couldn't seem to focus his attention on anything else. He had to know exactly why she was meeting Geoffrey, exactly what she meant to do.

He tried to gauge his wife's state of mind from the way she stood waiting for Geoffrey, to spot some clue to her true feelings. She was still dressed like a squire, his directive be damned, so she had taken no pains to look pretty. But vanity was not one of her more prominent sins, and besides, perhaps annoying him gave her more pleasure. Her face was pale in the moonlight, and her expression was troubled, but perhaps she was just nervous. She looked up at the cloudless starry sky, the hood of her mantle falling back, and he had to swallow hard, a lump of feeling that was worse than his rage stopping up his throat.

"Stay awake, mon ami," Raynard muttered from his post nearby. Will had wanted to come here alone, and his friend could well understand why. But killing Henry's cousin in cold blood wouldn't be wise, even in this instance, and Raynard had an idea that if Geoffrey made love to Mark's daughter, that was exactly what Will would do. Or maybe he expected Geoffrey to bring troops and spirit the girl away, wanted to catch him in the act. This explanation made more sense to Raynard, but the look in Will's eyes didn't support it, alas. His friend was jealous, plain and simple, jealous for the heart of a woman he barely knew. "Here he comes."

"You make a beautiful boy," Geoffrey said, close enough to murmur in Alista's ear before she realized he was there, so lost was she in her own thoughts.

"Geoffrey, just stop it," she ordered, turning to face him and move out of his reach. "We haven't much time."

"No, my love, we do not."

Raynard took a step in the direction of the pretty couple, but Will reached out and stopped him, shaking his head. Not yet . . .

"Pettengill has gone for his troops," Geoffrey continued, his voice carrying easily on the cold, crisp air. "They will besiege the castle at dawn, and we must be gone, or your husband will make you a hostage."

"Troops?" Alista echoed, too horrified to think about keeping her own voice down. "Michael has no troops. He specifically said—"

"FitzCammon's troops, then," Geoffrey interrupted. "My troops, to be perfectly accurate. They were supposed to take the castle without putting you in danger." A line she had never seen before appeared between his golden eyebrows. "Imagine my surprise when I heard they had marched on."

Alista could scarcely believe her ears. "You tried to help me by sending mercenaries to attack my castle?"

"To attack Will Brinlaw," he corrected, looking hurt as he reached for her. "To rescue you."

"Geoffrey, you might have asked—" The crossbow bolt whizzed past her ear so close she felt it more than heard it. "Geoffrey!" she cried as it buried itself in the young knight's shoulder. Before she could react, someone had grabbed her from behind and flung her face first into the snow as swords clashed above and behind her.

Naturally, the whoreson is left-handed, Will thought as he struck at the younger man again with his broadsword. Killing Henry's cousin was probably imprudent; that was why he'd only shot him in the shoulder, meaning to disable his sword arm and take him captive like the cowardly little beast that he was. But if he didn't yield soon, Will thought he might reconsider.

Raynard still had a grip on Alista, but not a firm one—Will had surprised him when he chose his moment to fire. He didn't want to break any of her fragile, feminine bones, and she refused to faint or even go limp like any reasonable noble lady would have done when so tackled and pinned. "Let me go!" she bellowed in most unladylike fashion, driving her boot heels into his shins as he got up, both her arms thrashing in his grasp. He managed to drag her to her feet, but she wrenched one arm free in the process. Whirling around, she managed by luck or fiendish design to drive her delicate little fist up into his jaw, making him taste blood and see stars.

Geoffrey was still fighting back, but he was weakening. Will outweighed him by a considerable margin, and the strain of fending off his more powerful attack blows was beginning to show, his parries coming more slowly, barely saving his skull each time. "So what say you, Sir Geoffrey?"

Will said, barely winded. "Will you yield, or shall I kill you?"

"No!" Alista flung herself between them without thinking—she couldn't watch a man die because of her, even an idiot like Geoffrey. And if she actually saw Will commit murder, she wouldn't be able to forget.

Will realized she had moved half a second before disaster struck, and he froze in mid-stroke, his broadsword trembling at her throat. Horrified, he let the blade drop, and Geoffrey took his best chance, ducking through the hole in the bailey wall and disappearing into the darkness without looking back.

"Damn it to hell!" Raynard swore, grabbing up his own fallen sword to go after him.

"Don't bother," Will said, his heart pounding in his chest. "Go raise our troops—we'll find him soon enough." He let his eyes focus on Alista. She was obviously shaken, too, panting lightly, soaked with snow, her braid coming loose, her black eyes wide. She was beautiful, the most desirable creature he had ever seen, and he could, in that moment, have happily strangled her to death. "No doubt he'll be joining Pettengill," Will finished, turning away from temptation.

Alista was snatching at breath as well as reason, but she managed to run after him. "Will, stop!" she pleaded. "Michael is a good man—"

"Enough!" he cut her off, a roar so loud and furious the very earth seemed to tremble. "Go back inside," he went on more calmly, his back still turned. "Be quiet and go back inside, or I swear before God and Satan, I will carry you in and bolt you into the smallest cupboard I can find."

Alista didn't doubt him for a moment, but she couldn't

seem to move. Her entire body seemed to be frozen and bloodless, the body of a dead woman, though her heart was pounding. Everything had happened too fast—how could everything in the world have gone so wrong so quickly? She tried to take a step and lost her balance, grabbed for Will's arm to catch herself. But he was moving away, out of her reach, and she fell, hitting her head on one of the wall's fallen stones hard enough to make the world go black.

Will saw Raynard react and whirled around, half-expecting to find his faery bride coming at him with her dagger drawn or worse. But apparently she had fainted.

"Is she alive?" Raynard asked doubtfully—weren't high-strung young ladies prone to expire from fright?

Will nodded, kneeling beside her. He touched her cheek with gloved fingertips, her lips blue with cold or shock. The same terrible pain he had felt before tore through his chest, and he hated her for making him feel it. He could almost hear Mark laughing at him from Hell or whatever pagan afterlife had claimed him. Will had believed he had won by living longer—little did he know what a trap his enemy had left behind. A faery trap baited with a tender woman's heart.

He slipped his arms beneath her, and she stirred as he picked her up, a sigh that almost sounded like his name rising to her lips. "I'll roust the men," Raynard said, turning away.

Alista was dreaming, and in her dream, she was flying. *I am fierce,* she cried in the language of flight. *I am free. I can fly.* She had dreamed this dream many times before, and it had always made her happy. But this time she was sad, the feeling she was soaring through the clouds wringing her heart with pain. Looking down, she saw a castle far below, and she longed to return there. But her wings wouldn't allow it, every beat carrying her higher and farther away. Weeping in frustration, she folded her wings across her breast, all her power focused on making no resistance as she suddenly plunged downward, rolling end over end through the whistling air toward the earthbound home she would not leave. Men were shouting, their cries growing louder, one voice rising above the rest in pain to match her own, and she opened her throat to answer—

And then she was awake.

"Be still, my love," Brother Paolo soothed, stroking her brow.

"Where is Will?" she demanded, sitting up.

"Gone to meet Sir Geoffrey's mercenaries before they can reach the castle," Brother Paolo said, moving away. "He and his captain have taken half of their forces with them, and the other half . . ." He paused as if loath to continue. "The other half are charged with guarding you lest you should try to escape."

"As if I would leave my own castle," she scoffed, bolting out of the bed.

"My lady, what happened?" He watched her throw open a trunk and start tearing through its contents.

"Somehow Will and Raynard knew I meant to meet Geoffrey," she answered, still searching. "They heard him tell me about those damned mercenaries; they just didn't wait long enough for me to tell him what I thought of them and him for bringing them." She emerged with her sword, put away since Will's arrival. "I don't know why I should be surprised."

"What is it you think you're doing?" the monk asked, alarmed. "You can't mean to go after them."

"No," she agreed. "But I will be here when they get back."

"And do what?" Brother Paolo demanded.

"Defend my home," she answered. The bump on the head she had received in the garden was throbbing steadily, making it hard to think. "Defend myself. Do something." She turned back to the Franciscan, searching for words to make him understand something she barely understood herself. "As soon as Will came here and told me Papa was dead, I surrendered, not just to Will himself, but to everything, to fate. I was so . . ." She couldn't think of a word bad enough to describe what she had felt. "I was just lost," she decided. "So I clung to Will, trusted him to do what was right, to take care of me."

"And he has treated you well," Paolo felt compelled to point out.

"Yes, except for murdering my father," she shot back. "Except for lying to me. Except for not trusting me—if he didn't see himself as my enemy, why did he ambush me and Geoffrey in the garden? Why didn't he listen to me when I tried to tell him about Geoffrey before? So long as we were alone, he treated me marvelously well, but as soon as someone else showed up, someone who knew the truth, he shut me out completely, and no matter how I tried to believe in him, he wouldn't let me."

"So I ask you again," the monk said more gently, understanding her better than she realized. "What do you intend to do?"

"I'm not sure yet," she admitted, raising her sword to see the light play along the blade. "But it won't be to sit in a corner and cry."

* * *

The battle, such as it was, was over very quickly. Will's soldiers ambushed the mercenary troops on the road while it was still full dark, beginning their attack by setting the catapult on fire with flaming arrows, along with a few mercenaries. FitzCammon lived up to his family name by turning his horse's tail and riding full speed for home, but Pettengill made a better showing, rallying his force into order with admirable efficiency. But it was a hopeless cause. Paid mercenaries fighting half-asleep were no match for the men who had followed Will to Jerusalem and back, particularly when Will led them like a man possessed by a demon. He seemed to be everywhere at once, charging Mark's warhorse into the thickest of the fight wherever it might be, slicing through the enemy with Mark's falcon sword like so much bloody wheat—somehow to use his old enemy's weapons made the fight that much more bitterly potent. In a matter of minutes, it was over. The Mark–Geoffrey partisans had thrown down their weapons and surrendered, Michael Pettengill among them.

"Where is Geoffrey?" Will demanded, riding up to him.

"You tell me," Pettengill shot back. One of his eyes was swollen half shut, and his forehead was sticky red with his own blood, but he still wore an expression of righteous indignation maddening to behold. "I left him at Brinlaw."

"You did hit him with that crossbow," Raynard pointed out, sounding unconvinced. "Maybe he bled to death."

"We should have such luck, but we don't," Will answered, grimly. His speech was slurred like he'd been drinking, and his eyelids looked hooded as he squinted into the rising sun. "Tell me where to find him, Pettengill," he demanded, drawing his sword.

"God's truth, villain, I know not," Michael said. "And if I did, I wouldn't tell you. Lady Alista is safe—"

"Lady Alista is at Brinlaw where I left her, and there she will stay!" Will cut him off loudly enough to make several of his men look up in surprise. Except in battle or sandstorms, their lord rarely raised his voice, and when he did, all hell was about to be unleashed. He wheeled Goliath around to look at the pitiful crew scattered in the roadway, battered and weaponless. "Kill them," he told Raynard, turning back. "Pettengill, too—and send someone after that coward FitzCammon." Goliath tossed his head as if to object, and Will pulled back gently on the reins. "Kill them all."

Raynard just stared at his friend, refusing to believe he was serious. "They have surrendered, Will. We can't just kill them—"

"Of course we can." Will got down off his horse with his sword still in his hand, Mark's sword, the one given to him by Mark's daughter, his false and lovely bride. He walked over to one of the mercenaries who was sitting at the edge of the road, nursing a wounded hand. In his mind, he could already see the man's head rolling into the ditch in a spurting shower of blood, the mouth still working in horrified surprise. "Watch and see," he said coldly as he raised the sword.

"No!" Raynard caught his arm in a grip of iron. "No castle is worth this," he said, meeting Will's angry eyes with his own, refusing to let go. "No castle, and no woman, either."

Will glared back at him for what seemed like an eternity. "Fine," he said at last, the fury in his gaze fading to something more like resignation. "Let them all go. Keep their weapons." He glanced back at Pettengill, now apparently dumbstruck with horror. "Give this noble knight a horse," Will finished. "The rest of these bastards can walk."

Alista stood at one of the tall, thin windows of the castle's second-floor gallery, gazing out at the road where Will and the others were riding back toward Brinlaw. Her sword dangled at her side as anger swelled inside her. *Murderer,* she thought as he rode into the courtyard, refusing to acknowledge the relief she felt as well. He was safe; he had won. Geoffrey could be dead; Michael Pettengill could be dead. Her father was dead. The wound in her palm throbbed with every beat of her heart, and her heart felt split in two. "I have to hate you," she spoke aloud, her voice echoing in the empty room. "I will hate you."

"Just what is it you mean to do, my lady?" Clarence was coming up the back stairway toward her, obviously incensed.

She looked over her shoulder at him, and her courage faltered a bit. He was strong and kind, and he had loved her father so, loved her for his sake. For a moment she wanted nothing more than to run to him and sob her heart out against his shoulder, to give him all her battles to fight as she had as a child. But she wasn't a child anymore. She was a woman, Mark of Falconskeep's daughter, and her father's blood in her veins demanded more vengeance than tears. "Will Brinlaw killed my father," she said.

"What makes you think so?" Clarence shot back as he reached her.

She looked at him, surprised. "You do not?"

He seemed to consider, his red-bearded face drawn in thought. "I cannot tell," he admitted. "If what Pettengill says is true, it looks bad, no question. But I thought you were not so convinced."

"That was before I spoke to Will himself," she answered. "He believes Papa caused his family's ruin by taking Brinlaw. He thinks Papa caused his sister's suicide."

"That could drive a man to murder, no question," Clarence nodded. A suicide was damned to Hell, a fate far worse than death. "And even knowing so little of him, I doubt Brinlaw would be squeamish about killing once he knew he had reason. But I just can't see him using poison to do it. An axe to the head, perhaps; a sword in the gullet, quite possibly; but poison? That doesn't seem like it would be his style."

Alista had already thought the same thing. Poison was a coward's weapon, and Will was certainly no coward. But she'd thought of an argument, too. "Perhaps he consulted with his king," she said. "A brawl with axes or swords would demand a royal response. A secret murder could be easily ignored and easily forgotten once Brinlaw was safely secured."

Clarence said nothing for a long moment, then he nodded. "That would make your husband a villain indeed."

She smiled bitterly. "That was my thought."

He put a hand on her shoulder and turned her to face him, his gaze taking in her costume and her sword. "If you fight him—"

"If I don't, I'm a coward and worse," she cut him off before he could finish. She knew what he would say, that Will would kill her, and she didn't want to hear it—perhaps she didn't care. "You don't understand; you can't," she went on, shame blushing red in her face. "I slept with him, Clarence. I gave him my father's sword. You and Papa brought me up to think better of myself than that, to have honor. I can't let him get away with that. I have to try."

The castellan was still frowning, but he nodded. "Then show me what you can do."

A stench to bring tears to the eyes assaulted Will as soon as he came into the Great Hall. "What the hell is that?" Raynard demanded, similarly appalled.

"Walnut hulls and tanner's acid," Sophie finally offered when no one else would speak. Indeed, everyone else was staring at Brinlaw's lord and his captain with undisguised suspicion, and their soldiers were being ignored.

"Why?" Will asked the girl, returning the household's looks in kind.

Sophie turned pale as milk, her eyes wide with apprehension. "For Lady Alista's clothes," she answered. "She told us to dye them all black, for mourning for Lord—for her father."

Will let this one lie. "Where is Lady Alista now?" he asked.

"Truly, my lord, I don't know," she said. "She went back upstairs. Brother Paolo is in the solar—"

"We'll find her," Raynard promised, giving the poor girl a wink to calm her down.

"I'll find her," Will corrected. "You assemble the household. Every man, woman, and child in this castle will swear their oath to me as lord, or they can take their chances with the snow." He met the eyes of one of Mark's guardsmen. "Any soldier who refuses my oath will be considered a traitor and an enemy to this house and will be put to death."

If Raynard hadn't just seen his friend threaten to hack off a mercenary's head, he would have thought this an empty threat made for effect, but now he wasn't so sure. Even so, he thought the plan a sound one. "As you will, my lord," he said.

"My lord, what of Michael Pettengill?" Brother Paolo's voice rose over the general murmur of dismay as he came out of the solar, clear and calm as ever.

Will stopped to meet his eyes as well. "Pettengill lives," he answered. "For that you may thank the captain." Looking around his hall once more, he turned to go and find his wife.

Alista's arms were aching, but the sword felt good in her hands, the chafe of the tight leather glove against her wounded palm a sweetly stinging goad. She brought the sword down with a scream from the bottom of her soul, a long arc from above her head with all her might flowing through it to crash into Clarence's parry, the clashing recoil powering another slashing stroke. She pushed on in her advance, every beam of concentration focused on the fight until the castellan's familiar face lost all meaning for her; all meaning in everything was lost in a pure desire to prevail, the rhythmic clang and scrape of swords no more or less than the music of her blood. *I am fierce; I am strong; I can kill.* Clarence was starting to tire, no longer fighting, only fighting back, backing ever closer to the rough stone wall, and her blood sang out with bitter joy. She was winning; she would beat him.

She heard someone approaching from behind her, running hard, and the metallic hiss of a sword being drawn, and she whirled around, her own sword raised, a circling swing into bone-jarring contact. "Alista, no!" Clarence roared as his pupil raised her sword against her husband.

To Will's relief as much as the castellan's, she froze, the

shrunken sword she wielded glittering in the early morning light. Will was frozen, too, his heart pounding behind his labored breath. He had been on his way to the master bedroom when he had heard a woman's shriek and the clash of swords coming from this long, bare gallery. He had broken immediately into a run, drawing his sword as he turned the corner, certain that Geoffrey had returned. But instead of the Angevin knight, Will found himself confronted with his own fragile wife, still dressed in tunic and leggings, armed with a sword, her delicate features in a grimace of murderous rage that left no doubt to her intentions. She meant to strike him dead.

"Alista, stop it," Clarence ordered, dropping his own sword as a pair of Will's guardsmen came clattering up the stairs with their weapons drawn.

"No," she said softly, her eyes locked to Will's.

"Alista," Clarence urged as the guardsmen froze, uncertain what to do next.

She slowly lowered her sword. "As you wish."

Will let his own sword fall, his heartbeat returning to something closer to normal. "You must be starved for entertainment, Clarence," he said coldly. "You're reduced to sparring with children." He turned his back on his wife to face his guardsmen. "Take him downstairs with the others."

"I don't need to be taken," Clarence answered, a dangerous reproach in his tone. "I will go." Sending his pupil a warning with his eyes, he led the guards away.

Alista watched him go, a lethal calm falling over her. Whatever was to come, it could hurt her no more deeply. "I have bad news for you, lady," Will was saying as they were left alone. Her black eyes narrowed, and her hand flexed on the hilt of her sword.

A smear of blood stained her forearm below her leather gauntlet—her wound from the pyre was bleeding. But she didn't seem to care or even notice, so focused was she on hating him. "Your lover has left you to your fate," he continued. "You and his troops as well."

She turned to him, almost laughing. "Which lover would that be, my lord?"

For a moment, his heart leapt up, but he would not be deceived. "Geoffrey d'Anjou," he said, scowling. "The knight you love so much you risked your life to save him last night, or have you forgotten? You're fortunate my reflexes are so quick."

"Aye, Will, I love Geoffrey," she said bitterly. "I love him so well that I married him the same night we met and took him to my bed the next. I hold Geoffrey in such tender esteem, I gave him my castle and my father's sword, entrusting him with the protection of everything I hold dear. I have Geoffrey so deep in my heart that when someone suggested he had murdered my father, the person I have loved above all others since I was four years old, I refused to believe them because I so trusted his honor." She stopped, an expression of mocking inspiration on her face. "But wait! That wasn't Geoffrey."

"It was Geoffrey you met in secret," he pointed out, refusing to be moved. "It was Geoffrey with whom you meant to flee—"

"I would never have left Brinlaw," she insisted. "I met with Geoffrey to make him leave me alone."

"Aye, lady, he looked positively heartbroken, you were repelling his advances so severely," he said sarcastically.

"I wanted him to tell me what happened to my father," she shot back. "I wanted him to tell me the truth."

"The truth is your father is dead," he answered, turning away from the accusation in her eyes. "What else could you need to know?"

She didn't allow herself to think or even to see him, only attacked, screaming wordless rage. Will turned barely in time to save himself from having the sword he had so maligned buried in his shoulder deep enough to cleave his heart. He knocked her blade aside with sufficient force to send her reeling; she did not fall but rather came at him again, slashing for his open side with the clever quickness of a seasoned fighter. He spun and feinted her back again, but still she refused to give way. "Alista, stop it!" he ordered, striking her blade away with his own, this time switching back to defend himself. "I have no wish to hurt you."

"Too late, you lying bastard," she swore back through clenched teeth. She desperately wanted to hurt him, to slice past his smug lies and false comfort until she saw him plainly, made him bleed as her heart bled. She struck at him again, and again he drove her back, but she could see fury dawning in his eyes, and she rejoiced in it, striking with all her strength.

Will had finally had enough. Lunging full force, he struck her sword hard enough to break her arms if she did not yield, letting his own fall as he drove her to the floor, pinning her down with his full length and weight. "I have never lied to you," he insisted, his face looming over her own, close enough for a kiss.

"Then tell me how my father chose you," she snarled, writhing furiously to escape. "Tell me how you were his friend."

"Stop it," he ordered, his grip tightening on the wrist of the hand that held her sword. He bashed it against the hard floor again and again until the fist unclenched and the sword skittered away across the stone.

"Finish me!" she screamed, tearful and furious. "Kill me if you want my lands! Is that not what you would do if I were my father's son?" She must have seen the horror in his eyes, for she laughed aloud through a sob, the sound of madness. "You murdered my father—is killing me this way any worse? You see how easily you can beat me; you won't even need to use poison."

She saw his eyes change, saw he meant to give her what she sought, and she reached for her dagger with her free left hand, meaning to take him as close to Hell as she might before he killed her. But as she drew the knife, he let her go, suddenly moved away, and the blade slashed across his cheek, opening a gash that immediately poured blood.

"Oh sweet Christ," she breathed, backing away across the floor as he stood up, the dagger still clenched in her fist, his blood wet scarlet on the blade. "Will . . ." A moment ago, she had wanted him dead, her very soul had howled for it, but now the sight of his blood sickened her, made her rage melt into horror. He was Will, her father's murderer—she should be thrilled to see him bleed, to know that she had slashed his flesh. But he was Will, her husband, and to hurt him tore at her heart.

Will barely seemed to notice the wound; his furious eyes were fixed without wavering on her face. He grabbed the front of her tunic and yanked her to her feet, the dagger falling with a clatter to the floor. "Your father did not choose me, any more than I chose you," he said in a voice as horribly cold and clear as the blue ice of his eyes. "But I didn't kill him. I wanted to—I would have, in time. But he died before I could, denying me the chance to win my castle back just as Henry denied me the right to claim it. So to have what was mine without committing treason, I listened to Mark's friend, my king. I took a wife I didn't want, a spoiled, unnatural brat I had never laid eyes on before so she wouldn't be turned out of her home and Henry wouldn't have to feel guilty. Only now it seems my wife does not thank me for this kindness. She wants to see me dead." His hand closed around her throat as she backed into the wall, no pressure but a threat. "This innocent creature for whom the King felt such pity is a faithless harlot whose lover brought an army against me." His grip tightened as he leaned closer, so close she felt his blood on her own skin. "You say you want me to kill you," he said so softly his voice was like the growl of a wolf. "What makes you believe I cannot?"

"Stop!" Brother Paolo cried, running up the stairs with no thought for his age or office. "I beg you, let her go!"

Will did as the Franciscan ordered, his grip on Alista's throat relaxing and falling away. He thought she would break free and run to the priest for protection, but she didn't budge, just stood and stared at him with her witch-black eyes.

Paolo saw the blood streaming down the knight's cheek like a flood of scarlet tears, and his hand went to his rosary, his heart pounding even harder. "Alista, what have you done?" he breathed. She had taken a weapon and shed her husband's blood; by the laws of man and even of the Church, this knight could take her life. "Please, my lord," he said, fighting back pride and anger as the sins they were. "She is but a child."

Will looked at him, then back at Alista. "Do you hear, sweet love?" he asked, his voice a deep-throated rasp that made him seem possessed by a demon. "Your priest would not have me oblige you. He would have me let you live."

"What do you care?" Alista retorted, her voice raw with tears or pain. "Don't you hate him, too?"

"Alista!" Paolo rushed forward and put himself between them. "Are you mad?"

Something about this question made the knight laugh so loudly the sound echoed through the rafters, but he said nothing, only turned and walked away.

Druscilla worked at her loom as the household and garrison assembled in the hall. The stench of Alista's clothes being dyed was making her stomach roll, and she struggled to concentrate on the bright threads of her weaving, gold and red worked with painstaking care into a background of deep blue, a falcon on a midnight sky—Mark's crest, the symbol of her despair.

Raynard was watching Druscilla so intently that for a long moment he didn't notice that the crowded hall had suddenly fallen silent. Then he turned and saw Will's face.

"Sweet Christ," he swore, all else forgotten at the sight of his friend's blood. "What did she—"

But Will wasn't listening, had walked straight past him to Druscilla. She was obviously appalled at the sight of him, blood soaking his tunic and rage in his eyes. She dropped her shuttle, and her face went white as milk, but she didn't get up from her seat, only looked up at him. "Tell me about Geoffrey," Will said with no preamble or effort to mask his anger, and no one in the hall could doubt just whom he meant. "Why did he come to Alista?"

"I know nothing of my lady's affairs," Druscilla answered, her chin defiant in spite of the quaver in her voice. "What Sir Geoffrey may have been to her is no business of mine."

"Will, you're bleeding," Raynard said. "Where is—"

"What is he to you?" Will interrupted, still glaring down on the girl.

"He was Lord Mark's friend, as you well know, my lord," she answered. She was trembling all over, and the hall seemed to waver behind Brinlaw's head until all she could see was his furious face, the cheek laid open almost to the bone. *He's killed her,* she thought, a fresh wave of nausea rising from her stomach. *She tried to fight him, and he has killed Alista.* She opened her mouth to speak, but no more words would come.

"Mark's friend," Will repeated. The pain in his cheek was getting worse, making him feel drunk. He had fought wounded in more battles that he could remember, the sting spurring the rage that made him lethal. His eyes focused on the loom, on the half-formed falcon's crest, Mark's crest, the traitor's banner being worked in Brinlaw's hall to hang over Brinlaw's hearth to comfort Mark's daughter, feed her hatred for her father's enemy.

He grabbed the loom and flung it against the table, barely hearing Druscilla's scream. He grabbed it again and dashed it against the gray stone chimney, the frame splintering and splitting apart, the threads tangling and twisting free. Raynard made a grab for him, but Will shoved him away, turned back as Druscilla tried to salvage her work, scrambling on her knees, and he snatched it back from her reach. "No!" she wailed as he flung the entire mess, broken wood and ripped tapestry and all into the fire.

Turning, he saw her weep, but he felt nothing. One of the other women came closer as if to comfort the girl, and he turned his gaze on her until she backed away again. "Leave it," he said, turning to include all who were present in the hall. "Let it burn."

Clarence had stood up as soon as he saw Will's face. Now he turned and quickly left the hall. Raynard saw a deadly flicker in his friend's eyes, a deadness in the blue he had hoped to never see again once they were back in England. "Come on, Will," he urged softly, not touching him for fear of setting him off again. "Let someone see to that cut."

Will looked at him. "No . . ." He turned and left the hall.

"Sweet Christ," Raynard repeated. Grabbing a rag from one of the stunned silent laundresses, he ran out after him.

Druscilla watched them go, felt the blood begin to flow back into her fingers and toes, the fist of fear begin to loosen from around her heart. The burning loom was splayed half out of the fireplace, and the flames were licking ever closer to her skirts as if reaching out for her. She stood up slowly, tried to take a step back, and fainted dead away.

By the time Alista reached the top of the narrow, winding stairs, her lungs felt raw from the climb, but still she gulped in the freezing wind as if she would perish without it. She leaned against the tower's jagged crown of stone and carefully unwrapped the bandage from around her hand and wrist, sticky again with blood. She flexed her fingers, wincing a little at the pain and the sight of the darkening bruises, a perfect pattern of her husband's fingers . . . her husband. The thought made her close her eyes and breathe deeper through her nose. She turned to lean out into the wind, let it tear at her hair and clothes. Opening her eyes, she looked down on the courtyard, saw a figure come out and head for the stables with another close on his heels: Will of Brinlaw and his captain. "May you break your neck, you bastard," she swore, the words torn from her lips by the raging wind, tears stinging her cheeks like crystals of burning ice.

She had never been so afraid in her life. She felt lost and trapped, not only in this castle that should have been hers but was not, but inside her own soul as well; her heart seemed to have been stolen from her as surely as her inheritance. "Dear Father in Heaven, help me know what I should do," she whispered, her hands clasped tight beneath her chin. "I want to do Your will, I swear it, whatever that may be . . ." She fell to her knees, her chin now level with the broken opening in the turret. "Papa, please forgive me . . . I swear I didn't know. . . ." Even now, she believed Will when he said he hadn't killed Mark—why would he bother to lie? She tried to remember the first time she had seen him, but the first image of his face wouldn't come clear, was lost in a memory-fog of pouring rain and the freezing shock of hearing her father was dead. The Will-face that haunted her had come later, bending close to kiss away her tears after the funeral, gazing down on her as she held him close after he dreamed of horrors. She threw back her head and screamed, her cry caught by the wind like the murder-scream of a hawk. How could that tender knight be the calculating bastard who had hated her father, who had only married her to capture a castle?

"It can't be true," she insisted to the wind, her forehead pressed to jagged stone, rolling back and forth in desperate denial. "He can't . . ." She grabbed the ledge to pull herself back to her feet and cried out in physical pain, her damaged wrist giving way with an ominous pop. "Damn you!" she swore, cradling it in her other hand. "Bastard . . ." Will was also the brute who had thrown her down and likely broken her wrist, his kisses be damned. That she'd been doing her best to kill him at the time was entirely beside the point.

She let out a dismayed little snort of laughter at her own folly. Even now she wanted him there, wanted to feel his arms around her and hear him murmur softly that all would be well, that tender lion's growl that had made her believe it was true, that he was her true heart's love. Unlike most churchmen, Brother Paolo had never lingered overmuch on the natural affinity for lust and evil that lurked in every woman's heart, but Alista was familiar with the concept, and now she knew it to be true. One night in a pretty devil's bed, and she was ready to betray a lifetime's love and duty. And he didn't even want her. He had called her an unnatural brat, a faithless harlot. . . . "Forgive me," she repeated, crossing herself, though even she couldn't tell which Father she begged for pardon. Lust was a grievous sin, and she owed her father all loyalty . . . but was hatred not a sin as well? Whatever Will might have done or felt or said, he was her husband. Could it be right that she should hate the man to whom she had sworn her obedience before God? But this was more woman's trickery—Will was a liar, had lied in their marriage, had lied before God in pretending to be her father's choice. His vows meant nothing, and neither should hers.

She looked up at the lowering, gray clouds the wind was sweeping across the sky, and her thoughts flew to the white falcon that had fallen to her death in a savage act of will. She remembered her screams in the mews, her desperate raging to be free at any cost, and her own heart seemed to cry out in perfect sympathy. She must escape; there must be a way to escape. . . .

She climbed up on the ledge, her uninjured hand clinging to the rough stone. The cold wind felt good to her, an element more natural to her spirit than any warm embrace. Her head fell back, her hair raked back from her face by icy fingers, and a cry rose to her lips, a challenge to the empty air. She didn't even feel the cold anymore, and the wind seemed to flow through her, a part of her, like blood.

She looked down at the courtyard so far below, and it seemed to be receding even farther, as if she were rising away, free of Brinlaw, free of care. She seemed to hear her mother's voice in the wind, a hundred voices that were both strange and familiar as her own secret thoughts, except she couldn't think. A moment ago, she had been unhappy and in pain, but now she felt light and whole, not happy, but serene, accepting of the wind that combed her thoughts into meaningless shreds like the clouds that now seemed close enough to touch. She reached out . . .

A sudden, sharp pain snatched her backward—her throbbing wrist as she let go of the stone. Suddenly she was afraid, dizzy and sick, clambering back down from the ledge, her body wracked with bitter cold.

Paolo had sent Alista to his rooms to wait for him to bring back a fresh bandage and placate the furious Clarence, but when he returned she wasn't there, and he wasn't surprised. This airy perch had been her favorite refuge since the day it was completed. But now that he'd finally made it to the top and saw her, he was alarmed—the fear on her face was like a kind of madness. "Cara mia, what is it?" he demanded, finding fresh reserves of strength to rush to her side.

At first she didn't answer, only turned and flung herself into his arms. "It's all right," she insisted at last, sounding as if she meant to convince herself as much as him. "I'm all right."

"Of course," he agreed, holding her tight. "Of course you are."

She drew back to look at him. "I don't know what to do."

He touched her cheek, trying to manage a smile. How cruel it was that in grief she should look more like her mother than she did at any other time. "Never fear, my child," he promised. "We will think of something."

Raynard rounded the corner just as a groom stumbled out through the stable door. "Never mind," he assured the poor man, shouting to make himself heard over the gusts of keening wind that seemed to have blown up from nowhere in an instant. "Go inside and get warm—we'll not take a horse out in this."

The man looked doubtful. "He's bleeding and mad as Satan," he warned.

"All the more reason to leave him alone," Raynard replied. "I only wish I could do the same."

Once the heavy door was shut on the storming fury outside, inside the stable was warm and still, and Will, when he found him, seemed to have quieted as well. He was standing in the stall of Mark's destrier, both hands laid on the horse's massive shoulder as if in a lingering caress. "He seems to be getting used to me," he said as Raynard approached the stall. He reached up to scratch the back of the powerful neck where the mane was cropped short to accommodate armor, and as if to agree, the horse let out a nickering snort and bobbed his head over his shoulder.

"Mark called him Goliath, I believe," Raynard answered easily, as if they were having the most casual of conversations with nothing at all amiss. Will's cheek was still bleeding, but not so much, and the cut, now that he was close enough to see it, looked deep, but not jagged, easy to stitch. "So tell me, how were you wounded?"

"Quite cleverly, since you ask," Will answered, running a palm along Goliath's back, gently checking for knots or abrasions a saddle might have rubbed into his coat. "I was taking away my wife's sword, and she slashed me with her dagger."

Raynard had to take several deep swallows of hay-sweetened air before he could calmly reply. "That was clever," he agreed. Will glanced back at him, and he held out the scrap of rag he'd brought out to stanch Will's wound. After a moment, Will took it, and for some stupid reason this made the Fleming feel better. "So what did you do then?"

"Nothing." Will dabbed his bloody cheek with the cloth and seemed surprised to see it stained bright red. "I left her with the friar." He went back to stroking the horse with his right hand while he held the cloth to his face with his left. "I think he believed I would kill her."

"I'm surprised you didn't," Raynard said bluntly. "She shed your blood, Will, the law gives you the right as her husband—"

"My right as her husband is why we fought," Will cut him off. He felt sick; his head was swimming, and he leaned closer to Goliath, resting his unwounded cheek on the warm, sleek coat. He could hear the steady rhythm of the massive heart, feel the rise and fall of breath, and it soothed and saddened him at the same time. In battle, he had often seen a beast like this charge forward in eye-rolling fury even after its master lay dead, and he had felt a love as pure and simple as the rage that drove him to fight just as these dumb warriors were driven to fight. He had thought no other earthly feeling could touch him so deeply and completely, and he wanted to weep, knowing now it wasn't so. He thought of Alista, fragile as a reed in her muddy shift, holding this great beast fast by the reins, thought of the fury in her eyes as she'd struck at him again and again. "I never wanted this," he said, speaking as much to Goliath as to Raynard. "When I swore I would fight for Brinlaw, I never meant—"

"Of course you did not," Raynard interrupted, brusque with relief he could admit and sympathy he could not. "Henry should have given you Brinlaw outright and found someone else to marry Mark's daughter."

"Like Geoffrey?" Will asked softly.

"Like who cares?" Raynard shot back. "At least now you don't have to pretend anymore. You can put her away as you always intended. Once your marriage to this lunatic is annulled, you can take a wife of your own choosing, a sane and proper woman who can give you that family you're so damned determined to have."

As he'd spoken, Will had turned to him with eyes like a frozen sea. "And that's what you advise me to do?"

Raynard thought of the unmistakable madness in his friend's eyes as he broke a woman's loom to pieces, the terror in Druscilla's face as he did it. He remembered that morning when Will had tried to murder a wounded mercenary just to ease his rage. "Yes," he answered. "I think it's the only choice you have now, with circumstances as they are."

Will continued to stare at him with no expression whatsoever on his face. "Thank you," he said at last, so softly Raynard barely heard. "You're right, of course. Any man would say the same."

"But you won't listen," Raynard said. "You won't do as I ask, even for your own sake."

Will looked away. "I don't know."

"Lord Brinlaw." Turning, they found Brother Paolo, a tall, thin accusation in brown wool whipping in the wind as he stood in the open stable door. "My lord, I would speak to you."

Paolo watched the younger man's face turn to stone—a defense or an attack? "Speak, then," he said, turning away again.

"I should warn you, Brother, we're neither of us over-fond of priests," Raynard said.

"No matter," Paolo retorted. "I don't particularly care for you, either."

"So why are you here?" Will interrupted, impatient. "What is it that you want?"

"To leave this place," Paolo answered. "To return to Florence and take Lady Alista with me."

Raynard couldn't have been more pleased if he'd devised the plan himself, but best to be cautious just the same. "What of Brinlaw, Brother, and your lady's marriage?" he innocently asked.

"The castle and lands will be yours," Paolo went on, still talking to Will's back. "Once Lord Mark's daughter is gone from England, none will dare dispute your claim. As for your marriage, when enough time has passed, it can be dissolved. I will write to the bishop myself."

" 'Tis sad to think of," Raynard said when Will still didn't answer. "But it may be the kindest solution—"

"What does Alista say?" Will turned, and though his expression was as blank as ever, his eyes were alive with powerful feeling. "This kind solution—does she wish it?"

"She believes it to be best," Paolo answered carefully.

"She is wise beyond her years, I think," Raynard said sagely, silently willing his friend to be the same.

Will looked at both of them in turn. "Where is she now?"

"She isn't well," Paolo answered. "She is resting—my lord!" He chased the knight across the courtyard with the captain close behind.

Will stalked through the hall and up the stairs. "Alista!" he yelled, pounding on the chamber door hard enough to bruise his fist. The friar, panting from his sprint, tried to pull him back, but he pushed him aside. "Alista! Open this door, right now!"

"Lord William, listen to me," Paolo persisted, refusing to be shook off. "If you break this door, Alista will never look on you again with anything but fear—"

The door opened. "I do not fear him, Brother," Alista said calmly. "What is it you want?"

"Nay, lady, not me, but you," Will said, stopping short. Her voice was cold; her eyes looked almost dead, they were so dull. Even when she had grieved for her father, weeping until her eyes were red and swollen, she had seemed warm and alive, a creature of magical vitality. Now she looked like a beautiful corpse. "What do you want?" he went on more gently. "Do you want to go to Florence?"

"Does it matter what I want?" she asked in that same deadened tone. "Do you not despise me?"

"Alista," the priest warned, turning pale.

"Whether it matters or not, I want to hear," Will answered her.

"I want you to go away." She looked up at him, her face like a mask. "I want my castle back. I want you to leave us in peace."

"Brinlaw is mine," he answered without raising his voice. "I will never give it up."

"Then yes, I want to go. I have to go." *I want to forget all the things that hurt me, the things I never wanted to know,* she spoke in her heart. *I want to go back in time to when I believed in you, just two days back to when I believed you were mine, that I could be yours forever.* "I hate you," she went on aloud. His expression didn't change—he didn't care. The torchlight danced over his features, turning his face to a mask of demonic cruelty in one instant and angelic beauty in the next. The gash she had put in his cheek only enhanced the illusion.

"I didn't kill your father," he said.

"But you wanted to kill him, and that is almost the same thing," she answered, cutting him off. "You would have." *You don't want me,* the voice inside her added. "And if I stay here, I will have to kill you or die in the attempt."

"Alista!" Brother Paolo cried, appalled.

In truth, Will's heart froze at this, not in fear but in hurt. But his face and manner didn't change. "You may hate me if you must," he said. "In your place I would do the same. But you won't leave me, not unless you do kill me or die."

"Santa Maria, stop it!" Paolo swore, shaken. "You must not say such things, either of you! You must not tempt God so—"

"Or what?" Will demanded, turning on him. "He will

grant our prayers? Believe me, old man, it isn't that easy."

"No," Alista agreed. "It isn't."

"I won't have you running to Geoffrey, inciting him to lay siege to my castle," Will went on, speaking to Alista like the others had simply disappeared. "But I will strike you a deal."

"What sort of deal?" she asked, taking a wary step back.

"I won't trouble you, and you won't trouble me." He pushed past her into the bedroom and opened her trunk, tossing through it until he found her sword. "No more surprise attacks." He held out his hand. "Your dagger, if you please."

"No," she said, backing away from him.

His face darkened. "Would you rather I take it by force?"

"Alista, please," Brother Paolo urged.

She took the weapon from her belt and handed it over to him. "Anything else?"

"No. Have we a deal?" When she didn't answer, he leaned closer, scowling, the dark gash livid against his sun-browned cheek. "Alista?"

"Yes," she said, struggling to find her voice. She saw his eyes close, watched, paralyzed, as he leaned closer. His mouth came down hard on hers, possessive and demanding, and for a terrible moment, her body longed to give in; her hands slid over his shoulders. . . .

He tasted her startled gasp of breath, but she was touching him, yielding . . . then the sharp little teeth sank into his lip. He jerked back, and she let him, a feral snarl on her pretty face with its halo of disheveled curls. "Aye, lady," he said bitterly, turning away. He walked out with his captain close behind him.

"Alista," Brother Paolo began. "You must—"

"No," she cut him off, a flash of anger in her eyes. "No more. Do not tell me anymore what I must do." His brown eyes looked stricken, making her feel worse. "Please, Brother, just leave me alone," she asked more gently, almost pleading. "Go and see to Druscilla."

"All right, my love," he said wearily. Kissing her once on the forehead, he left her alone as she wished.

She listened to him go, silent tears sliding a well-worn path down her cheeks. She met her own eyes in her wavering reflection in the mirror. She remembered him untangling her hair, watching her reflection in the mirror, watching him. She closed her eyes, and she could see his face, feel his touch on her skin, his heartbeat so close it had felt like her own in the darkness.

She opened her eyes and looked at her reflection again, trying to see what Will saw, what he would remember. She unfastened the clasp that held her braids and ripped the waves free with her fingers. Opening a box on the table, she found another, smaller dagger Will hadn't known was there. Raising it, she she touched the blade to her cheek, remembering the way Will's cheek had bled. With another deep breath, she hacked off a thick, black lock of hair and let it fall to the floor. She reached for another . . . but she couldn't do it, not even this much. Letting the dagger fall, she dropped her head to her hands and wept.

Seven

A letter of Fra Paolo Bosacci to his sister, Serena
Brinlaw Castle

February 1, 1155

My dearest friend,

Again, I come to you with troubled heart and mind. This house remains split in two, and I can see no means of bringing it together again. My sweet Alista is miserable, and for once nothing I can say or do can comfort her. She remains certain that while William Brinlaw may not have murdered her father with his own hands, he wished him naught but ill and took joy in his death as well as his castle, lied to her to have it, and for these things she cannot forgive him. And there is something else, something I wish you, with your many daughters, were here to see and put right, for it is beyond my ken. I am so accustomed to thinking of Alista as a child with a child's simplicity of passions, it is hard for me to imagine and sympathize with all the layers of feeling involved in her relationship with this Brinlaw. She has not confided in me (another source of anguish for both of us that I cannot hope to ease!), but I know that for the brief time they were truly together, she believed him to be her soul mate, that her father had seen him as such. Now she believes he never cared for her at all, that he only married her for the sake of convenience and pity and that in fact he has come to despise her. I believe that this as much as Brinlaw's enmity to Mark fuels her hatred of him. She has not said again that she will actually do him harm, nor has she made another attempt to harm herself (may God be praised!), and I trust in her good virtues enough to believe that she will not, but to see her, a pure soul that has never known anything but love, feel such bitter hatred breaks my heart. Sometimes I believe it is more than either of us can bear.

Brinlaw, for his part, while he seems to take pleasure in his role as this manor's lord, continues to believe Alista meant to disregard her forced marriage vows to be with Geoffrey d'Anjou, and nothing I or anyone else can say will dissuade him. He has made his room in the castle tower, leaving the room Mark once used to Alista, including the massive bed. The only furnishing from that room he has insisted on having is the bedrug, the pelt of the wolf Alista somehow managed to slay so long ago. I do not know if he has taken it because the thing itself pleases him or because to lose it hurts Alista, but in either case she is sorely vexed, seeing the wolfskin as a kind of talisman of her father.

But Mark has left a far more powerful symbol of himself behind. His young mistress, Druscilla, is with child. Needless to say, Brinlaw's new lord is not pleased. I would hesitate to even relate the words that passed between him and Alista when he heard of it except that from them you can see just how hurtful their relations have become.

She told him in the hall at dinner before the entire

household, all but daring him to make a scene. "The child is my father's, of course," she finished. "Dru says it will be born in August."

He did not disappoint her. "Not in this house, it won't."

She put down her knife as if to stop herself from stabbing him with it. "You would turn my friend and my father's unborn child out of my house into the woods?"

"My house, lady, and no, I would not." He looked at Druscilla with no trace of shame, as if he didn't know or didn't care how deeply his words must wound her. "She and her child may go to a convent or return to France or wherever she came from in the first place."

"Whatever great wrong may have been done your father by the King who is dead, this house is only yours because you are my husband by authority of the King who lives," Alista answered, standing up to face him. "And if this child is not born in this house, I swear to you no other ever will be."

Everyone could see his face go pale, but Brinlaw kept his seat. "That seems highly unlikely in any case, wouldn't you say, dear wife?" he answered her quite calmly as he went back to his meat. "Or did your father and the friar neglect to tell you how babies are made?"

"I thought I knew, but nothing I have seen for myself resembles what my father's women described," she replied. Serena, living in the gentler society of Florence, you cannot begin to imagine the reaction of the people in the hall to this confrontation. They were like spectators at a public duel, eagerly waiting for blood to be spilled. "But then," Alista continued, "they all rather fancied my father."

Brinlaw actually smiled. "And since he never married any of them, we can assume they were chosen for something other than property."

Alista went red as a berry, and I could happily have throttled him, priest or not. "But I am your wife, and while I live this property is mine if it is yours," she said. "This child will be my kin, and I will see it born and reared safely in its own home."

He was still smiling, but his eyes did not look amused. "We shall see. I look forward to being convinced."

So you see, dear sister, what a chaos this castle has become.

Time passed, and the winter grew colder, both outside Brinlaw Castle and within. The old lord was dead; the new lord was either a hero or the devil incarnate, depending on who was asked. The young mistress, who by all rights ought to have been the one to reconcile the two opinions, had apparently lost her mind. None of the castle's longtime residents could believe that Alista had plotted romantic treachery with Geoffrey d'Anjou or anyone else; all of the newcomers were certain of it. None of Will's men could begin to believe he was a cold-blooded murderer; every castle servant and old guardsman knew it must be so no matter what Will or even Alista said to the contrary.

"What good would it do to marry her if her father weren't dead first?" Sophie demanded of Rolf the soldier as he kept her early morning company in the kitchen. "He killed him sure as the world."

"He has the King in his saddlebags, girl. He didn't need to kill anybody to have his own way." Rolf also knew that if Will Brinlaw had taken a notion to do a killing, he'd have whacked off the old goat's head in the middle of London at noon before he'd resort to poison, but this he prudently kept to himself.

" 'Twas the King's own cousin who accused him, in case you've forgot," she scoffed, punching her bread dough.

"For all that means," Rolf chuckled. "The King has more cousins than French Louis has pimples on his arse, love. He can't be expected to keep his eye on every one."

"So Sir Geoffrey is a liar?"

"Aye, and a dog besides." Rolf took a long swallow to quench his rage on his lord's behalf. "Your lady should count herself lucky to be rid of him, no matter what she thinks."

"Now, see, I'm not certain she's so sorry Geoffrey's gone." She heaved the dough into a bowl and scooped another lump into the kneading trough. "You don't know Lady Alista; none of you do. She liked Sir Geoffrey well enough, but love him? I don't see it." In truth, Sophie had only seen her young mistress doe-eyed over one man—this scoundrel's lord. But she'd die and be damned before she'd say as much to Rolf. "She's barely more than a child with not a treacherous bone in her body."

"I'd expect a pretty wench to say as much, Sophie," Rolf grinned over his cup. "Every bone in every woman's body is treacherous from the day she is born, and the flesh over the bone is what leads a man to ruin."

The wad of dough was big enough to make three loaves and it caught him squarely in the face, bashing his cup against his teeth and sending him over backward. "There's a bit of women's treachery for you," Sophie laughed. "May you take good nourishment from it."

This exchange might have lightened Will's spirits had he been there to see it; as it was, he was still worried. "This can't go on all winter," he was complaining to Raynard in the privacy of his tower room, meaning his wife's behavior.

She didn't shirk her duties as housekeeper overmuch, when she deigned to come downstairs, and since their public brawl about her father's bastard, she rarely passed a cross word with her husband—indeed, she rarely spoke to him at all. Her bedroom door remained bolted against him, and her manner was even more forbidding. In short, she was playing the martyr, making him the villain, and anything he did to stop her would only prove her point. "The entire household is in chaos—I can't wait any longer for her to come to her senses."

"Assuming she ever does," Raynard agreed. Will still seemed determined to believe Alista's current manner was no more than a symptom of her grief. After a month, the captain was more inclined to consider it a permanent condition.

"Assuming that, yes," Will conceded, unwilling to reopen the question. "Either way, we all need more to do than huddle by the fires and make faces at one another. That's why I have the men rebuilding the walls, trying to keep them busy."

"I know, my lord, I know," Raynard said sympathetically. In Will's place, he fancied he would have had no such worries. Requiring the new oath of fealty had been a definite step in the right direction, but Will hadn't properly followed up, at least not to Raynard's way of thinking. Everyone in the house and garrison had sworn their oaths with sullen courtesy, but there were still many obvious malcontents dragging about the castle and whining that their beloved Lady Alista was being horribly abused. These Raynard would have treated to a refreshing dose of the flogging rope, and any that still couldn't find something to smile about would find themselves making whatever accommodation they could manage with the bitter winter weather, just as Will had threatened. As for Mark's murderous brat, he would slap her in the nearest nunnery for the good of her twisted little soul. Before they had come to Brinlaw, he had fully expected Will would do the same—they had learned such methods together. But now he feared something far less satisfying and more complicated would be more to his friend's liking. "So what do you mean to do?"

"Finish fixing the wall, no matter how much they complain," Will began, counting off his list. "Open up all the unused rooms in the castle to accommodate a larger household. If Henry sends me any more knights to keep warm, I'll have to start setting them on fire. Build collapsible shelters to be stored inside the walls for villagers in a siege or troops in an invasion—like the ones we saw in the East."

"And turn two garrisons into one by training them together so hard they hate us too much to hate one another," Raynard grinned, relieved. "That part I can help you with, and the building, too, but I'm a dead loss cleaning house."

"The household isn't your job, or mine either," Will said grimly, setting his jaw for battle. "But I do know whose it is."

A similar conversation was taking place upstairs. "Where are they all coming from?" Druscilla was complaining, spinning by the fire in Brother Paolo's room. "Holes in the ground?"

Brinlaw was crawling with new arrivals with more turning up every day. Many of King Henry's new-made knights, having neither wife nor war to think of, had come to ally themselves with Will, to swear service and tie their hopes to his success. More unexpected were the common people who seemed to just appear out of the forest, sometimes alone but more often as whole families, two or three generations' worth.

"I suspect they feel they've come home," Brother Paolo answered mildly. "Most of them tell me they were born here; some of the older men say they helped Lord William's father build this castle when he first came here from France."

Alista, who'd been staring out the window again, turned to him at this. "Will's father built Brinlaw?"

"Yes, of course," Paolo said, watching her. She wore a thick, black tunic with a heavy cowl over her shirt and breeches to ward off the chill, and with her hair braided back from her face, she could easily have passed for a delicate boy, a sickly young scholar perhaps. "You knew that, Alista."

"I knew old Henry made him lord when the manor was created," she said, turning again to lean against the window frame, arms folded across her chest. "I suppose I never considered how it was built."

"Perhaps some of these ancient villeins can rebuild the bailey wall," Druscilla suggested.

"Better them than my father's best soldiers," Alista agreed. If the people of Brinlaw had a practical complaint about their new lord, this was it. Unwilling to wait for spring like any reasonable person, Will had ordered that the hole in his castle's defenses be repaired in the midst of the winter's snows, and for the most part the men of Mark's garrison were the ones being ordered to do it. "I just hope our stores will feed them," she added, chewing her lower lip in thought. When her father had left her in December, the larders and storehouses of the manor had seemed stuffed to bursting, an abundance that was almost embarrassing. But since the castle garrison had literally doubled, plus Henry's surplus nobles, plus these new villeins, most of whom arrived with little more than the clothes they wore, she'd begun to be concerned. So far she had been able to manage—game was plentiful, and the last year's harvest had been good. But if her husband intended to continue welcoming newcomers at the current rate, they were facing a more lean than pious Lent and spring.

Paolo carefully kept his eyes on the page before him. "Lord William is a soldier," he remarked in a neutral tone. "Perhaps he doesn't realize the complications of keeping a manor."

"Perhaps he doesn't care," Alista muttered.

"Either way, someone should tell him," Paolo finished, dipping his stylus into the ink pot to begin another line.

Alista turned sharply, but the friar was bent over his writing, innocent as a dove. "Someone being me, I suppose you mean," she grumbled.

"You are Brinlaw's lady," he pointed out. "You have managed this castle through many a winter with little help while your father was away at war."

"I would hardly call you and Clarence little help," she retorted.

"Even so, neither of us is in any position to go to Lord William with your concerns," Paolo pressed on. "He is your husband—"

"As if I had forgotten—"

"You have not, but has he?" He set the stylus aside. "My lady, I have given this matter a great deal of thought. In truth, I have thought of little else these past few weeks. I believe you must stop being this man's prisoner."

"You think she should run away?" Druscilla asked.

"Not at all," Paolo hastened to reply. "You should stop hiding, stop behaving as if you are afraid, as if he is some ogre you fear to disturb lest he devour you."

Druscilla snorted delicately over her skein of wool. "From what I've seen, he might," she muttered.

"I am not afraid of him," Alista said.

"Then prove it," Paolo insisted. "I believe you are not, but your lord doesn't know you so well. Show him that you will not be intimidated, that your home is still your own."

"She tried, remember?" Dru said bitterly.

"No," Alista cut her off. "I attacked him for myself, Dru, and for Papa. If I had been thinking of the manor, I never would have done it." Paolo's approval was figured so plainly on his face, she couldn't help but smile. "So yes, dear Brother, you are right. I must talk to him."

As fate would have it, Will and Alista's paths came together in the middle of the hall in front of a fascinated audience. "Well met, lady," Will grumbled, trying to just not see how she was dressed.

"My lord," she replied with a nod. "I must speak with you." She glanced at the rapt faces all around them. "In private."

This was so unexpected, Will almost laughed, but the look in her eyes made it plain she wouldn't take this kindly, and Heaven or Hell only knew how she'd strike back. There were men present he'd prefer not to think him entirely unable to control his wife, nor did he want the first time he gave her the whaling she so richly deserved to be in front of the entire household. "Of course," he said instead, leading the way to the solar.

Raynard was now taking his ease by the solar fire, his nose buried in one of Mark's old books. "Get out," Will ordered without further ado.

His captain didn't seem offended. "Are you sure?" he grinned, glancing Alista's way. "You might need my protection. Do you at least have a sword?"

"No need, Captain," Alista answered for him with a sweet and deadly smile. "I have no more weapons, remember?"

This was true. Unsatisfied with Will's efforts, Raynard had gone through Alista's belongings himself, finding another infant sword, another dagger, even a tiny flail obviously only good for hunting squirrels the hard way. "I wouldn't call you entirely without resources, my lady," he said, making a bow before taking his leave.

"You wanted to talk to me?" Will asked blandly, settling into a chair when he was gone. "Forgive me if I'm surprised."

"I don't particularly want to," she answered with equal candor. "But . . . Will, I'm worried."

Compared to the rare and stilted quality of her conversation of late, this was tantamount to a confession of love. "What about?" he asked, still wary.

"Brinlaw," she answered. "We barely have enough flour and vegetables to last the winter as we stand now. If we continue to add new people—"

"You would have me turn them away?" he interrupted, a stubborn set coming to his jaw. These were his father's—no, *his* people. No wonder she didn't want them here. Better to keep the castle and village well stocked with only those who pitied her and hated him.

"Of course not," she protested. "But as lady of Brinlaw, I have an obligation—"

"Since when does your position as Brinlaw's lady concern you?" he shot back, cutting her off again. "Half the time no one sees you, and when they do, you appear like . . . I don't even know what like." He almost laughed. "Alista, I swear I have never seen anything like you."

"Many thanks, my lord." She sketched a sarcastic curtsey made more pointed by her boyish clothes. "If I promise to make myself seen in a proper gown, will you promise not to let us starve?"

"We're in no danger of starving," he grumbled, somewhat set back on his heels.

"Forgive me, my lord, but I have been keeping this holding's larders since I was a child, and I believe we are," she insisted.

"If you have to say 'my lord' like it's a curse, I'd prefer to be called Will, if you don't mind," he said, looking away.

"Will, if things go on as they have, by April the serfs will be grinding acorns to make their bread," she answered. "You no doubt know all there is to know about provisioning an army on the move, but you must trust me in this. Meat can be found, but grain only ripens in summer, and flour can't be hunted with a bow."

He looked back to find a smile flirting with the corners of her mouth and a hint of mirth dancing in her eyes. "Indeed," he grumbled, almost letting himself smile back, his scowl deepening instead. "I shall send to the King for more grain, if he means for me to feed his retainers—"

" 'Tis probably the reason he sent them to you in the first place," she warned. A darker thought seemed to occur to her. "But maybe you think he owes you a favor."

"More than one," he agreed, missing her meaning entirely; he assumed she'd just remembered how little she liked him and meant to take her smile back. "I'll send a messenger at once."

"Then I shall go change into a gown," she answered briskly, bobbing another curtsey and turning toward the door.

"Alista, wait." He wouldn't humble himself to chase after her but was relieved when she stopped on her own. "You need not wear a gown on my account."

"I would not wear it for you but for Brinlaw," she said evenly, her back still turned. "I would not have these strange knights think ill of this holding or my father because of my habits." She turned to look at him. "Besides, I have no need for breeches if I am to have no sword."

"Can you blame me for taking it?" he asked, surprised into a laugh.

"Can you think me, a woman, such a threat?" she retorted, leaping at the bait.

"Aye, lady, and a sneak besides," he shot back. "Or have you forgotten where I got this scar?"

This seemed to set her back a bit, but only for a moment. The slash she had given him had superficially healed, but he still carried an ugly, purple mark and likely would for some time to come. "I remember well, and 'twas not by deception that you received it," she said, true bitterness in her tone. "I only wish my own scars could be shown so plainly, then maybe you would not seem so hard-pressed."

"Your scars show right well, sweet, you may be sure," he replied, answering her in kind. "No one in this house will let me look away from them for so much as a moment."

"Is that why you seek to fill my home with strangers?"

All the dullness was gone from her eyes and stance—this was the witch he had married. "Is that why my father's soldiers are made masons?"

"Your home?" he demanded, letting his own temper fly free as hers. "By whose right? Whose authority? A false thief, an usurper who stole it from an honorable knight, then stole his life as well—"

"Then 'tis my home indeed," she shouted, no tearful shriek but a full-throated roar. "For the same can be said of me!"

"Aye, and see how dearly I pay for my sin," he shouted back. When she had struck at him with her sword, he had been furious, but he had known he could crush her, that there was a mad glory in her foolish courage, that he would be a villain no matter what he did. But this was a fair fight, and the rage he felt was clean and just, a kind of liberation.

"Not nearly dear enough, sweet," she snarled, aping his twisted endearment.

"And yet you think I should give you back your sword," he said, moving closer, his face barely inches from hers. "You complain that your father's men are put to work on the walls. No doubt it vexes you sorely that I do not set the loyal assassins of my sworn enemy to guarding my holding—"

"My father was not your sworn enemy until you made him so," she answered hotly. "He would have kept King Henry's peace until Doomsday had you not tried to take his lands."

"They were never his lands to take." His jaw was set, his eyes blue ice. "And I did not mean your father."

She stopped for a moment, then an almost feral smile that did nothing to lighten his heart came over her lovely face. "Indeed," she said slowly. "My retainers are no more assassins than they are brick masons, but 'tis true that for you they might make an exception." She turned to walk away again, and he caught hold of her arm above the elbow. "Let go!" she demanded, looking back at him in fury.

"I will not." He kissed her hard enough to bruise her mouth, holding her still as she struggled then holding her tighter as she stopped.

Alista's brain was still bellowing righteous fury, but the rest of her didn't want to listen. *He wants me,* she couldn't help thinking, her heart coming alive with bitter joy.

Mine, Will thought fiercely, his touch still angry as his hands pushed under the heavy woolen tunic she wore to find the soft flesh underneath. She shivered as his tongue made contact with hers, and he crushed her back against the table, longing to break her beneath him, dying to shelter her safe.

He broke the kiss to nuzzle her throat, and Alista opened her eyes. She saw the light and shadow of the fireplace flames dancing on the ceiling, mindless animation, heartless life like the animal heat racing through her. "Stop," she said, pushing at Will's shoulders, her fingertips scrambling for purchase on hard muscle as she struggled to push him away. "Stop it, please . . ."

She sounded so distressed, Will did as she asked without thinking, though in faith it wounded his soul. "What?" he asked her, his voice gruff with unconscious tenderness as he touched her cheek. "What is it?"

"Don't touch me!" she screamed, slapping his hand away. She crumpled to the floor in front of the table, weeping at his feet. He crouched to touch her, and she pushed him away again. "Leave me alone!" she sobbed, covering her face by crossing her arms before it, a childish, ungraceful gesture that tore at his heart even in his present distraction. "Please, Will, just leave me alone."

"Alista?" Dru came running in and froze. "What did you do to her?" she demanded of Will, courageous in fury.

"Nothing," Alista insisted, still crying, as Will straightened up. "He didn't do anything, Dru, I promise. Just go away."

"I'll go," Will said quickly, embarrassed, furious, and generally wishing he were someplace far away, preferably with an enemy to kill. Ignoring Druscilla's blue-eyed glare and Alista's lingering sniffles as best he could, he made a hasty retreat.

"Cherie, please, tell me," Dru said, kneeling beside her friend with admirable grace in spite of her condition. "What has happened?"

"Nothing," Alista insisted, embarrassed and miserable. "I'm fine. I'm a fool, but I'm fine."

"You are not." She pulled a snowy linen napkin from her sleeve and handed it over. "Now wipe your eyes and tell me what is wrong."

"Will kissed me," Alista admitted, taking it. "He tried to . . . Dru, I can't."

"Then you'd better do away with him and quickly," the pretty blonde crisply advised, "for he will try again soon enough."

"I tried that already, remember?" Alista muttered as she got up, Dru's acid practicality bringing her back to her senses more quickly than a sharp slap in the face.

"Not in any serious way," Dru pointed out. "Surely you knew you couldn't just hack him to pieces." She sat down in a chair and picked up Raynard's book. "If you weren't such a ninny about sharing his bed, you could have cut his throat long ago."

Alista laughed, incredulous. "I think Captain Raynard might suspect it was me who did it; don't you?"

"Poison, then," Dru went on unperturbed, setting the book aside. "You spend enough time in the kitchens; it should be easy enough to manage without arousing suspicion. He could simply get sick and die."

Like my father, Alista thought but didn't say. Reason and Will himself both told her that Will couldn't have poisoned Mark, but she still couldn't dismiss her doubts. Her father had been so strong, and Will had wanted Brinlaw so much. . . . "I couldn't," she said aloud, shaking her head. "To kill him in combat for honor is one thing; to murder him in cold blood is quite another."

"Are you a knight now, that you may make such nice distinctions?" Dru scoffed. "Like it or not, cherie, you are a woman, and you must use what you have. Either you want him dead, or you don't. If you do, kill him. If you don't, lie with him and be done with it."

"A lovely set of choices," Alista answered, feeling a little sick. "Remind me never to cross you, Dru."

The other woman smiled. "You needn't worry, cherie," she promised. "You will always be safe with me."

The next party of London knights brought a minstrel with them, a merry-eyed young man whose talents tended more to mischief than melancholy. Performing in the hall after dinner, he caught Dru's eye early on and was apparently smitten, trotting out an endless string of ballads in praise of blue-eyed blondes. Dru, for her part, apparently found his performance charming, rewarding him with her laughter and most dazzling smiles.

"This troubadour is broken, my lords," Raynard grumbled after half an hour of this. "He only knows one song."

"Not so, Captain," the minstrel pointed out with a bow as the laughter died away. "See if this likes you better." Making another bow to Alista, he began again:

"My true love's hair is raven's wing;
Her eyes are darkened stars.
"No rest nor joy my heart can bring
'Til she rests in my arms.
"Another holds her soul in thrall,
Imprisoned by a vow.
"A pile of stones, a broken wall—
These all her loves endow.
"But he shall find her faithless, too,
As surely I have done.
"But let her kiss a thousand new,
My heart is hers alone."

Throughout this performance, Will's face had steadily darkened, a change lost on neither his captain, whose grin steadily widened, nor his wife, who seemed ready to sink under the table. "I like it very well," Raynard said when the song was done. "When was it made?"

"Just recently," the minstrel answered. "The King's cousin made it, and Queen Eleanor likes it very much."

"She would," laughed Sir John Tweedy, one of the new arrivals. "London has become just like Aquitaine, crawling with poetic puppies all dying of love for the Queen. King

Henry says he hesitates to take food in his own court for fear he shall gag from the smell of horse dung and rose petals."

Alista was quietly getting up from her seat, but Will clamped a hand down on her wrist. "Which cousin?" he asked politely.

"Geoffrey," another of the knights offered before the minstrel could answer. "His mother's second husband is rich as Midas, a Flemish merchant, and he pays young Geoffrey handsomely to stay away in England. He has no estate, so he amuses himself at court. And a pretty fellow he is, too. All the ladies love him."

"How much would he charge to go back to France?" Raynard muttered.

"We are simple, country folk, minstrel," Druscilla said, glancing at Alista's miserable face in sympathy. "These fashionable lays offend our morals. Have you no songs about ladies who do love their lawful husbands?"

The minstrel had been watching how his lordship restrained his lady and how quiet she remained, and it rather offended his artistic sensibilities. "I do know one," he answered. "But it isn't—"

"Sing it," Dru urged before he could finish.

The minstrel looked over at the dais and the beautiful brunette whose husband looked ready to thrash her. "As you will," he said, raising his lute again.

"Lully, lulley! lully, lulley!
The falcon hath borne my mate away!

"He bore him up, he bore him down,
He bore him into an orchard brown.

"In that orchard there was a hall,
That was hangèd with purple and pall.

"And in that hall there was a bed,
It was hangèd with gold and red.

"And in that bed there lieth a knight,
His woundés bleeding day and night.

"At that bed's foot there lieth a hound,
Licking the blood as it runs down.

"By that bedside kneeleth a maid,
And she weepeth both night and day.

"And at that bed's head standeth a stone,
Corpus Christi *written thereon.*

"Lully, lulley! lully, lulley!
The falcon hath borne my mate away."

At the first chorus of this, Alista tried to get up again, but Will was still holding her wrist. She tried to keep still, but when the falcon chorus was repeated, she couldn't stand it any longer. She picked up her meat knife and rapped Will sharply across the knuckles with the handle. He let go with an oath, and she snatched herself free, running from the hall as quickly as her heavy skirts would allow. Forgetting his wounded hand and his audience, Will charged after her, his chair tumbling over in the process.

Clarence laid a hand on the shocked minstrel's shoulder. "You might want to consider another profession."

Will chased Alista through the corridor, catching her on the stairs. "Leave me alone!" she shrieked, clawing at him to get away. In her mind, falcons swooped and screeched, a white at the center of them all flying higher, bearing a soul away.

"Not a chance," Will snarled back, pinning her against the curving wall. "Have you written him? Who is his spy? Who brings you his letters?"

"What are you talking about?" she demanded.

"Geoffrey, little wretch," he said, glaring down at her, her arms still locked in his grip. "Must I sing it?"

"Yea, my lord, 'twould help," she shot back. "Perhaps then you wouldn't sound like such an ass!" She was losing her reason, and this lummox was still worried about Geoffrey? Incredible . . .

"An ass I may be, but not so stupid as you think." His grip tightened, and he leaned closer. "Now tell me—"

"There is nothing to tell!" she insisted. "As Christ be my judge, the last word I had of Geoffrey came from you when you told me he had run away." His face was so close to hers, she could barely make sense of it, and his eyes became part of the chaos swirling in her mind. Her hands were pressed to his chest as if to push him away, but now her fingers closed around the fabric of his shirt as if to hold on. "If you want to berate someone for that stupid song, go to London and bash away at him—kill him if you like; I don't care."

He laughed in her face. "Do you think me such a fool—?"

"Aye, and a brute besides if you will not let me go," she retorted.

His eyes narrowed, but in truth she had him at a loss. He could either beat the truth out of her, assuming she was lying and that she couldn't outlast him, neither of which seemed certain at the moment, or he could do as she asked. "As you will, my lady," he said coldly, letting her go.

She saw hurt in his eyes beneath the fury, and she didn't think, just moved. "Will, no," she said softly, kissing his cheek, framing his face with her hands. She kissed his eyelids, his brow as he bent to her, everything else forgotten. She moved to kiss his mouth . . .

"No." He pushed her away, stepping back. She looked so innocent, gazing up at him in grief and something a fool might see as love. Darkened stars, Geoffrey's song had called those eyes. Turned dark from the black of her soul, or only black with sorrow? In either case, he supposed he was the cause. "You can't have it both ways, Alista."

That night, he dreamed of falcons. Waking, he could still hear their cries, a piteous wail turning into sobs from somewhere outside his room. Rubbing his eyes, he could make out words in a strange tongue, an almost-singing lilt, and the cries were not a falcon but a woman, Alista, pounding and scratching at the bolted tower door.

He ran down the short flight of stairs and threw back the bolt. "Alista," he said as he opened the door and she fell forward into his arms.

"I want my father," she wept, trying to push past him as if to climb the stairs. "I have to find my father. . . ."

"Hush now," he scolded, scooping her off her feet and carrying her back to her room. "You're having a nightmare, sweet."

"No," she protested, though she had gone limp in his embrace, her arms around his neck. "I'm awake. I'm dreaming awake."

"Shhhhh . . ." He lay her down on Mark's bed and crawled in after her, wrapping his arms around her. "Go to sleep," he murmured, his voice rough with love as he kissed her cheek. "You can hate me again in the morning."

The next morning, Clarence and Brother Paolo both stood outside Alista's door, wondering what to do next. Will Brinlaw couldn't be found, and he was needed. "Allow me," Raynard said, joining them. He knocked briskly on the door. "My lady?"

After a moment, a hesitant voice answered. "Yes?"

Raynard winked at the monk. "Have you seen your husband?" he asked politely.

Another long pause. "Yes."

"If you see him again, tell him to come down to the courtyard," he finished. "Something has happened, and it has to be seen to be believed."

Inside the bedroom, Alista and Will were staring at one another, both of their expressions somewhere between hopeful and aghast. Alista had a vague memory of him holding her, a sensation entwined in the horror of her nightmare, but she hadn't realized this was real. He had said something to her, kissed her cheek. . . . She looked up at him, met his eyes with her own. "Will—"

"I'll go see what he wants," he said abruptly, getting up.

"Will, wait!" But he was already gone, the door slamming shut behind him.

Raynard was as good as his word. Out in the snowy courtyard, what looked like the entire garrison was being held at bay by a dwarf. Drawing closer, Will saw his face—not a dwarf, but a child, a boy of no more than ten with a broadsword as long as he was tall and a war-horse to rival Mark's Goliath standing at his back. He would have seemed to have been alone except for the piteous wail coming from a bag of woolens perched on the horse's back.

"He came riding over the drawbridge like he meant to take Jerusalem," one of the guards told Will.

"Are you all deaf, or just stupid?" the boy shouted. "Will no one answer me?"

Will walked out, grabbed the sword before the child could raise it, and wrenched it from his grasp. "I am lord of this castle," he said, tossing it away. "And I didn't hear your question."

The boy fell to his knees in the snow, but his face remained defiant as his challenge. "Forgive me, my lord," he said with more courtesy. "I only seek William Brinlaw."

Will studied his face, trying to remember if he'd ever seen him before. Delicate, freckled features under a wild, red shock of hair . . . something was familiar, but he couldn't place him, and he'd had very little contact with children, in any case. "What is your business with him?"

The boy looked up at the bundle on his saddle, still hiccuping grief. "His niece needs his protection."

Alista came running outside, still fastening her mantle over her boyish clothes, the easiest to throw on. Will was standing at the end of the drawbridge, conversing with a child. "What is going on?" she asked Druscilla, herself loitering in the doorway.

"Your guess is as good as mine," Dru answered, giving her a speculative look. "The boy was threatening him a moment ago—do you suppose he will throttle him?"

"Don't be ridiculous," Alista scoffed. She knew very little of Will, and little of that was good, but she couldn't imagine that he meant to hurt a child. Leaving Dru, she moved closer as Will lifted an even smaller creature from the horse's saddle, a little girl barely bigger than a baby.

"Her name is Nan," the boy said, looking nervously between the man and woman. "Please, is William Brinlaw here?"

"He is Will Brinlaw," Alista said, laying a comforting hand on the boy's shoulder as she watched Will holding the little girl. "What's your name, lad?"

"Tarquin," he answered, gazing up at her in wonder.

"I'm Alista," she said with a smile. "Welcome to Brinlaw Castle."

Nan had gone to Will without a peep of protest, her tears drying up at once. "Hullo," she said, wrapping her arms around his neck. "My bottom hurts."

"I shouldn't wonder," he agreed, smiling helplessly. He felt like God Himself had just thumped him hard on the head. His niece? May's daughter?

"We rode all the way from London," Tarquin explained, still staring at this strange, beautiful woman who disguised herself as a boy. "And before that to London from Cornwall."

"Sweet saints!" Alista started bustling, trying not to see the way Will held little Nan like she was a golden treasure, trying not to see Mark in the way he looked at the child. Trying not to remember how tenderly he'd comforted her. "Come on, let's go inside," she urged. "It's a miracle you've made it here at all."

Inside, over a heaping trencher of breakfast, Tarquin explained that Nan's father was dead. "Fell drunk down the stairs," he said, swallowing another monstrous bite. "Broke his fat, stupid neck."

Alista looked anxiously at Nan, but the mite seemed utterly unperturbed from her perch on her uncle's lap. "Who was he to you?" Will asked the boy, sensing in his tone a kindred soul. "Your master?"

"Something like," Tarquin answered, meeting his eyes. "My mum said I was his son." He took another ripping bite of bread. "Not that I say it with pride."

"You're smarter than you look," Will agreed. He had served as the dead man's squire for little more than a month before deciding he'd be safer at war with his father.

"Will!" Alista scolded, offended on the boy's behalf. She and Dru had done what they could to clean the children up, and Nan now looked as pretty as a cherub. But soap and fresh clothes could do nothing for the fading bruises on Tarquin's face and skinny ribs, or the raw marks on his wrists. "Was there no one in Cornwall to help you, no one you could send?"

"I didn't wait to ask." He glanced at Alista as if he feared to shock her. "I heard his friends talking, dicing like. They meant to cast lots for my Nan."

Alista was shocked. "Sweet saints—"

"They figured if one of them could get a priest to betroth him to her, they could keep her castle," Tarquin hastened to explain. "They knew they had to be quick now Lord Will is back in England and looking to make a name—" He broke off, blushing. "Or so they said, such like," he mumbled into his cup.

Alista was looking at Will, but he was prudently not looking back. "So you thought you'd find me first," Will said, absently wiping Nan's greasy chin with his sleeve.

"I'd heard you were with the King, so we went to London," Tarquin explained. "But when we got there, all the word was that you'd come north to Brinlaw."

"I still can't believe you made it all that way alone," Alista marveled. "You're very brave, Tarquin, and your sister is lucky to have you."

The boy looked at her for a moment with pure, unvarnished love before his wary scowl returned. "I couldn't very well let those bastards have her," he muttered. "She's half my kin, and it isn't her fault what her father might have been." He glanced sidelong at Will. "Her mum was a sweet, pretty lady."

"Aye, she was," Will agreed with a scowl to match the boy's. "I had no idea she had a child before she died."

"He didn't want it known, Nan's being a girl and all." He licked the last drops of gravy from his fingers. "But you'll keep her safe, will you not? Lady May always said that you would."

"Of course we will," Alista answered for him. "And you will help us."

"No, my lady, not me," Tarquin said quickly, getting up from the table. "I'll be on my way . . . the horse is mine by right—"

"Of course the horse is yours," Alista said, confused. "But you must be exhausted." She got up and went to him. "Stay with us and rest for a while at least. Nan would be miserable without you in a strange place, no matter how kindly she was treated."

As if on cue, Nan started to cry. "Tarquin, no!" she wept, holding out her arms. "No leave me!"

"Stupid baby," Tarquin muttered, taking her up in his

arms. The four-year-old was two-thirds as big as he was himself, but he held her with practiced ease. "Stop crying. You make my head hurt."

"No go!" she wailed, clinging tight.

"I'm not going anywhere," he promised, rocking her back and forth. "I'm here, Nan, I swear it. I'm here." The little one finally fell quiet, her head on his bony shoulder.

"Dru, will you take them upstairs?" Alista asked her friend, who was watching all that happened from her loom. "The poor little girl is exhausted."

"Come along, sir knight," Dru said with a bit of her old, flirtatious spark. "Bring your damsel along for a nap."

"Will, we can't let that child leave here alone," Alista insisted as soon as they were gone. "You didn't see—he's been horribly abused."

"I'd be shocked if you said he had not," Will answered. "Of course he isn't going anywhere, but you can't treat him so like a child. He won't bear it—he's thought of himself as a man too long."

Something in his voice gave her pause. "His father was really a monster?"

He smiled bitterly. "Not a monster, lady, just a man. A very stupid one." He took a sip from his cup. "When my father was disgraced for his loyalty to Maud, the man who was supposed to marry May broke their vow and married someone else. My father was in France with Henry's mother, and my mother was left in a convent in Anjou with two children almost grown and no money. May didn't want to be a nun; it wasn't in her nature." His tone was as pleasant as she had ever heard it when not in jest, but his eyes told a very different tale. "My mother thought she was doing right, I suppose. Bruel—Nan's father—was her distant cousin, a fence-rider who had never chosen a side in the war. She wrote and convinced him to take May as wife and me as squire so we could both come back to England."

"I take it things didn't work out as she had hoped," Alista said, sitting down again.

"He had no more use for a creature like May than a bear for a butterfly, and I—" He pushed back his sleeve to show her a nasty, irregular scar worn into the flesh of his wrist seemingly to the bone. "He had to keep tying me up to keep me from killing him for her."

"Tarquin has a mark just like this," she said softly, barely touching the scar. She had been living here at Brinlaw then, playing in their garden, sleeping in May's own bed for all she knew. A pampered brat . . .

"Finally, I broke free and ran away to find my father," he finished, her touch racing through him like fire. In truth, he hadn't yet recovered from the look in her eyes when Raynard woke them that morning. She had said his name, reached out for him. He had fled the room at a coward's sprint before she could bewitch him again, before he made a move toward her and felt her push him away. But now she was touching him again, and her manner was tender. Was this gentleness for him or the boy? "I wasn't as brave as Tarquin. I was with Henry fighting your father when I heard that she had died." His mouth twisted at the corner. "If anyone ever suggests to you that to take the pilgrim cross will cleanse your soul, laugh in his face for a liar."

Her hand closed over his. "But you didn't go to cleanse your soul," she said gently. "You went to save May's." He looked up at her, speechless with wonder at the way she reached into his heart and touched the truth. "Now we will save her child as well."

* * *

Will and Raynard had determined that Raynard should go to Bruel's castle in Cornwall and turn out his hangers-on, then leave a garrison behind. "How long do you think you'll be gone?" Druscilla asked, watching him pack by candlelight.

"I couldn't say," he answered, examining a crossbow. She had just appeared in the armory and had yet to state her business, so he was keeping an open mind. "It all depends on what I find."

"But you are coming back," she persisted.

He couldn't help but smile. "You never know, dearling. I may like it so well I'll get myself made castellan. Would you miss me?"

"Like I miss the toothache," she retorted. "Have a fine journey—don't fall off your horse."

"Druscilla, wait!" He chased her to the door and caught her arm. "You may well never miss me," he said, touching her cheek. "But I will most cruelly miss you."

"What will you miss most?" she asked with false sweetness. "My scorn or my contempt?"

"There's no telling," he said, leaning closer. "They both are my delight." He kissed her, half-expecting a slap, but she kissed him back with shocking tenderness. When he drew back, her eyes glistened with tears.

"I told you you wanted to kiss me," she said with a wry smile. "Have a safe journey, Raynard."

Will had passed by the door to the master bedroom earlier and heard singing, Alista singing in the same strange language she'd used at her father's pyre. But this song wasn't sad or scary but tender—a lullaby. He laid his hand on the door . . . she sounded so peaceful, almost happy. He wouldn't spoil it by knocking.

Now on his way down from bidding the lookouts good night, he passed that way again, and the heavy oaken door stood ajar. He touched it, and it swung open.

An empty pallet lay on the floor by the fire. Tarquin, a blanket wrapped tight around his shoulders, lay sleeping at the foot of the bed. Will could hardly blame him; at his age he would have moved heaven and earth to lie at the feet of such a woman.

For Alista was lovely. Her arms and shoulders were bare above the blankets to keep Nan from being smothered. The little girl was curled beneath her chin, snoring softly, obviously content. Her protector was sleeping as well, her lips slightly parted, her breathing deep and even.

Will sat gently on the edge of the bed, his legs suddenly too weak to hold him. "I'm sorry," he whispered, bending to kiss her cheek.

Her lashes fluttered, but she hardly seemed awake. "Come to bed," she mumbled, reaching for his hand. "I'm freezing."

"You don't—" But she was sleeping again, still holding his hand. Moving slowly as time, he slipped out of his boots one-handed and crawled into the bed.

"My lady?" a tiny voice was calling in Alista's sleeping ear. "Alista? Are you awake?"

She opened her eyes to find Nan nose to nose with her. "I am now," she whispered back, smiling. She liked children very much as a general rule, and this one seemed particularly good-natured—a miracle considering where and how she'd lived so far.

"Look," Nan said, her eyes wide with wonder and elation. "My uncle is asleep."

Alista lifted her head to look. She vaguely remembered Will coming in, but she'd thought maybe it was a dream. But there he was, fully dressed except for boots, lost to the world. "So he is," she answered, lying down again, a queer mixture of apprehension and relief coming over her.

Nan rolled over to face her uncle. "Isn't he lovely?" she said, laying a tiny hand on his cheek.

Alista couldn't help but smile. "Yes, he is," she agreed. "Now go back to sleep."

* * *

At dawn, Will opened his eyes. Nan was now curled like a hedgehog under his chin, sucking her thumb and snoring. He shifted her carefully as he got up, transferring her back to Alista's side of the bed. "It's all right," Alista mumbled in her sleep as the child snuggled close, kissing the top of Nan's head.

Will leaned down and kissed Alista's lips. "It will be," he whispered, a promise.

Wide awake and huddled by the fire, Tarquin watched the rumored best knight in the world, and he didn't know what to think. Will Brinlaw didn't look particularly happy; in fact, he was scowling down on his lady in a way that made the boy's stomach feel queer. The scar on his cheek only made him look more sinister.

But when he noticed Tarquin was watching, he didn't seem angry. "Are you hungry?" he asked him brusquely, getting up. Tarquin nodded, unable to find his voice. If Bruel had found him watching him with his mother, he'd have whaled the life out of him. But Brinlaw just nodded. "Come on; we'll find something to eat."

A few days later, Alista was passing by the stables when she heard what sounded like a full-out war coming from inside. "Alista!" Nan cried, running out to her in obvious distress. "Tarquin is going to kill him!"

The "him" in question was Tom, newly promoted from the mews to the stables, and he did indeed seem to be in danger of being killed by Tarquin, who was sitting on his chest and pounding away with both fists. "I yield, you devil!" Tom was howling, using his arms more to guard his face than to fight back. "I yield!"

"Tarquin!" Alista grabbed the little hothead by the collar

and dragged him backward. "Stop it! Stop it now!" He thrashed around and raised his fist as if he would strike her as well. Then he froze in horror and burst into tears. "Will you stop it?" she demanded, refusing for the moment to be moved.

"He will stop, won't you, Tarquin?" Nan said, wringing her little hands.

"Ye-yes," Tarquin sputtered, staring at the floor.

"I should hope so," Alista scolded. Leaving the winner for the moment, she went to have a look at the loser. "Tom, are you killed?"

"No, my lady," he mumbled, wiping his bloody nose on his sleeve.

"Here, let's be certain." She sat down on a groom's stool and drew him to her. "This nose isn't broken, and you still have all your teeth." She smiled. "You'll be a handsome rogue even yet, barring any further disaster."

"Thank you, my lady." He was still keeping a wary eye on Tarquin, who pointedly turned his back.

Alista looked at each of them in turn, suppressing a sigh. As if she knew the first thing about boys and their foolishness. She briefly considered turning the matter over to Will, who it could be presumed had more experience, but Tom was one of her father's charges. She wouldn't give up on him just yet. "Who will tell me how this began?" she asked wearily.

Tarquin's head snapped around. "I never will, even if you kill me," he said, shooting the other boy an unmistakable threat with his eyes.

"Nor I," Tom said quickly.

"I see." She stood up. "Nan, will you please take Tom to his mother so she can wash his face?"

"Come, Tommy," the little girl obeyed, taking the boy's hand as if he were the baby. "Let's go and see you fixed."

Alista waited until she knew they were gone before sitting down again. "Tarquin, come here, please." He came and flopped at her feet, obviously miserable. "You truly won't tell me what happened?" He shook his head, his eyes fixed on the floor. "Very well. I can't force you and wouldn't if I could." Fat tears rolled down his cheeks. "But I can't have you whaling on the servants, either. You and Tom are of an age, and it's only natural you should occasionally have a falling out. But because you are a noble—"

"I'm not," he interrupted hotly.

"You are if I say you are," she retorted. "And because you are, you have an obligation not to abuse those who are not. Do you understand what I mean?"

It was painfully obvious from the look on his face that he thought she was out of her mind. "You can't make me noble by saying so," he said, instead of answering her question.

"Lord William and I have become your guardians," she said. "When you are a little older, I suspect he will make you his squire—"

"I don't want to be his squire," he cried, springing to his feet. "He hurt you, and I hate him, no matter what anyone says!"

"Tarquin!"

"You don't have to pretend for me as you do for Nan—Lady Dru told me all about it."

Suddenly things were making more sense. "What did she tell you?" she asked, keeping her tone neutral with an effort.

"That he killed your father and nearly killed you when you opposed him," he answered at once. "Everyone knows 'twas you that gave him that scar, but you're only a lady. You can't really fight."

"Indeed?" she said mildly. "I think someone may have mentioned that before." She reached out to him. "Tarquin, give me your hand and listen," she began. "No matter what you may have heard or from whom, I do not want to fight Will Brinlaw." As she said it, looking into the child's hazel eyes, she realized with sinking heart that it was true. "What's more, he is your guardian, and he wants what's best for you, no matter how he may feel about me. You don't have to love him, but to hate him would be a grievous sin."

"Worse than murder?" he asked stubbornly.

"Murder?" she echoed, appalled. "Tarquin—"

"He murdered your father who you loved," the boy insisted, his eyes dark with rage on her behalf. "Everyone knows it, even—" He broke off and stared at the ground.

"Even Tom?" she guessed. He didn't answer. "Tarquin?"

"He said I was against you," he said softly, his voice thick with tears. "He said you hated Brinlaw, and if Nan and I did not, you would hate us, too. I didn't want to hate him; he's been so kind to Nan, and me too, more than I thought, even, but—" His words broke off again.

"Oh, Tarquin," she sighed, feeling rather guilty and misunderstood herself but mostly bad for him. "Tarquin, listen to me." She turned his face to hers. "First of all and most importantly, I could never hate you or Nan, no matter what. We will never be against one another, you and I, Will Brinlaw be loved or damned, I swear it on my father's soul. Do you believe me?" He was looking at her with such naked love and hope it broke her heart. "Do you?" she pressed.

"Yes," he finally answered, wiping his nose on his sleeve.

"Secondly, as far as I know and I believe, Will Brinlaw

did not murder anyone," she went on. "If Lady Dru told you he did, she was being very wicked."

"But if he didn't, why did you attack him?" he persisted. "Was that a lie as well?"

"No, that was a truth, though not so simple a one as Lady Dru believes," she admitted, wishing she had more experience with children. Someone who knew more how to comfort him could have done it without making herself quite so confused. "I thought for a while that Will did kill Papa, and some other things besides, and he thinks I did some things that were naughty as well."

"Really?" the boy asked, his eyes widening.

"Nothing you need worry about," she said firmly. "The point is that I loved my father so much, everyone here loved him so much that when we heard that he was dead, we didn't want to believe it. We wanted someone to blame, so we blamed Will. But Will and I have talked about it, and I have thought about it a great deal, and . . ." She paused, the truth coming out in the words as something of a painful surprise. "I think now that Papa just died," she admitted. "It wasn't Will's fault, and it would be wrong to hate him for it."

Tarquin didn't say anything for a moment, but she could see from his face that he had something more to say. "But you don't love him," he mumbled at last, blushing as he stared at the ground.

"I love you, and I love Nan, and that will have to be sufficient," she said crisply, closing that subject as quickly as possible. In the grand scheme of bitter life experiences, Tarquin probably had her beaten hands down, but he still didn't seem the proper person to consult about her love life. She stood up. "Now go and find Tom and beg his pardon."

"His pardon don't deserve to be begged," he grumbled.

"His pardon doesn't, and do it anyway," she ordered, softening her tone with a kiss.

As she passed through the Hall on her way upstairs, she saw Will conferring with several of Henry's knights around the hearth. Perched on his knee was Nan, sipping milk from her own little mug and soaking up every word. "She reminds me of someone I knew once," Brother Paolo said, coming up behind Alista as she watched them, a strange look on her face.

She turned sad eyes on him. "And Will?" she asked mildly. "Does he remind you of my father?"

She looked so unhappy, he almost wished he hadn't spoken. "In some ways, very much," he admitted. "In others . . . but then, I didn't know Mark as a young man."

She smiled a little. "Neither did I." She thought of Druscilla, the woman she was on her way to scold. Mark had bedded her with less just cause than Will had felt in bedding Alista. And Will had at least married her—if he didn't love her, at least he hadn't dishonored her. Mark hadn't loved Dru, not the way he'd loved his darling Blanche, and he'd made no secret of it. And when he died, Dru was left with no home but his daughter's charity and a baby on the way. Yet Druscilla still cried for him, cried for vengeance for his death, while Alista treated Will so coldly even a child could see it and believe she hated him. *But you don't love him*, Tarquin had said. If only that were true. "No, he isn't like my father," she said aloud.

"Let me help you, cara mia," Paolo urged, desperate in his helplessness. "Talk to me—"

"I can't," she interrupted, touching his mouth to stop his words. "I wouldn't know what to say." Kissing his cheek, she left him helpless as ever.

She found Dru in the room that had once been her own, weaving. Her new loom took up most of the tiny space, but she refused to let it be moved, and seeing the tapestry taking shape there, Alista understood why. It was her father's falcon crest, transformed from a crudely-drawn symbol serviceable for identifying troops to a work of art. Even half-finished, the white bird seemed to shimmer in shades of silver-gray and gold on its field of midnight blue. "What do you think?" Dru asked her as she came in.

"It's beautiful," Alista admitted.

"Who knows?" Dru said lightly as she worked. "Someday it may hang in the Hall."

"Nothing would please me more," Alista answered, sitting down on the bed. "But I won't get my hopes up. Dru, we both have to face that Will is here to stay." Just saying this aloud made her feel sick and wicked beyond salvation that she didn't feel worse. "My father is gone."

"Not entirely," Dru insisted, a hand straying to her swelling shape. "He could still have a son."

"But it wouldn't matter," Alista reminded her gently. "Dru, I just spoke to Tarquin. He said you told him that Will murdered my father and that I hated him for it."

"And do you not?" Dru demanded, letting her shuttle fall to face her.

"No, I do not," Alista answered, suddenly angry herself. The other girl looked so damnably self-righteous, as if any who opposed her way of thinking must be evil, when her thinking was so twisted. Looking at her, Alista was suddenly seized with a nearly irresistible urge to shake her until her teeth rattled in her pretty head. "And even if I did, I wouldn't tell his fosterling as much. Those children are Will's family; they belong to him. He is their only security, and however he may feel about us, he seems to care for them. We will not poison their feelings for him—"

"Why not, in heaven's name?" Dru cried, incredulous. "Why should I not do anything I can to hurt him? Shall I not think of protecting my own child, the child he hates?"

Alista was fast losing what little patience she had left. "How is hurting Will protecting—?"

"I don't know!" she all but screamed as she got up from her chair. "I only know that I hate him, that I will do anything to see him suffer, to see him leave us in peace." She looked at Alista, a desperate plea in her eyes. "Brinlaw killed your father to have his way, and he all but killed his daughter. Can you imagine what he might do to be rid of your father's son?"

"He did not all but kill me," Alista protested.

"Indeed?" She grabbed Alista's still-tender wrist, making her cry out in pain. "What do you think he would have done if Brother Paolo had not come in time? Choked the life out of you, is what."

"Dru," Alista pled, desperate not to hear this. "Will has had plenty of opportunity to wring my neck since then and cause as well, but he hasn't—"

"You he can take to his bed," Dru said bluntly. "In the end, you aren't much of a threat."

"Indeed," Alista murmured, stung silent.

"But a son—can you imagine?" Dru went on, a hard light coming into her sapphire-blue eyes. "Knights like Pettengill already know your husband for what he is. If your father had a son—"

"Dru, stop it! You mustn't think this way—"

"You said it yourself; we must be realistic," Dru insisted. "Will Brinlaw will most surely think this way."

"No," Alista protested. "He will not. He would never hurt a woman or a child, not even to keep this castle—"

"What makes you think not?" Dru laughed. "His sweet, tender treatment of you?"

Yes! Alista wanted to shout but didn't dare. As Dru had so gently pointed out, lovemaking was the most convenient method Will could have chosen to keep her quiet and content. Why should she think for a moment that for him it could mean something else? "He has treated Nan and Tarquin as kindly as his own children," she pointed out instead.

"Of course he has," Dru answered, unimpressed. "They brought him another castle." She reached out and took her friend's hands. "I don't believe he is an evil man, but he is a man and a soldier besides," she went on more gently. "What we think of as murder, he will see as war. What is one more death if it means he has what he feels is rightly his?"

Alista slowly pulled free of her grasp. "You are wrong, Dru," she said. "If I believed for a moment that my husband could murder an innocent child, even to keep Brinlaw, I could not live in this house. I would take those children and you and run as far from here as I could reach, and I would die myself before I let anyone stop me."

"Brave words, cherie," Dru said with a tiny, bitter smile. "But you were going to kill him, remember?"

"Have I failed you?" Alista demanded. "Have I ever shown you anything but friendship? Have I ever once hesitated to defend you or speak up on your behalf to my father or Will or anyone else?"

"No," Dru admitted, her blue eyes filling with tears.

"Forgive me, cherie." She moved to hug Alista, and Alista allowed it. "I am so sorry," she wept. "Please, don't give up on me."

"Of course I will not," Alista promised, hugging her back. "But you must trust me."

That night Alista dreamed of Falconskeep. She was walking down the winding stairs of the tallest tower, holding her mother's hand, but she was not a child. Looking up, she could see a full, yellow moon shining through an arrow slit, but they were headed down the stairs, down under the earth. "I don't like it," she said, speaking in her mother's lilting tongue.

Blanche stopped and turned to her. "Of course you do not, little bird," she answered, touching Alista's cheek, a brush of fingertips like wings. "You are a creature of the air."

"I want to go back," Alista insisted.

"You will," Blanche promised, heading down again.

At the bottom was the well, just as she remembered, the water's reflection throwing their torch's light in demon patterns on the mossy walls. "Give her your hand," Blanche ordered, and though she didn't want to, Alista put a hand into the freezing water. "You must love her, but never trust her too much," Blanche's voice went on as icy fingers closed tenderly over hers. "Your sister will be jealous of your soul."

"She must be so lonely," Alista said, looking down but seeing only water.

"Time means nothing to her, so she is never alone," Blanche answered, reaching into the water as well. "We are always with her." She smiled, taking Alista's other hand in hers. "And here we are always together."

When she opened her eyes, she was at home, in Will's bed at Brinlaw, Will's niece snoring peacefully beside her. Slipping from the bed, she opened the shutter and looked out at the full, yellow moon, a possibility dawning in her mind.

Tarquin thought his heart might well burst with excitement. He had been on boar hunts before, but never at the front with the hounds. Any hunt had been cause for drink in his father's household, and by the time he was old enough to hunt, he was old enough to duck a drunkard by making himself scarce. But at Brinlaw, all the hunters apparently intended to stay sober until after the beast was killed, and he had been handed a spear of his own, not some modified gardening hoe but a real boar spear with an eighteen-inch steel blade and a shaft and cross pieces of solid oak. "Do you know what to do with this?" Will had asked him, handing it over.

"Aye, well enough, I reckon," he had answered bravely. But now, kneeling in the snow with the others as the dogs charged into the thicket they insisted held the boar, he wasn't so sure. He glanced around the circle of men, each with his own spear braced on the ground, and he couldn't help but notice he was the smallest two-legged creature in evidence. If he were the boar, he wouldn't need a moment to decide which way to run. Will Brinlaw was across the way, looking meaner than any boar could hope to be with that nasty scar of his. Tom the stable boy said 'twas Lady Alista who'd given it to him. After his talk with Alista, Tarquin wasn't sure what to believe. One thing was certain; there was no wooing and such going on that he could see, and this made Will a fool and a villain besides, at least in Tarquin's books. Any man who could be married to Lady Alista and not be in love with her had no love in his soul to find.

Clarence caught his eye and gave him a solemn wink just as a rustle came from the brush. Catching a deep, ragged breath, he braced his spear in the mud just as the boar broke free. The beast's red, beady eyes scanned the circle, and Tarquin thought of his father, the comical look in his eyes as he started to tumble backward down the stairs, and suddenly he wasn't afraid anymore. "Come on, you bloody bastard," he whispered through his teeth, bearing down on his spear with all his might. "Come and get me."

But the boar had bigger game in mind. He charged straight for Will, his stubby legs churning up the snow, and Will was ready for him, driving his spear into the mighty chest up to the cross pieces. The furious creature began to thrash like a demon, and Tarquin's heart leapt into his throat as both man and pig did a full, sideways somersault. "Hold on, boy!" Clarence roared, rushing forward to help with the rest, Tarquin included, though he hadn't the foggiest notion what to do. Will was trying to regain his footing on the slippery ground without letting go of the spear—even Tarquin knew what would happen if he let go. One of the cross pieces gave way, and suddenly the boar was pulling to that side, smelling his chance, one razor-sharp tusk tearing a gash in Will's leather sleeve and probably the flesh underneath. "Not today, you don't," Clarence scolded the raging thing, stabbing it in the neck with a knife as long as Tarquin's forearm, and it collapsed, half in the snow, half on Will's lap like a spaniel.

"What a mess," Alista grumbled, binding up the cut on Will's arm. In truth, she had just stopped shaking. Will had lost a great deal of blood in the woods so that by the time the hunting party came across the drawbridge, he was supported on either side by Clarence and John Tweedy (horses being unsporting and more trouble than help at a boar hunt), his face as white as chalk. Seeing this and the blood soaking his leather tunic, she had nearly fainted herself. *Sweet Christ, I didn't mean it,* she had thought as they helped him into the solar. *What would I do if he should die?*

But once she'd gotten a closer look at his wound and realized she could stitch it, she'd stopped being so worried. In fact, she was more than a little annoyed at him for getting himself wounded in the first place and herself for being so upset that he had. "All your years at war, and you couldn't dodge a pig?" she muttered, sewing briskly.

"Does it hurt?" Nan asked with wrinkled brow, much more flatteringly concerned. She held a wad of fresh bandages at the ready, just in case, and stood at her uncle's other elbow, eager to lend her support.

"Not so much," Will lied, trying not to wince as his sweet, unloving bride tightened the knot.

"Were you always so accident-prone?" Alista chided, most unjustly, he thought. He hadn't been able to determine just how she'd manipulated that boar, but it wouldn't have surprised him in the slightest to learn she had. Even Raynard would have made a better nurse, or at least a more tender one. "Since you were a child, I mean? Or is it just since you've come here?"

"It's you," he retorted.

She almost smiled. "Then perhaps you'd better leave me alone before you kill yourself."

"Lord William!" Clarence came into the solar still filthy from the hunt. "A delegation from King Henry has arrived."

* * *

Ned wasn't what Will would have called a friend, exactly, but they knew one another, and his greeting was friendly enough. Once the initial pleasantries were completed, he asked to speak to Will "in private," casting a weather eye toward the lady of the manor. When they were alone, his manner turned serious. "Where is Captain Raynard?"

"Gone to Cornwall to secure my niece's inheritance," Will answered, handing him a cup. "My brother-in-law is dead."

"Was dead when Raynard found him?" Ned inquired.

"Was dead when Raynard left here," Will answered with a frown. "One of his retainers brought my niece to me with the news."

"Ah, well, that's good then," Ned nodded, satisfied. "Scurvy bugger—should have been dead an age ago." He still hadn't taken a seat, as if he feared to be too easy. "Tell me, Will, the girl . . . Any particular reason you have her dressed in black?"

"I don't, not that it's any of your business," Will said, forcing himself to smile. "She dresses herself so, mourning her father."

"Of course, of course," Ned mused. "I thought perhaps 'twas something else. They say Mark's wife was strange—"

"So I've heard," Will cut him off. "Ned, why are you here?"

"Henry sent me." He finally sat down on a bench. "The thing is this. Some knight named Michael Pettengill has been raising a stink at court, saying you murdered Lord Mark. He also says . . . well, never mind that, it's just silly. The thing of it is, he has absolutely insisted that Henry do something about it, so . . . technically speaking, I'm here to place you under King's arrest."

Will could not believe his ears. "You must be joking," he

laughed. "Henry knows full well I had nothing to do with Mark's death—"

"Of course he does, of course," Ned hastened to agree. "But this Pettengill, he's gone to Henry's mother, and she has taken up his suit, heaven only knows why. Plus Henry apparently has a cousin—"

"I know all about Harry's cousin," Will snarled. "So am I to be hanged?"

"Don't be ridiculous," Ned scoffed. "The King has made it plain he thinks Pettengill is a fool. He only wants you to come to court to answer his charges and put the whole matter to rest."

"Put the Duchess's tongue to rest, you mean," Will grumbled.

"Just so," Ned grinned. "A simple matter, over in a week, I should think."

"And if I refuse?" Will couldn't resist asking, one eyebrow raised.

Ned turned a most amusing shade of purple all the way up to his bald skull. "If you refuse the King's arrest, we . . . well, obviously, Will, we shall have to take you away by force. But surely there's no need—"

"No," Will agreed, smiling enough to settle the poor knight's nerves. "There is not. But this is damned inconvenient, and I intend to tell His Majesty so."

Ned smiled back, obviously relieved. "He would expect nothing less."

Alista was helping to get a bedchamber ready for their guest when Dru came running in as quickly as her little slippers would carry her. "Cherie, you won't believe it," she cried, obviously thrilled.

"What is it?" Alista asked, peevishly eager for news. She wasn't accustomed to being shut out of important conversations like a child, and she didn't care for it one bit.

Dru glanced at the other two women who were making the bed. One was a familiar friend from Alista's childhood, but the other was the wife of one of Will's soldiers, newly come to join her husband now that he was settled. "Come," Dru said, hooking her arm through Alista's and leading her into the dark corridor. "I managed to get a word with the squire of King Henry's knight," she confided.

"How clever of you," Alista giggled. "However did you do it?"

"Ah, well, you know me," Dru giggled back. "At any rate, he was very helpful."

"And what did he tell you, mistress?" Without his armor, Will could be quiet as a cat. "Never mind; I think I know already."

"Do you mean to tell Alista?" Dru asked, her little chin defiant.

"Yes, as a matter of fact," Will replied. "If you will excuse us."

Dru obviously wanted to protest further, but she didn't. "As you will," she said, giving Alista's hand a final squeeze. "We'll talk later," she whispered in her ear as she went back into the room.

"Whatever can the matter be?" Alista said when she was gone, patting her own breast in a parody of dainty alarm. "Are you certain my delicate nerves can bear it?"

"No," Will admitted, opening the door to another room. She went in, and he followed, closing the door behind him. "I'm being arrested," he said as he turned around.

Alista just looked at him for a moment, stunned out of

mockery. "For what?" she said at last. "What have you done?"

"For murdering your father," he answered, watching her face, trying to gauge her reaction. "Your friend Pettengill has accused me to the King."

She sat down hard in a dusty chair, but her face was the picture of calm. "And does the King believe him?"

"The King doesn't know," he answered, uncharacteristically perverse, but he couldn't keep it up. "Sweet saints, Alista, I told you I never—"

"I know you did, and I believe you," she cut him off, sinking into a chair. "So the King is taking back my fine present, taking you back to London."

"At first light tomorrow," he agreed, studying her face for the smallest flicker of emotion. "And if the King decides I'm guilty, he'll have me put to death."

She froze to her bones, but her expression never wavered; she made sure of it. "And that's a possibility?" she asked coolly.

"Anything is possible," he answered, scowling. Could she really be so unconcerned? He had never known her to mask her feelings before . . . perhaps what she was hiding was hope. Perhaps in truth she was as thrilled to hear of his arrest as her vicious little friend, Druscilla.

"So I may have my castle back after all?" she said lightly, unconsciously fueling his suspicions with the sweetest of feminine smiles. *He's only trying to frighten me,* she thought, her heart racing. *He just wants to see me break down and make a fool of myself over him so he can be sure of me while he's gone.*

"No, lady, you will not," he answered, his own expression grim. "If I were to be executed, Brinlaw would revert to the King. Either he would make you his ward, which seems rather unlikely, seeing that all you've ever had is Brinlaw, or he would find you another husband and forget all about you again." He made himself smile back at her. "Maybe you'll do better next time."

"Indeed," she said, making herself stand up as the walls seemed to rush in on her. Damn Henry's eyes . . . he wouldn't dare; he couldn't. A terrible thought occurred, and for a moment she thought she would be sick. But she made herself look up at him and smile again. "I suppose I couldn't do much worse."

She managed to finish putting things in order for the King's delegation, making sure enough places to sleep were made up and enough food was prepared that word of Brinlaw's continued prosperity would return to London with them. But as soon as the evening meal began to be set out, she slipped from the Hall. "Make my excuses," she whispered to Dru in the archway. "If anyone asks, I'm ill."

"Of course you are, cherie," Dru said with a smile. "Your husband has been arrested."

The girl looked positively radiant with delight, making Alista feel even sicker. "Exactly," she answered, managing a smile.

Luckily, Brother Paolo had stayed away from the Hall as well. The door to his room was ajar, but she still tapped it lightly. "May I come in?"

He looked up from his book. "Of course," he smiled, putting it aside.

She came inside and closed the door behind her, but she was uncertain where to begin. She had kept the beloved monk shut out of her heart of late, ashamed of what he might see there, afraid he might force her to look. But now she had nowhere else to turn, no one else to trust, and she needed his good counsel, no matter how painful it might be. "You've heard about Will?" she said at last, pacing the tiny room.

"Yes," he said, watching her, his heart aching for her. "Perhaps the King can discover the truth—"

"The King doesn't care about the truth," she cut him off, desperately unhappy. She sank to her knees beside his chair as she had been wont to do as a child. "If he did, he would have discovered it before he sent Will here. But it was more convenient for Henry for Will to be here, so Will was sent with royal proof of his right to marry me and claim Brinlaw, and my father was assumed to have died of natural causes." She leaned her head against his bony knee. "If the King believes otherwise now, if Michael has been able to convince him that Will is the villain he believes him to be, it can only be that he has a better reason to want Will gone from here."

"What sort of reason could there be?" the friar asked, silently taking note that she said Michael believed Will to be a villain, not that she believed it.

"That's what frightens me," she admitted. "Stephen gave Brinlaw to my father in the first place because of its strategic location—any King of England will want it held by his own man. And as my loving husband just pointed out to me, if he should now lose Brinlaw along with his head, the castle comes not to me but to Henry, to dispose of as he will, with me included or not as he sees fit. If Will is killed; I'm back to being a side chair, it seems." She unconsciously clutched at the hem of his robe. "Geoffrey is Henry's cousin," she continued, so softly he could barely hear, as if she feared some evil spirit of fate might be listening.

"What's more, he worships Henry, would do whatever he ordered without question."

"Unlike Will Brinlaw, who defied him openly at court," Paolo had to agree.

"Will shot Geoffrey with a crossbow and wounded him, the King's kin," she went on hopelessly. "My father's murder, if there was one, would in itself mean little in the grand design of Henry's reign. Can we suppose Henry has done no murders to gain his throne or had them done for him? Some even say old Stephen's son was poisoned."

"But a defiant nobleman, one who would not hesitate to unleash his temper on the King's own cousin if he chose, could be deadly," Paolo said, laying a hand on her hair.

"If Henry believes Will has moved out of his control, he could mean to—" She broke off, the words choked off by tears. "Why should I care?" she said miserably. "I try so hard to hate him—"

"Then you must stop trying," Brother Paolo urged. "No matter what your husband may have done, Christ does not want you to hate him."

"Good, because I don't," she sniffed, her mouth twisting up at one corner in a bitter grin. "I'm a fool and a traitor besides, but I can't help it—"

"You are neither a traitor nor a fool," the monk insisted.

"Yes, I am, because I love him." Just saying the words out loud was like a kind of incantation that unlocked her heart. She felt more miserable but less like she was smothering under the weight of a secret she couldn't even tell herself. "My father didn't choose him, but I did, and now, no matter what he says or does or might have done, I can't make myself take it back." She looked up at him, pleading with her eyes. "Am I a horrible creature?"

"Of course you are not," he promised, his voice breaking with emotion. *May God make you worthy, William Brinlaw*, he prayed. "Tell me how to help you, cara mia."

"You can't, no one . . ." Her voice trailed off as an idea lit her eyes. "Or maybe you can." She sat back on her knees, still lithe as a child for all her woman's troubles. "Will you go with Will to London?" she asked. "Stay with him—I know you can't keep him safe; he'll have to do that for himself. But if you're there to see—" She broke off, tears spilling from her eyes. "Papa just died, and I can never be sure what happened to him," she explained. "I have to know what happens to Will. Whatever it is, I have to know."

"And so you shall," he promised, hugging her close. "I will never leave his side."

Alista was still hiding with her priest, so Will was tucking Nan into bed. "Where are you going?" she asked as he pulled the blankets up. "Lady Dru says you're going away."

"I'm going to London to see King Henry," he said, privately cursing Dru's soul. "I'm going to tell him all about your castle so he can help me keep it safe so you can have it when you grow up."

"But that won't be for a long time. You should just send him a letter," she decided. "I don't think you should go."

"I don't want to go," he admitted. "But a letter won't do this time."

"Too bad," she said with a womanly sigh that made him smile even in his current black mood. "Will you come home soon?"

"Very soon." He brushed her baby-fine hair back from her brow. "Will you do something for me?"

"Anything," she said quickly, her face utterly serious.

His smile widened. "If Lady Alista should ask, will you tell her what I said, that I will be home very soon?"

She frowned. "Aren't you going to tell her?"

"Yes, but she might forget." Only a girl child could have looked so skeptical. "She might," he insisted, laughing. "She's very absent-minded, you know."

She giggled. "I'll tell her," she promised.

"Only if she asks," he warned.

"I won't forget." She sat up and kissed him, then snuggled back under the covers. "But I don't think she'll forget, either."

The children were sleeping, lost to the world, but Alista couldn't even think of lying down. Throwing a thick mantle over her shift, she went out to prowl the house.

Someone had a candle in the solar, throwing flickering lights into the Hall. Going in, she found Will tying up a bundle. "What are you doing?" she asked, closing the door behind her.

"You said Henry was taking back your present, so I thought I should leave you another one," he answered. "You'll be asleep when we leave in the morning."

I'll wager not, she thought but didn't say. "What is it?"

"Come and see."

She untied the bundle warily. Inside were her sword and dagger. "Oh dear . . . Captain Raynard would not be pleased."

"No," he agreed. "But what he doesn't know can't hurt him, unless you decide to hunt him down." This earned him a smile, but she didn't look up from the weapons. "Keep looking; there's something else."

Wrapped separately in faded silk was the strangest sword

she had ever seen, as small as hers but curved like a sickle with notches cut near the point. She picked it up and gasped—it was so light she could hold it easily in one hand. The hilt was beautifully carved and set with tiny jewels, and the blade was etched with fat, curling symbols halfway up. "I've never seen anything like it," she admitted, turning it in the light.

"An Arab prince no bigger than you are almost sliced me in half with that," he said, indicating a line on his side. "Be careful." He dropped the silk across the blade, and it fell in two pieces to the floor.

She turned to him, the point poised just below his chin. "Are you certain you want me to have this?"

"Yes," he nodded, his voice barely more than a whisper. "I'm sure."

She raised up on tiptoe and kissed him, her mouth barely touching his, but it was enough to make her want to cry. He was hers; she knew it in her soul, but she wasn't supposed to have him. "Thank you," she whispered, starting to turn away.

"No." Catching her sword arm first, he pulled her back to him and kissed her. The scimitar fell, but she was trying to push him away, to free herself from his arms. "Bear me, Alista," he murmured against her cheek. "You may never have to look at me again."

"Damn you," she wept, pounding on his chest with her fist. "How dare you say that to me?" He kissed her again, and she opened her mouth to his, clutching his shirt in both hands as he crushed her in his arms. "Will," she cried softly as his kiss moved to her throat.

He lifted her off her feet and up, suckling her breast through her shift as her mantle fell away. The taste of her was so familiar, so sweet, he wanted to weep himself, and her hands were touching him, tenderly stroking his hair, then pulling as he grazed her nipple with his teeth, returning pain in kind, the theme of their every touch.

"Yes," she whispered as he lowered her to the floor, the word half-lost in a kiss. He tore her shift away and gazed down at her, lost in contemplation, his fingertips tracing over her breasts and stomach and along her arms and the curve of her hip as if he were learning her shape. She reached up and touched his mouth, her fingers slipping between his lips as he touched her below and her eyes fell shut, every sense focused on the warm wet of his mouth and the tender pressure of his touch.

He needed to feel her skin on his, but he couldn't wait, couldn't stop now. Still dressed, he leaned over her, capturing her mouth, and her hands slipped under his shirt as if she were as eager to touch him as he was her. Her nails were bitten short, but her fingers were strong, kneading the muscles of his back and pressing the path of his spine and down, pushing his clothes away. Breaking the kiss, he tried to pull back to simply see her, but she wouldn't let him go, raising up from the floor to hold him, her arms around his shoulders.

He was perfect, a scarred and battered angel. Tracing his skin with delicate touch, she could feel every scar, every hurtful imperfection. He kissed her cheek, her ear, sweet breath stirring tendrils of her hair, and then he was moving inside her, opening her up, a sword into its sheath. Her body wept for all the time they'd lost, all the time they might never have. Her legs entwined around him, and his fingers laced with hers, a gentle counterpoint as he pounded her into the floor. She arched her back, and his kisses fell on her throat, along her jaw and chin, sweet, wet worship. Her heart was pounding; she couldn't breathe; and then it came, the killing heat that exploded at their joining to consume her. She cried out, and he kissed her mouth, let her wrap him tighter to her, joining her in the fire.

Brother Paolo came out into the courtyard just as the sun was coming up. "What are you doing, Brother?" Will asked, trying to be polite. "Did you come to say goodbye?"

"Not at all," the friar said cheerfully as his mare was led out from the stables. "I am going with you."

Will just looked at him for a moment. "No, you're not," he decided, going back to check Goliath's tack.

"Oh yes, I am," Paolo answered, unperturbed. "Your lady has sent me, and I will go."

" 'Tis never a bad thing, you know," Ned allowed. "Having a priest along on a journey."

"You must not have traveled much," Will grumbled, swinging into the saddle.

As they rode out over the drawbridge, the rising sun cleared the trees and its light fell on the castle. Looking back, Will saw a tiny figure in black at the top of the tallest tower. The wind was billowing through her wrap, and she seemed ready to take flight at any moment, a thought that suddenly chilled him to the bone. He wheeled Goliath around, half-intending to ride back. Then the feeling passed, and he saw that she was waving. Raising his own arm in salute, he turned and rode away.

Nine

Alista stood at the top of her tower and watched as Will and Brother Paolo rode away with the others, shrinking smaller and smaller, then turning to shapeless dots she couldn't have recognized one from the other if she'd taken her eyes away, then altogether gone over the hills. The sun had climbed higher as she watched until now it shone full on her face. She looked down at a dark stain on the broken stone wall before her—her blood. She opened her fist to see the white scar on the palm. . . .

The last time she had stood in this spot had been after she and Will had fought—not so long ago, really, less than two full months, but it seemed like another age. She had been desperate to escape, to leave Will and his castle—and herself most of all. She had wanted to fly away, and something strange had happened. For the first time since that terrible day, she let her mind return there, to think and feel her way through the Alista she had been. She had been thinking about the falcon, Papa's beloved white, and the way she had fallen to earth. She had climbed up on the ledge . . . had she meant to fall? She touched the stain, remembering, but she didn't think so. She hadn't wanted to fall; she had wanted to fly . . . but that was insane, was it not?

Something else was nagging at her brain, something about her mother. *She flew away,* a child wept inside her head, a child that was herself. Closing her eyes, she tried to be that child again, to remember what exactly she had meant, but no image would come clear. Her mother had been very ill, and she had died. All she could remember now was standing by the remains of her father's pyre, weeping in frustration because she couldn't remember what these words meant. The pyre, the words, the words she'd sung, her blood, the falcon—all of these broken shards of meaning were important, and the connection was her mother, but the pieces wouldn't fit together; the picture wouldn't come clear. "My mother wasn't evil," she had promised Will, and he had kissed her and told her he believed her in that moment before she had learned to doubt him. He said that this broken magic of hers didn't matter, and she had loved him for it. But it did matter; otherwise why were the pieces of it still haunting her? In her dreams, she flew, night after night . . .

"Lully, lulley; lully, lulley," she sang softly to herself, the wind snatching the words from her lips. "The falcon hath borne my mate away." The song had frightened her badly, made her want to run away. That night in her dreams, she had searched for her father; waking, she had tried to climb the tower to search for him in the stars. Half-dreaming, she had questioned none of this. She had known it was right just as she had known the words to sing at the pyre and the lullaby that would quiet Nan's fears, all in her own mother's tongue. If she tried now to speak this language, the words wouldn't come, but in her dreams it came to her more easily than English or Latin or even Norman French, the language of her father and Will.

She had dreamed of Falconskeep, and in the dream, she had spoken to her mother. The details had been lost when she woke, but now they came back to her—the stairway and the moon and the spirit in the well that had touched her hand. As the wind whispered in her ears, she seemed to hear her mother's voice again. *Little bird,* she had called her, just as she had done when Alista was a child. *You are a creature of the air.*

"Falconskeep," she said aloud as she opened her eyes. *All you ever had was Brinlaw,* Will had said, making her heart tremble, but it wasn't true. She still had Falconskeep.

She ran down the stairs, letting her mantle fall behind her, lifting her skirts to run faster. Barely pausing to knock, she went into Druscilla's room, the room that had once been hers. "Good morning, cherie," Dru said, just getting out of bed.

"I hope so," Alista answered, going to the window. "I hope I'm not about to damn my soul."

"What are you talking about?" Dru asked, half laughing.

Alista drew the folded page from its hidden crevice and opened it again. "Alista," her mother had written so many years ago, but the words were still fresh. "Little bird." The woman in her mother's drawing walked naked at the edge of the sea, and in Alista's mind she saw herself—the dream of her first night with Will, her own beautiful, naked body just born but fully grown. She could hear the sad cries of the falcons overhead, see the shadow of her lover on the sand . . .

* * *

Will was dozing in the saddle, Goliath's reins slack in his fist. Ahead of him, Brother Paolo and Ned were happily debating philosophy, but he had lost the thread of their arguments long ago, miles back along the London road. Now his eyelids were too heavy to lift, the horse's gentle motion like a kind of warrior's cradle.

He was walking along a rocky beach, and it was no longer cold. The sun was beating down on him, and he stripped out of his mantle and the armor underneath, fearless in this strange place he had never seen before as if he knew he belonged there. The wind was caressing his face, and looking up, he saw falcons circling overhead, their cries drifting down as if in welcome or warning. Looking back down the beach, he saw a woman standing at the edge of the surf, and his first thought was, *Alista!* But Alista's hair was so dark brown it looked black; this creature's hair was golden, like a mantle around her shoulders and falling down her back, hiding her naked body from his eyes. But she was Alista just the same, and he broke into a run, elated and alarmed, desperate to reach her before she disappeared.

She turned just as his boots splashed into the breakers, and she smiled, opening her arms to him, falling into his embrace as the falcons screamed in triumph.

"Brinlaw, look out!" Ned shouted. Will's head snapped up just as a peregrine falcon bulleted past his head, swooping down from the air as if he'd been called. Instinctively, Will put out his arm in the falconer's manner, and the bird settled there with a ruffle of wings, blinking his yellow eyes in perfect calm.

"That's the damnedest thing I ever saw!" Ned cried.

"Brother, did you see? He flew at him like he meant to pluck his eyes out."

"Or as if he knew him," Paolo agreed, a cold shadow falling over his heart.

"Is it one of yours?" Ned asked Will. "It has no trappings I can see, but it certainly seems tame."

Will scratched the falcon under his regal chin. "Hector?" he ventured, feeling ridiculous and still dazed from his dream. It certainly looked like the bird Alista had released, but why would that bird be so far from Brinlaw Forest? And why would it suddenly come to him? "Is it you?" The bird continued to look around unconcerned, shifting a bit on his perch.

"A magnificent creature, wherever it came from," Ned said. "You should bind it quickly—"

The falcon suddenly took flight with a screech that sounded like fury to Will. "I don't think he likes that idea," he said. "And I can't say I blame him." He held out his arm again and whistled faintly, and after a minute or so, Hector swooped back to his perch. "Relax," he told the bird softly. "She'd never forgive me if I tried to keep you tied." Brother Paolo was staring at him strangely, and Ned looked utterly flummoxed. "Let's go," he said, launching the falcon again. "He can come or not as he pleases."

Will and Ned started off again, Ned still shaking his head in wonder, but Paolo hung back. Sure enough, the falcon stayed above them, making short flights from tree to tree, always keeping Will in sight.

Alista blinked, still standing at her own window. "It's Will," she said softly. "It's always been Will."

"What has?" Dru asked, touching her arm. "Cherie, are you well?"

"Yes, I—" She looked at the other girl, finally seeing her. "You must come with me," she said.

"All right; of course," Dru answered, still mystified. "But where are we going?"

"Home," Alista said. "I am going home."

To his credit, Henry had Will brought directly to his private chambers as soon as he arrived. To Will's dismay, Eleanor was there as well. "Bonjour, Lord Brinlaw," she said as he came in, giving him a dazzling smile. "How was your journey?"

"For the dead of winter, very pleasant, Majesty," Will answered, dropping to his knee to kiss her hand.

"Manners and clean-shaven, too," Henry marveled. "Marriage agrees with you, Will."

"Thank you, my liege," Will said with significantly less warmth. "Would that I were still with my wife."

"You like her, then?" The King offered him a chair.

"She is beautiful," Will said, taking it. "Henry, what am I doing here?"

"Didn't you miss me?" Henry countered. His own wife was eyeing Will with an interest he wasn't quite certain he liked. "I thought you might be ready for a visit."

"There were easier ways to invite me." He took the cup he was offered but didn't drink. "It seems I am under arrest."

"Oh, that," Henry grinned. "A trifle, I assure you."

"Not to me," Will said stubbornly. "Far be it from me to question the motives of God's Anointed, but you know damned well I didn't kill Mark."

Henry frowned, annoyed. "You know, Will, technically speaking, I do not," he said, sipping his own wine. "From the time you threatened his life to the time I brought you here, you might have been anywhere, doing anything, with me all unaware. I was rather busy, if you'll recall, it being my coronation day."

"Bollocks, Harry," Will retorted, looking ready to melt glass with the fury in his eyes. "If this is a joke, it isn't funny. Do you have any idea the trouble I've had because of your damned letter to Alista? Then your idiot cousin and his popinjay turn up with the truth of the matter and all but accuse me of murder in my own house—"

"I knew nothing about that, believe me," Henry cut him off. "And incidentally, Geoffrey isn't precisely my cousin. His mother was one of my mother's ladies-in-waiting. Have you noticed how he favors my late father?"

Will looked over at Eleanor, who was shaking her head with a sigh. "Ah."

"Ah, indeed," Henry muttered. "Still, when he brought this Michael Pettengill to me with this tale of your treachery, I told him to forget it, to leave the thing alone. That's when he took it on himself to go with Pettengill to Brinlaw."

"Treason, I called it," Eleanor put in. "Direct defiance. But Henri wishes to spare his mother embarrassment."

"I want Geoffrey to shut the hell up for good and all," Henry put it more bluntly.

"Does this extend to having me hanged so he can have my wife?" Will inquired politely.

"Of course not," Henry scowled. "It just means the issue must be dealt with publicly before it can be put to rest for good. Pettengill must have his chance to air his grievance; you must tell him he's mistaken, that you were in church or fishing for pike in the river or making merry in a bawdy house to celebrate my crowning on the night Mark died. Then I will say I believe you, declare the matter closed, and that will be the end of it."

Will didn't want to smile, but he almost couldn't help it. Henry was truly vexed, for all he tried to hide it. "And who will convince my wife?" he asked, all innocent.

The King was not fooled. "I will," he grinned. "I shall write her another letter. I'm sorry, Will, truly, but we'll soon put it all right." He stood and offered Will his hand.

"I have no doubt, Majesty," Will answered with good grace as he took it.

"Lord Brinlaw, may I ask you a question?" Eleanor asked as he was leaving.

"Of course, Your Majesty."

She smiled. "You say Lady Alista is beautiful." Will nodded, his expression guarded. "Has she no other qualities to speak of?"

The knight just looked at her. That damned minstrel had said the Queen very much liked Geoffrey's song, that he was quite the favorite at her court of love. Now it seemed that this young Geoffrey was also the bastard of the late Geoffrey the Handsome. Rumor had long held that back when Eleanor was still Queen of France, long before she fell in love with Henry, she had been quite torridly involved in an illicit affair with his father. Perhaps she saw qualities, as she called them, in dead Geoffrey's baseborn son that she found lacking in his heir, the King of England. In any case, he was not inclined to make her his confidante. "No, Majesty," he said at last. "Nothing to speak of. Is that all?"

"Of course," she nodded. "Thank you."

"What, pray tell, was that all about?" Henry asked when Will was gone.

"Idle curiosity," Eleanor answered with a reassuring kiss.

"I see." He drew her into his lap over the arm of his chair at great risk to her queenly dignity. "Did you notice the scar on his cheek?"

"I did," she said with a secretive smile.

"What?" he demanded. "What is it you think you know?"

"Why nothing, dear England," she said. "How should I know anything at all?"

Alista took the scimitar out of its wrappings and held it up to the light. After midnight the armory was deserted, but a blazing fire still burned in the massive hearth, its flames gleaming like brimstone on the lethal curve of steel.

Grasping the hilt in both hands like a broadsword, she wheeled around to slash the straw and leather mannequin behind her. The weapon sliced deep, but when she tried to parry, the shape of the blade made her clumsy, and when she yanked it free, she overbalanced and nearly fell over, the sword was so light. Mumbling an oath, she stepped back to try again.

She extended her right arm with the weapon balanced in her open palm, waggling it lightly to test its weight and roll. With the handle placed across the back of her hand as seemed proper, the tiny jewels of the hilt cut into her palm, but when she rolled the hilt a quarter turn, her fingers found four grooves that seemed custom carved to her grip. Still holding it in one hand, she attacked the popinjay again, this time pulling back with little trouble.

"Better," Clarence said, coming in. "But hardly perfect."

"You think not?" she laughed, relaxing her stance. "I see you received my message."

"That's a pretty toy you have," he said. "Where did you get it?"

"Will gave it to me," she answered, handing it over. "Maybe he thought I would cut my own throat trying to learn to use it."

Clarence smiled without looking up. "A heathen scimitar . . . a right pricey one, I'd say."

"He said it belonged to an Arabian prince. Is it truly just a toy?"

"No, my lady, nothing of the sort," he assured her, slicing at the air. "I've seen rougher blades than this cut out an Englishman's guts while he was still raising his broadsword." He tested its weight much as Alista had done. "It's not much good against armor, not at all on plate, because it is so light, but you can maneuver it into the chinks like a butcher, once you know how."

"Really?" Alista said with a wry grin. "I was thinking with that curve it was rather like cutting down a tree with a ladle."

"That's because you want to slash your opponent's sides the way I taught you with a broadsword, taking him down to your size very much like you were hacking down a tree," he said. "Look at the shape of your blade. You get one downward slash, across the body, so, which you can do because you can lift it over your head one-handed—but that's just to hurt him. The coup de grace is the upward thrust into the stomach with this point—you see these notches?" She nodded, making a queasy face he would know was all for show. "You can catch all manner of dainties with those before you yank it out again." He handed it back to her. "Give yourself time; you'll learn." He ruffled her hair, ruefully shaking his head. "A lady grown and married, and she still thinks she ought to be a boy."

"No, I don't," she answered, putting the sword aside. "Clarence, I need your help. Will you help me?"

"That all depends on what you mean to do," he answered. "If you mean to kill someone we both know, then no, I will not, for it's a damned foolish idea."

"I don't want to kill anyone, not anymore," she promised. "But I have to go away—"

"Running away is almost as foolish as murder," he began.

"Maybe, but I have to just the same," she cut him off. "I must go to Falconskeep." She watched his expression change from shock to dismay to a grim determination she associated with fruitless attempts to weasel out of her lessons. "Clarence, I must."

"I don't see that," he said stubbornly.

"You don't have to see it," she retorted, just as stubborn. "What if Will didn't come back? What if King Henry means to execute him? Should I just wait here for his successor to show up to bed me or put me out of my house and my kin with me?"

"Druscilla, I suppose you mean," he grumbled. "I might have known she'd put you up to something foolish—"

"She didn't put me up to anything," she cut him off, offended. "But yes, she is coming with me."

"And what if your husband does come back?" he demanded.

"If he does . . ." She stuck her sword lazily into the popinjay's stomach. "Either he wants me or he doesn't. If he does, he will come and find me. If he doesn't . . ." She pulled it out again, easing around the blade's curve this time instead of against it. "He can leave us in peace."

The castellan took a deep, obviously disgruntled breath.

"I can't just leave," he pointed out. "My duty is here—"

"I know," she hastened to assure him. Her father had put him in charge of Brinlaw Castle when they'd first come there, and he'd never once abandoned his post. She wouldn't dare ask him to do so now. "I just need you to remind me of the way."

"The way?" he asked doubtfully. "You mean to go to Falconskeep?"

She took a deep breath, bracing herself for his most heated protest yet. "Yes, Falconskeep," she answered, not meeting his eyes. How could she make this soldier understand her reasons, the dreams and visions that compelled her more surely than any authority she had ever known, the desperate need she had to know herself, to know what these mysteries meant?

But Clarence surprised her. "Falconskeep," he repeated with an air of resignation, as if he'd expected as much. "I suppose I should draw you a map."

Henry's court was crowded, and quarters were scarce, leaving Brother Paolo no choice but to share the suite of rooms reserved for Will's "incarceration," and Will no choice but to let him. "Like living in a beehive," Will grumbled, polishing off the last of the wine as Hector polished off a mouse he'd found in the corner.

"No bee could live here," Paolo agreed, opening a second bottle. "Too much smoke." He filled their glasses again. "Not that I mind cities as a rule. I was born in Florence, after all."

"So you've said," Will mused, just drunk, tired, and lonely enough to be mildly interested. "So how did you end up in England?"

Paolo laughed. "It could have been much worse, signor—I started out headed for Ireland." He chewed his mutton thoughtfully. "I was a young priest, barely ordained, when God spoke to me in a dream."

"God Himself?" Will asked, amused. "Personally?"

"I thought so, but what did I know? Had I ever seen Him before?" He shook his head. "But no, that is blasphemy. It was God, and He told me my destiny lay in the north, across a cold, gray sea. I told the leader of my order of my dream, and he said that God must mean Ireland—he was very taken with Saint Patrick, I believe."

"Perhaps he had a horror of snakes," Will said with only the most friendly touch of sarcasm. "So why didn't you go to Ireland?"

"I tried," Paolo protested with a laugh. "But I am a Franciscan; I had no money for travel. At first, this wasn't such a problem. People on the Continent were willing if not always happy to help me in my quest for the sake of a blessing. But when I finally came to England, I found a civil war and people barely able to feed themselves, much less a priest. They had priests enough already, none of whom seemed able to do them any good; why should they worry about a foreigner? They believed God had abandoned them, so they abandoned me. By the time I made it to the Irish Sea, I was too ill to sail, even if I had been able to find passage. I was starving, freezing, furious with God for sending me on such a quest. I stood on the beach and shook my fist at the sky, telling God that if He wanted me to serve any better purpose than to give a few seagulls a very poor dinner, He had better send an angel to save me, and quickly." He smiled. "And so He did."

"An angel?" Will asked doubtfully. "Did you recognize him?"

"Her, signor," he corrected, taking another sip. "The Lady Blanche, Lord Mark's wife. Alista's mother."

"An angel?" Will repeated.

"The most beautiful creature I had ever seen," Paolo insisted. "At first I thought I must be seeing things—a vision. She came walking toward me on that horrid, rocky beach, a woman all alone, no man, no attendants even."

"That sounds like someone I know," Will muttered into his cup.

"Just so," Paolo agreed. "She took one look at me and said I must come to her castle. She fed me, gave me clothes that kept me warm in your hideous, English climate, and taught me to speak English by speaking to me in Italian—an Englishwoman who spoke Italian; can you imagine?"

"You said she was beautiful?" Will innocently inquired, a smile at the corner of his mouth.

"I know what you are thinking," Paolo retorted. "Yes, very beautiful—tall, with hair so blond it was almost white, and long, slender hands. A most elegant figure, but warm and kind."

"But you weren't in love with her," Will chided.

"It would not have mattered if I were," the friar laughed. "Lady Blanche was too in love with her husband. Alista was just a baby, barely able to walk, and Lord Mark had already been away fighting for months when I arrived at Falconskeep, and was to stay away the entire three years and more I was there. But his wife spoke of him constantly as if he had only left that moment to go hunting and would be back in time for dinner. I believe Alista's first words were 'As soon as my papa is home.' " His expression clouded, and he took another long drink. "As soon as her papa came home, her mother was an angel indeed."

"How old was she?" Will asked. "Alista, I mean."

"Four years old," Paolo answered. "Her mother died; her father came; Falconskeep was burned." He smiled sadly. "A very long time ago, signor. Sometimes I wonder what Alista remembers of that time and her mother and that castle by the sea. She never speaks of it, but there are signs . . ." He let his words trail off.

"She isn't four years old anymore," Will pointed out, suddenly feeling he didn't much care for this tale. He didn't like to think of Alista as a homeless baby, particularly since his own father might have been among those who made her so. It interfered overmuch with his own sense of righteous indignation.

Paolo shook his head. "No, she is a woman, with a woman's problems, and I find myself less able to help her with every day that dawns." He smiled again. "That is why I have come here."

"To help her how?" Will asked peevishly. "By keeping me from killing her lover?"

"Which lover did you mean?" Paolo countered, trying not to laugh outright.

"Does she not fear for the safety of Geoffrey d'Anjou?" Will said, getting up.

"Not as I noticed, signor," the friar said dryly. "Indeed, I don't think she ever worried over him much. Sir Geoffrey . . . there isn't much of Sir Geoffrey to speak of, taken all in all."

"I think not either," Will muttered, opening the shutter to look out at the stars. "But we're neither of us much judge."

Paolo could only shake his head and smile. "Believe as you will, my son. I am going to bed."

* * *

Armed with instructions from Clarence and her fascinating sword, Alista met Dru in the archway of the Great Hall, and together they slipped out of the castle. "Is Clarence seeing to the guards?" Dru whispered when they had reached the relative safety of the stables.

"Yes," Alista whispered. "All except that one."

The soldier had just put away his horse. "Hey, what are you doing out here?" he called out, catching sight of Dru. "It's the middle of the night."

"Is it?" Dru asked sweetly as Alista faded back into the shadows.

"Aye," he said, grinning foolishly at her as he approached. God save him, he was one of Will's. "Aren't you afraid you'll catch a chill out here in the cold night air?"

He doesn't recognize her, Alista thought, drawing her sword slowly and silently from her belt and praying she wouldn't have to use it. *He thinks she's a servant.*

"I'faith, sweeting, I was feeling rather warm," Dru replied in perfect peasant English, her lowered lashes at odds with her lascivious smile. "The night air suits me fine."

"Not so well as the moonlight," he answered, his tone turning soft with lover's menace.

Suddenly a huge pottery jar that had once held oats came down on the back of his neck, shattering to bits and sending him sprawling in the straw. "Why not have a look at the stars?" Tarquin muttered, giving him a kick for good measure.

"Tarquin, that was bad!" Nan protested, obviously appalled.

"Tarquin, that was magnifique!" Dru laughed, giving the boy a kiss.

"And timely," Alista agreed, bending over the casualty. He was out cold, but his pulse was steady and his breathing even. He'd be fine in a very few minutes, and someone was likely to come looking for him even sooner. They had to hurry. "Why aren't you children in bed?"

"Why aren't you?" Tarquin retorted. "You can't just be leaving us."

Nan suddenly seemed to realize why they were all up playing with horses in the middle of the night. "We can't leave!" she cried, running to Alista, stepping across the fallen guardsman's back in the process. "Ask me when my uncle is coming home," she ordered, yanking Alista's hand.

"Nan, what are you—?"

"Ask me!"

"All right." She bent down to the child's eye level. "When is your uncle coming home?"

"Very soon," she answered in triumph. "I promised him I would tell you if you asked."

"Alista, please," Dru urged. "I think that we must be gone."

"So we can't go, because he will be back, and if we aren't here, he will be very sad," the little girl pressed on.

"Nan, you aren't going anywhere," Alista began.

"Oh yes, she is," Tarquin said stubbornly. "I'm not going without her, and you two are not going without me."

"Tarquin, don't be ridiculous," Dru protested. "We can't take you with us."

"You can, and I'll tell you why," he shot back. "For one thing, if it weren't for me, you'd have been caught already and never get to go at all. For two, neither of you fine ladies has ever been anywhere without a troop of soldiers to protect you." He looked at Alista and blushed. "Your disguise is very good, my lady, but I don't think the bandits will be impressed. I've ridden from one end of England to the other. I know how to hide and survive."

"He makes a good point, Alista," Dru admitted.

"Don't you start, too," Alista snapped.

"And third and most important, if you try to go without us, I shall pinch Nan," Tarquin continued. "I'll pinch her and pinch her until she screams loud enough to wake every man jack in the castle."

"Tarquin, no!" Nan squeaked, holding her arms in alarm. "Don't you let him, my lady!"

"You wouldn't dare," Alista breathed.

"Try me," he snarled back.

If she hadn't been in such a hurry, Alista thought she would have taken him over her knee and spanked him. As it was, she was forced to consider what he said. If she took the children with her and Will came back to Brinlaw, there was no question he would come after her whether he wanted her or not. But if it wasn't Will who returned as Lord Brinlaw but Geoffrey d'Anjou, did she really want to trust Will's niece and her half-brother to his tender mercies with no one to defend them? "All right," she grumbled in surrender. "But do come on and hurry."

Alista led one horse with Druscilla in the saddle; Tarquin led the other with Nan. They stayed in the shadow of the wall until they heard Clarence call out and the guardsmen answer. Then when the two guarding the breach went to see what the castellan wanted, they led the horses out through the half-mended hole and down to the frozen moat. A hoof slipped in the mud and made Tarquin's horse scramble as he stepped onto the ice, and Nan clamped both her hands over her mouth to keep from crying out. Then he found his footing, and all was well again.

They walked the horses until they were well into the forest, then Alista stopped. "Are you all right?" Dru asked, touching her shoulder as she looked back at her tower, still visible over the trees.

"Fine." She climbed up in front of her friend. "Let's go."

Ten

A letter from Fra Paolo Bosacci to his sister, Serena
February 10, 1156

My dearest friend,

London continues to be an education to me, old as I am. King Henry has again postponed actually trying Will Brinlaw on the charges brought against him, preferring to keep him a guest at court. In one way, this is encouraging. The King's affection and regard for Brinlaw are obvious—indeed, many more constant courtiers are beginning to complain that this "country knight" exercises too much influence. But I still worry nonetheless. If Henry intends without question to rule in favor of his great friend, why not do so and be done with it? These delays could just as easily mean the opposite, that he means to find Will guilty for the sake of politics in spite of his personal feelings and therefore means to put it off as long as possible. So I am keeping my eyes open, my prayers constant, and my mind as sharp as effort can make it.

I know you must be curious to read about these monarchs, the most famous lovers in Christendom just now, so I will attempt to give you my impressions though I have no talent for gossip. Henry is not a particularly handsome man, nor is he physically large, yet he is one of the most imposing figures I have ever encountered. His manner, brusque and rather theatrical, more than make up for any deficits in his figure, and his will is legendary. If he should decide tomorrow to reduce his realm to sand by grinding down every tree and castle with his own teeth, he would commence chewing without the slightest hesitation, and everyone around him would despair, confident he would finish the task. While this personality is no doubt the key to his success as king, I imagine it makes him a rather trying husband. But if any woman could hold herself intact against his assault, it would be Queen Eleanor. I'm certain you've heard she is beautiful. This is an understatement. To look on her is quite literally to lose one's breath, a fact of which she is obviously aware and which she uses to its full advantage. She has a kind of cult to feminine beauty in general and her own lovely self in particular surrounding her at all times, ladies who serve her and the gentlemen who so desperately wish to. These pretty creatures of both sexes spend their days engaging in complex romantic play where what they term love is quite separate from God's rite of marriage, a religion unto itself where the female is divine, the male her abject slave. I am assured that very few of these elaborately choreographed romances are ever consummated, but I have my doubts. As our mother used to say, anyone who spends all his time cooking will eventually eat something.

At any rate, King Henry seems to have very little patience with his queen's games, preferring statecraft and other, more traditionally manly pursuits. He keeps Brinlaw with him, and I follow Brinlaw like a shadow whenever possible just as Alista asked, so I am mostly spared these unseemly, childish, and to my mind dangerous displays. However, I have seen Sir Geoffrey.

Brinlaw was hunting with the King, an activity I cannot share, so I was taking the opportunity to explore the late King Stephen's extensive library. I was admiring the illuminations on a French text when I suddenly realized I was being watched. Looking up, I found Geoffrey. "Well met, my lord," I greeted him, though in truth he had given me a fright. "I did not think to meet you here."

"Nor would you have done, had I not followed you," he told me, and though he was smiling, something in this gave me a pronounced feeling of dread. When he used to visit Lord Mark, I always thought of Geoffrey as a rather empty young man, good-natured enough, charming, certainly, but lacking in any true character. I believed he needed a purpose to determine who he would be. Now I fear he has found his purpose, and it is not a happy one. His face, once picture-pretty, has taken on an older, more melancholy appearance that young ladies at court are said to find fascinating, but to me it seemed more a quality of cunning in the lines around his eyes, the set of his mouth and chin. In short, he looks as if he has been gravely disappointed and means to have revenge. You, my sensible Serena, are probably laughing at me as you read this, but I swear it is true, and looking at him, I silently thanked God Alista never fell in love with him. "I wished to ask you about Lady Alista," he went on as if he'd read my thoughts.

"Perhaps you should ask her husband," I offered cautiously.

He laughed. "You must be joking; no priest could be so

cruel," he said, but his green eyes were not amused. "I must know; is she well?"

"Alista is fine," I told him. "You must believe me when I tell you this."

"Must I?" he mused softly, his gaze drifting from me. "And Druscilla? How are she and her child?"

"Also well," I said without thinking at the time, but Serena, how could he have known Lady Dru was with child? The last time he was at Brinlaw, it was hardly obvious, and in any case, he barely saw her. The longer I think about this, the more it worries me.

"Good," he nodded, seeming to barely hear me. "Will your virtue grant me one favor, Brother?" He looked back at me. "Will you remember me to Alista? Will you tell her she is in my thoughts?"

I considered my answer for a moment. "I will say you wish her well."

He smiled again as if he thought me a very funny old man. "Then that will have to do."

Tarquin proved to be every bit as much help as he had promised, leading them along less-traveled and therefore safer roads without ever losing his sense of direction, so they never strayed far from the path Clarence had sketched out. But he was a hard leader, nonetheless, insisting they ride almost without stopping at all for a week. "Are you certain you know where you're going?" Dru complained as another dawn broke behind them.

"I know exactly," Alista answered, smelling the sea in the air. She had forgotten how much she had missed it, she had been away so long, and yet now it seemed to have always been a part of her, like her blood. "We're almost there."

She half-expected to find Falconskeep still burning, was almost surprised a few hours later to see no smoke rising over its black and broken towers, the image of the last time she had seen it was still so vivid in her mind. "That's it?" Tarquin asked doubtfully.

Alista smiled. "Alas, it is," she said. "I told you you didn't want to come."

He looked again and shrugged. " 'Tis not so bad, I guess," he said, spurring his horse again.

"Compared to what?" Dru grumbled, holding on more tightly as Alista's horse broke into a gallop.

Most of the castle was indeed uninhabitable, but remarkably, the central tower was virtually untouched inside, as if the flames hadn't dared to pass its arch. "The best bedroom is up here, anyway," Alista said, starting up the stairs.

Dru had been looking steadily more uneasy every moment since they arrived. "Alista, wait," she said now, catching her arm. "Might I have a word?"

Her friend stopped, surprised, but she didn't argue. "Tarquin, you and Nan go on up and see what's there," she told the boy. "We'll be right behind you."

Dru looked around at the broken benches in the hall, the tapestries hanging in scorched ribbons from the walls, and slumped against the archway in despair. "No, don't," she demurred when Alista moved to fetch the charred remains of a chair. "I may never sit again."

"Poor Dru," Alista said with a sympathetic smile. "Only a little farther, and you can sleep for days, I swear."

"Assuming there's still a bed," Dru agreed. "I'm fine, cherie, truly, but I wonder—how long do you think we must stay here?"

Alista looked around as well, only slightly less dismayed.

"I wish I knew," she admitted. She had confided most of her reasons for leaving Brinlaw to Dru before they left—the practical ones, anyway—and her friend had agreed they were sound. If Brinlaw Castle was destined for yet another new lord, neither of them wanted to be there to greet him; Dru didn't even particularly want to be there if Will came back. But still, seeing the state of their refuge, Alista could certainly understand if Dru had doubts now. Even so, Falconskeep was hers, and in spite of anything she saw, she felt she was meant to be here. The answers she needed were here, not at Brinlaw, and not in Henry's court. "Once Brother Paolo returns from London, Clarence will tell him where we've gone."

"And he will tell your husband, whoever that might be after the trial, because Brother Paolo has seen this place and knows we can't possibly live here." She tried to soften her words with a smile, but it was a poor effort. "We need help, and not from Brother Paolo," she said more gently. "Send Tarquin to London, to Geoffrey—"

"Are you mad?" Alista cried.

"If he knows our trouble, he will come and take us to Anjou," Dru pressed on eagerly. "At least that would be better than this; at least we would be safe—"

"I would rather be safe here, if you don't mind," Alista said, turning back to the staircase. The very idea of turning to Geoffrey for help made her sick to her stomach, and the thought of facing Will after she did was even worse.

"I do mind, very much—"

"Druscilla, I will not!" A beam of sun fell across her face from an arrow slit above, turning her dark eyes purple with its light. "I will not send that child anywhere alone, and I will not beg help from Geoffrey. These things will never happen, no matter how sorely you chide me, so you may as well save your energy." The other woman looked so stricken, Alista felt like a perfect beast, but she couldn't back down. "Now do you need me to help you upstairs?"

"I think I can manage," Dru said, following. "But when I do reach a bed, I intend to lie down for a whole week."

When Brother Paolo returned from the clerk's where he had posted his letter to Serena, he found Will alone in his rooms. "My trial has officially been set," he announced as the monk came in, sitting on the window ledge with Hector perched on his fist. "I will be accused tomorrow." He let the falcon fly out the open window. "So either way, you should be headed home soon."

"You don't seem terribly concerned," Paolo said, warming his frozen hands at the fire.

"I'm not," Will answered, closing the shutter. The bird wouldn't return for hours, but he would return and to this very window without fail—after more than a week, he had yet to make a mistake. "Does that disappoint you?" Will asked with half a grin.

"Disappoint me? No, not at all. Worry me?" The Franciscan took a seat. "I just hope you do not place too much confidence in your friendship with the King."

"So do I," Will admitted. "But why should you care, Brother Paolo? Don't you wish to see me hanged or beheaded or whatever it is they're doing to murderers these days? Isn't that why Alista sent you, to see her revenge carried out?"

Paolo just stared at him. "You cannot truly believe that," he scoffed. "No man as old as you could be so stupid."

Will scowled, not answering this insult until he'd filled

his cup. "Very well then," he muttered after a swallow of wine. "What should I believe?"

"Alista did send me as a witness, but she wishes you no ill," Paolo answered. "She fears for you, in fact. From what she knows of King Henry's character, she believes he may intend to remove you from Brinlaw, to put someone more agreeable in your place, someone who doesn't defy his king and cause trouble with other knights. Otherwise, why summon you here at all? Why not just tell Pettengill to take his charges and choke on them?" The monk broke off for a moment before he finished. "Hopefully, you do know your sovereign better than Alista does."

That Henry could himself be planning to do him harm had never occurred to Will, but now that he thought about it, he had to admit it was possible. "My heart thrills to think my lady so frets about my safety," he said aloud, sarcastically.

"It should," Paolo shot back.

"So she sent you here to protect me, to call down one of those angels you know so well?" Will laughed, emptying his cup.

"She sent me so someone she trusts would know firsthand what happened to you, whatever that might be," the monk said. "Her father left her so many times, and she never knew what might befall him. Then when the day came that he didn't come back, no one would . . ." Again he let his words die unfinished. "She wants to know for certain who to hold accountable if you should fail to return." He picked up his book and stood again. "And whether you believe it or not, she would take losing you very ill." Before the knight could answer, he left, slamming the door behind him.

Will stared at the door for a long moment, stunned. Then he went to the table where the monk had left his vellum and stylus and began to write.

Dear Alista—

If Brother Paolo brings you this, he will tell you what has become of me. At this moment, I wouldn't dare to guess what he will say. But I can write you what has happened to me before and what I know of what happened to your father.

I lived at Brinlaw Castle until I was ten years old. My father, like yours, was often away at war, but my mother and older sister, May, were there with me, and I thought our lives were very ordinary and tedious. I longed and prayed for the day I could leave Brinlaw and be a knight like my father.

When I was ten, in the spring, a troop of Stephen's soldiers came and said our castle was forfeit to the Crown because my father was a traitor. I tried to fight them, but I was a child, and I failed. Again I prayed to be a knight, the best knight in the world so that no one would dare to oppose me once I won our castle back. My mother thought me very foolish, but May said she believed in me, that she knew God would grant my prayers. My mother, unwilling to wait for this miracle, made a marriage for her to Bruel, and I went with her to be her husband's squire. But as I have told you, this didn't last very long.

I ran away to war and finally found my father. He was very angry with me for breaking my oath to Bruel no matter how badly I had been treated, but he allowed me to stay with him. In truth, I believe he was as relieved to see me alive as I was to see him. I had always respected and admired my father; in the next few weeks, I grew to love him. He taught me everything I could ever hope to learn of honor. I was even bold enough to ask him how he could support the Empress's claim to England's throne when so many men called him a traitor for it. He explained it very simply, "I swore an oath to her father. At his bidding, I swore an oath to Maud. I will never break my oath."

A week later, he was dead. I was with him on the battlefield; I watched him die; and with his blood still on my hands, I swore my oath to Henry, swore to make him king. The only time I have ever doubted my course was when I heard my sister was dead. I thought God was angry with me; I thought it was my fault. So I took the cross to fight for God instead, to fight for May's salvation, just as you said. But the things I saw in the Holy Land . . . that fight was not of God, no matter what the priests might say. If I do live and you do someday wish to hear, I will tell you of Jerusalem. For now, suffice to say the desert proved to me that Brinlaw and England were the only causes worth my family's blood. So I came home and claimed Brinlaw from my king, and I didn't care about your father or you or politics or anything else. I could not. If the choice were before me again, I could not but choose the same.

I know you have heard already how your father and I quarreled at the coronation. Afterward, I didn't even stay for the King's celebration banquet, I was so enraged. I found Raynard, and the two of us went to a tavern and proceeded to drink ourselves blind. Sometime after midnight, we were summoned to Henry's private rooms. He told us Mark was dead and that if I would take his body home and marry you, Brinlaw would be mine. Again, I did not consider you, Alista. I hope that if I had known you then as

I do now, I would have, but even now, I can't be certain. Brinlaw was too important.

We were taken to the house where your father had died. Some of his guardsmen had already fled, and of those who remained, none had been with him when death came. He was still fully clothed, lying on the floor—one of the guards said they had rolled him onto his back but he was otherwise untouched. His sword and armor were laid out on a bench, though whether he had just removed them or had placed them there some time before to be ready for the morning, I couldn't say. There was an open bottle of wine on the table, and a cup had fallen over and spilled beside it as if he had set it down clumsily as he fell. He had fallen beside the table, and though he was white when I saw him, a servant of the house said that his face had been very red and that he had complained of a headache before retiring. He had also made them remove a bowl of dried fruits from the room because he said they were turned, that the stench hurt his head. More than that, I didn't ask. Forgive me, lady, but I did not care.

So that is what I know. It isn't likely to make you think any better of me, but at least it is the truth, and this is true as well. You told me once you did not deserve to be hated. I have never hated you. Coming to you, I imagined what you would be like, but nothing I could have dreamed could be like you. In the time before you came to despise me, you were everything any man could ever wish his wife to be. If Henry does fail me and I lose Brinlaw and my life, I will still regret the loss of you more than anything else.

Your husband in soul as in name,
Will

Dru and Nan were both sleeping, and Tarquin was building up the fire. "You know, it really isn't so bad here," he said, sitting back on his heels. "I'm surprised no thieves have come in to strip it bare."

"So am I," Alista admitted. In truth, her mother's old room wasn't even particularly dirty, with only a light layer of dust over all. The shutter had been open when they came in, the icy wind whipping around the circular walls, but the tapestries still hung just where they had when she had last seen them. Everything was just the same. Looking at the bed, she didn't see Dru and the child but a dying woman raising her slender, white hands to catch the wind.

"We need water, though," Tarquin said, breaking into her remembering. "Our skins are almost empty, and the only stream I've seen nearby is salt. Is there a well?"

Isn't there? she thought but didn't say, remembering her dream of her mother and a spirit that lived in the well and had touched her hand. But that was a dream. Reality was Nan waking up thirsty. "Come on," she said, getting up and taking a torch from the wall. "I'll show you another miracle."

The boy followed her down the stairs to the foot of the tower without comment, but when they reached the archway to the ruined hall and she continued downward, he looked doubtful. "What's down there?" he asked, picking up a bucket from the stairs.

"Wait and see," Alista answered, not sure what else to say, not sure what she expected. She picked up a bucket of her own and led the way again.

The upper stairs were as clean as if they'd been swept that morning, but as they ventured deeper, the steps grew slick with damp moss and mud. And when they reached the bottom, the well itself was sealed off with a great, moss-covered boulder, seated so snugly in the shaft it seemed to have been carved by a giant to fit it. As soon as Alista saw it, her heart sank. Clarence and Will together might have been able to move it, but a woman and a ten-year-old boy?

"I take it the spring is under the rock?" Tarquin asked, sounding as dispirited as she felt.

"We may as well try," she decided, setting her bucket on the floor and her torch in a bracket on the wall.

But as soon as they leaned against the boulder, it rolled easily away. "There must be a trick to it," Tarquin said, examining the well's jagged lip.

"A trick, but no rope," Alista agreed, looking around. "There used to be a chain." She remembered coming here with her mother when she was so tiny, she couldn't walk down the stairs without holding someone's hand. *I don't like it,* she had said in her dream, a woman full-grown and frightened. *I want to go back.* They had lowered their bucket on a thick, rusted chain, her mother singing, making her voice ring on the stones. "To comfort the water," she'd said. "The water can't bear the chain."

She took down the torch again and peered down the shaft, trying to shine light into the darkness, but the well was so narrow, it was impossible. "I suppose we'll have to go back up and find something."

"Wait," Tarquin said, leaning in. "Look there—there's something metal." He set his bucket down, too. "Lower me down, and I think I can reach it."

"I don't know," she frowned, unconvinced. "I don't think I see anything."

"It's right there—just hold on to my feet," he insisted, climbing onto the ledge.

"All right, but be careful." She grabbed his jerkin first, then his boots as he eased his way down. "Can you see it?"

"I feel something," he answered. "Just a little more . . ."

Suddenly he started to struggle, thrashing in her grip as if he meant to dive down the well. "What's the matter?" she protested, using all her strength to hold him and trying to yank him back up.

"Let me go!" he yelled, his voice echoing like something heard in dreams, both feet kicking madly to be free. "I have to go to her!"

"The hell you say," Alista said, breathless with exertion as she gave another mighty tug, and suddenly it was as if something that had been pulling back suddenly let go, and the two of them fell backward on the floor. "Are you mad?" she demanded angrily, untangling herself to get back to her feet. "You could have killed yourself!" *You mustn't trust her*, her dream mother had warned. *She will be jealous of your soul.*

The boy was staring at her, blinking, still sprawled on the floor, his eyes so wide white showed all around each hazel iris. "Yes," he agreed, choking out the word. "I meant to, for a moment." He looked down at something clutched tightly in his fist. "I found this," he said, offering it to Alista.

She recognized the pendant at once, and every other thought was lost. "Mama's heartstone," she breathed, taking it.

Her mother had always worn it, every day of Alista's life until the day she died, and Alista had loved it, loved to touch it, to lift it away from her mother's skin to see it sparkle in the light. "This will be yours someday," Mama had said, smiling at her, glad she liked it. "In a way, it already is." The chain was as bright as ever, but she remembered the stone when her mother took it off, the dullness of it and the deep, red flaw. These were gone. Now the entire stone was worn back to its ruby brightness, its heart shape worn sharp again.

"It was caught on what felt like a lever," Tarquin explained, catching his breath enough to get up at last. "I was about to pull it when I heard someone calling to me."

"That was me, trying to bring you back up." She slipped the chain around her neck, and the stone felt warm against her skin, as if someone had just that moment taken it off.

"No," he insisted. "It was a woman, but not you. She was at the bottom of the well, and she wanted me to come to her. And I couldn't stop myself from going."

Alista just looked at him. He looked perfectly in earnest, and she knew he was telling the truth; she just didn't want to admit it. Something was in the well, something that thought itself her sister. She shivered, dizzy . . . could such a thing be real? How was she to live with the knowledge once she knew for sure?

"How far down is that lever?" she asked him aloud, trying to stay practical, to put these frightening, dream-thoughts from her mind. "Did you touch it?"

"Yes, but—"

"Here, hold on to me." Tucking the heartstone into her shirt, she leaned over the rim of the well.

"This is not the best idea you ever had, Alista," he warned, springing to grab hold of her waist.

"All right, Tarquin, all right." She leaned in farther. "Hold my legs—I can see it, but I can't quite reach it."

"Just be very careful, please?" he said, doing as she asked.

"Quite careful—just don't let go." She should have been afraid, and she did feel a slight shiver of recognition as she put herself deeper into the dark. But no voice called to her; no icy hand touched hers. She felt her way down the rough stone wall until her fingertips brushed something smooth and made of wood jutting out of the side. Something about this was familiar, as if she'd been told about it long ago, but unlike her dream, this image wouldn't come clear. "Just a bit more," she murmured, stretching her arm until the muscles popped in protest. Her hand closed over the handle. "Here goes . . ."

Water came bubbling toward her in a rush. "Come back up!" Tarquin yelled, pulling her so quickly she banged her head on the edge. "Are you all right?"

"Except for the knot on my head," she grumbled, rubbing it. Her face and the front of her hair were dripping wet, the well had filled so quickly.

"Sorry," he muttered, looking embarrassed.

"Not at all," she relented, giving him a hug. "See, I told you it would work."

"It worked, all right," he grumbled. "So what would you call that?"

Floating on the surface was a large, leather-bound book. "No," she said, letting him go to pick it up. "It can't be." The outside was dripping wet, and she thought surely it must be ruined. But when she opened it, the pages were perfectly dry and turned easily, not even swollen or warped from damp.

"What is it?" Tarquin asked, raising on tiptoe to peer over her shoulder. "What sort of writing is that?"

"My mother's," she said softly, the strange text swimming in her sudden tears. "All of these things belonged to her." She had forgotten . . . the heartstone she remembered, but the book she had forgotten.

More than half of London's noblemen were crowded into Henry's main audience chamber, eager for gossip to while away the tedium of peace. None of them felt any particular ill will toward William Brinlaw, few of them even knew Michael Pettengill. But a nobleman killing another and then being taken to task for it? That was something to see. Plus Henry was still a brand new king—how would his justice be dealt? All in all, a most informative experience was anticipated by all.

"Sir Michael, you have made a serious accusation against a man I have long held dear," Henry was saying from the stern height of his crown. He looked every inch the King, as much here as he had in battle, and his manner was magnificently grave. "What evidence do you bring now that he stands accused?"

"The evidence of Your Majesty's own eyes, for a beginning," Pettengill began with admirable courage, looking very much a man secure in his beliefs. "On the great day of Your Majesty's coronation, this same William Brinlaw did threaten the life of Lord Mark in this very room before many of the same men who stand here now." A murmur of agreement rumbled around the room.

" 'Tis true," Henry agreed. "But if my ancient memory does not begin to fail me, Lord Mark did threaten his first."

"Yes, Majesty," Pettengill said with a bitter smile. "But Lord William is not dead."

"Not yet, anyway," Will said with a smile of his own, and the assemblage chuckled appreciatively.

"Even so," the King said dryly, giving a disapproving

look. "If I were to hold every man who ever threatened another accountable for that man's eventual death, I would soon have no nobles at all." Now he grinned. "And you would have no king." This earned a heartier laugh. "Will, where were you that night? I confess I was otherwise engaged."

"Drinking, Majesty," Will said, eliciting a softer murmur, but friendly nonetheless. "I confess I was angry with you, and since you were king, I couldn't tell you so."

"Not immediately, anyway," Henry answered. "Did you drink alone?"

"Captain Raynard was with me," Will replied. "And most of Cheapside at one time or another—we pretty well covered the district."

"No doubt your disgraceful behavior was witnessed by even more men than we have here," the King nodded. He turned back to the accuser with an air of paternal understanding. "Is this all you have, Michael, truly?" he asked, being Harry for a moment.

"No," Pettengill answered with conviction, but from where he sat, Brother Paolo thought he saw misgivings in his eyes. "I would ask England to hear what I have heard, the testimony that brought me to make this accusation though I knew the Crown would never wish to hear it."

"You needn't make a speech, Sir Knight," Henry grumbled. "If you have a witness here, bring him forward."

A man Brother Paolo recognized as one of Mark's former guardsmen came to the foot of the throne. He turned and looked at Will's face with theatrical malice, but the friar saw no recognition in the younger man's eyes. "So who are you?" Henry asked as the man made his bow.

"Richard Kite, Your Majesty," the man said, looking down at his boots. "I served Lord Mark as guardsman."

"You were here with him in London?" the King asked. "You know something about his death?"

"I was with him the night he died," Kite answered, looking up. "He was about to retire when this William Brinlaw showed up at his rooms, demanding to be let in." Paolo saw Will's impassive expression flicker ever so slightly, but he made no move to speak. "As tired as he was, my lord would not break Your Majesty's peace on such a night, and he bade me admit him. Once he was inside, his manner changed, became more friendly-like—he had brought a bottle of wine, and he asked Lord Mark to drink with him. He wanted to be friends for Your Majesty's sake, he said, and my lord believed him. They did drink together for an hour, then he left. An hour later, my lord was dead." He looked at Will again. "I cannot help but think that he was poisoned."

Another wave of speculation swept the court, this one not nearly so merry, but all eyes were fastened on the King. "I see," Henry said, rubbing his chin, obviously deep in thought. "When Lord Brinlaw appeared, did he have another man with him, a disreputable-looking fellow with a beard and beady little eyes?"

Paolo saw Will smile again—Captain Raynard would no doubt be highly insulted. "No, Your Majesty," Kite asserted. "He was alone."

Henry nodded. He looked over and caught Eleanor's eye and suddenly broke into a smile, as if newly besotted, and she returned the look in kind. "Where were we?" he said, returning his attention to the court. "Oh, yes . . . so, Richard Kite, you say Lord William came to Lord Mark's rooms alone, and an hour after he left them, your lord was dead, and you knew at once that he must have been poisoned."

"Yes, Your Majesty," Kite answered with another bow.

"Why did you not come to me at once?" the King asked, his tone deceptively mild. "Did you not imagine I would be interested to hear that one of my best-loved retainers had not died peacefully in his sleep as I believed but had indeed been murdered?"

"I . . ." The man looked helplessly around the crowd, his gaze stopping unmistakably on the face of Sir Geoffrey d'Anjou. "I did not wish to disturb—"

"So you went immediately to Sir Michael, without delay, and he is the one who chose to wait three whole days before bringing these charges to me," Henry said, all pretense of good humor gone.

"I wasn't certain," Kite said weakly.

"And yet you sound so certain now," Henry finished, his tone thick with sarcasm. He looked at Geoffrey, too, and not with fond affection. "William Brinlaw, in all your drinking on that night, did you ever share a bottle with Lord Mark?"

"No, Your Majesty," Will answered, the very picture of truth beside the suddenly stammering Kite.

"No," Henry repeated, glaring down on Kite. "I think we've heard enough—"

"What about Brinlaw's attack on the London road?" a young man suddenly shouted, standing up from his seat—a squire, from the look of him. "He brought his troops against Sir Michael and a band of men lawfully hired to liberate a castle stolen by a Welsh bandit." At the realization of so many eyes on him, the boy blanched a bit, but swallowing hard, he pressed on. "We were attacked on the road before sunup and nearly butchered. Even after we had surrendered, Brinlaw still meant to murder us all, even Sir Michael himself. He would have done, if his captain hadn't stopped him." He looked at Pettengill, his throat working with emotion. "Sir Michael, why don't you tell them?"

Will came forward, and though his face remained a mask, his eyes glittered with unconcealed fury. "Perhaps Sir Michael hesitates to tell his king that the castle he meant to liberate was mine," he said. "Or is it the attempted abduction of my wife that went with this so-called liberation that he doesn't wish to tell?"

Henry was actually smiling. "I don't know what's harder to picture, Will," he said. "You as a Welsh bandit, or Pettengill as the sort of chap who might abduct a wife."

"Mon âme, I have a thought," Eleanor suddenly interrupted, bringing the proceedings to a stunned and silent halt. "What about a trial by combat?" she asked when she had everyone's attention.

"My love?" Henry asked, as if he hadn't quite heard.

"Why not let God decide?" she suggested. "Obviously no earthly judge can ever know which of these men speaks the truth. But if Lord Will and Sir Michael were to meet in single combat, God Himself could judge between them."

This idea was obviously met with quiet but intense enthusiasm by the audience—the only thing better than a trial was a tournament. But Henry did not look so pleased. "Sir Michael only asked for a hearing, my love," he answered his wife, struggling to hide his irritation. "I would hardly ask him to defend his opinion with his life—"

"I will do it," Geoffrey shouted, standing up, and every pair of eyes now swept to him. "Knowing my affection for Lord Mark, my king asked that I come to this hearing unarmed."

"Very wise," the old knight sitting beside Brother Paolo muttered to no one in particular.

"But if someone will lend me a sword, I will happily

defend these charges with my life," Geoffrey continued, winning his own admirers in the crowd.

"I will!" The squeak came from the back of the room—Harold FitzCammon the Younger. "I have a sword right here."

Henry was glaring at Eleanor so intently, it seemed unlikely he still cared about the trial. "What say you, Lord William?" the Queen asked the accused when the King still did not speak. "Will you fight?"

Paolo watched Will's face as he turned to look at Geoffrey. It was obvious nothing would have pleased him better than to lop his handsome head off like a pumpkin. "I trust the judgment of my king in this matter as I do all things. And I will not kill one fool to prove I did not kill another," Will said. "But if anyone holds any doubt that I was right to defend my castle and my lady's virtue by every power at my hand, then yea, I will gladly fight to prove him wrong."

"Your lady's virtue," Geoffrey scoffed, taking another step forward. "Your lady's imprisonment, more like." The ladies present in the galleries above who, it must be said, had found the whole proceeding rather tedious till now, suddenly came alive with interest. "Your Majesty, I beseech you," Geoffrey continued, addressing the throne. "Do as Queen Eleanor suggests. Allow us to settle this on the field."

Henry was glaring fury at his wife and making no attempt to hide it. "Very well," he said at last. "If you are both determined to fight, England will not say you nay. But for the matter of Lord Mark, I say I have heard enough. While my judgment will never be godly, it will have to serve. I can see no reason to believe Mark was killed by

Brinlaw or anyone else, no matter how dearly we all loved him. Every man must die, and he is dead. I consider the matter closed." He leaned forward on his throne. "And I shall take it very ill indeed if I hear any more about it. Am I understood?"

Geoffrey was so pale, he looked like his own ghost. "Yes, Your Majesty," he said, his mouth hard and thin with rage. "I understand you well."

Henry nodded, his color returning to something closer to normal. "As for the other, Lord William Brinlaw and Sir Geoffrey d'Anjou shall meet in single combat on the tilting field at dawn tomorrow." He looked back and forth between them, then to the other nobles. "Let no man interfere, and may God render His judgment."

Druscilla stood at Alista's shoulder as she paged through her mother's book. "I can't believe the water didn't destroy it," Dru marveled, touching the corner of a page, still damp but perfectly intact.

"Nor can I," Alista admitted, flipping back to the front. On the first page was a thick column of strange characters she could not recognize, but after that the text was mostly Latin, with some English and French closer to the back. The final few pages were blank. "It's written in different hands . . . look, these last are my mother's; I'm sure of it."

" 'A Glamour for to Vanish,' " Dru read. "Do you suppose it works?"

"I do not," Alista scolded, quickly turning the page.

"Oh, come on," her friend laughed. "Surely you'll try—"

"Dru!"

"Why not?" Dru demanded.

"Because," Alista answered, still feeling queer from

finding the thing in the first place. Looking down at it, she thought of when she'd seen it last . . . Mama had given it to Brother Paolo and told him to hide it. "No English queen must ever have it," she murmured, barely realizing she had spoken aloud.

"And you are a queen now?" Dru laughed, but when she saw Alista's face, she was suddenly not so amused.

"Not me; Maud," Alista explained, looking up. "At least I suppose that's who she meant. It was during the civil war, and Maud's troops were coming." She stood up and turned toward the bed. "My mother was dying, and everyone was gone." She turned again, this time toward the window. "She told me to climb up and open the shutters so she could see the falcons."

"What falcons, cherie?" Dru asked gently as she touched her arm.

"There are always falcons here," Alista said. "They were flying all around the tower, and I was watching them, and suddenly I wasn't afraid. I knew my mama wouldn't die after all." She looked at Dru, her eyes wide. "Brother Paolo came," she went on in a more normal tone. "Mama gave him the book and the heartstone and asked him to hide them. He must have put them in the well."

"And yet they are returned to you," Dru pointed out. "You must be meant to have them."

"Yes," Alista agreed, touching the stone at her breast. "But that doesn't mean I have to use them."

"No, but you are a more godly woman than I could be if you do not," Dru laughed, more uneasily this time. "A woman must use whatever power she has, remember?"

Alista was staring at the bed where Nan now lay dreaming. "Yes, I remember," she said softly.

"Alista?" Dru said, touching her again. "Did your mother die that day?"

Her friend looked at her, her eyes an impenetrable black. "Yes," she said simply. "She did."

Brother Paolo watched as Will checked Goliath's armor and tack as the sky turned purple-gray behind them. "This is madness," he scolded, fairly certain he was wasting his breath. The wooden arena was already full to bursting with spectators in spite of the predawn hour and a clammy, misting rain. "What's more, it's murder—murder for the amusement of a mob."

Will looked back over his shoulder at him. "I'd dance, but I don't know how," he answered. "A man should stick to his talents."

"And now it's all a joke," the monk muttered.

"No, Brother, it is not a joke," Will said, turning around. "Geoffrey d'Anjou made love to my wife—that is not a joke. He hired mercenaries to attack my castle—that is not a joke. He had me arrested and tried to have me executed so he could have both in one fell blow—that is not a joke."

"So now you will kill him if you can," Paolo said.

"Yes!" Will roared, incredulous.

"But you have beaten him already," Paolo insisted. "Brinlaw is yours. Alista—you cannot believe that Alista loves Geoffrey."

"Whether I believe it or not, Geoffrey does," Will said stubbornly, his fury losing a bit of its righteous edge but still palpable. "He will go on believing it, writing his love ballads and hatching his schemes until I put a stop to it once and for all."

"So you will kill him to save your pride," Paolo

answered in a tone thick with disapproval. "Assuming he doesn't kill you."

"Assuming that, yes." Two of Henry's own squires came and helped him into the saddle, and Goliath stamped an impatient hoof on the frozen mud. "Tired of the sweet life already, Goliath?" Will asked, scratching the horse behind the ear at the curved edge of his armor before putting on his own metal gauntlet. "I know just how you feel."

"May God in His mercy protect you," Paolo said, making the sign of the cross. "In nomine Patris, et Filii—"

"No," Will cut him off. "Don't do that."

"Why not, in heaven's name?" Paolo asked, astonished.

"In heaven's name, I will not have a blessing I do not deserve," the knight answered grimly, lowering his visor so the last came out as a disembodied echo. "I will mock you, Brother, but I will not mock God." Taking the falcon sword from one squire and a lance from the other, he rode into the lists.

The monk saw the falcon, Hector, swoop over the field in a wide circle, then come to rest at the top of a banner pole. Hanging from it was the Brinlaw dragon. "Be with him, Almighty God, I beseech You," Paolo softly prayed. "He has only lost his way."

Will looked across the tilting field, the lance balanced easily in his grip. If he'd hoped to beat Geoffrey with his own sense of fashion, he was to be disappointed. The Angevin's style of dress at court was elaborate past all reason, but his armor was as plain as Will's own, smooth plate with an unornamented helm and shield—no gaps or curlicues to catch a lance point. "So he isn't joking either, eh?" Will muttered, and Goliath stamped and snorted. "I suppose we'll have to beat him for real."

One of Henry's heralds stood up in the royal box, a silk scarf in his hand. "Make ready!" he shouted, and the crowd held its great breath.

"Trust me, friend," Will went on softly as Goliath's velvet ears twitched, listening. "I trust you with my life." The horse strained forward as if in agreement, and Will smiled. "We're on our way home already."

"Commence!" the herald shouted, dropping the scarf to the ground.

The shouts of the crowd rivaled the sound of hoofbeats as the two great steeds came together. This first blow was as much the horses' test as the knights'. Goliath did not flinch, thundering full speed toward the other animal's head, leaning in even closer as Will's knees pressed in at the moment of contact. This caused Will's lance to drive against Geoffrey's breastplate with the full force of Goliath's great weight as well as his own strength behind it. Geoffrey's own horse, a gorgeous white stallion, flinched at the last moment, causing his rider's lance to strike a glancing blow to Will's shield, shattering the shield, but leaving Will in the saddle while Geoffrey tumbled over his horse's tail to the ground.

Wheeling Goliath around in a storm of shouting from the stands, Will briefly considered just riding over the son of a bitch without further ado. But this technically wasn't war; it was a tourney, and such unchivalrously practical behavior was expressly against the rules. Geoffrey was making no effort to get back in the saddle; he was drawing his sword instead. "Sorry, Goliath," Will sighed, trotting toward the other knight just to spare himself the walk. "It looks as though you're done."

Geoffrey made his first attack as Will pulled to a stop, grabbing Goliath's bridle and swinging his sword toward the horse's throat—a clever strategy, perfectly acceptable, intended to send the horse crashing over on his side with his rider pinned beneath him. But Goliath had been in enough battles to see this one coming even if Will did not. He tossed his great head, yanking the Angevin's arm nearly out of its socket, and brought his hooves up to drive him back, trusting Will to have the grace to keep his seat. Will did, just barely, and he laughed, impressed. "Well done!" He slid to the ground, giving the horse a slap on the rump to send him out of harm's way.

Geoffrey raised his sword again, preparing to strike, but Will was faster, turning and striking in a single movement, the falcon blade ringing on the steel over Geoffrey's arm with a blue explosion of sparks. The blow drove the Angevin aside a step, but he didn't stumble, bringing his sword down on Will's shoulder. The blade bounced off Will's armor as well, but the blow didn't exactly tickle, even so, and a sharp edge dug into his flesh as the metal bent. Raising his sword again, he felt a warm trickle of blood down his arm.

He made as if to strike at Geoffrey's side, then drove an elbow into his visor instead as he feinted away, taking another glancing blow from Geoffrey's sword in the process. But this brawler's strategy paid off even so, just as Raynard swore it always would. Geoffrey's visor was so bent, he had to raise it or give up breathing, and when he did, Will saw a marvelously satisfying stream of blood pouring from his pretty nose. Several ladies shrieked in horror as he moved to smash him again, but Geoffrey was ready this time. He drove his own sword up point first, so that Will had to fall back at the last moment or risk having his throat pierced or his own helmet popped off.

"You learn fast, boy," Will said, circling him, ready to strike as soon as he saw an opening.

"I'm not wounded this time, brute," Geoffrey shot back, crouched and waiting. "And I fight for love."

"Good for you," Will answered pleasantly, his visor hiding most of a near-maniacal grin as he struck. His sword came down on Geoffrey's left arm again, but this time they both heard a horrifying, splintering crack. The younger knight's face went pale as milk, but he quickly transferred his sword to his right hand and struck again, the flat of his blade crashing into Will's helm, making his ears ring. Will snatched the helmet off and tossed it aside, and Geoffrey thought fortune had smiled on him indeed. He raised his blade while Will was still turning around, using all his strength to bring it across and cleave the other man's head from his shoulders. But Will ducked into a squat at the last moment, knocking Geoffrey's legs out from under him with the flat of his own blade. Before he could catch a breath, Will stomped down hard on the arm that now held his sword, effectively pinning him to the ground. The crowd first screamed, then fell silent as Will didn't move, just stood over his immobilized opponent, his sword raised for the killing blow.

"Do it," Geoffrey urged, his handsome face twisted in fury and pain. "Kill me, and she will hate you forever. Alista's heart will always be mine."

Will looked down into the face of this single-minded child, and he thought of Alista. She, too, had demanded death from him in much this same position. Then she had gotten up and gotten on with living. She had both fought him and suffered him for the sake of her people in spite of her passions. She had taken his child-kin into her home and heart because they were innocents who needed her. She had hurt him, but she had kissed him good-bye. He heard a cry above the breathless silence, and looking up, he saw Hector circling in the newborn morning sky. "She doesn't love you," he said aloud, looking back down at Geoffrey. "There's not enough of you for her to love."

The green eyes widened, and Will's blood suddenly ran cold. He had never seen such hatred in a human face. "Sir Geoffrey, will you yield?" The voice was Henry's own, not the herald's.

Geoffrey continued to glare at Will as if to will him to hell. "Answer your king," Will said, raising his sword higher. "Or I will assume your answer is no."

"Yes!" the younger knight shouted, sending a sigh of relief through the stands. "I yield."

"Then it is finished," Henry said, his voice carrying well in spite of the frenzy of cheers. "Brinlaw, step back."

Will obeyed. "It is finished," he echoed as Geoffrey's attendants rushed out to them.

Geoffrey smiled weakly, the charmer again, but his eyes did not warm. "Aye, my lord," he said as his sword was taken and his helmet removed. "I suppose it is."

In the royal box, Henry sat down again. "Thank God," he muttered, glaring over at his queen. "I ought to strangle you, you know. This could have ended very badly."

"Bollocks," Eleanor retorted, the vulgar oath made a hundred times more shocking by her delicate accent.

"My love?" Henry asked, surprised into a laugh in spite of himself.

"Your friend Brinlaw is either a fool or has no soul, but which I cannot tell," she went on bitterly. "He could have done away with his rival in a single stroke but could not be bothered to do it." Her husband was staring at her aghast. "Say what you will, Henri. He deserves whatever ill may befall him."

Night had come again, but Alista couldn't sleep. *Did your mother die?* Dru had asked her; *Yes,* she had replied. But if that were true, if it was so simple, why didn't she remember?

She went to the window and threw open the shutter, mindless of the cold. The moon was full, and a solitary falcon passed over the glowing, yellow circle as if painted there by her mind. She remembered the falcons circling outside this window on that day, how loudly they had shrieked, and she put her hands over her ears, the woman reliving the memory of the child. Turning, she could see her mother lying on the bed again, saw her raise her hands to the wind, a wild look in her eyes. She had looked at her child, and her mouth had opened, but the sound wasn't words but the shrieking of a falcon. Her wasted body fell back on the bed, but the falcon rose higher, beating the air with her soft, white wings. "She flew away," Alista had wept to the friar, but he hadn't understood. Only Papa had known what she had seen, and he could not or would not explain. In time she had forgotten, just as she had forgotten the reason why his body must be burned and the words to sing his soul into the air. He had gone into the air and left her to be joined to the falcon again, the falcon who had thrown herself to the ground to be with him when she knew he was dead.

Her mother's book was still on the table, and she opened it, turned to the first, unintelligible page. Through tears she saw the symbols change, the words flowing together and resolving themselves into a tale her blood already knew . . .

In the time before men came, some of the faeries were falcons, and they lived among the rocks above the white-tipped sea. Their magic was very strong, and they were very wise, and all of them were women.

One day the men came to the beach in boats from across the sea, and they settled on the beach and in the forest. At first the falcons paid them no more mind than they would a new breed of wolf or gull. But then a man came who was more beautiful than the others, and the queen of the falcons fell in love with him. She suffered very much with love. She flew near the man and let him touch her, so often that he began to believe he had tamed her, but she only loved him and could not speak his words. She cried out her love to him in all the many tongues of the forest—mouse and hawk and even lizard—but he could not understand.

At last she could bear her pain no longer; she must have his love or die. A spirit of water and earth more ancient than even the falcons lived in a spring on the cliffs, and the queen asked her for help. This spirit hated the men because they made her afraid with their iron and harsh speech, and in the queen's request she saw a way to be safe from them forever. The spirit gave the falcon queen the Heartstone and with it a woman's form and voice. So long as the Lady or her daughters should wear the Heartstone, she should be a woman with a woman's voice to speak. But if ever she removed it, she could return to her true form. Only she must be certain she really wished to fly, for once the magic was done, she could never be a woman again.

All the spirit asked of the Lady in return was her protec-

tion for her magic spring forever, and the Lady most eagerly agreed. So when she had appeared to her beautiful man and he loved her in return, she caused him to build her a castle on the cliffs over the spirit's spring. It was in this tower that she held her man to her breast and in this tower that she bore his sons and her daughter. And when the time came that her mortal form must die, it was from this tower that she flew. She rejoined her faery sisters, leaving the heartstone in her daughter-woman's hands.

And so it has been and always must be.

Alista reached into her pocket and took out her mother's drawing with her own name written above it. A falcon faery, reborn in mortal form. A pretty story, but . . . *She is you,* her mother had smiled. *You are a creature of the air.*

"No," she said aloud, slamming the book shut with the drawing inside.

She took the heartstone from around her neck. A gift from the spirit of the spring who hated mortal men . . . she thought of Tarquin insisting there was a woman in the well, calling him to join her, calling him to his death. Not a story, but the truth. She thought of the terrible day she had fought with Will, when she had only wanted to escape. *I have to fly away,* she had thought, the words that had no meaning, and she had climbed to the top of her tower, the tower her father had added just for her. Standing on the ledge, she hadn't been afraid. She had felt the wind calling her away, lifting her in its embrace, trying to help her to escape.

"I don't want this to be true," she said softly. She had wanted answers; she had needed to know, but now that she did, she couldn't bear it. "I want to be just myself, not . . ." She broke off, unable to even say the words.

She dangled the heartstone on its chain, holding it out the window, its depths catching blood-red flashes of starlight, and once again she could feel the pull of the sky, feel the arms of the wind seeking to enfold her. All she had to do was let go, let it fall, and she could be free. She could fly away.

Then she thought of Will. *One man came who was more beautiful than the others . . . he believed he had tamed her, but she only loved him and could not speak his words. . . .*

She pulled the heartstone back, closing it tightly in her palm, tighter and tighter until it seemed to be burning, pulsing like a living heart.

In London, Will sat up in bed, his heart pounding. He had been dreaming, something about a night sky with a yellow moon, and Alista was falling, falling away from him, her hands reaching out, and she was screaming like a falcon. Even now, wide awake, he wanted to take hold of her, remembering the horrible sensation of grabbing empty air.

He dressed quickly, sent the page who was dozing in the hall to Henry's rooms, never mind the hour. "Brother Paolo," he said, giving the sleeping friar an inconsiderate shake. "Wake up. We're going home."

Eleven

Alista stepped aside and let Tarquin go tumbling past her like a windmill taking flight. "Mind your sword," she advised as he flailed his way to the ground.

The sun was shining on the beach, taking the edge off the chill, and she'd brought the boy down to practice with one of her small swords. He'd sworn he'd been getting instruction from various bored knights since he'd learned to walk, but apparently none of them had taught him much that was useful. "You think you should beat me easily because I'm a woman, and it makes you angry that you can't," she patiently explained.

"Beat you? I can't even get at you," he grumbled. She offered him a hand up, but he ignored it, preferring to struggle on his own.

"That's because you're angry," she said. "Now, because you haven't had much practice, it puts you at a disadvantage. Someday, when your body knows where to go without your mind to tell it, anger will make you stronger, but now it only makes you clumsy." She reached out and corrected his grip, and he allowed it. "That's why you're getting worse instead of better."

"Maybe I'm just naturally clumsy," he muttered.

"You are not," she said sternly. "Slowly this time . . . don't try to win, just concentrate on the beauty of the stroke . . . there, you see? You're strong, and you can feel where the sword ought to fall. You just need practice."

"So I can fight very old men who move very slowly?" he asked, feinting each stroke she made in a steady, monotonous rhythm.

"Learn to do it perfectly this way, and you'll do it perfectly and faster when you find yourself in a real fight." She suddenly turned her attack and flipped his sword out of his hands. He blinked, shocked, then narrowed his eyes, impressed but not amused. "Take heart, Tarquin," she urged as he went to retrieve his sword. "When we go home, perhaps Clarence will teach you, give you a more worthy opponent."

He had turned, but now he left his sword point drop. "Are we going home?"

"I hope so," she said lightly, raising hers.

It was a good question; unfortunately, she still didn't have an answer. The problems that had driven them from Brinlaw weren't going away. They still had no way of knowing what was happening in London, but it had been a month; surely the matter was settled. Will could be dead . . . no, he could not. She would know, somehow she would feel it. So he was alive; she would remain convinced of it, and if he was alive, he was on his way to Brinlaw—he might be there already. And when he reached the castle, he would know she had run away and taken Tarquin and Nan with her. "He's going to be furious," she said aloud, lost in worry.

"I'd think so," Tarquin agreed, easily following her thoughts. "Alista? Will you tell me what's down in the well?"

"No," she said coming back to herself. "Keep away from the well; that's all. Now come, let's try again."

"Hullo, you boys!" An ample-figured woman with curly red hair was making her way down the cliffside toward them, her dirndl hitched up to her knees. "What is it you're doing down here?" she demanded as she reached them. "Wherever you came from, you'd best—" She stopped short, her eyes round with shock. "Alista! My lady!" She caught Alista up in a hug, paying no mind to her sword or her surprise at being so addressed. "Little bird," she sighed, holding her back at arm's length. "You made it. You've come home."

An image of someone dressing her in a red silk gown came into Alista's mind. "Mind your lady mother, and never be afraid," she had said, kissing her on both cheeks as tears streamed down her own.

"I remember you," she said. "Your name is Gwyneth."

"Yes, of course," Gwyneth laughed. "But bless us, who has turned you into a boy?"

"I'm in trouble, Gwynnie," Alista confessed, trusting her completely. "I've run away from my husband."

This made her laugh even harder. "Never mind, lovey," she soothed, hugging her again. "He'll catch you soon enough."

Henry had sent a few more knights with Will and his friar, along with a wagonload of flour adequate to quiet the fears of Lady Brinlaw. Now less than a day's journey from home with an almost springlike sun shining overhead, Will's spirits were on the rise, his nightmare all but forgotten. "I heard Old Griffin is arming his Welshman for battle directly after Easter," one of the new knights was saying.

"Aye, and some say 'twill be Scotland instead," another laughed. "What do you think, Will?"

"No one ever lost much betting on the treachery of either," Will said. "If I had to guess, I'd say we'll end up fighting both by summer."

"That's just what the King said," the first one said, obviously elated. "He said our only comfort is that they hate one another more sorely than either one hates us, so 'tis unlikely they'll ever join forces."

"That is a comfort," Will agreed. Like Henry and unlike these two puppies, he had fought against both Welsh bowmen and Scots berserkers and had no great desire to ever fight either again.

Another band of riders was coming toward them on the road, and he recognized his own dragon on their banner. "Stay here with the friar," he ordered, spurring Goliath ahead.

"I was hoping we'd run into you," Raynard joked as Will reached his party, but he wasn't smiling. "How was London?"

"Boring, stupid, and full of Eleanor," Will answered, trusting his friend to know exactly what he meant. "How was Bruel's castle?"

"Boring, stupid, and full of pig shit," Raynard said. "But that we put right quick enough."

"So what's wrong?" The Fleming seemed to be choosing careful words, not a good omen at all. "Raynard?"

"They're gone," Raynard finally said, seeing no better

way to tell it. "Alista, Druscilla, and both the little ones. They've been gone for weeks."

"Gone?" Will repeated, doubting the good of his ears. "Gone where? Gone with whom?"

"Gone with themselves, for all I can tell," Raynard said. "Gone to the Indies or Eden, for all I know. By the time I got there, they had two weeks' start already; everyone else at the castle was still there; no one saw or heard or knew a thing."

"Are you certain?" Will asked grimly.

"As certain as I could make myself without your specific permission," the captain answered. "They are your retainers now. We spent a week searching the village and the forest for miles around the castle, but other than some hoof prints around the moat, we haven't found a thing. So we were headed for you."

Looking back, Will could see Alista's priest on his little brown mare surrounded by knights in armor, serene as St. Francis himself. Wheeling Goliath around, he galloped back up the hill like he was riding into battle.

"Where is she?" he demanded, grabbing the friar by his woolen robe as if he meant to yank him out of the saddle. "Where is my wife?"

"Not at home, I take it," Paolo answered with laudable calm.

"Will, take a breath," Raynard advised, catching up. "She wouldn't have left him in your reach if she'd told him anything."

"Very astute of you, Captain," the friar said as Will let him go.

"The only one anyone saw was Druscilla," Raynard went on. "She batted her lashes at one of the guards to distract him while someone else bashed him in the head."

"I wonder who that could have been?" Will muttered sarcastically.

"And the children?" Paolo asked, ignoring him.

"Alista was seen taking them to bed like always," Raynard answered. "But in the morning they were gone as well."

"My lord, think," Paolo said, turning to Will. "What of Nan's father's cronies? Perhaps they were kidnapped—"

"With Druscilla's help?" Will cut him off. "No, Brother, I don't think so. You and I both know who planned this escape. And when I catch her, I am breaking her sweet neck."

Gwynnie's coming had changed everything. Druscilla was cosseted and pitied as much as she needed; Nan was petted and admired and urged to eat her porridge; Tarquin was kept too busy running errands and carrying furniture to worry about the well spirit or anything else. And Alista had a friend who apparently knew everything.

"You're wearing the heartstone, I see," she said, cutting up turnips in the little kitchen she and Tarquin had set up downstairs in what was left of Falconskeep's Hall. "You must not want free of your husband too badly."

"You know about that?" Alista asked, shocked.

"Of course I do, lovey. We all do." She sighed. "Or we did. There aren't so many of us anymore. When your mother died with you so young, we were afraid our time was over. A lot of the older ones just finally gave it up and died."

"How horrible," Alista said, not sure she understood.

"Not at all," Gwynnie laughed. "Most of them were a thousand years old or more. It was time for them to go. No, the days of faery are almost done." She came and kissed Alista's hair. "We are among the last."

"I'm no faery, Gwynnie," Alista protested.

"Not by half, anyway," the older woman teased. "What are you afraid of?"

"I'm not afraid," Alista protested. Gwynnie pulled a doubtful face. "All right, I am," she admitted. "I don't want all this magic and faeries and falcons—I just want to be myself, the same as I've always been."

"But sweeting, this is what you've always been; you just didn't know it," Gwynnie pointed out.

"Yes, and it almost killed me or . . . something." She picked up a turnip to give her hands something to do. "I can't be sure, of course, but I think . . . I think I almost turned into a falcon before I knew I could."

This at least was enough to give the faery woman pause. Putting her own work aside, she took the turnip from Alista and took her hands in hers. "Tell me."

"I . . . I was miserable and afraid," Alista began, the words coming hard to her even now. "I wanted to escape."

"Escape what, sweeting?" Gwynnie urged.

"Everything," Alista half-laughed, half-sobbed. "My father was dead; my castle was lost; my husband—" She stopped. "He doesn't love me, Gwyneth," she said, crying because she couldn't help it.

"As if he had a choice," Gwyneth laughed. "But we'll get to him in a moment. Tell me about your changing."

"I climbed to the top of the tallest tower in our castle, and I was crying, and the wind was blowing," she went on, the words coming faster and faster, suddenly desperate to get out. "I heard voices in the wind. All of a sudden, I wasn't unhappy anymore." The details had started to fade, but still she was trembling. "I wasn't happy, either, just rather . . . peaceful, I guess is the word. And that's when I felt it."

"Felt what?" Gwynnie prodded, a shadow in her eyes.

"The wind," Alista answered, looking up at her. "It was reaching out to me, lifting me up, and I felt myself changing." She shook her head, pushing the memory away. "At the time, I didn't know what it was, but now . . . if Brother Paolo hadn't come looking for me when he did, I don't know what would have happened."

"You would be a falcon, most likely," Gwyneth sighed, going back to her turnips.

"That isn't very comforting," Alista grumbled. "Now do you see why I don't want to know all this?"

"But sweeting, it isn't the knowing that could have hurt you but the not knowing," Gwynnie protested. "If you had known, you would have recognized those voices for what they were, could have known the choice before you. If you had been wearing the heartstone, you would have been in no danger of changing without meaning to fly." She swept the turnip pieces into a pot. "No, love, you'll never convince me stupidity is for the best," she said, setting the pot on the fire. "You need to learn who you are. Then you won't be so afraid, not of magic, anyway." She grinned. "Now tell me about your husband. Why do you want rid of him?"

"I don't, really," Alista admitted. "He doesn't love me, though—it isn't like that."

"Nonsense," Gwyn scoffed with a smile.

"He just wanted my father's castle," Alista tried to explain. "Now I've run away and taken Nan and Tarquin. If he finds me, he really is going to kill me."

* * *

"You don't really mean to kill her?" Raynard was asking Will as they sat by the watchfire.

"With my bare hands," Will said curtly as he stared into the flames. "She's on her way to Anjou." To think he had been so certain . . . he had let the bastard live, he had been so certain he had nothing to fear. And all the while, Alista, wise and clever and practical Alista, had already escaped him and taken his niece and her half-brother besides. He ought to have let Geoffrey have her; nothing else would serve him as he deserved.

"I thought you said Geoffrey was with you in London," his friend pointed out.

"She's meeting him somewhere, or his agent," Will insisted. "She wouldn't just flee without having some destination."

"So we're headed for Anjou?"

"We're headed in that direction." He looked over at Brother Paolo, on his knees saying his rosary at the edge of the trees. "But she'll never make it that far."

But when they reached Southampton, no one knew anything of Lady Alista Brinlaw or Sir Geoffrey d'Anjou—it being the dead of winter, no ships had sailed toward France in weeks. No one along the docks had seen any women or children matching the description of his wife and her little band of fugitives. "If they'd been here, someone would remember," Raynard pointed out as gently as he could manage—Moses could not have glared at the Red Sea with more fury than what Will was throwing at the Atlantic now. "Even if Alista disguised herself as a man and managed to bring it off, a pregnant woman and two children—"

"So where are they?" Will cut him off. "You tell me, Raynard. Did they just vanish?"

Raynard leaned back against a piling, at a loss. "How should I know?" he said rather peevishly. "I wasn't at Brinlaw when you left. How did you and your lady part?"

Will looked at him. "Well enough, considering," he answered. "I gave her a sword."

Raynard looked up at the sky as if begging strength of the angels. "Did she think you were coming back? Did you say you were coming back?"

"I told her I wasn't sure," Will said a bit defensively. "I wasn't, entirely." He looked back at Brother Paolo, who was still questioning an old fisherman. "And I know she wasn't—she told her priest she didn't trust Harry not to give Brinlaw to someone he could control more easily."

"And what do you suppose she thought would become of her if that happened? And Dru, and the children?" Raynard pressed. "Will?"

"I told her Henry would probably marry her off to someone else," he answered, feeling sick. "I was angry. She seemed so damned happy to see me arrested—"

"You wanted to scare her," Raynard finished. "So you scared the hell out of her, gave her a sword, and left. Did she say anything to you? Did she say good-bye?"

"She waved," he answered grimly. In his mind, he saw her standing at the top of the tower, and he remembered the sudden foreboding that had almost made him turn back. The night before, she had clung to him so tightly, weeping as she called his name. But that meant nothing; she never said anything. Hector was swooping over the water like a seagull, and he watched him dive for a fish. "She's with Geoffrey," he finished. "She has to be."

"Will, Geoffrey d'Anjou is in London!" Raynard said, losing patience. "Our own agents saw him there not three days past—"

"Then she is waiting for him somewhere, hiding," Will cut him off as he walked past him up the dock. Brother Paolo was staring out at them, and Will stopped to stare back. "Somebody knows where they've gone," he said, scowling. "We're going back to Brinlaw, and that person is going to tell us. Alista cannot just vanish."

Alista was trying to vanish, but under a certain amount of duress. "This is ridiculous," she protested to Gwyneth as Dru and the children looked on.

"Naught of the sort," Gwynnie insisted. "This is a faery spell, no conjuring required. It's all in the blood."

"Is anyone but me cold?" Tarquin inquired from his perch on the ground. Faery magic apparently required practice in the woods.

"No, not a bit," Alista said sarcastically, clad only in her shift. Clothes were apparently impossible to glamour away, but she wasn't prepared to prance naked through the forest, faery or not.

"Here, sweeting," Gwyneth said, tossing her own cloak over the children—Nan was perched on Tarquin's lap.

"I want to see!" Nan protested, fighting free.

"You needn't try so hard," Gwyn went on to Alista. "You're not conjuring. It's just as your mother wrote—let it happen, and it will."

"Come on, Alista," Dru urged, a slight edge to her tone. "Knowledge is power."

"Knowledge is safety," Gwyneth retorted with a sharp look.

"Holy Christ!" Tarquin swore, tumbling his little sister to the ground in his haste to stand up.

Alista was gone. Her shift was still standing in the same place, but the woman inside it had disappeared. "Well done, little bird," Gwyneth smiled.

"Can she talk?" Dru asked, helping Nan up.

"She can, but she doesn't want to," Gwyneth answered sagely.

Alista opened her mouth to say this wasn't true, then realized that it was. Her first thought had been that she didn't feel any different, but she did, completely different, a whole different creature. She wasn't cold anymore, for one thing. She still felt the earth and stones under her bare feet, but the sensation was no longer unpleasant. Indeed, she felt perfectly comfortable, perfectly at ease. She unlaced the top of her shift and let it drop to the ground.

"There she goes," Gwyneth said approvingly.

Tarquin took a step toward the fallen garment. "Alista, I don't like this," he called, an edge of fear to his voice. A caress swept over his hair, and he whirled around, almost falling. "Stop it!"

"Leave her be, Tarquin," Dru scolded, laughing.

"She's fine, sweeting," Gwyneth soothed. "Come, bring your sharp eyes over here." She put an arm around his shoulders and pointed. "Look there, where the light shines through the trees. What do you see?"

"Nothing," he began impatiently, then stopped. The beams of sunlight seemed to waver a few feet above the ground, to turn a softer, pinker shade of white. "I see it!"

"A glamour is just a way to hide, like putting on a cloak," Gwynnie explained. "She can fool us, but not the light."

Alista brushed her hand across a budding branch, making it shiver, and she felt its sleeping life race through her. Touching Tarquin in this state had been a revelation, like breathing him in like air. Her own breathing and heartbeat seemed to have vanished more completely than her form, leaving her an empty vessel of spirit eager to fill herself up, an intoxicating thirst.

"You keep talking about magic and conjuring as if they were two different things," Dru said. "What's the difference?"

"Faery magic is like breathing—it just happens," Gwyn explained. "Conjuring is harder and more dangerous. You need components, elements, concentration—sometimes you even need to call up an ancient spirit. It's risky business with too many factors the conjurer can't control."

"Black magic," Tarquin said, scowling. His own mother had imagined herself a conjurer of sorts, cutting the tails off black cats and reading fortunes in the kitchen fire. The castle women had called her a witch, and they hadn't been eager to run out to the woods to watch her practice.

"No such thing," Gwyneth answered. "Only black magicians. The problem is that any mortal fool can conjure, given the right rituals, and most of the fools who are stupid enough to try have evil intentions and no idea the power they're cutting loose in the world."

Alista had fallen to her hands and knees, utterly fascinated by the feel of the earth itself, the timeless power that seemed to slowly pulse there, silently waiting. "The daughters of Romans loved to conjure spirits," she said in the language of faery. "They fed them their own children."

"Yes, they did," Gwyneth answered in plain English, turning toward the sound of Alista's voice. "Dru, take the little ones inside."

"Alista?" Nan called, starting to cry.

"Come, Tarquin," Dru said, taking the little girl's hand, too unwieldy herself now to pick her up.

"No," Tarquin said, throwing off Gwynnie's hand. "Alista, come back, right now!"

"And who are you to give orders, little mortal?" Gwyneth laughed, fixing him with a look when he opened his mouth to argue. "She's perfectly all right; you needn't worry," she promised. "Now go inside with the others."

"Tarquin, please," Dru said, putting a hand on his shoulder and giving the faery woman a wary look.

The boy wasn't pleased, but he did as he was bade.

As soon as they were gone, Alista faded back into view, still sprawled on the ground. "Why didn't you tell me?" she asked as Gwyn threw her cloak over her shoulders.

"I thought you already knew," Gwyneth answered, helping her stand. " 'Tis always thus with faeries—we can feel what has passed on the earth as clearly as life when the magic is on us. I would have thought you had felt such things long since."

"No, I have not," Alista said, bitterly cold and still sickened by the images she had seen, the blood of innocents soaking into the loamy ground.

"Once you're used to it, you can shut the past out," Gwynnie promised.

"I don't intend to get used to it," Alista said, putting on her shoes. "I've had my fill of magic."

That night in bed, she still couldn't get warm, and she slipped an arm under Nan, drawing her closer. "I miss my uncle," Nan whispered, snuggling back against her.

Alista kissed the top of her little head. "So do I, sweet love."

The child drifted back to sleep, but Alista still couldn't stop shivering. She took the heartstone in her hand, clutching the stone in her fist. "Find me," she whispered to the midnight sky. "I need you. I don't want to run away."

Once again, Brother Paolo awakened to find Will Brinlaw bending over him, on the road back to Brinlaw Castle, but this time he looked very like a lost child. "I had another dream," he said, an edge of desperation in his tone. "You have to help me, forgive me, whether you will or not." He looked at the friar, his blue eyes wild with fear. "Tell me where to find her, Fra Paolo," he said softly. "She's frightened, and she wants to be found. I don't know how I know it, but I do."

"And what will you do if you find her?" Paolo asked, still not quite convinced. "Break her to bits?"

"Take her home," Will answered without a moment's hesitation. "Love her . . . I love her, Paolo, more than my own heart."

The priest smiled, his own heart flooded with sweet relief. "Then all will be well," he promised. "There is only one place she can have gone."

Alista and the children were walking on the beach. "I love the sea!" Nan shouted, running into a gossiping village of gulls, scattering them in every direction.

"So do I!" Alista said, running to catch up.

"So do I!" Tarquin yelled at the top of his lungs as he spun on the sand like a dervish.

"Don't get your feet wet, Nan," Alista warned, sitting down on a smooth, gray rock. She felt more herself today, as if things were getting better somehow. She had expected to dream of flying and the atrocities of Roman mothers, but once she had fallen asleep, her dreams had been sweet, and she felt rested, almost reborn.

"I won't." Nan squatted at the very edge of the surf, watching the bubbles gravely.

"Why wouldn't Lady Dru come with us?" Tarquin asked, collapsing at Alista's feet. "Doesn't she love the sea?"

"Not this one," Alista said. She brushed sand out of his hair. "This sea leads to Ireland, you know. Not France." She and Dru had quarreled again that morning about their eventual destination, and she was still feeling rather cross about it in spite of her good mood. "Perhaps that's why she doesn't like it."

"What's in France?" Tarquin scoffed.

"French people." Alista snickered. "French castles."

"French cows," Nan put in happily. "French fishes."

"Fresh French fishes!" Tarquin cried, collapsing in contagious giggles.

"Look!" Nan said suddenly, pointing up the beach. "I told you my uncle would come!" She started running, but Alista was faster. Before she could even see his face or think long enough to be cautious, she raced across the sand and threw herself into his arms.

"Are you mad?" Will thundered, trying to shake her, trying to stay angry, but it was hopeless. Her arms were around his neck, and she was kissing his face, and this time it was him she meant to hold, him she had run to welcome home. "What in God's name were you thinking?" he demanded just as her mouth captured his, but he was already lost; he was hers.

"Madness," she agreed when the kiss was broken. "I'm sorry . . . I'm so sorry."

"You mustn't scold Alista!" Nan scolded, overtaking them at last. "She didn't mean to be naughty. Look, you've made her cry!"

"Oh no," Will said. "You're right, Nan; I mustn't do that." He brushed his wife's tears away and tenderly kissed her mouth. "Please don't cry, Alista."

"That's better," Nan said, squealing with delight as he scooped her up for a kiss of her own.

Raynard, Brother Paolo, and the new young knights stood on the cliff above, their faces exhibiting various degrees of amusement. "That was what he meant when he said he would break her neck?" one of the younger ones asked as Will swept his bride off her feet.

"He'll do it later," Raynard decided.

Brother Paolo was beaming. "Forgive me, Captain, but you are mistaken," he said. "I think he will do nothing of the sort."

Tarquin came into the castle first, storming through the Hall and out the other side. "Here, now, what's the matter?" Gwynnie called after him.

"My uncle has come!" Nan shouted, running in at the heels of the man she announced, who was himself busy kissing the woman he carried in his arms. They, too, went straight through, headed for the stairs.

"Wait there, you," Gwynnie said, catching Nan before she could follow. "You must stay and introduce me to the rest of these fine gentlemen."

"Mon Dieu, I knew it," Dru began, getting up as Raynard came in.

"Oh, do hush," Gwynnie scolded, giving her a swat to

the rump that startled her past all speech. "You've caused enough trouble already."

"Druscilla must think I'm insane," Alista said, touching Will's face as he carried her into her mother's old room. "Actually, I'm pretty certain of it myself."

"Shhh—" He kissed her, savoring the weight of her in his arms, the solid reality of his momentary possession. Soon he had no doubt she'd be fighting her way free again, but in this sweet moment, she was his. "Don't talk," he ordered, sitting on the bed with her cradled in his lap. "Not yet."

She nodded, tracing the contours of his face, drunk on the want in his eyes. His beard was growing back, a thousand prickles beneath her fingertips, and his hair had grown longer since she'd first seen him, long enough to cover his ears and fall across his face when she brushed it forward, silky as her own or even Nan's.

He was touching her stomach, her side . . . woman's softness under a boy's leather jerkin. Eleanor had asked if she had qualities to speak of—the Queen would never know. She was looking at him with a tiny smile, as if she knew what he was thinking. He must look a lovesick fool, but this was no courtly vixen who would torture him for it, but his honest love, his faery. He closed his eyes as her hands framed his face, felt her kiss on his brow, his eyelids, his lips, and he burned to embrace her, to tumble her to the bed. But she was moving away, standing with her mouth still feeding on his, sliding and wriggling out of her clothes. He moved to help her, and she reached for his tunic, undressing him as well.

She bared his skin in the daylight, fascinated—she had

never really looked at him before, and he took her breath away. She took one of his hands between her own and studied it, starting small, a beauty she could manage. The palm was callused from the sword, but the shape was perfect, and she traced the delicate web of lines, turned it over to trace the blue veins and the curve of a scar just below where the fingers began. She touched a single vein, followed it, found another at the wrist and followed it up the arm, his sword arm, curved and hard with muscle, an arm that could lift her or drive her to the ground. She looked up into his eyes, suddenly too weak to stand, willfully relinquishing her strength to be held by him.

She looked at him, touched him as if he were some new creation, some wondrous thing she had never seen before. She seemed to melt against him, and he caught her close, cradling her against his shoulder, drawing her legs across his lap. He kissed her cheek, her mouth, her jaw delicate as eggshell in his hand. He cradled a creamy-soft breast in his palm, and she sighed against his chest, preening under his caress. But when he moved to push her back on the bed, she demurred again, turning in his lap to face him, hot silk of her thighs torturing his sex. She kissed his throat, grazing his flesh with her teeth, her hands sliding over his shoulders, then her mouth moved down to his chest, her arms around his waist, her tongue circling and suckling each nipple in its turn.

A sense of almost angry possessiveness swept over her, a fierce will to protect this beautiful giant who was hers. She rubbed her face against the rough, curly hair on his stomach, nuzzling like a cat, running her palms over the hard muscle of his thighs, delighting in the smell and feel and even the taste of him. Pulling back, she looked at him, confronting this strangeness she only knew by touch. It was a ridiculous-looking thing at first glance, but studying, she found it beautiful as the rest of him was beautiful. Blue-veined and curving upward, it pulsed with power beneath her touch. She bent close and kissed him, tasting his salt on her lips as he had once tasted her.

He was dreaming . . . this couldn't be real; she could not be of this world. Fighting to hold himself in check, he reached for her, drew her back into his arms.

He was holding her, crushing her, and his head bent to her breast, taking her into his mouth, and love twisted through her like a living vine, changing the very shape of her soul. His hands slid over her so tenderly she felt exquisite, perfected by his touch, but trembling, lost to the world. She shifted in his arms and felt him push inside her, delicious pressure, making her whole.

She held him to her, urging him closer, her thighs clamped hard against his sides, and the pendant stone she wore burned against his cheek, seemed to pulse with life. Suddenly she cried out, her head falling back, and he rolled over her, pressing her to the bed and kissing her desperately as she writhed and trembled beneath him.

It was too much; she couldn't bear it. She felt as if she were falling, but he had caught her, held her to him, held her to the world. "Don't let go," she begged as she felt him rush inside her. "Don't let me go, my love." He kissed her, answer enough, every inch of her embraced.

Nan had finally given up pacing the floor waiting and fallen asleep in her brother's lap, her thumb stuck firmly in her mouth. But the boy seemed ready to keep his vigil all night, staring into the kitchen fire, his child's face fixed in a scowl that was frighteningly adult. "Well, I'm done in," the woman, Gwyneth, yawned, getting up from her seat. "Here, lordling, let me have that precious bundle." To Paolo's surprise, he surrendered the child without a word. "Aren't you coming?" Gwyneth urged. Tarquin shook his head, not looking at her. "You're being a little donkey; you know that, don't you?" To this he didn't even bother to respond. "Good night, then," she sighed, leaving him be. "Good night, Friar."

"Good night." Watching her go with the child still sleeping on her shoulder gave Paolo another of the queer shudders of the mind he'd been experiencing ever since they had arrived at Falconskeep again. The little one might have been Alista. . . .

"She's a witch," Tarquin suddenly spoke. When Paolo turned, the boy's hazel eyes were fixed on him, the reflection of the fire wavering in their depths. "She doesn't serve Alista; she belongs to the demon in the well."

The boy was being eaten alive with jealousy and making up stories to make himself feel better, the friar told himself. "There's a demon in the well?" he asked lightly, as if this were an interesting matter, certainly, but of very little consequence.

"I heard her," Tarquin answered. "She tried to drown me." He looked back at the fire, his expression genuinely troubled. "She wants Alista, too. She gave her a necklace and a book with strange writing. I couldn't read it, couldn't even make out the letters, but Alista could. It's magic." His scowl deepened. "*Black* magic."

Paolo's heart felt like it was battering its way through his breastbone. "Did she tell you what it said?"

The boy glanced over at him, then looked away. "She

won't tell me anything except to stay away from the well."

"Excellent advice," Paolo muttered.

"But she never takes the necklace off, not since the moment I—since we found it in the well. Not even to sleep." He looked toward the stairs, his scowl returning. "I'll bet she's even wearing it right now."

Tarquin would have won his bet. Alista was absently rubbing the heartstone between her fingers as she read the letter addressed to her she had found in Will's tunic, the letter he had apparently written the night before his trial. Tears trickled down her cheeks as she finished. Poor Papa . . . to die so alone. Will was sleeping, or so she thought. Looking up, she found him watching her. "That was mine, you know," he said.

"Then why is my name on it?" she retorted, smiling, but her expression sobered again as she looked back at the page. "Thank you, Will," she said softly.

"I should have told you long ago," he answered. He started to sit up, but she pushed him down again, rejoining him under the covers. "So I take it the King didn't hang you, after all," she said.

"I never really thought he would," Will admitted, marveling at the feel of her shoulder with a single, reverent finger.

"Then you're twice a beast for letting me think that he might."

"I didn't think you'd care—"

"Bollocks," she cut him off, making him laugh, which didn't seem to please her. "I shouldn't have cared," she began, moving to get up.

"Wait, love, please." He caught her arm gently. "I'm sorry," he promised. "I wanted to think you would miss me, but I couldn't think of any good reason why you should."

After another moment, she relented, snuggling back down in the pillows. "Well, now you should be able to think of at least one."

He smiled. "In truth, it wasn't as easy proving my innocence as I had thought it would be," he admitted. "A man named Richard Kite had told Pettengill I came to your father's rooms and poisoned him, but that isn't true."

"I know Richard Kite," she said. "He's a liar and a drunkard besides." She touched his face, assuring herself he was real.

"So Henry determined," Will answered, kissing her wrist. "I did have to fight Geoffrey, though."

"Geoffrey was there?" she asked, seeming genuinely surprised. "He had the nerve to face you?"

"He's quite the popular fellow, and braver than he looks," he answered, rolling onto his back again, not certain he wanted to see her face. "When I disputed the notion that I had attacked Pettengill and his damned mercenaries without provocation, Geoffrey challenged me to a trial by combat." He pointed to the healing scrape on his shoulder. "He gave me this, thank you very much."

"You're joking," she laughed. "Geoffrey did that? Were you drunk? What did you do to him?"

"I could have killed him, but I didn't." He sat up so he could look down on her. "I was fighting for your honor, Lady Brinlaw. He announced to the entire court that he was your lover."

"He did not!" she breathed.

"Well, he pretty well did," he admitted. "I certainly took it that way, and so did everyone else."

"Sweet saints," she breathed. She sat up and pressed a kiss to his wounded shoulder. "Thank you, then, for defending me."

"You aren't upset, then?" he pressed, settling down again and pulling her to him.

"About Geoffrey?" She nestled close. "Is he alive?"

"Yes," he answered, waiting to hear the rest.

"Then he got better than he deserves," she said. "Will, you don't still think—" She looked at him. "You do! Will, for pity, I do not love Geoffrey. I don't even *like* Geoffrey."

"He certainly seems to like you," he grumbled.

"If that's so, I can't imagine why," she shot back. "I've never given him cause, believe me. That night he was at Brinlaw when you almost killed him the first time, I only met him so I could make him leave me alone and so he could tell me what happened to my father. I even took a sword with me in case he tried to kiss me." She fought a smile. "I was fairly certain I could take him," she went on. "I can't imagine why he gave you so much trouble."

"He did not give me so much trouble!" he growled, rolling on top of her, making her shriek with pretended alarm. "So you truly don't care for him?" he asked more gently, caressing her hair.

"I truly, truly do not," she promised.

"Then why did you run away?" he complained.

"Because I was afraid you wouldn't come back," she admitted. Gwyneth said he had to love her, and he had come looking for her. Surely he cared a little. "In faith, I thought Geoffrey might have convinced King Henry to let him have Brinlaw and me with it, just to spite you."

"That's ridiculous," he scoffed.

"Well, I never would have thought it if you hadn't all but told me it was so," she retorted. "You said if Henry didn't find you innocent, he could kill you and take Brinlaw—"

"I know what I said," he grumbled.

"So I left your castle and came to mine to wait and see what happened," she finished. "I supposed if you survived and if you wanted me, you'd come find me."

"If I wanted—? I went all the way to Southampton!" he shouted, getting up. "I threatened to murder poor Brother Paolo—a priest, if you'll recall. I was on my way back to Brinlaw to slap Clarence in hot irons when Paolo finally told me where to find you." *Tell me about my dreams, Alista,* he thought but didn't say. *Tell me why I always dream you're flying away from me.* He looked down at her, smiling up at him. "If I wanted . . . ," he muttered, turning away.

She had never been so happy to be yelled at in her life. But there was still one more matter to be settled while he was still so agreeable. *And what about the heartstone, sweeting?* Gwynnie's voice chided in her head. *When will you tell him about that?* "Will, what about Druscilla?" she asked.

"What about her?" he grumbled.

"I can't go back to Brinlaw without her," she pressed, sitting up. "I have to know she and her baby are welcome there."

"Can't go—? You'll go where I tell you, lady—"

"Will, please," she cut him off, paying this bluster no mind. "It's only a little baby."

"A little baby with a possible claim to Brinlaw," he said stubbornly.

"Oh, dam-NA-tion!" she swore, flinging herself out of bed. "Dru said you would think this way! She knew it! I, poor fool, said no, you would not, could not possibly be such an ass, but Dru, she knew!"

"Alista, calm down," he ordered, following her more slowly.

"Why should I?" she demanded. "Can I never trust you with anything that isn't that damned castle? The bloody King of England, Ireland, Scotland, Wales, and various pieces of France has given it to you without reservation for all time, and I, for one, wish you joy of it. Why isn't that enough?"

"He has given it to you as well," he pointed out, trying not to lose his temper again. "Don't you care at all that Druscilla could try to use your father's son to put you out of your home?"

"Dru would never do that," she scoffed.

"I wouldn't be so sure of that if I were you," he muttered.

"Damn it, Will, just stop!" she cried, all but pleading. "Dru says I must not trust you; you say I ought not to trust Dru. What of Fra Paolo, shall I suspect him as well?"

He couldn't help but smile. She was naked, impossibly lovely, and so completely enraged. "Now that you mention it, I've given the matter some thought," he began, "and I give you my permission to trust Paolo."

"Thank you ever so much," she said, starting to laugh, thinking suddenly what a picture she must make. "Alas, poor Brinlaw," she sighed. "I am a terrible wife, am I not?"

"Yes," he agreed, dragging her back into bed. "The worst I've ever had." He kissed her, and she kissed him back, but suddenly she pulled back. "What?"

"Promise me," she demanded. "Promise Dru is safe."

"I promise," he said, resigned. "Your friend has nothing to fear from me."

Brother Paolo felt his way down the narrow stairway, his torch painting demons in shadows and light along the moss-covered walls. At the bottom he found the well where he had disposed of Blanche's relics, looking not so different from when he had left it. Only the details had changed. The great boulder he had used to seal it lay to one side again. On the other side were stacked several wooden buckets banded tightly with reeds instead of iron. And rather than being sunk so deep in the shaft it could barely be detected, sweet water filled the well so completely it lapped and spilled over the brim.

"Paolo . . ." A woman's voice, Bianca's voice, echoed through the tiny cavern. "My friend . . . why have you returned?" Looking down into the silver water's depths, he seemed to see her, her white-blond hair floating like a halo around her face, even more beautiful than he had remembered.

"A phantom, a trick," he muttered through lips dry with fear. Yet gazing down, he could not resist the vision, and put his hand into the icy water. Something even colder took hold of his wrist as Blanche's face dissolved into a beam of blinding light. "No!" he roared as the demon tried to pull him into the well with terrifying strength. Just as he felt he could hold out no longer, something else grabbed him from behind.

"In the name of Christ, begone!" Gwyneth shouted lustily, giving him a mighty heave. She shouted something else in a language he didn't understand, and the thing let go, sending them both reeling over backward.

"Well, that was exciting," Gwyneth said, getting up and brushing herself off. "Shame on you, Friar, for not thinking of it yourself." Before he could answer, she had left him, laughing as she went back up the stairs.

"Wait!" he cried, running after her. "What was that? Who are you?"

She stopped, the hand that didn't hold a torch propped on her hip as a fist. "That was something that has no love for you that you'd do well to leave in peace," she answered. "And I am the only creature left in the world who knew Alista's mother other than you, and I love her child every bit as much as you do." She softened her scowl. "That's all you ever need know."

"No, madam, it is not," he retorted, but he was still trying to catch his breath and couldn't follow when she went on.

"Go back to bed, Brother Paolo," she called over her shoulder as she disappeared around the curve of the stairs.

Twelve

Raynard was more than pleased that things were working out so well for his friend. He was even more relieved that none of his worst fears had proved true, that the women and children were perfectly safe. He just couldn't shake the feeling that the world had reordered itself while his back was turned, leaving him utterly unable to make sense of it. Coming into Alista's burned-out excuse for a keep after his morning patrol, he found Druscilla alone in what was passing for a kitchen, bent over a pot of porridge. "Careful there," he said, catching her by the apron as she stumbled. "You need better ballast on the back, or you're liable to tip on over."

"Oh, shut up," she said, jerking free with such violence she almost sloshed the porridge over and reduced all her efforts to naught. "Better yet, go away."

"Better still, why don't you inform me why you didn't just tell me your troubles when I asked you?" he said, helping himself to breakfast and settling into a chair.

"Why should I have done?" she scoffed. "You wouldn't have cared."

"Now I am offended," he protested. "I thought I made my interest perfectly plain when last we met."

"Before you knew I was pregnant," she pointed out.

He grinned, trying to look innocently pleased and failing miserably. "That needn't have made such a difference."

"Beast!" she swore, flinging the piping hot ladle directly at his head. "Pig! You are disgusting!" Pushing past Gwynnie, who was just coming up from the well, she ran out the door.

"I don't know what you said, dear, but I don't think she liked it," Gwynnie said picking up the ladle.

"You think?" he grumbled.

"You'd better hurry and go after her," the faery advised, tossing him Dru's forgotten mantle. "You may never get another chance."

He started to say something clever about how Dru ought to guard her chances with him, but suddenly that seemed a terrible waste of time. Snatching up the mantle, he fairly sprinted out the door.

Outside, a soft rain was fast becoming a stinging sleet, and by the time he found her, Dru was visibly shivering. "Dramatic exits work better in summer," he advised her. She looked around, furious, but he cut her off before she could reply, softening his approach. "Here, my lady," he interrupted, wrapping the mantle around her shoulders.

She drew the woolen folds tighter, willing her teeth to stop chattering. "If you're waiting for thanks, you're wasting your time," she informed him.

"Oh, I know," he agreed. "You know, poppet, things

seem to have gotten turned around here somehow. You're treating me like I've hurt you when it's you who ran away from Brinlaw and led us the chase of a month."

"You left first," she pointed out, looking away.

"I never," he answered, confused.

"You went to Bruel because Will sent you," she said. "Even after you knew I cared for you, you left me. What was I to think—?"

"I had no choice!" he cried, incredulous. "What do you want from me?"

"I want to be first," she answered, her blue eyes alight with feeling. "Just once in my life, I want to know how that feels." He just shook his head, still mystified. "Do you think my father asked me if I wanted to leave Paris before he traded me and a sack full of silver for his tiny little title in Normandy? Believe me, he did not. Do you think my husband thought of me when he plotted treason and got himself killed?"

"From the way you talk about him, perhaps he thought he was doing you a favor," Raynard quipped, trying to deny how deeply touched he was.

"Oui, idiot, I am certain he did—the favor of prison, starvation—he never gave it a second thought," she retorted, not amused. "I was nothing to him, less than nothing to anyone else. But by that time I was used to it; I thought I deserved no better. Then Mark came, and he was so kind, a real man of honor with a brain and a heart. I felt so lucky to be his whore, to belong to him." She was crying, the tears that had broken his heart the first time he had heard them, he who had no heart to break. "But all he ever was to me was kind, and his heart was never mine. He didn't love me—he couldn't! After his dead wife and his darling daughter, he had no love left. But I didn't blame him; I swear I did not."

"Yet you blame me," Raynard said softly.

"I thought for a while that you were different." She laughed, a brutal, bitter sound, stinging cold as the falling ice. "I thought perhaps you were as bad as I am." She looked up at him. "But I was wrong. You are a man of honor, too."

She started to turn away, but he caught her by the shoulders. "Are you finished?" he asked, holding her fast in an almost-painful grip. "May I speak?" Her eyes narrowed, but she nodded. "You apparently know nothing about me, Dru, so let me tell you—I don't read minds. If you had ever once asked me not to leave you—"

"What?" she demanded. "What would you have done, liar? Deny your best friend?"

"No, of course not," he answered. "I would have taken you with me!" She looked so shocked, he almost laughed. "Aye, poppet, as simple as that." He touched her cheek. "The world does not have to be so complicated, you know."

She shook her head, smiling through tears, but her eyes were even sadder than before. "The whore of a Fleming whose soul is already damned," she sighed. "And to think I missed my chance." Raising up on tiptoe, she kissed his cheek. "I take it back, cherie," she murmured. "You're not a pig. Just a fool."

She started to back away, but he caught her, kissed her mouth, holding her tight until she returned his embrace. "You make pretty speeches, Dru, but you're the liar," he said, his expression dark but his eyes soft with love.

"Someday you will tell me the truth." She raised a hand to strike him, and he abruptly let her go. "Don't catch cold, poppet," he advised, walking away.

Alista shifted to a more comfortable position on Will's lap, the razor poised a precarious inch from his throat. "You realize this isn't necessary," she pointed out before she began. "Your beard suits me perfectly well. My father always had one."

"All the more reason to shave it," Will said.

"Ha! A bit of courtesy, if you please, sir, or I may be moved to slip." She scraped the delicate skin just beneath his chin. "I wonder how you'd look without a nose?"

"Be careful," he ordered, steadying her by the hips, pushing the shirt she was wearing well up her thighs in the process. "You could stand up, you know."

"You could keep your peace, you know," she retorted, concentrating on his jaw. "If I'm doing this, I'm doing it my way."

"You should have Druscilla work that in Latin on a banner for you—methinks it is your motto."

"If you don't hush, I am seriously going to hurt you," she scolded through a laugh. One of his hands slid up her side. "Will, be still!"

"Alista!" Nan called, pounding open-handed on the door. "Uncle! Are you asleeping?"

"Wait a minute, dearest; I'm coming," Alista called back, stripping out of the shirt she wore so Will could put it on before she threw on a gown.

"Where did we get all these children?" Will grumbled, dragging the shirt over his head.

"Bless me, sweet, I don't know," she retorted. "I thought

they came with you." She threw open the door just as Nan was about to start pounding again. "Did you climb all those stairs by yourself?" she said, picking the little girl up. "Does Gwynnie know where you are?"

"I don't like sleeping with Gwynnie," she announced by way of an answer. "She snores."

"Does she indeed?" Will asked, taking her himself. "Well, I know a secret—so do you." He buried his face in Nan's neck and made a hideous noise either meant to represent a snore or a dragon in a temper, making her shriek with delight.

"Gwynnie, by the way, was my nursemaid when I was a little girl," Alista explained for Will's benefit. "She and her family still live near Falconskeep, and she came to help when she found out we were here."

"Tarquin says she's a witch," Nan added.

"Tarquin is very wrong!" Alista said, shocked and appalled. "Why would he say such a thing when she's been so kind to him?"

"He doesn't say it to be mean," Nan explained from the crook of Will's arm as Alista finished his shave. "He just thinks she knows the demon in the well."

"He says there's a demon in the well?" Will laughed. "I think your brother has been telling you tales, Nana."

"No, Uncle, it isn't a tale," Nan said. "There is a demon in the well, isn't there, Alista?"

"There is no demon in the well or anywhere else," Alista scolded.

"But there is—she gave you your pretty necklace." She reached up and freed the heartstone from Alista's bodice. "Isn't it pretty, Uncle?"

"Very pretty," he agreed, giving Alista a quizzical look.

"Alista, I have to speak to you," Brother Paolo said as he came in, obviously agitated.

"When we get home, we're moving our bed downstairs into the Hall," Will muttered, setting Nan on her feet. " 'Twill be so much more convenient for everyone."

"Forgive me, my lord," Paolo said grudgingly, though it was obvious he couldn't have cared less. "This cannot wait."

"Will, why don't you take Nan downstairs?" Alista suggested, troubled by the haggard look of the friar's eyes. "She probably needs her breakfast."

The friar's appearance hadn't escaped Will, either. "I have a better idea." Tucking his niece under his arm, he went to the top of the stairs and called down. "Sir George! Come and take this baggage and make her eat her breakfast!" He came back as Nan was heard giggling her way down the stairs.

"Take that off at once," Paolo ordered, pointing to the heartstone around Alista's neck. "Throw it back down the well and that devil's book along with it."

"I will not!" She held the stone as if she thought he meant to snatch it by force. "It is not a devil's book; it was my mother's—she left it for me."

"She gave it to me to be hidden where no one would ever find it," the friar insisted. "She wanted to protect you—"

"No, she didn't," his former charge cut him off. "Not from this—you don't even know what it says, or you couldn't think that."

"My God, you read it?" Paolo cried. "Holy Father, forgive her. Alista, listen to me. You must never, ever open that book again. I forbid it."

"Just a moment, Brother," Will said before she could

answer. "With all due respect to your vocation, Alista is no longer a child to be forbidden by her guardian to do or not do as she likes."

"Forgive me, signor," Paolo said with uncharacteristic sarcasm. "I forgot—that is your job now."

"Stop it!" Alista ordered. "I forbid either of you to say another word until you know what you're talking about." She went and got the book from the chest under the bed. "Look at this," she said, opening it and holding it out to the friar.

"I will not," he answered, appalled at the very suggestion.

"Give it to me," Will said, taking it from her. "What am I looking at?"

"You tell me," she said, looking over his shoulder. "What does it look like?"

"Here, my love, have another bite of apple," Paolo muttered with fatalistic humor.

"Writing of some sort," Will said, shooting him a look of annoyance. "But I can't read it. Can you?"

"Every word," she answered. "Just like I can remember every word of every song my mother sang to me in that speech, even though I haven't heard them since I was four years old." She turned to look at Paolo. "Just like I knew the words to sing over my father."

"And you believe this is a good thing?" the priest demanded, aghast. "You believe you should encourage this? Put it away from you, cara mia, and pray it is not too late."

"It is too late," she insisted. "It was too late before I was ever born and before my mother was ever born and before any of the women who have lived at Falconskeep were ever born."

Will remembered the sound of Mark's death chant, the wild light in her eyes as she sang it, shedding her own blood on the flames, and suddenly he was afraid. "What is written here?" he asked her.

"You should not ask," Paolo warned. "You cannot—"

"Why?" Alista demanded. "I am not a heathen fool; I can see the danger in such things, but will ignorance keep me safe? I assure you, it will not." She touched the friar's arm. "When I was a child at court, a Jew was burned for blasphemy; do you remember?" she asked in a gentler tone. "Do you remember what you told me? You said King Stephen's ignorance had caused him to blunder into a sin far greater than the Jew's because he was afraid to face the truth."

"Here," Will said, holding the book out to her. He wasn't much concerned with burned blasphemers, and after his Crusade, he wasn't moved overmuch by the priestly definitions of sin and evil. But his dreams would not be ignored, and neither would the fear mixed with fury he saw now in Alista's eyes. "Read it." He looked at Brother Paolo. "You can go if you want; you don't have to listen. But I have to know."

Paolo looked at the two of them united against him, this stranger allied with his child. "I will listen," he told Alista. "For your sake, I will hear."

She read them the story of the falcon queen, the words as legible to her now as Latin script. At first, Will was relieved. For all the friar's ravings, this so-called devil's book was no more than a faery tale, the stone his wife now wore no more than a trinket crafted to make it seem real. But as she read on, he remembered his dreams of Alista falling away, flying away from him, her cry like the scream of a falcon. He thought of his half-waking dream of walking along a beach, then running to catch her, and cold prickles raced over his flesh. He had seen that beach yesterday when Alista had run to his arms. "Do you believe this?" he asked when she was done. "Do you believe it's true?"

"I know it is," she answered. "I saw it happen when my mother died. I saw her change. The falcon came out of her dying body—"

"Blasphemy!" Paolo breathed in horror.

"Maybe, but it's true," Alista replied. "I tried to tell you what I had seen, remember? I told you she flew away. Could a child have imagined such a story?"

Blanche's death, however it had come, was of little concern to Will. "What about you?" he asked. He wanted to take hold of her, to reassure himself that she was solid, safe, but he restrained himself. "This could happen to you?"

She reached for him, taking his hand. "Yes," she said, so softly they barely heard. "It almost has already. The day you . . . the day we fought, I ran away to the top of my tower, the tallest tower of Brinlaw—that seemed the best place to go, though I didn't know why. I was hysterical; I wanted to escape. I climbed up on the ledge without thinking. . . ."

"Sweet Christ," Paolo groaned, crossing himself.

"The wind came to take me, to help me fly away," she went on. "I felt it, and I didn't care. It seemed right, the only thing to do. And for just a moment, I could feel myself changing, and I was happy. I wanted it to happen. Then suddenly something happened, I don't know what, and I remembered where I was, and I was so frightened. I almost lost myself; I knew it even then, though I didn't know just how."

"You were out of your mind," Paolo protested. "If you had fallen, you would not have become some demon bird. You would have been killed."

"Either way, she would have been lost to us," Will said. He should be concerned, angry, afraid. His wife was some magical creature; his daughters could be cursed. Either this was true, or Alista was insane and had somehow dragged him into her madness, made him dream things that made this faery tale seem true. He thought of the falcon, Hector, who had followed him to London and beyond as faithfully as the priest, and he almost laughed at the sheer absurdity of it. But looking down at his faery, all he could feel was relief. Whatever else was true or wasn't, she was his; he hadn't lost her. He drew her into his arms, and she came gratefully, shivering against him as if she could still feel the wind. "Do you truly think you need these things, this book and this heartstone?" he asked her gently.

"I know I do," she answered, weak with relief. She had been so afraid of what he would say, so afraid he wouldn't want her anymore. She hated that Brother Paolo was so worried, but she knew she could make him understand, that he would never forsake her, magic or not. But she hadn't been so sure of Will—how could she have been? She wrapped her arms around his waist, silently praying thanks.

"Then you'll have them." Paolo opened his mouth to protest, but Will cut him off. "They are hers, Brother; we have no right to take them."

"No right but her salvation," Paolo said, refusing to be convinced.

"Brother, there's nothing so terrible; I looked," she soothed. "But I'm no more in love with the idea of sorcery than you are. I tried one spell—"

"Sweet saints!" Paolo roared, sitting down hard in horror.

"What was it?" Will asked, more calmly but rather taken aback himself.

"It isn't even a spell, really," she said, half-wishing she'd never mentioned it, except of course the children would. "It's just something I can do—faery magic, Gwyneth calls it. The other is called conjuring—"

"Alista, what did you do?" Will interrupted before Paolo could.

"I disappeared," she admitted. "Not really, of course. I was still there; I just couldn't be seen." Both of them were staring at her with identical expressions, eyes and mouths agape, and they looked so silly she couldn't help but giggle. "I didn't like it, actually," she insisted, trying to wipe the smile from her face.

"Sweet saints," Paolo repeated, unable to say anything else.

"Why not?" Will asked, trying not to overreact. For all he knew, she was making the whole thing up to tease the monk. Then again, she had sounded serious, and taken with everything else, he supposed the idea of her making herself vanish was no more insane than the rest. "Why didn't you like it?"

"It made me feel queer, like I really *wasn't* there," she explained. "I seemed to feel other things more clearly than I felt myself." She shook her head. "I just didn't like it, and I'm not going to do it again." She went and took Brother Paolo's hand. "I'm not going to do any of it," she promised. "No spells; no conjuring—I won't even read the book if it upsets you so."

Paolo looked up at her, looking far more ancient than

his years. "And the well?" he asked. "Is that harmless, too?"

"The well?" Will repeated, remembering Nan's demon.

"No, it isn't harmless," Alista admitted. "In fact, I think she may have meant to drown Tarquin. But I stopped her—"

"She?" Will pressed, taking her arm to get her attention.

"The spirit in the well," she explained, turning to him. "From the story, remember? The one who gave my ancestor her human form—"

"The one that tried to drown me last night," Paolo interrupted.

"What?" Alista cried. "What were you doing down there?"

"Young Tarquin told me about his adventures with this demon," the monk answered. "He also said you and this Gwyneth had been practicing black magic."

"So how did you escape?" Will asked before Alista could respond.

"Gwyneth pulled me back before the thing could pull me under," Paolo grudgingly admitted. "She cast it back in the name of Christ."

"Odd behavior for a woman who practices black magic," Will said dryly.

"Gwyneth does not practice black magic," Alista said sternly. "As for the well, you should all leave it alone. The legend says it hates men, and that much at least seems to be true."

"We're all going to leave it alone, you included," Will told her. "We're going home to Brinlaw."

"Alista!" Tarquin yelled as he trudged up the stairs. "Gwynnie wants to know if you need help packing!" He came in and froze at the sight of the three of them looking so serious. "What's going on?"

"Nothing much," Alista said, for once not smiling at the sight of him. "We were just talking about your demon."

He blushed, glancing at Brother Paolo. "He's a priest," he offered weakly. "I thought he should know."

She nodded, but she was obviously not pleased with him, and his heart sank. "Will, forgive me, but could you and Fra Paolo excuse us for a moment?" she said. "I think Tarquin and I need to talk."

Will wasn't thrilled, but he surrendered. "As you will," he said. "Come on, Brother."

Tarquin stared at the floor as they left, a sullen scowl on his face. "I'm not sorry," he muttered when they were gone.

"If you believe what you told Brother Paolo, then I shouldn't think you would be," Alista answered. "Do you believe it?" He didn't answer. "Do you think there's a demon in the well?"

"It ain't no angel," he muttered.

"And Gwynnie and I are witches, practicing black magic," she went on.

"That's what my mother would call it," he said with an obvious effort. "Making yourself disappear—she used to say she'd sell her soul to Satan to be able to disappear."

"So that's what you think I have done," she said.

He looked up, stricken. "No," he protested. "But—"

"I can't help what I am, what I was born to be, just as Gwyneth says," she cut him off. If she hadn't just been accused of the same things in sweeter words by her lifelong guardian, she might have been a bit more understanding, questioned him a little less sharply. "Do you think I'm evil?"

"No, never," he swore with tears in his eyes.

"Then why . . ." The look on his face broke her heart, made her really see him. "Darling, why are you so angry with me?" she asked.

"I'm not . . . I am . . . I don't know!" he cried. "Why does everything have to change? Why did they have to find us? If you've got all this magic, and it's real, why couldn't you use it to keep them away?"

"Will and the others, you mean?" she asked, more confused than ever. "Tarquin, I wanted Will to find us. Don't you want to go home?"

"Not with him, I don't," he muttered.

"Tarquin FitzBruel, listen to me," she ordered, putting her hands on his shoulders. "Stop this at once. You have no reason in the world to dislike Will—" He looked up at her with such hurt in his eyes, she stopped. "What then?" she asked more gently. "Tell me; I want to help."

"No, you don't," he said, pulling free. "You don't even want to know." Before she could stop him, he ran away down the stairs.

Brother Paolo, meanwhile, had stopped Will on the landing. "If you love her as you told me you do, you will not allow this," he warned.

Will started walking down the stairs again, then he stopped. "I will spare you the pain of trying to convince me," he said, turning on the monk. "I like this madness no better than you do. Given a choice, my wife would never under any circumstances have the ability to turn herself into a bird and fly away. But she does." He stopped, the full import of what he was saying slowly sinking in. "She does, and I will not drive her away."

"I'm not asking you to drive her away," the monk protested. "I'm asking you to save her soul."

"I am no one to save anyone's soul, not even my own, certainly not a pure soul like hers," Will retorted. "I am not in God's favor, 'tis true, but these things, this magic, it makes my blood run cold just as it does yours. Given my absolute preference, Alista would not be cursed or blessed or just simply born with this. But if she were not, she would not be Alista." He paused, rather embarrassed. "Alista is who I have chosen."

"Alista lived for fifteen years without the slightest taint of evil," Paolo insisted.

"How do you know?" the knight demanded. "She must have remembered some of her mother's magic, or else how does she understand it now? And how do you know so certainly that this is evil? The first night we met, you told me Alista dreams very close to the angels—a strange phrase I've always remembered. Did you not believe those words?"

"Yes," Paolo admitted with an effort.

"As I do," Will went on. "And your own long-worshipped Bianca; have you now decided she was evil as well?"

"Don't you dare," Paolo warned, his face going white with rage.

"Dare what, Brother?" the knight taunted him. "Dare suggest that the beloved of your soul could be a witch, controlled by some demon in a well? Very well, I will not." His scowl deepened. "And I would ask the same of you."

Sir George, oblivious to the felicity of his timing, chose this moment to come back through the arch downstairs with a happily crowing Nan perched on his shoulders. "Hullo,

Brother Paolo!" she called, waving her porridge spoon.

"Hello, cara mia," the monk answered, smiling but sad. Perhaps Brinlaw was right; perhaps Alista, with her faery's blood, knew best. Perhaps he was wrong. He fervently prayed that he was. But he still would be very glad to leave Falconskeep behind.

"Hullo, Tarquin!" Nan called as her half-brother ran down the stairs. "Where are you going?" she demanded as he passed her by without stopping.

"Here, my lord, I'll go fetch him," Sir George offered, lifting Nan down from his shoulders.

"No, let him go," Will said, taking Nan even so. He remembered only too well what sort of temper was required to drive a boy out of the house and into an ice storm, and sweet-natured Sir George was not up to the challenge. "He'll come back when he's ready."

Tarquin half-ran, half-stumbled down to the beach, his boots sliding precariously over the icy rocks. He ran to the very edge of the water, just as he and Nan and Alista had done the day before. But today instead of being with them, he was alone, completely alone—Alista hated him. Today instead of the first sun of spring, he stood in the last ice of winter.

"She'll find out," he muttered, breaking up a stick of driftwood and flinging the bits into the surf. "She'll cry and cry, and I'll just laugh." Alista was the smartest person he had ever known in some ways, but apparently where men were concerned, she was dumb as this driftwood, dumb as dead, drunk Tabby, his mother, had been. Tabby had always said she hated Bruel when he was gone, that she'd die and be damned before she let him back into her cot.

Then he'd come back, and she'd fall all over him, and out Tarquin would have to go to beg his dinner where he might. Bruel would be all sweetness for a day or so, giving her wine with his sloppy kisses, calling her his pussycat. But such bliss could never last. Before a week had passed, the pig would lose interest in tupping and start pounding instead, and Tabby would be muttering gibberish over her cats' tails and clutching Tarquin to her sweaty bosom, making him promise to avenge her.

"I'll kill him," he muttered, unconsciously stabbing his stick into the sucking sand. Alista hadn't said she hated Will Brinlaw, but she had run away from him as soon as his back was turned. Something was wrong between them; she had tried to peel his face off at some point. Lady Dru was frankly terrified of him, and she didn't seem to scare easily, and Alista loved her, he knew. But as soon as Brinlaw showed up, there went Alista, running down the beach to throw herself into his arms and let him carry her off upstairs like the rest of them didn't even exist anymore.

But it wouldn't last. Alista was beautiful, and Brinlaw wasn't a total pig, so she could probably keep him interested a lot longer than Tabby's charms had fascinated Bruel. But eventually even Brinlaw would get drunk or tired of her or just plain mean, and then . . .

"I'll kill him," he repeated, no longer feeling the cold.

Alista had started packing when Gwyneth came in, carrying a platter of breakfast. "I never got an answer, so I thought perhaps you were prostrate with weakness," the faery teased.

"What? Oh," Alista answered, remembering Tarquin's original message. "I'm sorry, Gwyn. I got distracted."

"I don't wonder," Gwyneth laughed.

"By Tarquin," Alista finished. "He's apparently furious with me."

The faery just smiled. "He'll get over it," she said sagely. "You mustn't let him worry you."

"I'll try not." She looked at the chaos of clothing around her and sighed. "Obviously I do need help packing, but I don't want to keep you from your own."

"My own what, love?" Gwyneth asked. "Eat your breakfast; you need your strength."

"Your own packing," Alista answered, tearing off a morsel of bread. "So you can come with me to Brinlaw, of course."

"Come with you?" she laughed. "No, little bird, not me. What would I do so far from the sea?" She folded Tarquin's extra trews into a basket. "Nay, love, my place is here." She composed her face in innocent lines, fooling no one. "That's quite some husband you have."

"You think so?" Alista asked, equally casual.

"Aye," Gwynnie laughed. "I do think. So do you still believe he doesn't love you, silly girl?"

"He never said he loved me," Alista pointed out, tying up the laces on a satchel.

"Said? What is said?" She shook her head as if Alista really were the thickest halfwit she'd ever heard tell of. "A man can say anything—it's what he does that you have to watch."

"Well, what he's done doesn't mean he loves me," Alista said. "My father was ever eager to see Dru when he came home, too, and I know he didn't . . ." She let her voice trail off before the words were spoken. "Besides, if he felt it, he would say it. He's very straightforward."

"He did seem so to me," Gwynnie agreed with a final muffled snicker. "Have you told him what you are?"

"I showed him the book and explained about the heartstone," Alista admitted.

"And did he believe you?"

"To be honest, I'm not really sure." She had brought very little from Brinlaw and had made nothing since she'd arrived, but she now had more clothes than she had space to pack them. "How did we fit this all in here?" Alista mused as she stuffed. "He didn't say he didn't believe it, and when I said I did, he didn't try to tell me I was wrong. And he wouldn't allow Brother Paolo to take my things."

"From what I know of mortal men, I'd say that's about the best you could hope for," Gwynnie sighed. "As for Brother Paolo . . . explain this to me, my lady. God the Father did make all that is in heaven and earth, and Christ the Son was charged with explaining the workings of it to us, men and women, too, and everything that is."

"Yes, that's the kernel of it, as I understand it," Alista said.

"Then did God not make the faery?" Alista had never seen her in anything but the kindest of humors, but now she seemed almost angry. "Is our salvation of no use to His Son? I suppose I can believe in Our Lord no matter how daft His earthly messengers might seem, but I won't just pouf away with a pop because He says I don't exist, or if I do, I must be evil."

"I don't think Our Father would say that at all," Alista said. "I've long suspected that the priests haven't quite figured out all that the Christ tried to tell them." She took the gown Nan had soaked on the beach the day before from the rack by the fire and smoothed its stiffening folds, thinking about how upset Brother Paolo had been by the very idea of her magic in spite of his liberal education. "Take Brother Paolo, since we're talking. He is handsome and kind, intelligent to a fault, the most gentle man I have ever known. Yet to serve Our Lord as he feels he must, he can never have a wife or child."

"I shouldn't worry about him if I were you," Gwyn smiled. "He's had a child and a true love, too. But if it makes him feel closer to heaven to pretend 'tis not so, it does no harm, I reckon." She sighed. "But it's a terrible waste, no question."

Alista smiled as well. "I do wish you would reconsider," she said. "Who will I talk to this way if you're not there?"

Gwyneth suddenly kissed the younger woman's cheek. "You don't need me, lovey, or you couldn't keep me away," she promised.

"I do need you," Alista demurred, hugging her tight. "But at least I'll still have Dru."

"For what good that will do," Gwyneth teased. She had made it plain long ago that while she liked Druscilla well enough, she didn't think much of her character. "So tell me, this good-looking rogue of a captain, is he the father of the babe?"

"Raynard?" Alista laughed, astonished. "No, of course not. My father was—is—she is having my father's child."

"Mark's child? Your blood?" She turned back to packing, shaking her head. "I don't think so."

"Gwyneth, she is," Alista insisted. "Dru was my father's mistress—who else's child could she be carrying?"

"I couldn't say," Gwyn answered, still looking doubtful. "But what do I know of mortal babies? I'm sure you must be right."

* * *

Tarquin came back into Falconskeep through what had once been the chapel, now converted to a temporary stable, and he didn't see Will Brinlaw with his horse until it was too late to escape being seen himself. "Alista tells me you're the mastermind who led her here without leaving any trail to speak of," Will said, checking Goliath's back and sides for burrs and scrapes.

"She didn't want us to be followed," Tarquin said, venturing a casual step closer. "How did you find us, anyway?"

"Brother Paolo knew she would come here," Will said. "Otherwise I'd be searching yet and might never have found you at all." He glanced over at the boy. "I'm not sure I'd have the . . . gumption to make such a journey with two women, one of them pregnant, and a baby."

At first Tarquin thought he must be mocking him, but the man didn't smile. "Yes, you would, if you had to," Tarquin scoffed, rather pleased at the compliment in spite of himself. "Lady May said you were the best knight in the world."

Something about this made him scowl, but he didn't lose his temper. "Lady May was a bit prejudiced," he said.

"She said you were modest, too," Tarquin pointed out. He had liked Lady May very much. She was one of the few people at his father's castle who always gave him something to eat if she could, and he had liked listening to her talk about real knights and ladies and her life before. She had talked about her brother like he was the hero of a legend until Tarquin, little cynic that he was even then, had almost believed it.

Will shook his head as he went for Goliath's bridle. "No one is the best knight in the world," he said, fitting the bit into place with a comforting caress. Goliath tossed his head once just to let Will know he was doing him a favor but otherwise didn't resist. "Hush, now," Will soothed, scratching under Goliath's chin as he fastened the straps.

"Someone has to be," Tarquin protested, coming close enough to pet the horse.

"Not for more than a moment at a time," Will said. "Hand me the blanket." He gave Tarquin the reins to hold while he dealt with the saddle. "Some knights are better than others, and some are very good indeed. But every fight is different, and every man changes, too. Say your best knight in the world stays up drinking the night before a battle because it's his grandmother's birthday. The not-nearly-so-great knight he fights in the morning may very well take off his head. And much smaller things can make almost as big a difference—the weather, the terrain. My men once beat a much bigger force just because we were already in such a miserable state, we didn't care anymore about the rain."

"Alista says being angry can help, once you know how to fight." He stroked Goliath's velvet nose. "Is that true?"

Will frowned. "Well . . . it's sort of true. Being angry can make you more brave, more willing to take chances, and these chances can win you the battle. But they can also get you killed. You see this?" He pointed to the scar on his cheek, and Tarquin nodded, fascinated. "Alista was very angry when she gave me this, and even though I'm a stronger fighter than she is, she fought well and did some damage. If she had been accustomed to fighting to do harm, she wouldn't have cut my face, she would have stabbed me in the eye, and I would be dead now. So her rage helped her, but not enough. She made me angry, too, and I'm accustomed to battle. So I almost killed her instead."

Why did she want to kill you? Tarquin longed to ask but didn't dare. "But you didn't," he said instead.

"No, thank God," Will agreed, actually crossing himself without thinking. "So Alista has been talking to you about fighting?"

"Some," Tarquin nodded. He wasn't sure what Will actually thought about his wife's skills with a sword; best not to make too much of it. "She said you might make me your squire someday."

Will looked at him from the corner of his eye. "Would you want to be my squire?"

"I don't know," Tarquin shrugged as if he had no opinion at all. "What's being a squire like?"

"It stinks," Will told him candidly. "You have to tromp around everywhere a knight decides to go with no say in the matter and no glory when you get there, no matter who wins the war. You have to be awake long before he is, and you get to sleep long after he does, yet he's the one who must be waited on hand and foot lest he be too tired to fight. When his battles go badly, he takes it out on you. When his mistress runs away with a minstrel while he's defending the Crown, he takes it out on you. When the food starts to run out, he eats, the horses eat, but you very likely go hungry. You are the one who keeps the weapons and armor in perfect order, but you never get to use them. And if you dare to complain, you get called an ungrateful wretch, as if you ought to think it some great privilege to work harder and be treated worse than the peasants who work his fields."

Tarquin knew most of this already from watching his father and his friends, but he'd never thought to hear a knight like Will admit it. To his mind, as much as he disliked him, Will was a "real" knight. "Why would anyone want to do that?" he asked.

"Only one reason," Will grinned, and Tarquin braced himself for the truth of chivalry. "To become a knight and get to do it to somebody else."

"Don't listen to him, boy," Raynard said, coming in. "He treated his last squire like the Baby Jesus, coddled him all the way from Bethlehem to Egypt."

"So what happened to him?" Tarquin asked.

"He fell off his horse in his first battle as a knight and got trampled to death before he could stand up," Raynard said. "But while he was a squire, he enjoyed himself very much."

"So now you know," Will said, squeezing Tarquin's shoulder and scowling at Raynard. "Perhaps you should give it some thought."

"You may as well unsaddle that horse," Raynard said, giving Tarquin a wink. "The sleet is picking up; we'll be going nowhere today."

Will shook his head, aggrieved and amused at once. He might have known he couldn't just ride away. "Then we have a mission to accomplish inside," he said, unfastening Goliath's saddle. "Tarquin, how would you like to introduce us to your demon?"

When Alista and Gwyneth came downstairs, they found Druscilla in the Hall holding court among the new young knights as if neither she nor they realized she was pregnant and thus technically no longer a demoiselle. "You needn't worry about our Dru," Gwyn confided in Alista's ear. "Happy or not, she knows how to land on her feet."

"Alista, come and meet Sir George," Dru called. "And Sir Linville and Sir Roger Hanley."

"Well met, milords," Alista curtsied, trying not to blush at their frankly curious stares.

"Indeed, my lady, 'tis glad we are to see you in one piece," Roger laughed. "Your lord was threatening to do you an injury all the way 'round England."

"Lord Brinlaw was concerned," Linville put in more tactfully.

"My lord was under the impression that I did not wish to be found," Alista answered with a smile, fighting back her natural shyness. "But we've put that mistake to rights."

"Aye, my lady, so we saw," Roger agreed, earning himself several brisk thumps from his companions.

" 'Twas Sir Geoffrey d'Anjou who needed to be broke in pieces," George asserted somewhat more shyly. Sixteen and newly arrived from France, he still found adult conversations a bit intimidating, particularly where ladies were involved. Nan had already claimed him for her own and currently had his purloined helmet set on the floor for use as a queer sort of bunting board cradle for her doll.

"And so he nearly was," Linville agreed. "You should have seen Lord Will, my lady. You would have been very proud."

"I'm certain I would have," Alista smiled.

"Seen him where?" Dru asked. "At the trial?"

"No, my lady, at the tournament," Roger enthused. "Brinlaw went at Geoffrey like a mastiff at a cat. If Geoffrey had refused to yield another moment, he would have taken his head off sure as the world."

"Roger, good heavens," George scolded, looking pointedly at Nan.

"I didn't realize there was a tournament," Dru said, a slight tremor in her voice. "I thought King Henry judged Brinlaw innocent."

"And so he did, in Papa's death," Alista said, taking both Nan and her dolly into her lap. "But apparently Pettengill's squire challenged Will on his master's behalf for attacking them on the road. Queen Eleanor suggested a trial by combat, and Geoffrey offered to fight on Pettengill's behalf."

"So you know all about it, then," Dru said. Gwyneth turned to stare at her, smiling a mysterious smile.

"Will told me," Alista admitted.

"Pettengill didn't want to fight at all," Linville said. "That was all Sir Geoffrey."

"And everyone knows why," Roger began, forgetting himself for a moment. Then he remembered Alista and turned an alarming shade of plum.

"It was a lawful fight, my lady, most fairly done," Linville explained in a soothing tone. "God judged aright, I'm sure. None can doubt your honor or your husband's affection."

"Assuming it was God who brought it off and not Brinlaw's superior strength," Dru said lightly. "Just think, Alista, a royal tournament fought over you, and you weren't even there to see it."

"I wouldn't have wanted to see it," Alista said, shuddering.

"Well, all's well as ends, I always say," Gwyneth said with another speculative smile.

Tarquin led Will and Raynard through a tiny back passage to the central tower and down the stairs. "Alista is not going to like this," he warned.

"Why not?" Raynard asked warily. Will still hadn't explained what he'd meant by "demon."

"She told me to stay away from the well," the boy explained.

"She suggested I do the same," Will said, taking the torch from him and holding it higher to light more of the mossy steps. "That's why we're going the back way."

"Have I been rendered mute without my knowing?" Raynard asked as they reached the bottom. "What are we doing down here?"

Will grinned. "We came to see the demon in the well," he said pleasantly.

"Except maybe it isn't a demon, exactly," Tarquin added. "Alista thinks it isn't."

Raynard peered frowning down the well shaft. "In truth, Will, what is this?" he demanded.

"In faith, Raynard, I'm not sure," Will admitted as he gave Tarquin back his torch. "Something in this well has grabbed hold of two men now—Tarquin here when they first arrived and Brother Paolo last night—and they both think it's a demon."

"She," Tarquin corrected. Brinlaw had said two men, and then to make it certain had said right out he was one of them. He could barely credit his hearing. He'd never been called such by any knight or peasant either. It was an interesting sensation. "And I'm not sure what she is," he continued. "I just know she didn't like me."

Will crouched beside the raised stone basin. "What were you doing when she grabbed you?"

"I was down in the shaft, looking for the lever that brought the water up," Tarquin explained, watching in tense fascination. "You'd never reach it now without drowning."

"So Brother Paolo couldn't have been doing the same." Will stuck his hand into the water and found it perfectly ordinary, wet and cold.

"I heard her calling to me," Tarquin said, taking a slow step closer. In truth, he had wanted to investigate this creature further from the beginning, but Alista had been so adamant, and he hadn't dared come alone. But surely these two knew what they were doing, and if they didn't, they could manage to fight their way out of danger. And he was with them; Brinlaw had brought him along as if it were the most natural thing in the world, as if he weren't just an inconvenient mouth to feed that his lady insisted he keep for the sake of his baby niece. . . .

"I think you've all gone raving," Raynard informed them.

"The monk, too?" Will asked mildly. He stood up and leaned over the well, peering into its crystalline depths. "What did she look like?"

"A woman," Tarquin shrugged. "Red hair, green eyes . . . like my mother, only prettier."

"That's a demon?" Raynard mused.

"I wonder if Paolo saw the same thing," Will said. His eyes were adjusting to the darkness, and he could make out the shapes of the stones far below, so slick they looked like silver. "Bianca?" he called softly.

"I wish you could see yourself," Raynard scolded.

Will was unlacing his tunic. "What are you going to do?" Tarquin asked, alarmed in spite of himself.

"What you did," Will answered, pulling the tunic over his head. The expressions on both their faces when he looked up were so appalled, he couldn't help but smile. "Why, do you think I shouldn't?" he asked Tarquin.

"I don't care," the boy said sullenly, his eyes going guarded again. "Do what you want."

"I'm not coming in there after you," Raynard warned.

"Just pull me out if I start slipping," Will ordered. Taking a deep breath, he plunged his head under the water.

Leaning well over, he found Tarquin's lever fairly quickly, but when he moved it, nothing happened. Below it, his hands found an opening, a rounded passage leading off the main shaft of the well. But he heard no woman's voice, and when he opened his eyes, he saw nothing but watery dark. His chest bursting, he straightened up again.

"Words cannot describe how ridiculous you just looked," Raynard said as he caught his breath and shook freezing water from his hair.

"What did you see?" Tarquin demanded.

"Nothing," Will answered. "I felt a hole—maybe whatever it is swims in and out." He put on his tunic again, trying to remember the legend Alista had read. *The spirit hated men, but why? Something about . . . iron.*

He unsheathed his sword, Mark's falcon sword, and plunged it into the water.

"That was dramatic," Raynard said dryly. "What was supposed to happen?"

Will raised his sword again, the falcon's jeweled eyes glittering in the torchlight. Mark's falcon . . . Mark who had burned on the pyre with this sword across his chest . . . "Give me your sword," he ordered.

"Since you asked me so nicely," Raynard grumbled, handing it over.

As soon as the tip of the blade touched the surface, the water shrank back with a great, sucking groan. Will pushed it in deeper, leaning over and bracing himself against the rim, and still the water receded.

"Stop it," Tarquin warned, his voice hollow with fear. "You're hurting her."

As if to agree, a screaming roar seemed to echo through the stones beneath their feet, and a thick, foaming spout of water burst from the well, flinging Will backward and pounding against the ceiling, dousing them all as it cascaded down the walls. Tarquin lost his footing in the sudden flood, and Raynard grabbed him by the shirt collar and hauled him back to the surface. "Will!" the captain shouted as the water receded, shrinking back into the well like a living beast returning to its lair.

"I'm all right," Will said, getting back on his feet, still clutching Raynard's sword, or what was left of it. The blade had been twisted into a shining spiral.

"I'm not," Raynard said, wide-eyed, as he let Tarquin go. "Holy Christ!"

"Hullo, down there!" Gwyneth's voice called from the stairs. "If you boys are done playing, the rest of us are ready for dinner."

As he trudged up the stairs, Tarquin felt someone ruffle his hair and nearly jumped out of his skin. "You're all right?" Brinlaw asked as he passed.

"Fine," Tarquin answered, brusque with shock. "Well, wet, but—"

The knight smiled. "Me, too," he agreed, continuing up the stairs. Tarquin just watched him for a moment, confused but pleased, before running to catch up.

Nan was snoring, and Tarquin was curled on his pallet with a flannel rag pinned around his throat for fear he'd catch a chill from his adventure with the knights at the well. "I can't believe after everything you heard this morning, you just went down and stabbed the thing," Alista was complaining quietly to her husband as she spread his clothes on the windowsill to dry.

"Neither can I," Will agreed. "I felt ridiculous."

She pushed his head to one side as she passed, ruffling his hair. "You could have drowned," she pointed out.

"Your spirit didn't seem interested in me," he admitted, drawing her into his lap. "I was beginning to think Tarquin and Fra Paolo had caught hysterics from one another."

"But now you believe me?" she said, taking his hand in both of hers and thinking the well spirit had horrible taste. If she'd been trapped in a well for centuries, this was what she'd have wanted to drag down to her lair, not a little boy or an aging monk.

"I always believed you." He kissed her brow. "I knew you were a faery from the time I married you."

She drew back to look at him, surprised, then frowning. "What kind of lover's prattle is that?" she said scornfully. "I suppose next you'll say I bewitched you."

"You did," he insisted, laughing softly.

"Aye, I'm certain," she grumbled. "That's why you treated me so well."

"It is," he said. "Imagine how I might have treated you if I weren't bewitched."

She smiled. "I can't even imagine." She traced the scar on his cheek. "Truthfully, Will . . . you haven't really told me what you think of all this."

"All what?" He tangled a hand in her hair and drew her mouth to his.

"All this magic," she answered, breaking the kiss with a soft, wet sound. "Does it not trouble you? You haven't said."

"Yes, I have." He laced his fingers with hers, turned her palm up to see the blue-white crescent of her scar. He remembered the dead ash smell of her father's burned-out pyre, the look in her eyes as she had given him her father's sword. "I told you the day after your father's funeral that I don't care." He pressed a kiss to her palm. "I told you it doesn't matter."

Her eyes filled with tears, but she smiled. "That was a long time ago," she said. "So much has changed since then."

He thought of his dream of the beach, racing desperately to catch her, and of the desert, his self-loathing and despair and the promise he had made to himself. "Nothing has changed," he promised. "You are still my wife."

But you didn't choose me, she thought as he kissed her, turning in the chair to face him. *You don't love me.* His touch slid up her sides as she knelt over him, and she framed his face with her hands, deepening the kiss.

Then Nan rolled over in the bed nearby, sighing through a yawn. "Oh, dear," Alista whispered, dropping her head to Will's shoulder.

"She's asleep," he whispered back, an edge of desperation in his tone that could be heard even in a whisper.

"She isn't that asleep," Alista answered, feeling rather desperate herself. She started to get up, and he kissed her again, wrapping her tighter in his arms. "Love, we can't," she protested as his mouth moved to her throat.

"I know," he groaned, letting her go.

She caressed his hair with a smile. "At Brinlaw, the children can have their own rooms."

He caught her hand to make her stop. "We leave first thing in the morning."

* * *

The moment of departure had finally arrived. Nan was already perched on Goliath's saddle, waiting for her uncle, with an extremely anxious Sir George in charge of holding the reins and keeping the great war-horse from tossing his burden obliviously over his head. After a brief but intense discussion, Tarquin had been induced to share a horse with Alista—for the sake of his masculine dignity, she let him sit in front. Now all that remained was to settle Druscilla. "Your mount, my lady," Raynard said, leading the remaining horse to her. "Unless you would prefer to share mine."

"And smell your stench all the way to Brinlaw?" she scoffed. "Je pense non—I feel sick enough already."

His mocking grin disappeared at once. "Are you truly ill?"

"No, fool; now help me up."

"Raynard, wait," Will said. "My lady, are you truly able to travel?"

As if you care, she thought. *Stop showing off for Alista.* "Yes, my lord, I'm fine," she said sweetly.

Will wasn't entirely fooled. "Alista told me you worry about your child's place at Brinlaw," he began. He glanced over at his wife, but she was adjusting Tarquin's hood. Apparently he was on his own. "Let me try to reassure you," he went on. "Lord Mark was never my friend, but he was a great soldier and Brinlaw's lord. You are Alista's friend. Your child will always have my protection, as will you, for as long as you wish."

Druscilla's smile was dazzling. "Thank you, my lord," she said, making a graceful curtsey in spite of her condition. "You do comfort me very much."

Thirteen

A letter from Fra Paolo Bosacci to his sister, Serena
Brinlaw Castle
Easter Sunday, 1156

My dearest friend—

Best wishes to you and your dear ones on this most holy of days. Tell all that I do remember them and pray they will ever be blessed. I send particular thanks and love to my niece, Teresa, for her kindness in the naming of her son. May God in His mercy smile upon this newborn Paolo as He has always done on this old one.

For I am content, Serena, in spite of all my fears. We are home again, away from that faery place, and that in itself is a great comfort. Alista has settled into a life as Lady Brinlaw that seems to be all we could have wished for her. Since we have returned from Falconskeep, I have seen no taint of sorcery upon her beyond the Heartstone which she always wears and which even I would not deny her. I am much haunted by her experience on the tower here. I saw her that day, and while I still cannot believe she would have been transformed, I cannot deny that she felt something that was not of this world. If she believes this Heartstone to be a talisman against that phenomenon, whatever it might be, I will not say her nay. Otherwise, she seems to be well occupied by her husband and the two children they have taken in, leaving her no time for magic. In short, all seems to be well.

And yet . . . I can hear you laughing at me as you read this. You will think me an old fool who cannot trust good fortune. But so much remains unresolved, so many questions unanswered. I hope that I am an old fool, that the doubts that haunt me are foolish, and in my prayers, I give them to God. But they still haunt me just the same.

Easter had passed, and spring had come to Brinlaw. The knights were all but leaping the walls in anticipation of war at any moment, but Alista somehow managed to ignore them, to pretend it wouldn't come, and Will was her willing accomplice. They were happy. Their days were full of work for the manor they both loved; their nights were full of each other. Why should anything have to change?

Alista came downstairs in her riding clothes to find a scene of domestic tranquillity in the Great Hall. Brother Paolo had begun of late to teach Tarquin how to read and write, and the two of them were sitting together at the table ruining a stylus and wasting a great deal of ink, both heads bent in concentration. Dru was working at her loom while Sir Roger watched, enraptured. And Nan was playing with her puppies and Sir George.

Dru's spaniel, through a shocking lack of discretion in her choice of companions, had recently produced three of the ugliest mongrels ever born on English soil. Nan had fallen in love at first sight, christening all three dogs Virgil. Why this should be, she either could not or would not tell, but she would not be dissuaded, as Sir George was discovering now.

"They can't all three be Virgil," he protested as she cradled one like a baby in her lap while the other two clambered to lick her face.

"Oh, yes, they are," she replied with the serenity of a madonna. "They can't help it; Virgil is their name." Weighted over with puppies, she fell over backward in the rushes, giggling like a fiend.

"Nan, that isn't very ladylike," Dru protested with a sigh.

"Oh, I don't know; I think she looks very domestic," Alista said. "The Virgils certainly seem to like it." Sir George was trying to rescue his charge, making her giggle even harder until he was laughing himself. "I'm going riding," Alista continued, feeling vaguely ridiculous. She still didn't see why being married meant she needed an escort to venture over the drawbridge, but in this case it was easier to comply with Will's wishes than withstand his wrath afterward.

"I'll go!" Tarquin announced, standing up before either of the knights could move.

"Is it all right?" Alista asked Brother Paolo, who nodded with an indulgent smile, waving a blessing. "Then wonderful, Tarquin; thank you."

Outside they found Will working with the crew on the wall. His wife had suggested to him that her half of the garrison might not feel so put upon about being used as masons if their lord were willing to lift a few stones himself, and he had taken her at her word. Stripped to the waist and streaming sweat, he was quite a vision to behold, and she pulled Goliath to a stop to admire him for a moment. "We're going riding," she smiled when he turned and looked back.

"So I see," he said, reaching for his shirt. "Wait and I'll come with you."

"Oh, no, my lord," she demurred. "I wouldn't dream of taking you from your work. Besides, I don't want you; I have Tarquin." Goliath pranced a step to one side. "And . . . I have your horse."

"I see that, too," he agreed. "Be careful."

"Goliath and I are old friends," she said, patting the horse on the neck.

"We'll be careful," Tarquin promised.

Will grinned. "Watch her, Tarquin. She's sneaky."

Tarquin thought of Alista disappearing in the Falconskeep woods, her phantom touch on his hair. "You're telling me," he muttered, urging his horse into a trot.

"We'll be back soon," Alista said with a grin of her own. "Maybe."

So long as they were in sight of the sentries, she rode at a dignified trot, the pace of a matron mindful of her coiffure. But as soon as they passed into the trees, she urged Goliath into a gallop, disappearing into the forest and trusting Tarquin to keep up. Urging his own mount forward with a whoop, Tarquin joyfully followed.

Turning aside from the forest trail, Alista crashed through the thinning brush, jumping Goliath over a fallen tree trunk to reach the open hills where they could truly run free. Bending low over the horse's neck, she nudged him with her heels to make him run even faster, the wind tearing through her hair. *Like flying,* she thought happily, the ground a blur of springtime green below her.

They finally stopped on the shores of the lake, Tarquin catching up just as she was alighting to lead Goliath to the edge for a drink. "I don't think that's what Brinlaw meant by being careful," the boy grinned, following suit.

"Probably not," she admitted. On the other shore, she could see what little remained of her father's pyre after the winter storms. When they had returned from Falconskeep, she had allowed Brother Paolo to bury Mark's armor and shield in the chapel, but all of the ashes had already been gone.

"Are you sad?" Tarquin asked.

"No," she answered, shaking her head. She looked back at him. "Are you?"

"No." He sat down on the grass, his horse's reins wrapped around his fist, and looked around him. The tops of the castle's towers could be seen over the trees, and the bang of the stonecutters could be heard faintly even from here. "I thought when spring came, I would leave."

Alista sat down beside him. "Where would you go?" she asked.

"I don't know. Anywhere, I guess." He shrugged. "But I didn't go."

"Why would you want to leave us?" she couldn't help but ask.

"I wouldn't, I guess." He looked at her. "Alista, are you happy?"

"Yes," she promised. She lay back on the ground and gazed up at the lamb's-wool clouds. "But if you went away, I would be very sad indeed."

I will never love anyone else, he silently swore, his boy-man's heart on fire with a feeling he was sure would never change. "Then I won't go away," he said aloud, lying down beside her.

They both dozed off, waking to hoofbeats. "This is riding?" Will teased, pulling up before them as they both sat up blinking. In truth, he had been a bit concerned, they'd been gone so long, but all seemed to be well.

"No, silly. This is napping," Alista said, yawning and unperturbed.

Will dropped to the ground beside her. "It looks lovely," he said. "I wish I had time to take it up." He tossed Tarquin a leather pouch. "Sophie and Dru thought the two of you might be hungry."

Tarquin opened the pouch and found bread and meat. "They were right," he admitted, tearing off a healthy chunk of each.

"So did you finish the wall?" Alista teased.

"As a matter of fact, we did," Will answered, opening a flask of wine. "Just in time, as it turns out."

"Why do you say that?" Alista asked lightly, as a shadow passed over her heart. "Are the Saxons invading from the lake?"

"No," Will said, taking a sip before handing it to her. "The Scots are invading from the north. A messenger from Henry just arrived."

"Will they come this far?" Tarquin asked, alarmed.

"No, no, not unless they're a great deal stronger than we expect," Will assured him. "But we'll have to ride north to meet them."

"We meaning who?" Alista demanded.

"Me, Henry's knights, part of the garrison," Will answered. "Raynard and I have discussed it, and he's going to stay and help Clarence here."

"You and Raynard have discussed it," she repeated. "What about me?"

"You were out riding," Will pointed out. "Why? Do you not want Raynard to stay with you?"

"Raynard may do as he likes," she said, getting up. "I want you to stay with me."

Will and Tarquin exchanged a mystified look. "I would prefer that, too," Will said gamely. "But we're at war."

"And if you don't go, Henry must surely lose," she said sarcastically.

"I am sworn to go," Will said, getting up. "That's how it works, love. Henry is king; I am Henry's lord. Henry gives me a castle and lands; I hold them in his name. Henry goes to war: I raise troops and go with him."

"You are Henry's lord, and I am your lady; therefore, I am meant to shut up," she snarled.

Will couldn't help but smile. "Well, that's how it's supposed to work," he allowed. "Alista, we've been talking about war with Scotland for months. What did you think would happen? Do you think me a coward, that I would send troops and stay home behind my wife's skirts?"

"No, of course not," she admitted. "But . . . to tell you the truth, I didn't let myself think about it at all."

He touched her cheek. "So you will miss me, then?"

"No," she retorted. "Not a bit."

"Am I going?" Tarquin asked. He had been acting as a sort of apprentice squire for Will ever since they had returned from Falconskeep, learning how to keep his armor in order and serve at table, all the slavish tasks of a nobleman's son.

"No," Alista said before Will could answer. "If Captain Raynard can stay, so can you."

"Alista," Will began, "if he wants to go—"

"I don't," Tarquin said quickly, beaming. Will raised an

eyebrow, and his smile faded a bit. "If my lady wants me to stay."

"Your lady does," Alista said with the air of an empress giving her final word. "So when are the rest of you leaving?" she went on in a more fragile tone, turning again to Will.

"Not for a week or more," he answered. "Henry is still putting his plans together. But he'll be sending more word soon."

"Good for him," she grumbled.

"Alista," Will began again.

"I know, I know," she interrupted. "I understand—I have understood all my life." She picked up Goliath's reins, preparing to mount. "That doesn't mean I have to like it."

That night, she dreamed of Falconskeep for the first time since they'd come home. She was in her mother's old room, and she was frightened. Looking down, she saw she held the scimitar, and the blade was red and slimy with blood. The window was open, and the wind was calling to her, calling in the cries of falcons. "I will not," she called back. "I will stay . . ." But suddenly she knew she had no reason to stay, that all her loves were lost. Dropping the sword, she went to the window and braced her hands on the frame, hands that were sticky with blood. The wind raked through her hair, and she reached up to free it from its combs, smearing blood on her cheeks and brow. The falcons were circling, calling her to them. She reached for the heartstone . . . but it was gone.

"No!" she cried, sitting up in bed.

"Alista?" Will mumbled, rolling over. "What . . . ?" He sat up, and she threw her arms around his neck. "What is it?" he said softly, holding her as she clung to him with all her might.

"You were gone," she said, still half-asleep. "You were dead, and it was my fault."

"You were dreaming," he promised, kissing her brow. "It was just a bad dream."

"A very bad dream," she agreed, still not entirely convinced.

"But now you're safe," he promised.

She loosened her death-grip a bit. "Sorry . . ."

"No, don't be sorry." She settled back on the pillows, curled on her side, and he lay down to face her. "Do you want to tell me about it?"

"No," she said with a shiver. "Maybe in the morning, in the light."

He took her hand and kissed it. "I know what you mean." He brushed the soft, black curls from her face. "I have dreams like that, too."

"I know." She touched his mouth, tracing its shape, reassuring herself he was real, that this was what was real. "About the desert." His blue eyes widened. "You talk in your sleep," she explained.

"Yes, about the desert." Something about her nearness and the dark made the words just come. "The Jihad are Muslim soldiers, like Crusaders, only heathen," he explained. "They are mighty warriors, but they can disappear into the desert like ghosts. Raynard and I led a battalion charged with running a group of them to ground. We marched into the desert, and they engaged us several times, but we could never seem to catch them all. They'd fight until the battle turned against them, then they seemed to just vanish among the dunes. Finally we realized they were joining the nomad tribes, losing themselves in these clans of desert people to regroup before coming after us again." He smiled bitterly. "This made us very angry," he went on in a voice dry as sun-bleached bones. "Englishmen have no business in the desert in the first place—we were half-mad already from thirst and the heat. We found a desert tribe, and we attacked." Tears rose in his eyes, but his voice was flat and cold. "We slaughtered them. Men, women, babies still in swaddling. When we were done, not a single nomad lived." His eyes met hers. "Not one of them was Jihad."

"Will, no," she breathed through tears of her own.

"I had given the order," he said. "I thought God would strike me dead—I actually fell on my knees in the sand and waited for it to happen. My men thought I had lost my mind, and I suppose I had. If Raynard hadn't been there . . ." His words trailed off for a moment. "We marched back to Jerusalem and gave up the cross."

If she hadn't known before, Alista knew now that she loved him, for as much as this tale sickened her, as deeply as she felt his wrong in it, her heart still hurt for him. It was Will she cried for as she silently wept. "That's why you won't take the Host." She took his hand between both of her own and kissed the scar across it. "You have to make confession. Brother Paolo—"

"God knows what I did," he said brusquely. "He was there."

"Yes, my love, He does." She pressed a kiss to his forehead. "And He knows how dearly sorry you are for it. But you must let yourself be absolved."

"I don't deserve absolution," he answered, shaking his head. "What penance could ever be enough?" He touched her cheek, adoring her with his eyes, his faery beloved with her pure, white soul. "Maybe Raynard is right," he said with a wry smile. "Maybe it is easier to give up and be damned."

"You will not be damned," she frowned. "I won't allow it."

He pulled her close and kissed her, rolling over her, aching for her in his very soul, damned or not. She wrapped herself around him, desperate to keep him close, to protect him even from himself. She cried out as he came inside her, calling his name, and he kissed her mouth as if to breathe for her. Her fingers tangled in his hair as she pressed him closer still, her tongue invading him as her hips arched up to meet him. *One flesh,* she thought as sweet tremors rippled through her. *One flesh . . . one breath . . . one soul.*

Raynard was sitting alone on the battlements, unable to sleep, trying to imagine how he'd gotten where he was. A year ago, he had been in the desert, fighting to live, living to fight, and he had been perfectly content. Now he was nestled safe in the green, sweet bosom of England, and he was perfectly miserable. He wasn't even going to fight the Scots, for pity's sake. He didn't even want to fight the Scots, and that was a hundred times worse.

He suddenly realized he was being watched. Drawing his dagger slowly from his belt, he turned fast and found Druscilla, who froze with a terrified gasp. "Bloody hell," he swore, dropping the knife. "Dru, what in hell are you doing?"

"I'm sorry," she said, still obviously shaken. "I just wanted to talk to you."

"So talk," he scolded, picking up his weapon. "Just don't sneak up on me."

"I'm sorry," she repeated as he put the blade away. "Raynard . . ." She grabbed him and kissed him on the lips. Startled, it took him a moment to catch up, and by the time he reached for her, she had pulled away. "Tell me you care for me," she ordered, a desperate light in her eyes. "Tell me you love me."

Obviously she thought he'd lost his mind. "Why should I?" he frowned, his own eyes narrow with suspicion.

"Please, my love, my soul," she begged, clinging to his shirt. "I know I am a monster, but please don't punish me, not now." Tears streamed down her cheeks. "Please, Raynard."

"I love you," he promised, pulling her close. "Of course I love you." She held on with all her might, and he stroked her hair, still at a loss. "Poppet, what is wrong?"

"Take me away from here," she begged. "I'll go anywhere you say, do anything you like."

He put his hands on her shoulders and drew back to see her face. "Dru, what are you—?"

"I can't stay here," she insisted. "We could go to France, or Jerusalem, even. We could be happy; I could make you so happy."

"You're not making any sense," he protested. "Even if I could leave, you couldn't possibly travel. Look at yourself—"

"You could," she insisted, pleading turning to rage in an instant. "You could leave if you wanted, but you don't. You don't want me."

"What does one have to do with the other?" he demanded. "Of course I want you—"

"Then prove it," she cut him off. "Take me away from here, and I am yours."

"I can't do that," he said, raising his voice in frustration. "Druscilla, tell me what has frightened you so. Tell me why you think you have to run away."

"You don't care," she said coldly, backing away. "If you did, it wouldn't matter why I had to go, only that I said I must."

"Dru, that's ridiculous," he scoffed.

"Aye, and I'm ridiculous." Fresh tears spilled from her eyes, glistening in the moonlight. "I must have been out of my mind." He reached for her, and she held up a hand, warding him off. "Touch me again, and I'll scream."

"Not if I scream first," he retorted, but he let his hands drop nonetheless. He turned away in hopes the urge to strangle her would pass. "Now stop this stupid game, and tell me—" He turned back, and she was gone. "Holy raging Christ!" he swore, flinging his sword against the wall.

A few days later, word came from Henry that not only was he on the move, but that he would stop at Brinlaw Castle personally to collect Will and his troops. Will went into the solar with the messenger to read the rest of his letters, and when he came out, Alista was gone. "Where is my lady?" he asked Sophie, expecting to hear that she was upstairs sorting madly through bed linens or in the kitchens frantically counting pies.

"Outside at the edge of the moat," Sophie answered rather sheepishly. "I think she wants to make a basket."

"A basket?" Will echoed, not sure he'd heard correctly.

"Yes, my lord. She's pulling reeds to make a basket," the maid nodded.

He paused, trying to work it out for himself, but nothing would come. "Sophie, why is she making a basket?"

The girl shrugged. "I couldn't say, my lord," she admitted sadly. "Do you want me to go tell her you wish her to stop?"

"No, no, I'll go," he sighed. "Is anyone making ready for the King?"

"Oh, yes, my lord," she said eagerly. "Captain Raynard has the men packing their supplies right now."

"Good," he nodded.

Outside, he found Sophie was perfectly correct. His wife, the lady of Brinlaw Castle, was yanking reeds out of the moat like she couldn't care less a royal progress was on its way. "I take it you're not impressed that King Henry is coming," he called to her from the drawbridge.

"I don't see why he has to come here at all," she complained, barely glancing up. "Couldn't that messenger have just taken all the knights who wanted to go to war back with him when he went?"

"Henry believes he is doing us an honor, love," Will said, smiling in spite of himself at the picture she presented. Her hair had come loose and was falling in her eyes; her skirt was sopping to the knees from wading in the edge of the water; her arms were muddy to the elbows, not to mention the mud she'd smeared on her face doing battle with her hair. In short, she was the most beautiful thing he had ever seen in his life. "You know, now that I think of it, he may even have Eleanor with him. Perhaps he means to leave her here with you while he fights Scotland."

This got her attention—she looked so horrified, he almost felt sorry for his joke. "Will, no!" she cried, so dismayed she almost lost her balance. "The Queen here? That's horrible. . . ."

He couldn't bear to see her suffer so for long. "Actually,

I'm joking," he admitted. "Truly, love, if Eleanor comes this far from her own court, I'll eat your basket."

She just looked at him for a moment, black eyes flashing, but he was too smitten to see his peril. "Oh good," she said sweetly, moving closer to the drawbridge as if to go back inside that way. "Will you help me up?"

Even then he didn't catch on. "Of course," he said, the very model of chivalry. He offered his hand; she smiled up at him . . . and then he was swallowing a large mouthful of the muddy moat. "You little wretch!" he sputtered, breaking the surface.

"Oops," she laughed. "You slipped."

"Aye, lady, it seems I did," he agreed, moving toward her, the water barely deeper than his waist as he drew closer. "Tell me . . . can you swim?"

"No," she lied, backing toward the bailey wall. "Not a stroke. I could drown in a basin. Will, no!" He grabbed her around the waist and dragged her into the water with her screaming all the way until he ducked them both. She came up laughing, her hair streaming mud, her arms around his neck.

"Shall I rescue you, Lady Brinlaw?" he inquired, laughing as hard as she. "You do seem to be in distress."

"I am," she agreed, looking into his eyes. "My stupid husband thinks I am a fish." She kissed him, and he carried her back to shore.

"I think you have to start over," he said, looking down at her reeds, now floating free on the surface. "Or perhaps you could start putting things in order for the King."

"Let him sleep in his tent," she grumbled, her arms draped around his neck.

"That would not reflect well on either of us," he

reminded her in his best husbandly tone. She kissed him again, and he began to think she was right; a royal progress was nothing to get excited over. . . .

"So how many noble knights is he bringing with him?" she asked with a sigh.

"I honestly don't remember," he grumbled, setting her back on her feet. "Oh, but one of them is Geoffrey d'Anjou."

She made as if to push him back into the moat. "That isn't funny—"

"I don't think so, either, but it's true," he laughed, catching her. "Henry wrote to warn me. Apparently his stepfather has bought him an army to play with, so Henry couldn't very well leave him at home."

"But does he have to bring him here?" she demanded. "That's outrageous!"

"Not at all," he said. "We fought; I won; he yielded; I accepted his surrender; Henry made us friends. We should fight side by side as brothers henceforward." She was giving him such a look, he started laughing again. "I know it's ridiculous, love, but it's true."

"It is ridiculous," she retorted. "And I hope Geoffrey is as well versed in chivalry as you and your stupid king."

When Henry arrived the next day, Will wasted no time sharing his wife's opinion over wine in the solar. "I couldn't very well send him on to Scotland without me," Henry laughed. Alone with Will and Raynard, with his royal boots propped on a bench, a cup in his hand, preparing to march into battle, he felt as happy as he had in months. "He might conquer the country and make himself king before we got there."

"His mercenaries must fight better than he does." Will grinned.

"They do," the King admitted with a grin. "He's annoying as all hell, I freely admit it, but truthfully he isn't a bad soldier, and I need all the troops I can get." He took a contemplative sip. "He'll behave himself, and if he doesn't, you have my permission to kill him."

"I said it was in poor taste to bring him, Harry," Will protested with a smile. "I never said I was worried."

"Though that last royal proclamation may be too good to pass up," Raynard mused. "Do you suppose we could convince Lady Alista to tempt him into evil so we can take His Majesty at his word?"

"She wouldn't have to do much," Henry said. "Sweet saints, Will, you should have told me."

"Told you what?" Will asked, casually filling his cup.

"Let's just say I now see what all the fuss was about," Henry said. "Who would have thought it of old Mark—no wonder Geoffrey kicked up such a ruckus. She's the only woman I know excepting Eleanor who may be as pretty as he is."

Pretty Geoffrey was in the Great Hall with the rest of the knights. "Brinlaw has changed," he remarked to Alista as she passed to fill his cup.

"Yes, well, it would, wouldn't it?" she said, smiling at him. "Hello, Geoffrey."

"That's all you have to say to me? 'Hello, Geoffrey'?" His tone was teasing and forthright, no effort made to not be heard by any in the Hall who cared to listen. "I'm crushed."

Alista had learned to play this game a little better since last they'd met, and she had made up her mind to act as if she knew nothing more about his so-called affections for her than what she had seen herself. "I thought you looked less tall," she laughed. "Actually, I did want to tell you how much I appreciated what you and Michael tried to do for Papa," she said more seriously. "It was very kind."

"Is that why you think I did it?" he asked, a different light coming into his cat-green eyes. "To be kind?"

"I can't tell why you did it," she answered, unruffled. "I only know why I am grateful."

He smiled, but his eyes narrowed. "Brinlaw has taught you to be cruel."

She was spared making an answer by the appearance of Sophie from the kitchen. "Forgive me, my lady, but you are needed," she said, giving Geoffrey a sidelong glance.

"Then I shall come," Alista answered, setting down her pitcher. "If we don't speak again, Sir Geoffrey, I wish you good fortune in Scotland."

"Then I shall surely have it," he said, making a courtly bow.

Once Henry had a hold on him, Alista didn't see her husband again until an hour before supper. He found her in the tiny closet they were using as a bedroom so the King could have theirs. "It does seem Druscilla . . . ," Will began after barking his shins on a chest for the third time in five minutes, ". . . has the bigger room."

"Druscilla has both children in her room," Alista pointed out, in no mood to argue. "Would you like to trade?"

"No," he admitted, keeping his peace. He watched her mending the hem of her best black gown, a look of unmixed irritation on her face that was charming to behold. "There's no one else who could do that?"

"No, blast it to hell." Her thread tangled again, and she bit it off with a most unladylike snarl before starting again. "Believe me, I asked."

"Take heart, love," he soothed, stretching out on the narrow bed. "By full sun tomorrow, we'll have left you in peace and gone to Scotland."

"That makes me feel so much better," she said, jabbing herself in the finger with the needle. "Damn it!"

"Here, let me see," he said, sitting up to examine her wound.

"I still don't see why he had to bring stupid Geoffrey," she muttered as he put the bleeding digit in his mouth to suck out the hurt.

He frowned. "Why, did he say something to you?" he asked, making sure the bleeding had stopped. "What did he say?"

"Nothing, nothing. I just—" Someone knocked on the door. "Now what?"

"Pardon, my lord," the royal squire said when Will opened the door. He handed over a bundle wrapped in silk. "For your lady, with the Queen's best regards."

"For me?" Alista asked when he was gone. "What do you suppose it is?"

"I shudder to even imagine," Will said, handing it over.

She untied the cords and opened the silk. "It's a gown," she said flatly, hardly the squeal of delight the Queen had perhaps anticipated. It was an exquisite gown, as lovely as one Eleanor might have chosen for herself, the color of burgundy wine. Alista lifted it from its wrappings, but she still didn't seem pleased. "Why would the Queen send me a gown?"

"Why does Eleanor do anything?" Will said, almost completely disinterested. "Look at the bright side—now you don't have to fix that one."

"I am not wearing this," she said, folding the gown.

"Oh yes, madam, you are," he retorted. "What's wrong with it?"

It's from Geoffrey, you ass! she wanted to scream. She could still see his face in the garden at Christmas—"You would be magnificent," he had said, looking at her like she was a statue he meant to buy. Was this his way of making peace?

"I'm in mourning," she reminded her husband. He was leaving in the morning; she didn't want to talk about Geoffrey.

"And it's damned insulting to me that you remain so," Will shot back. "But when we're alone at home, you can dress yourself as you please—"

"I thank you, my great and terrible master," she said with a curtsey.

"But when the King and half of England is in my house, my wife will appear in proper dress," he finished, unimpressed by her sarcasm.

"And this is suddenly the only proper dress I own?" she asked, beginning to truly lose her temper. Why should he care what she wore? Was she an infant, that she couldn't dress herself?

"Since it happens to be a gift from Henry's wife, yes," he answered, feeling a little silly. "Honestly, Alista, can't you just for once do as I wish without re-creating the Saxon

Invasion? Can't you just smile and say, 'Yes, Will,' just once in your life? Other wives do such things; I've seen them."

"Do they?" she asked, taking the gown out again. Just who was he trying to impress?

"You'll wear it, then?" he pressed, leaving nothing to chance.

She gave him a smile to make his blood run cold. "Yes, Will."

At first he thought she would not appear at supper at all. She had taken her new gown and gone to Druscilla's room, and he hadn't seen her since. "Is Lady Alista ill?" Sir Geoffrey asked politely after the second course had been served with her place still empty.

"Not that I noticed," Will answered with deadly courtesy of his own.

"I would say not," Henry said, looking toward the archway. "If she is, may every woman in England be so struck."

If he could have spoken, Will might have agreed. Alista was gorgeous. The gown fit her well, and the color complemented her complexion, but that was only part of her transformation. Her carriage as she moved through the Hall was regal, gracious, ever-so-slightly cold, and every glossy, black hair on her head had its place. Her skin had never looked so white, her lips so red, her eyes so full of unknowable secrets barely hidden in their depths. Will's wild faery was gone, replaced by a woman of fashion.

"Forgive me for being so late, Majesty," she said, making a deep, perfect curtsey at the dais. "I wanted to be worthy of Queen Eleanor's gift."

"I do forgive you anything, my lady, if this is the result,"

Henry smiled. "Your husband can make do without you; come and sit by me."

Marvelous, Alista silently groaned as Geoffrey moved to make room on the bench. *And Will just sits there eating his beef like he couldn't care less.*

In truth, Will didn't dare even glance in their direction for fear he would go mad and murder Henry and his cousin, too, before he could stop himself. And Alista continued to make it worse—had she ever laughed so musically at his jokes? Not that he was given to making jokes, but even so . . .

"Your husband tells me you have taken his fosterlings quite under your wing, Lady Alista," Henry said, making her sputter the tiniest bit over her cup before she regained her composure. "It warms the heart to think of someone so young and beautiful having that kind of maternal instinct. But when can Will expect an heir of his own?"

Her father had told her Henry made a charming art of rudeness; now she knew precisely what he had meant. "I am certainly doing my best, Majesty," she answered. "But if you will take him off to Scotland, you undo me, I'm afraid."

Henry roared with laughter, but Will was staring at her aghast. "I shall have to send him home quickly," the King promised.

Geoffrey suddenly stood up. "My lady, will you dance?" he asked. "With Lord William's permission, of course."

She looked over at Will, trying to send him a message with her eyes, but the idiot refused to receive it. "My lady will do as she likes," he answered. "In this as in all things."

"Do not believe him, Majesty," Alista said lightly. "But yes, Sir Geoffrey, I will dance."

If the world had been what it should be, this would have made Alista happy. She had always enjoyed having music at Brinlaw, and Geoffrey was in fact the one who had bothered to teach her to dance in the first place—her father hadn't known himself. But nothing, it seemed, could be simple and fun when love and the royals were involved. "How do you like your gown?" Geoffrey murmured, turning her in the figure. "I told you that color would suit you."

Her eyes widened—he was daring to admit it? Here, in the middle of Brinlaw's Hall? "It's lovely," she said when he passed close again. "But when did we ever discuss colors, my lord?"

His smile was wicked, but friendly, the Geoffrey-smile of old that had always made her laugh. "So you contend you do not remember."

"'Tis no contention," she said lightly. "I do not."

"A flirt and a liar as well," he said, lifting her hand to his lips.

"Would you call that behaving himself?" Will asked his king from across the room.

"As well as could be expected, under the circumstances," Henry said lightly.

"So now I'm to be insulted as well as challenged with riddles," Alista was saying, her skirts swirling around her as she turned. "I remembered you having better manners." She glanced at the dais, silently willing Will to get up and rescue her, for heaven's sake, but he just sat there with Henry and Raynard, the three of them staring in a row like she were some sort of monkey brought in to dance for their amusement.

"Leave it alone, Will, she's only trying to make you jealous," Henry advised, the voice of experience. When his friend didn't answer, he looked at his face. "And it's working beautifully," he finished with a sigh.

"Forgive me, my lady," Geoffrey answered, drawing her a few inches closer. "How shall I make it up to you?" The figure required that he move behind her, and as he did, he brushed so close she felt his breath on her skin. "Shall I tell you that you are the most beautiful creature I have ever seen?" She could feel herself blushing, but she made herself smile, refusing to let on that he upset her. "Shall I tell you how dearly I love you?"

She whirled around too quickly for the music, her eyes alight with anger, but her smile never wavered. "Shall I tell my husband?" she said sweetly, touching Geoffrey's cheek.

"I'm not jealous," Will said tersely, a muscle jumping in his cheek, his jaw was clenched so tightly.

"I'm glad to hear it," Henry gave up, exchanging a wry grin with Raynard. "Even so, why don't you put a stop to this before not being jealous gives you a stroke? This is your manor; I will not interfere."

Will was up before the words were spoken. He didn't speak; he didn't stop. He walked straight out through the dancers, caught hold of his wife in mid-figure, threw her over his shoulder, and walked out of the Hall, leaving Geoffrey standing alone, gaping at his cousin, and Raynard and Henry laughing so hard they were in peril of falling from their chairs.

"Are you mad?" Alista protested as soon as they were out of earshot. "Put me down." He still said nothing, carrying her up the stairs. "Will, for pity's sake!"

When he reached their temporary room, he kicked the door open, cracking it back against the wall. By this time, Alista had gone limp, refusing to give him the satisfaction of a struggle. "What can you be thinking?" she demanded as he carried her into the tiny room. He tossed her on the bed with all the tenderness he would use on a sack of corn. "Do you never intend to speak to me again?" She started to get up. "Don't be an ass, Will—"

"Trust me, Alista!" he said, turning on her with such fury in his eyes she shrank back onto the bed. "You don't want me to speak." He glared at her another long moment, and she crouched warily at the edge of the mattress, not sure whether she would fight, flee, or surrender. Then he turned and left, slamming the door behind him. Nonplussed, she jumped up just in time to hear the outside bolt slide home.

"You bastard!" she roared, banging on the door. "You wouldn't dare!" Apparently he would; there was no answer. "William Brinlaw, come let me out at once!" Still no answer, and the castle was full of eager ears. "You'd best hope I starve to death before you come back," she muttered, flinging herself down on the bed. "Otherwise you are dead."

Tarquin had felt no desire to dodge a lot of strangers in the Hall, so he had been allowed to have his supper upstairs with Nan and Druscilla. He had fallen asleep on his pallet by the fire as Dru sewed a shirt for her new baby. But she was singing . . .

He rolled over, careful to keep silent. She was sitting in front of the mirror, singing under her breath so softly he couldn't make out the words. A polished copper bowl sat on the vanity table before her, and she seemed to be watching something inside it as she sang.

She stopped for a moment to consult the book propped against the mirror—Alista's book. He started to say something, but then she looked up again, and something about her face in the mirror made the words dry up in his throat.

Tendrils of smoke or mist began to rise from the bowl, framing her reflection, and she smiled. Tarquin rolled back toward the fire and dragged his blankets over his head.

By the time Will circled the battlements a dozen times in the bracing, midnight air, he felt more like himself, better equipped to correct his wife with kindness and calm. Unfortunately, Alista's confinement had given her the opposite effect.

The pottery basin missed his head by inches before shattering on the wall. "How dare you?" she shouted, launching herself at him after this warning volley. "You will not lock me up like I might be your . . . your . . ." She crashed full weight against his chest, making him stagger back against the door. "You bastard!"

"You would have preferred I let you make a fool of me before the King and all his council?" he demanded, grabbing for her as she came at him again. Another woman would have clawed at his face, but not Alista—she was making a fist. "I think not, dearest."

She sank her teeth into his wrist, making him let out a most satisfying yelp of pain, but the monster wouldn't let go. "As if I cared a tinker's dam what Henry thinks," she raged, kicking and struggling with such violence her feet completely left the floor. "You're the one who's Henry's puppet, not I."

"I . . . am no man's puppet," he said, heaving them both toward the bed.

"What would you call it?" she demanded. He had her by the hair with one hand to keep her from biting again, making it impossible to immobilize both of her hands for long. She broke a fist free and drove it backward over her shoulder and into his jaw—a sloppy blow, but an effective one; he let go, dropping her in a heap on the floor. "Henry has done nothing but thwart and betray you at every turn to suit his own purposes," she pressed on, getting up. "Refusing to give you Brinlaw, lying to me, making you stand trial, bringing stupid Geoffrey here."

"What's your point?" he asked, still seeing stars.

"My point is that after all this, you still intend to march off to Scotland just because he asked you," she said, shoving him back on the bed while he still looked marginally dazed.

"He didn't ask me; he ordered me," he said, grabbing her and pulling her down with him. "He's the King; he can do that."

"And if you said you'd rather not, that you'd rather stay here with me?" she asked, holding herself away from him, just out of reach of his kiss, one knee planted dangerously against his stomach.

"He'd assume you had castrated me and have you burned at the stake." She was breathing hard from fighting, her lips parted, a sheen of perspiration on her face and throat and half-bared breasts as she loomed over him, and he remembered her dancing with Geoffrey, her smile as the French fop whispered secrets in her ear. "I'm one of his knights, remember?" he said, dragging her down to him to kiss her mouth.

"I am in earnest, Will," she protested when her lips were free.

"So am I." He rolled her onto her back and rolled over her, his hands running over her possessively, her flesh still wrapped in velvet. She turned her face away, and he kissed her ear instead, catching the tender lobe between his teeth.

"You don't fight fair," she protested, reaching up to

push at him and enfolding him instead. "Mean-spirited brute . . ."

"I love you," he agreed, kissing his way down her throat.

"What?" He was pushing up her skirt, his leg laced between hers, and sweet, lethargic want was spilling through her, but she had to hear what he'd said. "Tell me what you said again," she insisted, pulling at his shirt.

He raised his head to look at her, his eyes dreamy with desire. "I said I love you," he answered as if she ought to have known already. He bent and kissed her softly on the lips. "I love you."

"Then how can you leave me?" she asked, tears spilling from her eyes.

"Leave you?" His voice was soft, the voice no one ever heard but her, not even Nan. "Never."

"Tomorrow." He kissed her mouth. "I love you," she protested as he kissed her cheek. "Stay with me." He was still kissing her, caressing her leg and upward, and she grabbed a fistful of his hair. "Say you'll stay with me!"

"You know I can't." He brushed the tears from her cheek. "You know that." She looked away, refusing to answer. "Alista . . . I'll be home in a month, I promise, and then—"

"And then we'll be happy here forever," she said, miserable and furious and longing to give in, to lose herself in his kisses and forget her fears, but she couldn't. Even though she knew she should, that she was behaving like an idiot child, she couldn't seem to stop. "One more battle, and you'll come home to stay; you swear it. It's a lie—even if you mean it, it's a lie."

"Alista, this rebellion . . . it is nothing," he protested. "Compared to the battles I've seen—"

"So no one will die?" she cut him off. "Every knight who rides away from Brinlaw in the morning will—"

"No," he admitted before she could finish. "Men will die."

"But none of them will be you. You can promise me."

"Yes." He was scowling and furious, and her heart ached for him more than any woman could have ever loved any prattling poet with his fond and fawning eyes. "That's exactly what I promise." He touched her cheek and made her look at him. "I won't die," he said in a gentler tone. "I will come home to you."

Her trembling mouth twisted in a smile. "Are you certain you want to?"

He smiled back, relieved. "'Tis my life's only ambition," he swore as he kissed her again.

The next morning, she couldn't even bear to stand on the battlements as they rode away, to see their pennants finally disappear over the forest hill. She sat in the solar with Brother Paolo and the children and Druscilla, a piece of much-detested needlework lying in her lap, and tried not to think of Will at all, to pretend he was somewhere about, would walk in at any moment. But it was no use. "Bastard," she swore, dissolving into tears.

"You don't mean that," Paolo said gently.

"No," she admitted, wiping her eyes. Her father had left her to go to battle a hundred times, and she had borne it; why was this so different? "But it feels like I do."

Dru suddenly got up and came to her. "My poor cherie," she soothed, her own tears bright in her eyes. "My poor, sweet, little love."

Fourteen

As time passed, Alista thought she would feel better, but she didn't. Every day she became more anxious, and every night she dreamed of falcons and blood until finally she feared to fall asleep. "Cara mia, this is not like you," Brother Paolo said, finding her alone in the chapel. He sat down beside her on the narrow bench. "You love your husband at least partly because he is a warrior, because he can protect you. Is this not so?"

"Yes, of course," she nodded. She had lit a row of candles, and their flickering light was hypnotic. If she let herself, she could drift into a trance just watching them, Brinlaw Castle and the friar were left behind as she was lost in the same waking dream—the falcons were calling, and Will was dead. . . .

"This is insane, I know," she said sharply, shaking her head to clear it. "I know how childish I'm being." She stood up, willing strength back into her exhausted limbs. "I remember when Papa used to leave, and Dru would cry all day. I thought she was the silliest creature I had ever seen. I would feel so sorry for her. . . ." She looked back at him with a wistful smile. "Now see how much worse I behave."

"What is it that frightens you so?" the monk said. "Have you so little faith in Brinlaw's skills as a knight—?"

"No, of course not; I would be a fool indeed if I didn't know he can fight. He has survived much worse campaigns than this." She looked up at the cross above the altar. "He promised me he would come home," she said softly. "He swore that he wouldn't be killed."

Paolo felt the flesh on the back of his neck tingle with apprehension. "You fear this was blasphemy," he said. "A challenge to God."

"That's part of it, I think," she admitted, sinking down on the bench again. "And something else, too." She looked up at him, the candles' flames reflected in the black of her eyes. "Will thinks he is damned," she said softly. "He did something in the Holy Land that he believes God cannot forgive. That's why he wouldn't take Communion, even before they left."

Paolo had suspected something like this. On the morning of their departure, he had presided over a great Mass with the King's own priest, giving the Blood and Body of Christ to all who would go to fight—all, that is, but Brinlaw. Will had spent his last hour before leaving in his own solar with Alista in his arms as if her love were his only salvation. "You must pray for him, cara mia," he said. "Pray he will accept the truth, that he will return to God."

"I do," she promised. "Every moment, and I still believe God hears me." She had cried so much, her eyelids felt raw and sore all the time now, so when fresh tears came, she barely noticed. "But I'm still so afraid." She reached for his hand, and he gave it. "I have this dream . . . if I closed my eyes right now, I could see it. I'm at Falconskeep, and Will is dead, and I have to fly away."

"My love, this is nothing," the friar soothed, much relieved. "You fear for him—it is only natural that you should have such a dream. Recognize it for the phantom it is, and it will haunt you no more."

"Do you think I haven't tried that?" she protested. "You said it yourself; this is not like me. I am not given to hysterics—temper, yes, but not hysterics. As dearly as I loved Papa, as many times as I dreamed he was killed when he was away, have you ever seen me behave this way?"

"No," he admitted.

"But I have seen visions these past few months, visions that were the keys to truth," she went on. "Do you remember the falcon, Brother? The white falcon who died at my feet?"

His blood ran cold to remember, but he wouldn't lie to her. "Yes, love, I remember."

"That's how I feel now, every minute," she said. "I feel exactly as I did in the moment I knew the falcon was dead—as if everything I ever loved were lost, as if I know a tiny part of something important, but I can't see the rest, and if I don't see it, I can't stop it. . . ." Her voice trailed off. "I don't think I can bear it."

"Alista, listen to me," he demanded, taking her by the shoulders. "These dreams and visions—they are illusions of the devil, meant to trick you into despair, or else they are just as I said, empty phantoms of your own mind. You must resist them, let them go."

"I can't," she wept.

"You can, and you must," he insisted. "Even if you were right; even if the worst should happen and Will Brinlaw should die, all would not be lost. What of Nan and

Tarquin? What of Brinlaw Castle and the village? What of Druscilla, of me?" He kissed her forehead. "You think I don't understand the love you feel, but I do."

"I know you do," she said softly.

"Then believe me when I tell you it is not all the earth and sky, no matter what your heart may tell you," he smiled, cradling her cheek in his hand. "You are more than this love."

She smiled through her tears. "I know," she admitted. "But I don't want to be."

The next day something happened that should have made her feel better. A messenger from King Henry on his way to fetch reinforcements stopped at Brinlaw Castle for a fresh horse, and he brought a letter for Alista from her husband:

Dear Alista—

Tell Tarquin not to worry about Scotsmen marching on Brinlaw; now that we have chased them back across their borders, we cannot induce them to venture out of their own Highlands. We spend all our time chasing ghosts among the rocks and mists, and our horses are all exhausted from the steep terrain. But I am well, and I remember my promise, so have no fear.

Even your admirer, Sir Geoffrey, seems to be concerned for my welfare. Yesterday I had lost Goliath—or rather, he had lost me. He knew quite well where he was; I had just gotten knocked off his back. I was fighting one demon in a kilt when another decided to assist him by coming at me from behind. They had me pretty well pinned against the cliffside when who should come riding up but Sir Geoffrey d'Anjou, leading Goliath behind him. Between the two of us, we made short work of my attackers, and I was forced to give him thanks—without question the most painful part of this campaign so far.

Tell Nan her Sir George is fighting well and enjoying himself very much. He asks that you kiss her on his behalf and give three-headed Virgil a bone in his name.

I remember my promise; you must remember it as well.

Will

She read this through twice in the privacy of her room, then hurried back downstairs. "Where is the King's messenger?" she asked Clarence.

"In the kitchen with Lady Dru," he answered. "Preparing to leave, I think."

She ran to the kitchen and found the messenger finishing his food with Dru sitting nearby. "Will you be returning to the front?"

"Aye, my lady, as quickly as ever I may," he said, scrambling to his feet.

"Can you take a message back to my husband?" she asked. "It will only take a moment—"

"I wish I could wait, my lady, truly," he answered, glancing at Dru, "but I've delayed too long already. But if it's not too personal, you could just tell me—"

"It is too personal, but I have to tell him, so I shall have to trust your discretion," she cut him off. "Swear to me you'll go to him straight after you report to the King."

"On my life, my lady," he swore.

She nodded, collecting her thoughts. "Tell him not to trust Sir Geoffrey d'Anjou, no matter how helpful he seems to be," she began. "Tell him I didn't tell him this before he left because he was already being so silly and we had so little time, but when we were dancing, Geoffrey said he loved me. If Geoffrey is pretending now to be his friend, it can only mean he's plotting something. Can you remember all that?"

The herald just stared at her for a moment, his eyes as wide as his smile. "Aye, my lady," he promised. "I won't forget a single word."

Dru's expression had grown progressively darker as Alista spoke. "Weren't you in a hurry?" she now said pointedly.

The herald seemed to remember himself. "Aye, lady, yes," he said. "I am. I thank you." He made a quick bow to Alista. "I will remember, my lady."

Will had been summoned to the royal pavilion to consult with his king before the morning's battle. Ushered into Henry's private quarters, he found God's Anointed bidding a lingering and fond farewell to a lovely redhead dressed in little more than the plaid of her clan. Breaking the kiss, the girl gave Will a solemn wink before making her escape. "Consorting with the enemy, my liege?" Will asked.

"A spy," Henry grinned. " I was questioning her, and things got rather out of hand."

"No doubt Eleanor would understand," Will couldn't stop himself from saying. A year ago, the presence of a camp follower in Henry's bed on a campaign would have given him no more pause than the presence of the bed itself. Henry was a grown man, and what his wife didn't know couldn't cause her grief. But now to his horror, he found he disapproved.

"She would not, the darling wretch," Henry admitted, but his smile never dimmed. "She would take it quite personally, I'm afraid, kick up all manner of fuss. But luckily she isn't here, and besides, whatever she may be doing to fill her empty hours is no business of mine, either." He cast a sidelong glance at his friend. "If I were, for example, to start carrying her bodily from my Hall every time some unmarried knight made eyes at her, I shouldn't have the strength left to rule."

"So that makes tupping whores your right," Will said, matching his humorous tone.

"My crown makes tupping whores my right," Henry retorted. "Having a wife with whom the whole damned world is in love makes tupping whores my pleasure." He shook his head. "Poor Brinlaw, smitten by his bride," he sighed. "Take heart, mon ami. It won't last." He took a swallow of wine. "Believe me." His smile returned. "But I wanted to ask you about Geoffrey. Has he given you any more trouble?"

"None," Will admitted. "He actually saved me from being hacked to pieces a few days ago."

"Good for him," the King nodded as a squire filled Will's cup. "Consider it his apology." He settled into a chair and motioned for Will to do the same. "I chastised him rather sharply after that incident at Brinlaw, and I suspect he took it to heart. He's expecting me to give him a manor in Anjou, a piece of my inheritance from our father, the duke. My mother thinks it's a good idea."

"Have you no manors in Greenland?" Will muttered into his cup.

"Come now, Will, be a sport," Henry laughed. "France should be plenty far enough—she'll have forgotten about him in no time."

"Alista has forgotten him already," Will said with the scowl his friend remembered so well. "What little she ever thought of him."

"So the lady has convinced you her heart is yours alone," Henry mused. "She seems a sweet-natured little creature; perhaps it's true. Still, any woman that attractive is bound to use it; she'd have no choice." He stopped, catching sight of Will's face. "God's bones, Brinlaw, pray remember that regicide is a capital crime," he laughed.

"You're safe, Majesty," Will replied with a small smile that barely touched his eyes.

"I'm glad to hear it," Henry said. "Have it your way—Lady Alista is a paragon of wifely virtue who could never entertain an adulterous thought no matter how many her beauty might inspire." He raised his cup in salute. "I'm sure she is home in your castle pining for you right now."

The King was, in fact, quite right. Sitting in the back garden watching the children play, Alista was pining for her beloved so intensely her heart literally ached. "Will's niece favors him, poor child," Raynard said, coming out through the arch.

Alista looked back, insulted on Nan's behalf, then she saw his grin and smiled back. "She is beautiful," she retorted.

"Yes, she is," he agreed, sitting down beside her. "But I can't say much for her dogs."

"No," she laughed. "Virgil is not a pretty beast in any of his incarnations."

The captain smiled. "I understand you had a letter from Will."

"Yes." She reached into her pocket. "Would you like to see it?"

"No, my lady, I'm sure it's private," he quickly demurred.

"No, it really isn't." She held it out. "Please, Raynard. I insist."

He took it rather warily and read. "He's not much of a poet, is he?" he grinned, shaking his head.

"No, thank heavens," she agreed, taking the letter back. "I've already had enough poetry to last a lifetime." She sighed, barely realizing she had done it. "He's a good solider, isn't he, Raynard?"

The Fleming was watching her closely. "Aye, lady, the best," he promised. "You needn't fear for him."

"I can't help it," she admitted.

Watching her dance with Geoffrey, Raynard had been suspicious. She had seemed so different, her beauty more obvious, more sleek, and he had thought perhaps this was the real Alista, the one Will could not or would not see. But watching her now, he thought he knew better. This simpler beauty was the woman in truth, and she loved Will with all her heart. "What was his promise?" he asked her with genuine affection.

She smiled. "To come home," she confessed.

"Then believe him," he advised. "In all the years I've known him, he's never broken a promise yet."

Will missed his beloved, but just at this moment he missed Raynard more. Some of the men were beginning to say the Scots could not be killed because they were never alive, that they were spirits of the dead risen up to avenge themselves against their Norman oppressors. Will took the more practical view that there were simply many more Scots than anyone could have reasonably expected, all of whom knew the contours and hazards of this rocky terrain better than Will knew the scar on the back of his hand.

Raynard would have said, Who cares; keep hacking at them, and they'll all fall eventually. That was why he missed Raynard.

Another clansman sprang screaming from the rocks, trying to get at Goliath's belly under his armor. Will kicked him in the face and sprang out of the saddle—he had given up wearing his own plate mail by the second fight, realizing it was a kind of suicide to keep it. The Scot had barely flinched, was raising his sword again, but Will was ready. He deflected the blow and swung his own blade in a single, circular motion, neatly cleaving the man's head from his shoulders.

He turned to find his next opponent, then he felt a sudden sting in his shoulder. Turning back, he saw a man running back toward the English encampment, but that was hardly unusual. He reached back and touched his shoulder—it hurt no more than a bee sting. He looked at his fingertips and saw only a tiny smear of blood. Then another Scotsman was on him, and his shoulder was forgotten.

Alista was putting her freshly washed clothes in the chest at the foot of the bed when she suddenly thought of something, something in her mother's book, a magic mirror that could be made to reveal one's true love. If she looked into such a mirror, she would see Will and know he was all right, and perhaps she could get a decent night's sleep. "It's only one spell," she said aloud, warming quickly to the idea, her very heart seizing on it like a lifeline. Resolved to just do it and be done before she lost her nerve, she dug deeper into the chest for the book. But the book was gone.

She found Brother Paolo in the solar. "Where is it?" she

asked him gently. "I know you think you're protecting me, but I need it."

"Need what, cara mia?" he asked, concerned more by the look in her eyes than her words.

"My book," she answered, her patience starting to unravel. "My Falconskeep book—what have you done with it?"

"It is lost?" he asked mildly.

"No, it is not lost," she said with an edge of acid. Suddenly it felt as though the more he thwarted her, the more it seemed that nothing would comfort her but to have the book back. "You have taken it. It's mine, Brother—you have no right."

"Cara, on my life I swear I do not have it," he promised, becoming deeply alarmed. Her manner remained relatively calm, but in her eyes she looked ready to throttle the book from him by force. "Have you been using it?"

"No, I have not," she said. "But it's mine, and I need it." Tears rose in her eyes. "Please, Brother," she begged. "I need it for only a little while—"

"Alista, listen to me." He caught her by the shoulders. "As much as I do not want you to use that book, I would never take it from you without your knowledge or keep it—"

"You're lying!" she cried, breaking free. He had to be—her mother's magic wouldn't torture her and then desert her; it wouldn't just disappear now that she knew how dearly she needed it.

"Alista!" Dru said, coming in with the children. "How can you say such a thing? Whatever may have happened, Brother Paolo is a priest; he does not lie."

"Cara mia, you are hysterical," Paolo soothed. "Stop and think—"

"I don't want to stop and think!" Alista cried, breaking free of his touch. "I want to do something!" She turned back to the friar. "Swear to me on my mother's soul that you didn't take her book from me."

"On Bianca's soul I swear, though it be blasphemy," he answered, deep hurt in his eyes.

"Now do you believe him?" Dru said.

Alista looked at them both, then at the children. Nan's lower lip was trembling fearfully, and Tarquin looked utterly miserable. "Of course; how can I not?" she mumbled as she turned and walked away.

She had taken everything out of the chest by the time Druscilla came into her room. "Are you all right, cherie?" She lit another candle by the bed. "What are you doing?"

"It's all right," Alista said, sitting back on her heels. "I'm not myself, I know. I'm sorry."

"Don't be ridiculous." She sat on the edge of the bed. "You miss him very much?"

Alista went back to her rummaging. "I don't want to talk about it."

Dru suddenly smiled. "Here, this will cheer you up," she said. "Quickly, give me your hand." She put her friend's hand on her stomach. "Do you feel that?"

First Alista felt a flutter, a shiver, as if Dru were cold. Then came a definite kick. "Sweet saints!" she laughed in spite of herself. "Dru, how do you bear it? That would drive me mad."

"I love it," Dru smiled. "You can't imagine, cherie. It changes everything."

"I would think so," Alista agreed. Would she ever have a little soul swimming inside her? She didn't now; would Will come home to make one?

"Here, I brought you this," Dru said, interrupting her thoughts. "Brother Paolo made it for you to help you not be so frightened. He would have brought it up himself, but he was afraid it might upset you again to see him."

"I should go and tell him I'm sorry," Alista said, taking the cup. "I didn't mean those things. I can't believe I even said them." Fresh tears sprang to her eyes just when she thought she'd fought them off. "I feel so foolish, but I know I'm right. I know this is important."

"He knows you didn't mean it," Dru soothed, helping her up. "Besides, he has already gone to bed and locked his door. You can tell him tomorrow." Alista drank the sweet-tasting brew, and Dru took back the cup. "Now, stop searching, get in this bed, and try to sleep."

"I have to find my book," Alista protested, already drowsy. "And the children, I know they're upset."

"I will see to the children," Dru promised, pushing her gently to the pillows. "You just go to sleep."

Dru had gone, and she was almost asleep, the dream she dreaded lurking just at the edge of her consciousness, when she heard the door open again. "Alista?" Tarquin said, creeping closer. "Are you awake?"

"What is it, beloved?" she asked, rolling over, trying to focus on his face.

He hesitated. "You . . . you mustn't be angry at Brother Paolo," he said, rushing forward. "He didn't take your book; I know he didn't."

"How do you know?" she asked, suddenly interested, but she still couldn't seem to wake up. What had Brother Paolo given her . . . ? "Tarquin, did you—?"

"No, my lady, may God strike me, I never touched it," he swore, so wretched he couldn't be telling anything but the truth. "But I saw it. I tried to get it back for you just now, but it's gone."

"Where did you see it?" she said, struggling to sit up.

"Please, my lady, I cannot tell," he answered, all but in tears as he helped her. "I cannot, though you kill me. But I swear the good friar had nothing to do with it, and I will get it back for you this very night, see if I don't." This idea seemed to cheer him somewhat. "Let me find it, my lady. If I don't bring it to you by the morning, I will tell you who—if I don't find it. But I will."

"All right, Tarquin," she agreed, sinking down again. Suddenly she was so tired, she couldn't even remember clearly what the child was talking about or why he was so upset. *Rest,* a voice whispered in her head. *Rest, and then we will fly.* "Tomorrow will be soon enough," she said aloud, giving Tarquin a pat as she drifted off.

Much troubled in mind, Brother Paolo climbed to the top of the castle walls to watch the sun set. "Well met, Brother," Clarence greeted him. "Have you a blessing for a storm?"

Paolo looked up at the sky, streaked with only the thinnest tendrils of pink and blue clouds. "You think we will have a storm?"

"A storm or a dragon," Clarence laughed. "Look there, just over the trees to the north." A thick-looking mist did indeed seem to have been poured over the treetops like cream on a pudding. "The Saxons spoke of such mists as the breath of dragons, saying they brought destruction. For myself, I am hoping for a storm."

To Paolo, the wind seemed to have grown colder as the

castellan spoke. "So am I," he answered, foreboding gathering around his heart like a phantom mist.

By the time the battle was over, Will's shoulder had started to throb with pain, but he still didn't think much about it—a stray arrow must have grazed him, a rock set flying by a horse's hoof, something of that sort. But when he went into Henry's tent and a squire offered him wine, his stomach suddenly twisted in revulsion.

"Well fought, Brinlaw," Henry was saying. "We may win this thing yet."

"May God so will," he mumbled, feeling dizzy.

"Amen," Henry echoed with a chuckle. "Of course, the stupidity of the Scots helps a lot. One of my heralds was murdered, but they didn't get him until after he brought me the message about our reinforcements—a wasted death."

"Which herald?" Will asked.

Henry seemed to see him for the first time. "Good God, man, what's wrong with you?" he said. "You look like death!"

"Harry, which herald?" Will insisted, sitting down before he fell, the cup falling from his hand. He lifted his arm with an effort, the flesh suddenly numb as if drained of blood.

"The one who went to Brinlaw, my lord," the squire put in anxiously. "But he did see your lady and deliver your letter, I know. He was looking for you to give you a message."

"Will, what has happened?" Henry asked, pushing the other knights gathered around him aside. "Are you hurt?"

"Aye, Majesty," another squire answered for him, seeing the blood on the back of Will's leather sleeve.

"'Tis nothing," Will insisted. "Where is the herald's body? Was there a letter?"

"No, my lord," the first squire said. "He did not have time to wait for a letter, but he said he had a message that was for your ears alone." He blushed a bit. "He said you'd have his head if it were told, you or Sir Geoffrey d'Anjou."

"Geoffrey," Henry echoed grimly.

"Where are his men encamped?" Will asked, remembering the man he'd seen running back toward the English tents.

"Show him," Henry ordered. "And someone find Geoffrey and bring him to me."

Tarquin had searched Druscilla's room from top to bottom but still hadn't found Alista's book, nor had he seen any sign of Druscilla. After a few tense minutes of consideration, he decided he had to have help.

Captain Raynard was on the battlements, but he could barely see him, the mist was so thick. It seemed to wrap itself around Tarquin like a blanket of snakes, writhing cold and wet, trying to drag him down to a place he didn't want to go. "Captain Raynard!" he yelled, a note of panic in voice.

"Tarquin! Sweet Christ, boy," the captain swore, grabbing him by the collar as if to save him from drowning again. "What are you doing out here?"

"Looking for you." The mist even seemed to want inside his mouth, a thought that made him feel sick. "I need your help. I have to find something."

"So do I," Raynard laughed, but for once he didn't sound amused. "The rest of the bloody garrison." He glanced down at the boy and saw the look of dismay on his face. "Whatever it is, we'll find it later," he promised. "Right now, I want you to go inside and find your sister. Take her someplace and hide, someplace even Alista wouldn't know where to look."

"Why?" Tarquin said, moving in an instant from worried to genuinely scared. "What's going on?"

"I don't know," the captain admitted. "But this fog isn't a real thing, Tarquin, not a natural, Godly thing, and it hasn't come by chance. Whatever brought it . . ." His voice trailed off, but the fear in his eyes spoke volumes. "Go find Nan and quickly. Hide and don't come out until you hear me calling you—and mind you're sure it's me calling, or Will, or the friar, but no one else, not even Alista. Do you understand?"

"Aye," Tarquin nodded. "You or Brother Paolo."

"Good man," Raynard nodded, squeezing his shoulder. "Now go."

Will and Henry's squire searched the tents of every mercenary known to be in Geoffrey's employ, but none of them looked like the man Will had seen. Meanwhile his vision was becoming steadily worse, his arm was useless, and the rest of his right side was beginning to go numb as well. When they returned to the royal pavilion, Henry had more bad news. "Geoffrey is nowhere to be found," he said, motioning his own physician toward Will. "I saw him myself during the battle; he fought near me, but now he is gone."

"Headed for Brinlaw?" Will asked, already knowing the answer as the healer cut his sleeve to probe his wound.

"We can't know that," Henry protested. "He could be dead in a ditch for all we know—we're still numbering the casualties."

"The cut is nothing," the physician pronounced. "Barely even a scratch. But it already festers."

"Poison," Will said, getting up.

"All the more reason for you to be still and let yourself be tended," Henry ordered. "Let me find Geoffrey, if he lives—"

"No," Will said, getting up. "Forgive me, Majesty—"

"No," Henry cut him off. "No need. Go, and hurry, Take whatever men you need."

Tarquin went and got Nan from Druscilla's bed. "Come on, and don't make a sound," he ordered in a whisper. He could already hear strange voices inside the castle, and somewhere a woman was sobbing to wake the dead.

"What is it?" Nan asked fearfully as he laced her shoes.

"If I knew that, we wouldn't have to hide," he scolded. "Now hush up and come on."

They crept down the stairs and through the chapel, the voices louder here. Slipping out the kitchen door, Tarquin tripped over something in the misty darkness. Clarence lay half-in, half-out of the doorway, his tunic soaked with blood, his eyes staring wide at the sky. Tarquin clamped his hand over Nan's mouth to muffle her scream. "It's all right," he promised in an urgent whisper. "We're just having a nightmare, Nana. We'll wake up soon."

"Hurry, Tarquin," she whispered back when he let her go. "We have to hide."

Thankfully, the stables were deserted. He ran, dragging the little girl behind him, to Goliath's empty stall. Kicking the straw aside, he found the tiny trapdoor. Will had shown him this, a hiding place dug during the war between Stephen and Maud.

"Look," Nan said suddenly. "That is not my uncle's horse."

The white stallion was restless, obviously no happier to be there in the middle of the night than they were. He was packed as if for a long journey. Tarquin crept closer, whistling softly under his breath. The crest on the bridle was a lion, the lion of Anjou. And Alista's mantle was folded neatly over the saddle.

"Nan, listen to me," Tarquin ordered, his mind racing. "I want you to hide and stay hidden until Raynard or Brother Paolo or your uncle comes to find you. Do not come to Lady Dru, no matter how sweetly she may call you. Do you understand?"

"Yes, but where are you going?" she fretted.

"Never mind that. When your uncle comes, tell him I have followed Alista and that I will leave a trail even he can follow. But only tell him." She opened her mouth to protest further. "There's no time, Nana. Do as I say."

"All right," she pouted. "But when we wake up, I'm going to be very cross."

Smiling, he kissed her and hustled her into the hollow under the floor. Then he crept back into the house.

The chapel was no longer empty. Druscilla was there, standing in the light. In the shadows stood Geoffrey d'Anjou.

"You didn't have to kill Clarence," Dru was saying.

"I didn't kill him," Geoffrey shot back. "And if my man had not, he would have killed me. Is that what you would have preferred?

"You know I would not," Dru said, running to kiss him.

He let her, but only for a moment. "Where is Alista?" he said, pushing her away.

"Sleeping, poor lamb," Dru answered, touching his cheek. "She won't awaken before morning."

"Good," Geoffrey said, extricating himself from her embrace. "By then we'll be long gone."

Dru laughed. "Cherie, have you not seen me? I cannot possibly travel—"

"You won't have to." Tarquin had never seen eyes so cold. "You're not going anywhere." He turned and headed for the stairs. Dru ran after him, and Tarquin crept behind at a safe distance, keeping out of sight in the shadows.

"You will not!" Dru said, grabbing Geoffrey's arm.

Without waiting to hear more, Tarquin slipped past them and up the stairs.

Alista was sleeping so peacefully, he wanted to weep. He ached to be grown and a knight—he would spirit her away from danger or better yet, spit Geoffrey d'Anjou like a pig on a pike for daring to come near her. But in his present ten-year-old state, neither of these plans was practical, and time was running short.

He threw open the chest at the foot of the bed and grabbed the scimitar, then sprinted for the stairs. Geoffrey had just reached the top with Druscilla in his wake, screaming at him in French, and Brother Paolo could be heard banging on the door of his room from the inside demanding to be let out. Tarquin melted into the shadows of another doorway as Geoffrey turned the corner, and was about to keep running when Raynard came running up the stairs. "There you are!" he laughed, drawing his sword.

But Geoffrey was quicker than any villain had a right to be. His sword was already drawn, and as he turned, he slashed at Raynard, slicing his chest and arm, opening the flesh to the bone. "No!" Dru screamed, rushing forward as the captain fell, putting herself between him and Geoffrey's sword. "Leave him alone!"

"Have him, then," Geoffrey said, wiping his sword clean on his leather breeches. "I wish you joy."

"You bastard," Dru wept, kneeling beside the fallen captain. "Deceiver—"

"You shouldn't fling such names about so freely, puss," Geoffrey said, a tremor in his voice. "They apply so well to you." He stared at Dru and Raynard as if he couldn't believe what he was seeing. Then he turned toward Alista's room again, and Tarquin raced down the stairs.

By the time Will made it to Brinlaw, the sun was up, and he was moving by sheer force of will. If Goliath hadn't known the way home, he doubted he would have made it at all. "My lord!" one of the guardsmen called, running to meet him in the courtyard. "Thank God."

"Where is Alista?" He got down off the horse and staggered, would have fallen if the guard hadn't caught him.

"Gone, my lord," the man said, helping him to the door without being asked. "Kidnapped by Geoffrey d'Anjou, and the children are missing as well. Captain Raynard is hurt, barely living." He looked at his lord's haggard face. "And you."

"And me," Will agreed. "Take me to the priest."

Brother Paolo was with Raynard in the solar, tending his wounds as best he could. Druscilla sat by the fire, her rosary in her lap, a guardsman watching her every move as if she might sprout horns and breathe fire at any moment. When Will walked in, she looked up, her face turning even more pale. "You are dead," she breathed. "You just don't know it yet."

Will ignored her. "What has happened?" he asked Brother Paolo.

"Druscilla used Alista's magic book to allow Geoffrey and his men into the castle," Paolo answered. "Apparently he and not Lord Mark is the father of her child. He promised that if she helped him kill you and take the castle, he would marry her and make her Lady Brinlaw. But she is betrayed, and Geoffrey and his troops have fled with Alista."

"The poison is magic," Dru said, her voice dull with defeat. "You should never have lived so long." Raynard made a coughing sound, and she looked up, showing the tears on her cheeks. "This was not meant," she protested. "No one was meant to die but you. Alista was meant to be safe."

"The children," Raynard said, grabbing Will's wrist, the first words he'd spoken since he'd been struck. "I told them to hide, to only come to you, me, or the friar."

"Thank God," Paolo said, crossing himself. "I'll go—"

"No," Will cut him off. "I'll go." Alista's book lay open on the table. "You look there and find a way to cure me."

Paolo blanched. "I cannot—"

"She will not submit to Geoffrey," Will said, his own voice thundering inside his swimming head. "What do you think he will do then?"

Paolo had no answer. "I will do what I can," he promised. "But if I do, you must do something for me."

"Anything," Will promised. He looked at Dru, wishing he had the strength to waste in wringing her neck. "If she can read it, so can you." He looked down at Raynard and grinned. "Watch him; make him do it."

"I'm coming with you," Raynard groaned, trying to get up.

"Not this time, auntie," Will said. "I'll be back with the children."

He started with the stables simply because he wasn't sure he could climb the stairs. "Tarquin?" he called, his throat thick and aching. "Nan? Nana, where are you?"

"Here!" The trap in Goliath's stall popped open, and Nan came out, running to him.

"Where is Tarquin?"

"He has gone, following Alista." She obviously expected to be picked up, but Will was afraid if he bent over to do it, he'd never straighten up again. "He said he would leave a trail for you," she went on with a frown. "I do not like this dream."

Alista was dreaming the same old dream, standing at the window at Falconskeep with blood on her hands, Will's blood . . . no, not Will's, but Will was dead. She turned to look back into the room, but the shapes there had no meaning. The colors were wrong, and the edges were curved . . . her perspective was wrong; everything seemed so huge. She opened her mouth to scream, and a falcon's screech echoed in her ears. *Wake up,* she desperately prayed. *Please, God, I have to wake up. . . .* But her eyes wouldn't open, and the dream continued on.

Paolo tied the compress to Will's festering wound, dismayed at the angry black network of lines radiating over his shoulder and down his arm. "Can you even lift your sword?"

"I will when I have to," Will replied, the sheen of sweat breaking over his skin belying his brave words. "It will work, Fra Paolo. You did well."

The priest wished he shared his confidence. The passage on the poison's antidote was even more vague and confusing than the one on the poison, a combination of herbs and singing and such trash as suet and crushed bone. But he had done it, praying for forgiveness every moment. "Now you must do something for me," he said as Will put his shirt back on.

"Whatever it is, it will have to be quick," Will answered.

"It will be," Paolo promised. "Come with me to the chapel."

The knight froze in mid-movement. "Why?"

The monk was as adamant now as Will had been when he demanded an antidote. "Because you have to make confession," he said firmly. "You have to accept Christ's grace, or you cannot save her." He could see in the young man's eyes that he wanted to believe him in spite of his scowl, and he pressed on. "Whatever it is, whatever your sin, is it worth more than Alista's life? Will you lose your love to keep it?"

Will wanted to tell this priest he was crazy, as out of touch with God's will as the Pope who had sent him into the desert to murder the innocent. But looking into the wise, brown eyes, he knew Paolo believed what he said, and try as he might to cast off the teachings of his childhood, to escape the bonds of faith that plagued him, Will believed it, too. The love of his soul was lost, captured by a murderer with neither honor nor sanity to his credit, and at this moment, her rescue depended on a small boy and himself, half-crippled by poison and not expected to live the day. They needed God's help, and Will was the one who must ask for it. "What if He doesn't forgive me?" he asked the monk aloud.

"He will, no matter what it is, if you are truly contrite," Paolo promised, his own heart warm with relief in spite of their trouble. "Do you regret your sin?"

To his added humiliation, tears rose in Will's eyes. "Aye, Brother," he admitted. "I regret it very much."

His confession took only a few minutes, once he began, and Brother Paolo had the elements ready. As Will swallowed the wine, he stepped back and made the sign of the cross. "In the name of the Father, and of the Son, and of the Holy Spirit. Amen."

Alista opened her eyes on dappled sunlight falling through new spring leaves. "Awake at last," Geoffrey said fondly, looking down at her. "You've been asleep for days, my love. I was beginning to think Druscilla had killed you."

She sat up quickly, her muscles aching in protest. "Where are we?" she demanded. All around them, men were gathered in groups, eating and caring for their horses.

"We are free." He pressed a kiss to her brow. "You are free, my love." He drew her into an embrace, and she let him, struck dumb with horror. "He is dead," he promised. "You are avenged."

I'm dreaming," she thought. *Paolo's potion has given me nightmares.* . . . She thought of the dream that had haunted her since Will left, but this was different. In that dream, it was night, and she was at Falconskeep. This was day, bright sunlight, and they were in a strange wood. *Falconskeep,* she thought. *I must go to Falconskeep. . . .*

"When Henry returns from Scotland, he will have no choice but to bless our union." He moved to kiss her mouth, and she flinched, pushing him away, barely seeing him.

"Will is dead?" she said, getting up on legs that felt like

lead. *I would know. . . . Didn't my mother know, even as a falcon?*

"Dead as Arthur," Geoffrey agreed. "Poisoned in battle—some Scot probably cut him in half." He touched her hair. "Are you not pleased, my love? Is that not what you wanted?"

She stumbled, her hand going to the heartstone at her throat. "Holy Saint Mary," she breathed, feeling it cold against her skin. It shouldn't be cold; it should be warm. Looking down, she saw the color was dull, barely pink, not even a flaw of red. "Can it be true?" Her head was still spinning; she couldn't think straight. He couldn't be saying her love was dead; he couldn't be smiling at her like she should be happy to hear it. She looked back down at the heartstone, lifted it in her palm, and the terrible truth seemed to flow from it into her blood like poison. "Will is dead," she said, letting it fall, her voice dull as death, dull as the stone itself. "You killed him."

"On my soul I swear it," Geoffrey said. He picked up her mantle and draped it around her shoulders. "He will never touch you again."

Something heavy was concealed in the lining of the mantle, lying against her leg. Something long and curved . . .

"You have done this?" she asked, looking into Geoffrey's eyes, so green, perfectly level with her own.

"All for you," he promised. He didn't try to kiss her mouth again, only her cheek, but his hands closed possessively around her arms. "Only for you." His lips moved over her hair. "Henry will forgive us," he promised in a whisper. "He will return your father's lands."

"My father's castle?" she said, trembling with revulsion.

Her first instinct was to fight, to reach for the sword she felt concealed in her mantle, but then he had troops. Even if she could hurt him, his troops would protect him. She had to get him alone. Suddenly, her dream made sense, the kernel of truth it held revealed clearly. Too late; again, she knew too late . . .

"Our castle," he promised. "Now that Brinlaw is dead, there is no reason why it can't be ours."

She smiled at him. "I should have known," she said in a voice that sounded like someone else to her ears. "I should never have doubted you."

He smiled back. "Never," he agreed. "Now we must only avoid your dead husband's partisans until Henry's return. I already dispatched the worst, left him bleeding to death at Brinlaw."

"Raynard," she said, feeling sick.

"Yes, Captain Raynard," he agreed. "But there are others—"

"Sir Geoffrey," one of the sentries said, coming into camp on the run. "We are being followed, I'm certain of it."

"Followed by whom?" Geoffrey demanded as Alista's heart leapt into her throat.

"We couldn't find them," the man admitted. "But there's a definite trail."

Tarquin, she thought, elation mixed with horror. If they should find him, if Geoffrey should find him . . .

"I know a place," she said quickly. She touched his pale, perfect cheek, longing to tear it from his skull. "I know a place we can hide."

"What are you talking about?" he asked, smiling at her indulgently.

"Send your men ahead," she said, smiling her most winsome smile. *Falconskeep,* her mind repeated like a witch's spell. "Let our pursuers follow them. You and I will be safe."

As they rode away, she caught the heartstone in her fist and yanked with all her might, once, twice, the chain cutting into her flesh. On the third pull, it let go, and she let it fall into the grass.

Tarquin wriggled out of a thicket too dense for a rabbit to penetrate as Geoffrey's horse disappeared, his breath coming shallow and fast with exhaustion and fear. Crawling out into the clearing, his hand found something smooth in the grass. "Thank you," he whispered, his hands closing around the heartstone. "Make her be wrong." He had little experience with prayer, but he made up for it in fervor. "Make Brinlaw be alive, and make him come."

Riding onto the beach at Falconskeep, Alista thought she was dreaming indeed. The light was failing, and the falcons were circling high above the tower. In their cries she heard the voices of women, calling comfort, calling her to come home. "I've never seen so many," Geoffrey said, looking up. "What is the name of this place?"

"Falconskeep," she answered. "My mother's home . . ." She slid from the horse to the ground. "I was born here." She looked up at him and smiled. "I have come home."

Tarquin was as good as his word. The boy had left a trail of broken limbs and bits of cloth torn from his mantle for days away from Brinlaw. But he was on foot and couldn't run forever. Will found him in a clearing, half-dead from exhaustion. "We'll find her," he promised, embracing the boy.

"It's all right," Tarquin insisted, holding on and all but weeping with relief. "I know where they went." He pulled back and smiled. "She's taking him to Falconskeep. He doesn't know she doesn't want to go. She thinks you're dead—he thinks she's glad you're dead." He held up his fist. "She left this."

Will took the heartstone, for the first time feeling fear. Alista's legend: So long as the lady wore the heartstone, she would keep her human form. But once she left it behind and took to the air, she would never be a woman again. "Come on," he said, flinging Tarquin into the saddle. "We have to hurry."

"None of Will's partisans know about this place," Alista was saying as Geoffrey built a fire. She had opened the window, and she could hear the falcons outside, a hundred or more it seemed, all of them calling her name, telling her not to be afraid. "Only Will himself and Raynard." She slipped the mantle from her shoulders and found the slit in the lining, reached down and slid the scimitar free.

"It's perfect," Geoffrey said. "We can wait here until Henry returns from Scotland. My men will engage whatever is left of Brinlaw's garrison when they catch up, and kill them while we wait here safe." He got up and turned around. At the sight of her holding the sword, his eyes widened. "What is this?"

"Your death," she said coldly, moving toward him. "Not that it matters, but answer me this. Do you really believe you care for me, or has this all been for the castle?"

His smile twisted into something like a grimace of pain. "The castle?" he echoed, reaching for his own sword. "Yes, love, I want the castle." He circled back from her, leading her into the room like a dance. "I thought it was all I wanted. Until the tournament in London, I thought my feelings for you were a game."

"But they were not?" she scoffed, holding the scimitar in both hands as if she wasn't sure how to control it.

"I had almost forgotten your face," he went on as if she hadn't spoken. "Even now, I sometimes find it hard to remember exactly what you look like. But I remember Brinlaw." He smiled, a horrible, madman's smile. "I remember the way he hated me, how dearly he wanted me to die, and seeing that, I loved you." He laughed. "You don't understand, mon âme," he said. "He had everything that should have been mine. A castle, a name." His smile twisted into evil again. "My royal brother's love. But I had you." His eyes turned soft, and a woman who didn't know him and couldn't hear his words would have thought him beautiful. "All that I had was your heart, and he hated me for it. And so I loved you."

"But you were wrong," she said. "You were both wrong—you had nothing. I love him."

"Don't say that," he ordered, his face turning cold in an instant.

"But it's true," she insisted. "I loved him even then. And I never wanted you, Geoffrey." She made a clumsy slash at him, the sort a woman who had never held a sword might make.

"Enough!" he ordered, springing back. "I have no wish to hurt you, ma chère," he warned, crouching into a more defensive stance. "Tell me what you want."

"I want my husband," she answered. "I want my love. I want you to die."

"No," he said, almost purring. "You do not—"

"I do," she swore, moving closer. "I hate you—"

"Stop saying that!" he shouted, his voice breaking like a woman's. "You will stop! I will make you stop—"

"No," she said, circling closer. "You won't." When he lunged to disarm her, her left hand let go of the sword and her right hand brought it up, then down in a slashing arc. Geoffrey roared in pain and shock, and she brought the point back up into his stomach, just as Clarence had described.

"Mon Dieu," he gasped, falling to his knees, his own sword clattering on the floor. She couldn't seem to let go of the scimitar, even when his hands closed over her wrist; she followed him to the floor, the twisting blade making a vicious, slurping sound as he finally slumped flat on his side.

She crawled backward, pulling the sword free, bile rising in her throat. Weeping, she slumped on her knees and was sick, the cries of the falcons echoing, deafening in her ears. She had done it; she had murdered Will's murderer. Will was dead, but Geoffrey was dead, too. Now only one thing remained.

She staggered back to her feet, letting the scimitar fall. The wind was roaring through the window, tearing the tapestries from the walls, and she could hear songs in the wind, distinct voices calling out in the language of her mothers, calling her to join them. She turned to the window, bracing herself on the frame, her hands thick with Geoffrey's blood, the blood of her love's murderer. This was the dream; this was the prophecy. Finding new strength, she began to climb the stairs.

Will saw flickering light coming from the window of the tower room and silently rejoiced. They were here; she was alive. Brother Paolo's reluctant conjuring had apparently been successful—his arm felt almost usable again. "Wait here, Tarquin," he ordered, drawing his sword. "I'll be right back."

The ruined castle was black as pitch inside, the wind dragging clouds across the moon, and the floor was wet, his boots splashing as he walked. Finding the door to the tower by feel, he pulled it open, and water washed over him in a wave, settling waist deep. When he tried to move forward, the freezing water seemed to pull him back, sucking him downward, down the flooded stairs, and he thought he heard a woman laughing, lunatic cackles echoing in the dark. Tarquin's demon had come after him at last. Dropping his sword to grab the railing in both hands, he hauled himself up with all his strength, finally breaking free. The water sucked and receded behind him as he continued up the stairs.

The tower room was torn to pieces, and Geoffrey's corpse lay on the floor, the scimitar he had given Alista lying by him thick with blood. But Will's wife was nowhere to be seen. "Alista!" he shouted, but the wind tore the word from his lips and blew it away before he could even hear it himself.

He looked more closely at Geoffrey, saw where his love had fallen and bloody footprints leading to the stairs.

Alista had never been so high. Unlike the tower at Brinlaw, this one had no protective wall; the stairs simply ended in a crumbling platform of stone that seemed ready to disintegrate at every step. She moved to the edge, the wind swirling around her, the cold embrace of a lover who was dead. She spread her arms wide, hearing the voices of the falcons calling her to join them—*sister . . . Lady . . . Queen . . .*

"Alista!" Her back was turned, and even with him screaming, he wasn't sure she'd heard. "Alista, stop!"

She turned to fall backward into the arms of the wind and saw Will. "No!" he roared, springing forward as she fell.

He caught her wrist, the one he had broken, and she reached up and grabbed on with her other hand. He should have been able to pull her back at once, but the wind seemed determined to snatch her from his grasp, and the platform was crumbling under his feet, a large chunk falling away as he tried to take a step back.

"Will, you have to let go!" Alista cried. The wind had her now; she could feel herself changing, wings folded inside her body, ready to rise free. "I won't die; you will!"

"Like hell you won't!" he shouted, holding on with all his might, trying not to feel the way her wrist was sliding through his grip even so. "I'll shoot you out of the sky with my last breath!"

"Will, please!" Her body was cold, but her spirit curled inside it was warming, unfolding to fly.

"No!" Another piece of platform broke off and fell away, and he slipped, barely catching his balance. "If you go, I go!"

"No!" The falcons were circling high overhead, holding themselves aloof. "I won't go!" Alista screamed, not at Will but at the falcons, her legacy of flight. "If I fall, I fall!" The falcon-faery inside her shuddered, a rattle of wings. "In the name of Christ, I say, let me go!" she screamed even louder, her throat raw with pain. "I want him! I will die!"

Suddenly the wind let go. Will had stopped fighting; she was his to hold. Dragging her up to the platform, he wrapped her in his arms.

Fifteen

That first night, Alista didn't think of Dru at all, didn't even know what she had done. All she cared about was that Will was alive, that she was with him. Stumbling down from the tower, leaning on one another and weeping in relief, she and Will found Tarquin with Gwynnie, her face almost haggard with worry in spite of her faery nature. She bundled all three of them home to her tiny cottage in the woods to scrub Alista clean of blood and examine Will's wound. "That old monk didn't do badly," she said. "The poison is almost gone."

Alista was clutching Tarquin so tightly she was in danger of breaking his bones. "My brave boy," she whispered, kissing his hair as he cried. "Thank you thank you thank you."

"Here." He pressed the heartstone into her hand. "I knew you'd want it back."

She smiled back at him, her hair wild, her freshly washed face now smeared with tears, and she was so beautiful, he thought his heart would break. "Thank you," she repeated, pulling him close to kiss his cheek.

"That poor child needs to sleep for a week," Gwyneth said, coming to take charge of him. "Let's find you a bed, my love." She led the boy to the bedroom door. "You two get some sleep as well," she teased with a wicked grin as she closed it behind them.

As soon as the door was shut, Alista was in Will's arms. "I thought you were dead," she wept as she held on. "He told me you were dead."

"I promised you I'd come back," he protested, kissing her cheek, her temple, her mouth. "Don't you dare try to leave me again."

"Never," she swore, kissing him back. "Never again."

Only after she had slept a whole night and day and night again in her beloved's arms did she hear what Druscilla had done, and even then she could hardly make herself believe it. Clarence was dead; Raynard was so badly wounded he might be dead by now. Will poisoned; Alista herself drugged and betrayed, and all with Alista's own magic. "Knowledge is power," Alista murmured, turning her face to Will's shoulder to weep as they rode Goliath toward home.

When they reached Brinlaw, they found Henry's favorite clerk, Thomas à Becket, there to mete out the King's judgment. "King Henry leaves the matter in your hands, Lord Brinlaw," he said as Dru was led into the solar. "Whatever punishment you see fit, the Crown will carry out."

"Dru?" Alista said, but the girl she had thought was her best friend wouldn't even look at her, and she looked away herself.

"The child is innocent," Will said, taking Alista's hand. "But once it is born—"

"No." Raynard hadn't moved from his bed since he'd been wounded, but he was up now, leaning heavily on Brother Paolo's shoulder, his face white as parchment. "She lives."

Dru looked up, her blue eyes wide with what could have been hope or horror. "She tried to murder your lord," Becket pointed out.

"He isn't my lord," the Fleming replied. "He is my friend." He looked at Will. "In all the years I've known you, I've never asked you for anything," he said. "I'm asking you now. I want this woman's life."

"No," Dru said, shaking her head. "I should die—"

"But you won't," Raynard cut her off with the ghost of his usual grin. "You are first in my damned soul, and I will not allow it."

Becket raised an eyebrow at Will, who nodded. "Imprisonment, then?" the clerk asked gamely.

Alista walked over to Dru. "Clarence is dead," she said flatly.

"I know," Dru answered, staring at the floor as tears spilled over her cheeks. "I never meant . . . I wanted him so much." She closed her eyes as if the memory burned. "I thought I loved him."

"And all the time I was telling you the things he said to me, all the time you thought I loved him," Alista said, incredulous.

"I thought he was pretending," Dru laughed bitterly. "I thought I could give him his castle . . . I was a fool, an evil miserable fool."

"So it seems," Becket said dryly. "But what are we to do with you?"

"Tell me you are sorry," Alista said, ignoring him, looking down at Dru alone, willing her to look back. "Make me believe you regret what you've done."

Dru looked up, her beauty twisted grotesque with shock. "You know that I do."

"I know you're afraid," Alista said, steeling herself against the other woman's pain.

"I'm not," Dru answered, no trace of guile in her eyes. "Not of being punished, anyway. I never thought you could be hurt, that Raynard . . ." She looked down again, fresh tears distorting her words. "I'm sorry, cherie," she promised. "More sorry than you can know."

Alista looked down on her for another long moment. "Forgive her," she said at last, turning to Will and the clerk.

"I beg your pardon?" Will said, his blue eyes going wide.

"I have to," Alista said. "She did horrible things, but she didn't do them alone, and Geoffrey . . ." She remembered the sound her sword had made as she pulled it free, the look of comic shock on his face. "Geoffrey has already been punished. Please, Will." She took his hand again. "Please?"

"She tried to murder me," Will pointed out, looking first at his best friend, then at his wife.

"And if she had succeeded, I would have already torn her to pieces with my bare hands, and Captain Raynard would have helped me; you know that," Alista said. "But you are alive, and I am so grateful, so happy. I have to try to save her if I can."

"Listen to her, my lord," Brother Paolo said gently. "You know what it is to be absolved."

Will's scowl was so fierce it would have made a stranger tremble in his boots, and Alista secretly smiled, knowing he was about to give in. "All right," he said at last. "She is forgiven."

Alista waited until all the others had gone before she went up to her husband. "Thank you," she said softly, raising up on tiptoe to kiss his mouth. "I know you think I'm insane."

"I'd think you were a saint if I didn't know you so well," he grumbled. "You truly believe her?"

"I do," she promised. "Not that I won't be watching her, mind." She took his hand between both her own and pressed her lips to the scar there. "I have you back," she said softly, her heart aching with love. "I can be generous."

He turned her face up to his and kissed her, anything that could hurt them forgotten. "I love you," he whispered, holding her in his arms.

Epilogue

The summer flew by as Brinlaw Castle recovered. Clarence and the other men of the garrison who had been killed were sorely missed and greatly mourned, and Druscilla, never a castle favorite, was hard-pressed to find a friendly face at first. But Lady Alista and her lord both made it plain that they believed Mark's mistress to have been duped and betrayed by Geoffrey d'Anjou and that they had forgiven her. Eventually a grudging truce was made. Everyone wanted to be relieved, to believe things were returning to normal. In July, the news that Alista herself was pregnant was more cause to rejoice, more reason to believe that all would at last be well.

Now Dru's child was about to be born. Alista passed a cool, wet cloth over Druscilla's sweating brow, the August air still and sweltering hot in spite of the open windows. "It's all right," she promised, taking the other girl's hand.

"Yea, sweeting," Gwyneth promised. "It won't be long now."

"Don't leave me," Dru whispered, too hoarse now for anything else.

"I won't," Alista promised.

"I'm going to die," she confided, making Gwyneth smile and shake her head. "I know I am," she insisted. "Alista, would you do something for me?"

"Yes, love, of course," she soothed. "What is it?"

Coming into the solar, she couldn't help but smile. Tarquin and Brother Paolo were making no attempt to hide their anxiety; the boy was pacing the floor, and the friar was holding his rosary over his book, whispering prayers as he read. Will was a little better, or worse, his map spread out before him but his eyes focused on the door. But Raynard was sheer brilliance. He was pretending to be asleep. "Gwyneth says it won't be long now," Alista said calmly, ruffling Tarquin's hair as he passed. "She sent me down to get you."

Brother Paolo rushed to his feet. "I'm on my way."

"No, Brother, not you," Alista demurred, her smile turning almost malicious. "You. Raynard. She wants you."

For a moment, she thought he wouldn't answer or even give up his ruse, but he finally looked up at her. "What does Gwyneth want with me?" he grumbled.

"Gwyneth doesn't want you at all," she admitted. "But Druscilla is quite desperate. She thinks she is going to die."

His eyes widened, his doubtful scowl dissolving. Then he lunged to his feet and sprinted toward the stairs.

"Is she truly going to die?" Tarquin asked as Alista sat down.

"Of course not," Alista promised. "Gwynnie says everything is going splendidly."

"Good," Tarquin muttered, leaving to wander in the courtyard.

"I don't know why he has to be so silly," Alista remarked, looking over Will's shoulder.

"He's a boy, and he's never been around anyone having a baby before," Will said sagely.

"Neither have I, for that matter, but Tarquin isn't who I meant," she answered. He was mapping out the Scottish campaign, trying to make a record of the terrain for next summer. After leaving Henry and refusing to return for this one, he thought it was the least he could do. "Why can't Raynard forgive her?" The rest of the castle had finally learned to at least be civil to Dru, and Alista treated her almost as warmly as she had before her betrayal, but the captain was not so forgiving. Since the day of her judgment, he had not spoken to Druscilla at all, not so much as a word. "He loves her; he admitted as much. He asked you to spare her life. But he never intends to talk to her again?"

"Raynard is a cynical soldier," Will said, looking back at her. "Druscilla has managed in less than a year to prove him right in every ill opinion he ever had of women."

"He could still give it up now," she said stubbornly.

"He will," he promised.

A scream echoed through the castle, and Alista shuddered. "Poor Dru," she mumbled, a hand going unconsciously to her own swollen abdomen. "And poor me, come to think of it."

"Are you worried?" Will teased, kissing her cheek.

"No, not a bit," she said sarcastically. "Go have a look upstairs, and you won't be either." She turned and put her arms around his neck. "But it's worth it, I suppose."

"I suppose," he agreed. "Another Falconskeep faery?"

"Another Brinlaw knight," she countered.

"One of each?"

"Will!" He laughed and kissed her again. "It isn't funny."

"Of course it isn't," he promised. "But it will be fine."

Return to a time of romance…

Where today's

hottest romance authors

bring you vibrant

and vivid love stories

with a dash of history.

Printed in the United States
By Bookmasters